NIGHT HAWK

By Jolene Loraine

ISBN: 1499705476
ISBN-13: 978-1499705478
Library of Congress Control Number: 2014909830
CreateSpace Independent Publishing Platform,
North Charleston, SC

Dedicated to all who seek to know what it means to truly live; to love, to dream, to hope and to take a stand for what is right no matter how dark the world.

PROLOGUE

A dimly flickering light dominated the darkened interior of the room, illuminating the boy's face as he sat transfixed on his bed. The holographic world of forested mountains dropped away to a vast field nestled against a massive lake that appeared to spill out across the child's bed. He pulled his knees up to his chin as he watched figures materialize and stand on the beach of this lake. His hazel eyes grew wide as he reached out to touch the figures, softly muttering each by name.

A sudden bang from the other room made him wince. There was no surprise in his soft features, only annoyance, only grief. Pausing the story, he twisted to face the bedroom door and listened, hugging himself all the tighter as he did.

"I don't have time for this," a man's voice boomed through the hallway. "If it's so important to you, you go."

The shrill, angry voice of a woman responded with equal harshness. "But he's your son. Don't you have time for your own…"

"Son? That…"

"That what? Huh? That what?"

At this, the boy slowly slipped from his place to creep across the plush carpeting to the door. A sliver of light glowed beyond. He pressed himself to this slight crack, but dared not open the door any wider.

"Hawk. Is that all you can ever say about him?" The woman's voice grew in pitch.

"I don't have time for this right now."

"You never have time."

"I didn't want this." The booming voice of the man challenged the volume of his wife's argument. "You did."

"Don't start those lies. You wanted children, too."

"If it wasn't for…"

"I won't listen to this again."

"And I won't go. I've got more important things to do."

The bang of another door and heavy footfalls signaled the arguing parents were getting closer. Jumping back, the boy hurried to his place on the bed to stare at the frozen images that were waiting patiently for his return – his faithful friends. As he wrapped a blanket tightly around his shoulders, he let them continue their story.

"It's all about you, isn't it?" the woman's voice shouted. "It's always about you."

With a groan, the boy covered his ears.

"And what about you and your kid?"

"*Our* kid."

With a final slam of a door, the fight ended. All was silent and after a short while the boy relaxed. He kept his eyes fixed to the images as his mother slowly pushed the door aside and leaned against the frame.

"David?"

The boy refused to answer, leaving his mother to stare blankly at him through bloodshot eyes.

"What story is this?" she finally asked.

"Natchua."

She remained at the door a moment longer, listening with little interest to the soft narration. Finally she approached to sit beside her son. Drawing him into her arms she smoothed his rumpled blonde hair before laying her cheek on the top of his head. Still David did little to acknowledge her presence though he did not push her away. Together they listened as the story generator continued the tale.

"There was little hope for the Humans, newly arrived on Telamier. Especially with…"

"Vairdec at war for the planet," the mother chimed in. "How many times have you seen this?"

"Shh." David's eyes remained fixed on the image as it changed to a strong, heroic figure astride a large, gray steed.

"But there was hope for the founding colony," the computer continued, "and his name was…"

David was quick to finish. "Jonathan Alsen."

"He's some hero, isn't he?"

For the first time, David glanced up at his mother. "The best." His eyes sparkled as he spoke

3

with the computer. "'When Humans came to Telamier they nearly died when the Vairdec armies swept through San Terres Valley, but Jonathan Alsen was ready for them, preparing an army of Humans and Candonians to meet the enemy head on – an army known as Natchua.'"

"You have this story memorized."

"It's my favorite."

He watched the battle scene for a while, the Humans bravely fighting back a fierce regiment of dark armored creatures in vicious-looking war masks.

"Mother," he asked carefully, "do you think the Vairdec will come back?"

She thought for a moment, watching the battle come to an end with a victorious group of Humans being joined by other species.

"The war was a long time ago. The Celehi won't let them return easily."

"The Celehi *and* Humans," her son corrected. "You know what?"

"What?"

"I'm going to be Natchua." He rose to his knees with pride. "I'm going to fight like Jonathan Alsen."

His mother only gave a sigh. "Sure, dear. Whatever you want."

CHAPTER ONE

David Jonathan Malard was not about to let a mere Faxon get the better of him, despite the fact the leathery brute weighed almost twice as much as he and sported an impressive arsenal of knuckle blades and an LB-87 rifle. Keeping a firm hold on the rifle barrel, David twisted low to the right, using the weapon to hold back a direct strike of the blades. In a single, smooth turn, he came up beside and slightly behind his enemy. The Faxon hissed as David drove the heel of his boot into the tendon below the hock, which was never as strong as the heavy-boned legs would suggest. The move easily dropped the larger creature to his knee.

There was no time to waste. An injured Faxon was a dangerous Faxon. Pressing his weight against the rifle to which he still clung tenaciously, David slammed his left elbow into the top of the creature's thick, black muzzle, blocking the flailing blades with an armored wrist cuff. The blow to the muzzle did exactly as David had been taught, and the Faxon was momentarily stunned. Using the precious seconds,

David yanked the rifle barrel upward and twisted it out of the Faxon's hands. The creature gave an indignant growl, lunging forward to receive the butt of the rifle across his nose. Flinging the rifle out of reach, David slapped a cuff around the Faxon's wrist. It immediately locked. Enraged, the Faxon lunged forward. David remained undaunted, having already thrown a second cuff around a thick, rounded beam. With a press of a button, an energy pulse locked the cuffs' signal together, keeping the Faxon from moving any more than a single step in any direction. David stood just out of reach.

  With a deep sigh, he examined his catch. Not bad for a night's work, but unfortunately the night was still young and this was not his main target. He allowed for a moment to catch his breath, preparing himself for yet another difficult task. Taking a couple steps back, he ran his hand through the sweaty strands of blond hair that stubbornly fell back over his hazel eyes.

  He was a handsome man by most standards. At the age of thirty-four, he was still quite young. His features were soft, yet well defined. A boyish charm glinted in his eyes that lay beneath a strong brow accented by smooth cheekbones and hard-set jaw. He stood a good six-foot-two in height and from head to toe he was a wonderful example of fitness and strength. While not massive in muscular bulk, his body was toned by the rigors of his active lifestyle.

  After wiping his brow with his uniform sleeve, he glanced about, his keen eyes picking up the subtle variations within the shadowy alley. A headband aided in his scrutiny of his surroundings.

Special sensors sent a holographic shield across his eyes, adjusting to the subtle changes in light to provide both shading in bright environments and superb night vision. Assessing that all was now quiet around him, David turned to the thick, military-style band on his wrist, watching the readout on the mission's current status. Taking a deep breath, he resumed his work, jogging hurriedly down a narrow street.

"Where's my team, Eatrax?" he called. His voice instantly carried through the black, military issue comlink he wore as a band around his neck.

"East side," a voice answered from a small band tucked behind David's ear. *"Low road. Watch for Kruestar. He doubled back."*

David allowed himself a slight half smile. This was exactly what he wanted.

"That Manogonite sob won't get far. Stay with the goods. Arzen."

Another voice broke in to answer his call. *"I'm with you."*

Almost immediately Sergeant Keven Arzen joined David on the street. He, too, was Human, standing just a couple inches shorter than David. He was squarer in the face with short, brown hair and muscular chest and arms. In his hand he clutched his regulation handgun.

"They fanned out," he said as he kept a steady pace beside David. "Eatrax has the east."

"We've got Kruestar," David answered.

As they neared the end of the alley, they pulled up short, barely avoiding a barrage of gunfire.

"Looks like they regrouped," Keven observed.

David gave his gun a quick check. "Cover me."

Doing as ordered, Keven responded to the gunfire with a barrage of his own, allowing David to make it to the other side of the street and around the far building.

"Hold them there," David instructed over his comlink as he raced down the concrete walk.

Various shipping crates and other debris lay in his path. It was an inevitable hindrance on the southeastern side of San Terres. This close to Livasy Bay, a giant lake despite its name, there were plenty of warehouses and shipping docks to hide among. And of course, not everything shipped was entirely legal, which was why David and his team from the Coalition of Law Enforcement were spending their night running about in the dangerous dark alleys of the city.

Coming around the side of the building, David immediately caught sight of his adversaries, still focused on the other side of the alley where Sergeant Arzen's shooting demanded their attention. He could only afford one clean shot. Singling out the apparent leader of the small group, he fired a numbing energy bolt that quickly dropped the gruff man. Instantly the other three split their defense between the two agents, and David was forced to retreat.

For a moment he held his ground against the wall, hoping for the crazed shooting to die down. However, the group was relentless, giving David no chance for a second clean shot. Carefully he scanned the wall on the far side of the alley. The glint of metal drew his attention to where a broken monitor consol hung limply halfway up the steel structure. Adjusting himself at the corner, David examined the angle of the metal and the positions of the shooters. It was almost perfect.

Without looking at his weapon, David switched the ammunition from laser to bullet. Taking quick aim, he fired at the bit of metal. The bullet clanged against the surface, twisting the consol slightly to the left. Just a little bit more. He fired again. The metal moved a fraction further. It was all he could afford for the shooters noticed his random shots and were taking the opportunity to advance on his location. In an instant, David switched the gun back to its laser setting and fired. The beam bounced off the reflective surface to strike the nearest shooter in the arm. He fell back against his fellow fighter, giving Arzen a chance to advance during the distraction.

"Nice shot," Keven's voice said through David's comlink.

"I can't believe it worked."

"Check your back."

David spun around, gun poised, to see a winged shadow streak by his head and disappear around a corner. David tracked the creature but could not get a clean shot.

"Not this time, Kruestar," he growled.

Shoving aside some loose pipes, David gave chase.

"Arzen, hold position till backup arrives."

"Copy. Be careful."

David didn't answer. Ahead of him flew a vehemently snarling Manogonite. He was a medium-sized creature with a stout, rounded body covered in a short, bristly fur. A tight vest draped over most of his body was his only clothing, which allowed full mobility of his thick haunches, bony arms and large, leathery wings. His face was round with a short, wrinkled muzzle giving him a perpetual snarl. Black eyes were wide with rage. Giant, fan-like ears caught the subtle sounds of his pursuer. Baring his fangs, he spat out a curse as he flipped in the air to catch hold of a wall. With clawed hands and feet, he scaled the building and disappeared over the rim.

David's eyes narrowed. Kruestar was a slippery adversary. Luckily David was up for the challenge. He knew the Manogonite's ways and better yet, knew the city's layout as well as his own house. He spent many of his young adult years wandering the streets just to learn its patterns. It was knowledge he always knew would be an advantage to him as an officer. Running on ahead, he used a stack of crates to catch a narrow ledge and hoist himself to the roof.

From there, the best way to the adjoining buildings was via the structural beams between them. Built when a proposal for more covered streets had been made, funding never fully found its way to the docks. Setting the beams was all the construction workers managed to complete. This was fine by David. All he wanted was the Manogonite. As he neared the edge of the roof he could see Kruestar doubling back down the alley underneath the beams. This was an unexpected benefit. Gauging the distance, David rushed out onto the beam and jumped, catching hold of the Manogonite as he sailed underneath.

A wailing scream erupted from Kruestar's throat as they fell. David was enveloped in a fury of beating wings and sharp claws, but he held on despite the battering he received. Tucking and rolling, he came up on his feet with one of Kruestar's arms and a wing held tightly in his grasp. He glared back into the fiery eyes of the creature, undaunted by the clearly visible rows of sharp teeth. A clawed hand struck out at his face and David ducked, getting a beating with the free wing all the while.

"Enough," he snapped angrily as he flipped Kruestar over to press his knee into the Manogonite's shoulder. "You are under arrest."

David's announcement elicited another vicious yowl from the Manogonite. Though smaller than David, he was strong and very flexible. Twisting in the officer's grasp, he lashed out with his fangs, forcing David back to avoid a bite to his face. Kruestar leaped into the air as the weight of David's knee relaxed. However, David refused to let go, and was lifted off the ground. Kruestar kicked and flapped madly, trying to free himself from David's grip.

David hung on, pushing off from a wall to twist and catch a bar with his feet. Using himself as an anchor, David yanked Kruestar up short and together they fell once more in a fighting, tangled mess. Striking the ground, the Manogonite righted himself to try and take off once more. His claws dug at the rough pavement that received a constant shower of saliva with each vicious Manogonite curse. David clung to the creature's shoulders, pressing himself against Kruestar's back and ignoring the fury of the wings on either side. A couple seconds later the wings dropped limply to the ground as Kruestar gave a resigned growl. Sergeant Arzen held his gun poised in front of the Manogonite's face.

"Right on time," David panted.

As the two agents secured their prize, David retrieved a small cylindrical reader device from Kruestar's vest. Holding it up to Arzen he gave a smile.

"I think we're through here."

Nestled in the western center of San Terres, capital of the Human's region of Earthenia, sat the city's Coalition of Law Enforcement headquarters. It was one of the few buildings that never lacked activity. Day and night agents went about their duties to protect their city and provide law enforcement wherever needed. The CLE was not a Human designed organization per say, and had only been adopted by them out of the necessity for keeping in proper standing with the planet's dominant species, the Celehi.

Operating under a strict set of guidelines, the CLE was essentially identical across the entire planet, regardless of what region one might be in. While the Celehi allowed some leeway by the private governments of other species, they continually emphasized the importance of keeping a universal law. This inevitably meant that a Celehi presence was felt in the coalition of Earthenia. It came with mixed feelings. Humans were by nature fiercely independent but, small in numbers, any extra help in law enforcement was welcome – though not always voiced. Thankfully the Celehi had been willing enough to leave the Earthenian CLE division hierarchy in the hands of the Humans, who had proven themselves quite capable of thriving during their nearly two hundred year growth on Telamier. They kept an eye on them from a distance, and in exchange, the Humans willingly hired many Celehi officers into their ranks. One of which was celebrating with his Human comrades upon returning to headquarters with Kruestar and his gang in tow.

David, Sergeant Keven Arzen and Celehi officer Eatrax Iera'Tora stood with their four agents in the midst of a boisterous group of their teammates who enthusiastically gathered to hear the tale and congratulate the successful officers. Captain Mordechi Korshek, head of the San Terres division, stepped through the throng to face his returning officers.

"Good work everyone," he said. "With the information brought in we can finally shut down that ring for good."

A heartfelt mixture of applause and cheers followed. Captain Korshek turned to face David.

"Malard. You did well today. I'm going to make sure the director hears of your accomplishment. Good work, lieutenant."

David stood at attention and gave a slight dip of his head. "Thank you, sir."

As the captain exited, the group relaxed to gather in a tighter ball around David. Keven Arzen slapped his friend on the back.

"The Mighty Malard strikes again," he announced proudly. "Let's hear it for the Hawk."

David shifted uncomfortably amidst the applause.

"You were pretty good yourself," he said, trying to draw the attention away. He glanced over at Eatrax. "It wasn't easy bringing in those Faxons, was it, Eatrax?"

The Celehi rippled a slight shade of purple. It was a unique characteristic of his species to show emotions through rippling colors that played across an otherwise pale bluish skin. His was a tall species, powerfully built but graceful in movement. His physique was quite similar to that of the Humans, though his nose was less prominent while his eyebrows and cheekbones were just the opposite. Dark, narrow eyes watched the world with a deeply intellectual bent. He sported no hair, a common look for the Celehi who naturally grew hair only in one or two small clumps on their head. Instead, a metallic tattoo pattern adorned his scalp.

"They show good combat," he answered casually.

The group's attention quickly turned from the calm, slower drawl of Eatrax as another Human sergeant sauntered into the room. With a wide grin he held up a case of liquor.

"Now we can celebrate," he announced.

With approving comments, they crowded around. Keven reached through the crowd to snatch up two bottles, handing one off to David. However, David wasn't paying the drinks any attention and was instead edging toward the door. Keven gave a knowing smile, though chose to ask the question anyway.

"What's the rush?"

"Where's your sister?"

Keven gave a nod toward the side door. "Probably the lobby."

"Don't wait up."

"I never do."

The lobby was a stark contrast to the meeting hall where the raucous celebration was taking place. It remained dark with only one light strip glowing along the upper edge of the far wall. A beautiful, shapely woman in a CLE uniform stood alone at the window. Her dark brown hair was pulled up in a bun, exposing the delicate skin of her neck. Slipping up behind her, David wrapped his arms around her waist and lovingly kissed her exposed skin. She lay back in his embrace with a smile.

"It's good to see you, Melina," David said softly.

"So," she sighed, "the hero returns."

"Hero?"

Melina turned to face David. "That's what they're saying. There's a rumor going around that you're up for promotion again."

"When did you start listening to rumors?" David questioned playfully.

"So you're not?"

David gave a shrug.

"You're taking this very casually," Melina continued as she slid her hand up his chest to his shoulder. "Are you going to still love me when you're a captain?"

"Of course." He pulled her tightly against himself and began kissing her neck once more.

"You'll always be my commanding officer," he whispered.

With a pleasant laugh, Melina pushed him back. "That's the best you can come up with? You didn't hit your head out there, did you?"

She ran her hand along the side of his head and he leaned into her touch. Reading his invitation, Melina drew close to kiss him on the lips.

"Your commanding officer," she mused as they parted. "At least you have your perspectives straight."

"Really?" David toyed.

She gave him a seductive look. "And I'm sure you'll be saluting after what I have planned on our wedding night."

"Twenty-seven days."

"You're keeping count?"

Straightening in grandiose fashion, David took up Melina's hands and waltzed her around the chairs of the room.

"Twenty-seven days and our current duties will finally be over. Then it's wedding toasts and an unforgettable honeymoon by the warm waters of Antidine."

Melina gave a laugh as her fiancé dipped her. "Twenty-seven days and counting."

CHAPTER TWO

Karnoss sat as a shimmering jewel in the northernmost lands of Earthenia. Around it spread the foreboding frozen desert of Tralex whose unconquered expanse lay as a rustic wasteland bordering Telamier's arctic north. Out on the desert floor high winds threatened to tear flesh from bone, and did much to shape the rocks that jutted out of its red-brown sands. Two-thirds of the year it lay in a subzero freeze, moisture so scarce that it left the red desert void of snow much of the time.

However, even here the Humans ventured to leave their mark. Karnoss had risen as a testament to their tenacity in conquering even the harshest environments. Through careful design, the towering buildings channeled the roaring desert winds into energy producing generators for both the immediate city and others across the vast reaches of Earthenia's landmass. It was a technologically wealthy city, full of a life steeped in shopping, gambling and entertainment.

Yet Humans were not the first inhabitants of the desert lands. That feat belonged to the Celehi and their ingenuity within Valor Peak, which lay in a short, jagged mountain range just west of Karnoss's plateau. In years past it served as a bunker carved into the highest mountain of the range. From there they engineered a strategic defense against their most notorious enemy, the Vairdec, when the two species had battled for control of Telamier some two hundred years prior. After the Celehi's victory, the bunker fell into disrepair, largely forgotten and left to ruin until the Humans arrival.

Eventually the bunker found new life through the Earthenian military. While San Terres's neighboring city of Eenosha oversaw the physical training of its Human military personnel and CLE agents, Karnoss's Valor Peak housed the classrooms necessary for the mental schooling. But it was not the required classes soldiers went through that gave Valor Peak its reputation. That remained the honor of SIERA, Earthenia's Strategic Intelligence and Enforcement Regional Agency. It was this specialized division that utilized most of the base, having renovated it with aircraft hangars, workout and training facilities, conference rooms, control center and barracks with full facilities.

As a regional agency, SIERA represented all of Earthenia's military, focusing on two specialized branches. Earthenian Covert Operations, or ECO, trained agents for secretive missions involving intelligence gathering and espionage. In the early days, their objective remained fixed on the Vairdec, the information obtained catching the eye of

Earthenia's allies with whom they shared the information. This openness conveniently kept the ECO's other operations involving spying on those closer to home from becoming dangerously suspect.

The ESF, or Earthenian Special Forces, drew in the strongest from the military's recruits. Cut off from their ancestral home world, Humans held status only on Telamier, causing their military development to often exceed their neighbors' whose Telamierian colonies sported smaller defense units. This caused SIERA to become a coveted place of learning and cooperative military work. It was a common sight to have Celehi, Oxyrans, Teshians and even Manogonites alongside the Humans within Valor Peak, all of which was overseen by SIERA's top commander, General Kyler Riechet.

As an active member of Earthenia's armed forces for over forty years, General Riechet was highly renowned for his wisdom and strength of character. Despite being in his mid-sixties, his physical body remained strong, though gray was settling in his short brown hair, and the creases were ever deepening on his careworn face. His experience in the field coupled with his deep understanding of SIERA's roots as a Vairdec defense unit made him indispensable as its leader. He kept a close eye on Earthenia's military recruits as they went through basics, assessing mental and physical stamina to carefully hand pick soldiers for either of the two branches within SIERA.

At the moment he stood at the back of one of Valor Peak's lecture halls while his daughter, Colonel Amber Riechet, finished her lessons on known

Vairdec war tactics. Her specialty lay in the ESF as both an active member and instructor. Her current fourteen students consisted mainly of Humans who were newly recruited into the Earthenian military. Interspersed were a few Oxyrans, Celehi and a young Teshian, all prepared to learn as much as possible on the ways of intergalactic warfare. They sat in a semicircle around the large, visual enhancement wall that, for the moment, remained blank to allow Colonel Amber Riechet to command the students' full attention.

"While a faction must hold a reasonable claim to an argument, and those without will not become involved in any declaration of war, it must be noted that subsidiary factions connected through family or marriage ties hold legal claims to land acquired by the warring faction. Knowing this, it is best to put down an aggressive faction immediately. Chances are, reclaiming will never be possible with the influx of Vairdec joining to hold the victor's spoils."

Amber's eyes trailed to her timepiece then to her father. Something about his stance made her uneasy.

"We are out of time for now. Be sure to read through section twelve by seven-o tomorrow. Simulated tactical runs will begin at that time. Check your data for your assigned space. Dismissed."

The class rose, saluting their superior before quickly transferring holographic notes that hung in front of each chair to their datapads and exiting quietly from the room. After accepting the salute from the last student out the door, General Riechet focused his attention on his approaching daughter. She was a tall woman in her thirties, slender, toned and well muscled, all results of the rigors of her military life. Her wavy auburn hair was pulled up in a sash that fell across her back, staying clear of her intense, dark eyes and hard-set features. The only life she had ever known was the military. Her bearing spoke clearly of that. She commanded respect.

"What are your feelings about this new batch of recruits?" he asked as she stopped before him.

"Average, I'm afraid. I don't see much potential for ESF from these. They apply themselves where needed, but don't show any extra application to their training. They just don't have the enthusiasm."

Riechet gave a disappointed huff. "Pity. They may be more apt to show enthusiasm for their training if they knew the extent of our insider information."

"Sir?"

"We're past the stages of rumors."

With a motion of his hand, Riechet signaled his daughter to fall into step beside him as they exited the lecture hall and began down the wide, main corridor of the underground base. Despite her growing questions, Amber refrained from speaking as they walked. Though there were few soldiers in the corridor at the time, she knew the importance of keeping her concerns over secret information to herself.

Turning sharply to the left, Riechet entered a brightly lit situation room with Amber right behind him. It was a circular room of minimalist features. Two rows of chairs sat around two-thirds of the perimeter, the middle being left open for computer imaging. Manning the current images from a side console was a stately Celehi woman named De'oolay Soe. She retained the title of SIERA's mastermind behind the computers; a specialist that Riechet relied on extensively to be kept up-to-date over happenings around Telamier and beyond. Upon seeing the general, she stood, brushing the single black, lavender-highlighted ponytail back over her shoulder. Beside her stood Lieutenant Colonel Jylin Py'guela, a Celehi whose stature and military demeanor made him an imposing figure in SIERA. As a member of the dominant species of the planet, he proved indispensable at keeping the peace among the various species training in Special Forces, where he partnered with Amber to manage training and organize missions. At the moment, his skin rippled a barely perceptible tint of anxious yellow.

"Sir," Jylin said upon seeing Riechet, "we have confirmation. Celharan High Command calls for their outlying colonies to send military aid to Celhara. The Vairdec have increased their numbers just outside the neutral zone."

Riechet took a moment to glance around the room, assessing the thoughts of those present. Along with the two Celehi was Mikander Soerin, a Human most commonly referred to as Mike among friends, of which he had plenty, for while he displayed a tough, physical bearing, his eyes betrayed his natural gentleness. At thirty-seven he had seen much of life, both good and bad, though he never allowed any of it to disrupt his calm mannerisms and playful wit. He possessed a natural ability to bring a calming presence with him. Even in the midst of such serious news, he refused to show any worry in his rugged features.

Mike withdrew his hands from his flight jacket and straightened slightly as Riechet's eyes passed over him. Riechet liked the young man. Along with his charming personality, Mike was the best fighter pilot in the unit. In fact he remained one of the Earthenian Air Force's top men whom Riechet fought hard to have transferred into SIERA permanently. The hard work and inevitable headaches came as a small price in Riechet's mind. He needed good pilots.

Standing near Mike was Riechet's only other fighter pilot permanently assigned to SIERA. Prysadeon-Marsoenian Alimar-Torsmod, known as Lash by most and going by Alimar for proper military address, was Teshian. He was a creature whose home planet of Hardiban lay within one of the closest solar systems to Telamier's own Ilus System. As a standard of the species he was slender and graceful with long white hair that he pulled back into a ponytail around large, pointed ears. He had a stout, rounded muzzle and piercing red eyes that glinted beneath an elegant spot pattern across his forehead. Riechet always found the Teshians a fascinating species, likening them to some of nature's most sinuous mammalian predators.

"De'oolay," Riechet said, keeping his voice calm and in control, "a super system map, please. Mark the colonies called to deploy."

"Sir."

A map materialized within the room's center, the different solar systems within the Chorbix Super System frozen in three-dimension before the general.

He examined it quietly, easily picking out Telamier that hung in its place in orbit around the Ilus star. Circling just beyond Telamier, the much larger planet of Ayzat, home of the Oxyran species, was clearly visible. Riechet ignored these features and with a motion of his hand, pushed the Ilus Solar System aside to draw the other systems across his line of sight. Like Ayzat, he ignored Hardiban, Borfax of the Faxons, Manog of the Manogonites and Airisus of the Airisons. Instead he focused on the marks where Celehi colonies were now preparing to send military aid to their home world. Only colonies furthest out seemed to be effected by the call, but the number still concerned Riechet. The Celehi were clearly taking this more seriously than past Vairdec raids. Carefully he measured off the distance until he stopped at the edge of the super system. There, three large planets circled the star, Jysah. Riechet's finger touched the image of the middle planet, allowing its name to flare up at the touch, though he already knew the planet well.

Celhara

It was the home world of the Celehi. As their numbers grew and their technology expanded, they ventured out to explore and settle new worlds. When they arrived on Telamier they found its rich natural resources much to their liking. Unfortunately, so did many other species. Colonies rapidly expanded, pressing against each other's borders. The territory skirmishes escalated into war, coming to a final showdown between the Vairdec and the Celehi. The Celehi proved the stronger, not by military standing, but by loyalty from Celhara. It was a large and well-fortified planet, able to send enough aid to finally drive the Vairdec away from the super system. Neither side forgot the outcome. Rumors of revenge increasingly found their way to Celhara. Still Riechet refused to jump to conclusions. Cupping his chin in his hand, he concentrated on the image before him.

"It's a long way for Telamier's reserves to go for the *possibility* of Vairdec activity entering the system." His eyes narrowed. "What are they not telling us?"

"Sir," De'oolay said, cutting into his thoughts. "Celehi Command requests an audience."

Riechet gave an approving nod. "It's about time they answered."

The map dissolved to be replaced by the images of several Celehi officials in government uniforms. Ambassador Agerbee, who knew the more obscure Human language, stood at the front. Everyone in the situation room spoke fluent Celharan and only out of respect did the Celehi Command choose to speak the language of the species they addressed. The ambassador was a tall, boney figure whose single, rich black ponytail now carried the luster of the typical maroon indicative of advanced years. His skin, too, had lost its light blue sheen of youth for a paler gray, though his eyes still held a great deal of fire.

"General Kyler Riechet," he began. "It is understood that you hold the knowledge of the Celehi's orders. "

"I have just been notified." He didn't try to hide his annoyance. "Though I would have preferred to be a part of the discussion, considering several top members of my division are suddenly moving out."

Agerbee remained unmoved. "We say sorry for your inconvenience. Regardless this matter belongs to Celehi. We believe we need not involve Humans in all situations, regardless of alliances we share."

"But as commanding officer of SIERA, I feel it is a matter of protocol to include me in the discussion involving members of this division."

"We agree your Human military does hold the division," Agerbee said. "You must remember Celehi funds to SIERA allow us to remove who and what we believe important to our needs. The current situation involves Vairdec, and SIERA-trained soldiers prove important to Celhara at this time."

"We do train for Vairdec aggression," Riechet agreed, "and I do not protest their going – only the lack of proper communication. If our societies are to work in close alliance, I would appreciate open lines of discussion. Furthermore, SIERA's numbers are taking a significant loss with the Celehi withdrawing."

"Your concern for this situation proves of lower importance. The battle is near Celhara, not Telamier."

Riechet calmed and placed his hands behind his back. "Then we have confirmation that Celhara is under Vairdec attack?"

"At this current time, no. Communications prove slow coming from great distances. Our knowledge includes the attacks of border stations.

More attacks took a Celehi cruise ship. Celhara calls for our soldiers. We send them."

"Have the Vairdec given a reason to attack?"

Agerbee gave a ripple of surprise. "Must I explain Vairdec reasoning to you?"

"As warring as they are, Vairdec do not attack without reason."

"We know Arct-Ieya commands the attacks."

At this the other officers in the room stiffened slightly, exchanging silent glances. Riechet remained stoic.

"It is a reason."

Amber studied her father's features. Her many years at his side made her a master of reading his unspoken thoughts and could tell that many serious matters lay heavily on his mind. Despite good reason for him to begin a debate with the Celehi Command, he refrained from speaking on any of his concerns.

"I do request that my two highest-ranking Celehi officers remain here. They are indispensable and I want a strong Celehi presence to remain visible within the division."

Agerbee gave a nod. "I will arrange your request be accepted."

"Thank you, ambassador."

The image faded but Riechet remained still until Jylin spoke.

"A strong Celehi presence to remain visible?"

Riechet relaxed and even allowed himself a slight smile. "Command likes the sound of it. If it keeps you here, I'll say it. De'oolay, did you know anything about Arct-Ieya leading this aggression?"

"No, sir," she said. "This is first news."

Keeping one hand behind his back, Riechet began to pace a few steps around the room, his eyes on the floor as he thought. "Arct-Ieya," he muttered.

"Is she not daughter of Arct-Morden?" Lash asked.

Riechet lifted his gaze in the Teshian's direction to give a quick nod. No further response was needed. Everyone knew the serious consequences that could arise from Arct-Morden, Supreme Commander of the Telamierian Colonization, having a surviving daughter now holding a position close to Celehi space. Riechet paced a couple more steps before drawing up short and turning on his heels to face his officers.

"Arct-Ieya's too skilled to attack a planet like Celhara without careful planning."

"She's had two hundred years," Mike said.

Longevity often played a key role in the reason the Vairdec tended to be so fierce – they had a long time to brood and plan. However, Riechet was not fully convinced of the strategy.

"She would have to control more factions than what her known social standing suggests."

"Can we question a vengeful female?"

Riechet chose to ignore Mike's whispered comment to Lash. "I doubt she has command over more than two, maybe three, factions. They would seriously hurt Celhara, but would not easily take the planet. Her losses would be too great. Her best tactic would be to strike the outlying colonies and weaken Celhara's allies before making an attack on the home planet. It appears she's allowing Celhara to know of her coming so they can rally their defenses."

"And after two hundred years of planning, you don't do that," Amber said.

"No, you don't." Riechet turned his attention to Jylin. "Py'guela, see to the Celehi soldiers. Make sure only Celehi equipment leaves this base. I won't tolerate them slipping away with any Human-funded supplies."

"Yes, sir."

"De'oolay, keep watch on those channels. I want to know everything that's happening on Celhara."

Riechet was already headed for the door as he spoke, motioning Amber to follow. The rest dispersed to their given tasks. Back in the main corridor, Riechet silently opened a line on his comlink. It needed no voice to activate, having picked up the mental number Riechet gave through the small piece tucked behind his ear. A slight vibration through the neckband signaled the connection was made.

"Darkracer, meet me in my quarters."

"I know that look," Amber said, having to quicken her step to keep up with the general. "What are you thinking?"

"Not here."

A couple minutes later they rounded the bend of the officers' quarters to Riechet's private apartment. Darkracer already stood waiting in the outer room as the general and Amber entered. In all appearances Darkracer resembled a large, black horse. He was well muscled with feathered feet, thick mane and wavy tail. Though horse he was not, and to call him one was a great offense. He was a Candonian, an intelligent creature whose kind formed the first alliance with the original colony of Humans who stepped through an enigmatic dimensional gate onto Telamierian soil two hundred years before.

The Candonians' appearance as horses gave a sense of comfort and familiarity to the founding colony, allowing for a strong bond to form between the two species. That alliance helped save the Humans from annihilation during the Vairdec War. Later it served to give them the regional status over the land they now called Earthenia. As the status could only be reached if a species population was no less than three-quarter million, joining with the Candonians allowed for the needed number to be reached. It did, however, mean that Earthenia was owned in part by the Candonians.

Thankfully, a peaceful coexistence developed rather quickly. Most Candonians happily left Humans to themselves as long as Humans agreed to leave the Candonian herds and their forest home alone. Interaction between the two species continued to lessen over the years, making Darkracer an exception to the norm. He and a younger male whose Human name was Phantom held the current distinction as the only Candonians serving in a Human facility. Unlike so many, they refused to forget the role their species played in the Vairdec War and the establishment of Earthenia.

"What's this about?" Darkracer asked.

He had studied and worked with Humans since his youth, allowing for flawless speech and a deep understanding of the species. Most of his time among Humans had been spent at General Riechet's side. It was as natural for Riechet to speak with Darkracer as it was for the Candonian to speak the Human's tongue.

"A suspicion I don't want spreading into rumor."

Darkracer's ears pricked forward. "Suspicion?"

"I don't think Arct-Ieya plans to attack Celhara. Why would she make her plans so obvious? That's not a Vairdec tactic. Why give the Celehi time to rally their forces?"

"Because she's not going after Celhara."

Riechet pointed firmly at his daughter. "Exactly. It's risky and complicated, but I think she could slip through the various defenses and make straight for Telamier."

Being in the privacy of her father's apartment, Amber allowed the persona of a colonel to slip away. She sank into a plush chair, worry etched on her face.

"Three factions might not destroy Celhara, but they'd make short work of us. Especially with so many Celehi leaving."

Darkracer wasn't ready to accept the bad news. "Can we be certain of this?"

Riechet, too, relaxed enough to lean back against a side table. "What better way to weaken Telamier than to send the Celehi reserves back to Celhara? The distance between our two planets can play well to Arct-Ieya's advantage. Send as many running in the wrong direction and when they're too far away to cause a problem..."

He finished by throwing up his hands.

Darkracer gave a shake of his head.

"How does she plan to send them all racing the wrong direction?"

"She already has," Riechet interjected. "She's made it clear that she intends to attack the Celehi. They assume her target is Celhara since that is where she is amassing her armies."

Darkracer refused to be convinced. "Perhaps she really is after Celhara. After all, it is right across the neutral zone – an easy target."

"She doesn't care about easy. Her grievances are with this planet. She was born here. Her mother was executed here. And like you said before," Riechet waved a hand toward Amber, "after two hundred years of planning, you don't take such a sloppy approach against a strong adversary."

"Surely the Celehi can see this, too," Darkracer said.

"I can't be sure of what they know," Riechet admitted. "Evidence says she's moving on Celhara. My gut says differently."

"Well if it's between your gut and their evidence, I'll go with your gut," Amber said with a huff. "No offense to the Celehi, they're smart, but let's face it, they're not always the quickest to catch a deception."

"Which the Vairdec are very good at," Darkracer added with a snort.

"Darkracer," Riechet said, straightening to take up the military persona once again, "I know you've been profiling possible recruits. We'll need them. I don't want to trust fully to our military pulling up all our reserves in time. Besides, I want specially trained individuals, not the average soldier."

"Won't this place us over SIERA's quota?" Amber asked. "The government's been pressing hard to balance unit numbers."

Riechet gave his daughter a firm look. "You let me worry about that. Hopefully the loss of the Celehi will count for something."

The twitch of the Candonian's ears signaled his concern. "The military won't like transferring, especially if they feel as you do about the Vairdec's plans. Most of those I've watched won't be easily brought to SIERA."

"Then look outside the military."

Darkracer blew through his nostrils as he thought. "There is one – San Terres. I've been watching him for some time."

"Malard?"

"Mhmm," Darkracer confirmed with a nod. "With him being CLE it'll be easier, but he's good. They won't like giving him up."

"Yes, I read of him. If he's as good as you say, I want him here." Riechet jabbed a finger at the floor to emphasize his words. "CLE has plenty of good officers and I'm finding myself suddenly lacking. With trouble brewing, I don't like the disability. Work with CLE and see what you can do. Amber, put some military brass behind that."

"Yes, sir."

"Racer, also see what you can do to get more Candonians to lend support. You and Phantom hardly constitute a reasonable representation of your kind."

"I always thought we were too much."

"I'll be in touch with the Earthenian government. And remember, not a word to anyone else at this time."

CHAPTER THREE

San Terres's CLE Headquarters buzzed with activity. Nine agents stood around the locker room, fitting on protective clothing and checking weapons. In their midst Melina Arzen stood gravely over a table holding a half dozen shock bombs and a sniper rifle. David wove his way easily through the hushed bustle to stand beside Melina. She snatched up the rifle to check the power cell once again.

"Heard you were joining," she said without looking up.

For several nahms she headed up the intelligence gathering for a drug operation that proved more serious than first thought. The decision had been made to strike immediately and the captain was calling in some of his best agents to assist.

"Disappointed?" David replied playfully.

A smile tugged at the corner of her mouth. "The captain hesitated, but this could be a difficult take-down. We need the best."

"Don't flatter yourself."

He leaned over to give her a quick kiss on the cheek.

"David," Melina scolded softly, pushing him back, "this isn't the time."

Melina's mood was tense and David knew when to back off. He turned his attention to his LB-49, a favorite weapon of his, to give him something to do in the awkward silence. The LB Class firearms possessed the unique ability to switch between lasers and bullets, giving them an advantage on a battlefield. Once perfected, the LB firearms quickly became the weapon of choice for both the CLE and the military. Though slightly larger than most handguns, its form made it easy to carry. Made from karnocite, it was lightweight, durable and sleek – all points David appreciated. His, being a 49, gave him one of the highest-level power cells available in handguns. Something in David told him he would need that extra power tonight. It was a feeling he wanted to suppress. Calmly he picked up a side arm and turned to Melina

"What are you worried about?"

Melina refused to answer. She kept her eyes on her work.

"Do you think the Pho'Max family's involved?" David pressed.

"Maybe behind the scenes," Melina finally said, "but they're nothing compared to this group's boss."

She gripped her gun tightly by the barrel, staring so intently at it that David began to wonder if she was trying to burn a hole through it with her mind.

"This is a big break," she muttered, "but if we're not careful, he'll take us out. The guy's ruthless."

"Does he have a name?"

"The underground only calls him the Assassin."

"The Assassin? Charming."

"According to the stories, he killed his own parents for the money."

"What's a guy like this running simple drugs for?"

"No idea. We're still learning about him. If we can bring him in…"

Melina took hold of David's arm, turning him to face her. David could see the tension in her eyes. She was always one to take her job seriously. He liked that about her.

"Just don't underestimate him."

A chill went down David's spine at her words, but he refused to show any fear or weakness in front of his future bride. "Well, he better not underestimate me."

He felt a hand press against his back. Keven stood alongside, his eyes remaining fixed on his younger sister. She tried to give him a weak smile.

"You two be careful out there," he told them.

"It's just another run," Melina answered, her harsher tone belying her obvious belief otherwise.

David jumped in to help ease the tension. "Exactly. We've done this before. Let's get it over with, okay?"

Keven gave him a gentle slap on the back then reached for his sister. After a quick hug he stepped back.

"Sorry I can't be with you, but orders place me elsewhere."

Melina touched his arm lovingly. "Don't worry about it." Her resolve strengthened. "Hey, I've got this crazy gun slinger beside me."

Keven eyed David with a smirk.

"Time to move," Captain Korshek called out before either could speak.

"Guess that's our cue," David spoke softly.

Melina gave her brother one last parting smile, a bit forced David observed, before slipping past. Keven placed his hand on David's shoulder.

"Take care of my sister," he said softly.

David gave his friend's arm a squeeze before stepping away. "Always," he said.

Less than an hour later, David and Melina took up their positions behind a small craft with weapons in hand. Night had fallen over the city several hours before, and with only one of Telamier's three moons barely above the city skyline, the landing dock remained shrouded in an eerie darkness – perfect for a sting operation. Surrounding the open space were a few low control buildings, a repair hangar and two docking bays. It was a private facility on the northeastern outskirts of San Terres, carefully selected to be away from prying eyes. David felt a thrill rise from the idea of playing a key role in the surprise attack the dealers were about to face. Their time of smuggling stolen Earthenian goods off planet in exchange for harmful drugs was at an end.

"That's where the contraband will be," Melina said softly, indicating the nearest docking bay across from them.

David glanced at the control building to the left. "Let's take higher ground."

Melina shook her head. "They control that."

"Not for long," he answered, moving stealthily into the shadows.

A firm grip on his arm drew him up short. He glanced questioningly at Melina, following her gaze to a platform to the right.

"A T-50," she said. "It's the first I've seen at an exchange."

Using a magnifier, David clearly saw what Melina's concern was. The T-50 was a rather large cannon to be present at a simple exchange of stolen goods. Most smugglers never went through the trouble or expense. Perhaps Melina's concern over this "Assassin" went deeper than David first wanted to believe. He gritted his teeth.

"Then we better shut these guys down fast," he said, trying to sound as optimistic as possible.

Melina was still not convinced. "I don't know. This isn't normal."

"You want to call it off?"

David could see the struggle in Melina. She had waited a long time for this moment. Not everyday did the smugglers' headman show at an exchange. This was an important takedown, for her, and for the entire agency.

"We could wait for a better opportunity." Her voice betrayed her dislike over her own thought.

"We lose this, we lose the boss," David reminded. He waited a moment, watching Melina glance between the cannon and him. A decision had to be made. "We're in place. We can take him."

Melina's eyes shone with sudden confidence as she studied David. She gave a firm nod. "Right. Like you said, the team's in place."

"I can call in air cover," David reassured in an attempt to put her more at ease. "Don't worry. Just stay with me."

"Heads up, everyone," Melina said quietly through her comlink. "T-50 on east tower ridge. Watch yourselves."

As Melina spoke, David made a call of his own back to headquarters to request air support to be placed on immediate standby. Once done, David looked to Melina.

"We might be able to take out the T-50's operators from the platform."

With a nod, Melina willingly followed him around the edge of the landing dock, staying concealed within the shadows as they approached a maintenance platform next to the control building. David moved quickly and silently to its base, keeping his eyes on a sniper stationed above. He enjoyed this part of his job; the hunt, the chase – he was a predator that was about to make his kill. Melina moved fluidly beside him. She was stealthy and sinuous in her movements, causing an excited chill to run down David's spine.

Keep your mind on your job, he ordered himself.

Reaching the top of the platform, David could see a Manogonite hunched over his rifle, focusing intently on the activity within the drop zone. Just perfect, David thought, another Manogonite. Their incredible hearing created unwelcome challenges to anyone trying to sneak up from behind. However, as David pulled himself over the edge of the platform, the creature did not move. His attention remained fixed on the activity below his perch. It seemed strange that he wouldn't think to watch his back, but David wasn't going to spend his time contemplating the lack of intelligence in criminal society. After all, could he really complain about his job being made easier?

Noiselessly he approached from behind. In one swift move he clapped his hand over the Manogonite's mouth while pressing his weight down across its back. As trained, he used his free arm and a knee to pin the wings securely to the body while Melina subdued the surprised creature with a tranquilizer. Feeling the muscles beneath him relax, David twisted his body around to pull his captive off his feet. The Manogonite's rifle dropped from his hands. Melina slid in to catch it before it clattered to the ground below, thus signaling their presence. She gave David a look of part relief, part annoyance. He gave a sigh as he cuffed the now unconscious sentry.

"That's why I have you," he whispered, hoping Melina remained unaware of how fast his heart was racing.

Taking up the Manogonite's position, and careful to stay in the shadows, they looked down on the landing dock.

"Now we wait," Melina said.

"Can your agent ID the boss?"

"He better, or this is all for nothing."

They watched in tense silence as the delivery of stolen goods changed hands. David studied the scene carefully, keeping watch for any sign of trouble. His breathing slowed to a steady, controlled rhythm. Long ago he discovered the value of training himself to breathe easy – to calm himself right before jumping into action. Be steady, be calm. Watch, wait… almost.

A sudden commotion sent a jolt of adrenaline through David's system. Shields sprang up out of nowhere on the dock. The agent spun in surprise, dropping dead before completing his turn. From the shadows a large contingency of battle-ready criminals emerged to attack the concealed CLE agents from two sides. Manogonites dropped from their high perches, screaming their war cries.

"We're tagged," Melina gasped.

She fired down one of the dealers as David focused on the T-50. Unfortunately the operators held secure positions behind the bulk of their weapon.

"Base," he called, "it's a setup. We're taking fire. Backup required."

At the sight of the cannon turning, David grabbed Melina's arm. Together they leaped for a second service platform. The structure behind them burst into flames, the impact throwing them to the edge. David frantically grabbed at Melina to keep her from slipping over the side and falling the fifteen feet to the dock's hard ground.

"Where's air cover?" Melina called over the noise of the fire.

"On their way."

Melina turned for the stairs leading down. A quick scan warned David that those with the cannon were not through searching for them. The stairs were too exposed. A short four-foot jump stood between them and a ledge to the control building's roof, its façade and upper floors providing protection against the cannon. If they followed the roofline, they could acquire a position above the weapon and hopefully disable it before air support arrived. Pulling Melina around, David motioned toward the ledge.

Melina gave no argument and together they jumped. The T-50 operator's attention remained on the activity below long enough for him to miss catching sight of the escape, giving David the chance to safely lead the way over the rooftop. A dark shadow moved off David's left shoulder. He glanced its way but when nothing else presented itself, he began to doubt his senses. Just get back in the game, he told himself. The CLE's aircrafts needed that cannon taken out immediately.

Suddenly the shadow reappeared, this time in front of them. A glint of metal in the figure's hand sent alarms screaming through David's brain. He pulled Melina down, avoiding the shot with only inches to spare. He fired back, but their adversary was prepared and easily blocked the shot with an arm deflector. Melina yanked David around a low wall as shots streamed around them.

"I think we found the boss."

David hurriedly adjusted his gun to its highest and deadliest power setting. Melina glanced back over her shoulder. The way remained clear and provided cover. Beyond the wall, the Assassin bided his time. This was their chance to escape.

"He holds the advantage. Let's go back."

David winced. Here stood the very target of the CLE's hard work. Agents had died that night trying to bring this criminal in. How could he explain running away now? After all, the Assassin was only a man.

"It's two against one. We just need to hold him a while."

"We don't have backup."

"They're on their way."

David smiled as much to calm himself as Melina. Quietly he reminded himself of the numerous situations he escaped from before, situations not unlike this. Just imagine this man as nothing more than so many other brutes successfully brought to justice. With Melina there, how could they lose?

Before Melina could argue, David jumped to his feet and vaulted over the barrier to take another position. Their opposition tracked him easily, using a high-powered night vision mask. He remained poised, even passive, as he positioned himself for the attack. David and Melina fired. Instantly the Assassin threw down a deflector shield, dispersing the shots. As the shield dissipated, he came to life. With a powerful spin, he flung a grenade at Melina while allowing his momentum to bring him into position with David in one fluid motion. He was moving fast, not allowing

David to switch tactics, forcing him to retreat from the barrage of firepower. Successfully evading the grenade's blast, Melina rolled to her stomach and fired low. Even while firing on David, the Assassin drew a second weapon he used to fire back at Melina. A pulse of energy struck her. Though uninjured, she found herself suddenly without use of the laser system of her gun.

David's heart beat madly against his chest. Never before had he seen anyone fight with such calm and deadly precision. Clenching his teeth he fought back the anxiety. This was only a man, he argued. David's successes included far larger opponents. He was good at what he did. He had to remember that. Switching his gun to bullets, David moved in. If this felon wanted to play hard, David felt more than willing to oblige.

The Assassin responded to David's turn to the offensive in the same calm, swift manner as before. Tossing his gun aside, he reached for a short, steel spike. With a flick of his wrist, one half went sailing forward on the end of a cable, striking David in the hand. David's shot missed its mark. The bullet passed harmlessly by its intended target to send Melina ducking to avoid friendly fire. The sight of her caused David to falter for a split second. The Assassin took full advantage, wrapping the cable tightly around David's wrist. David's gun clattered to the rooftop.

Melina rose shakily, holding her gun at ready. However, the Assassin anticipated her attack, shifting behind David and using him as a Human shield. David staggered blindly as the Assassin delivered a smashing blow to his face, pivoting enough to allow

Melina a chance to shoot. Spying the threat, the Assassin flipped a switch on his weapon and whipped the handle at her. A strong magnetic pulse yanked the gun from Melina's grasp. Keeping hold of the cable, he instantly drew the handle and gun back to his outstretched hand. Placing David between himself and Melina once again, he fired her own weapon at her.

Rarely had David ever felt so enraged. This creature dared to get the better of him. Worse, he attempted to kill Melina. David's desire for an arrest vanished. This was a fight to the death. He smashed himself back against his enemy as he grabbed for the gun hand. The Assassin wisely released the gun to avoid sustaining any serious injury in a disarming. Having replaced the spike on his belt, he turned on David in hand-to-hand combat.

As David twisted to face his opponent, he got his first real assessment of the man he fought. The Assassin was the same height and build as David, but despite the appearance of an even match, he quickly proved his superiority in battle. He was a killer. His skills and training far surpassed anything David possessed. This only enraged him further. He blindly struck at anything within his reach, each move blocked and countered with painful precision. David found himself slamming against the rooftop before he knew he had been thrown off his feet.

With the Assassin open, Melina raced in, firing her backup weapon. Her target dove out of the line of fire, his momentum sending him on his knees to slide toward Melina. He yanked the spike from his belt, smashing the sharp point into her chest as he and

Melina collided. David felt as if a wall of fire had slammed through his body. Searing heat rose through his entire being. White light blinded him. He cried out, unaware that he made any sound as he leaped for his enemy. The handle of the crime lord's weapon smashed him in the side of the head, sending him rolling.

David's hand landed on one of the fallen guns and he raised it in a blind rage. The Assassin kicked it from his hand, sending a second kick into David's ribs. He never felt the pain. Grief and fury drove all other senses from him. The impact rolled him once again, but he quickly stopped himself on his hands and knees. David never made it to his feet. The spike slammed down through his left shoulder, its point driving deep into the rooftop. David lay pinned and helpless. The sudden realization that he was about to die washed over him. How could this be the end?

To his surprise, the Assassin calmly walked away, leaving David to watch Melina drag herself toward him. The physical pain he felt didn't matter. Every fiber of his being longed to hold the one he loved. He tried to speak, but the words choked him and never came. Weakly David reached out to Melina. She reached for him as well, her fingertips almost brushing his before her body slackened. The light in her eyes faded in front of David.

CHAPTER FOUR

General Riechet walked quickly down the main corridor. He refused to run. Running was a sign of panic. It was an emotion he would not show to any in his command. Regardless of the urgency of De'oolay's call, he would move only with purpose and control. Upon entering SIERA's control room, he found her sitting in front of the main computer with ripples of yellow betraying her anxiety.

"It is now official," she said as the door closed behind the general. "Reports arrived stating one of Celhara's Command Posts is destroyed. Other attacks caused two high-ranking officials to die. An attack focused on a large civilian population. No confirmation on casualty numbers. The Vairdec claim responsibility and declare war on Celhara. Celehi armies from Telamier are deploying immediately. SIERA's Celehi unit is ordered to depart at thirteen-oh tomorrow."

"Is Arct-Ieya's army within range of Celhara?"

"The attacks come from smaller units. Celhara only views the full army through long-range scanners at the neutral zone. The Vairdec move fast – three factions, like you predicted."

"She's attacking Celhara with only three factions? And announcing it beforehand?"

Riechet could feel the instinctive unease washing over him. This was unlike any Vairdec behavior he had seen before, especially from a well-documented military mind such as Arct-Ieya's. Catching movement out the corner of his eye, he glanced over to watch Amber's approach. Her mannerisms remained stoic as she stepped alongside.

"Colonel."

"Sir."

"I think we're due for an unscheduled call-in, wouldn't you say?"

"Which reserves would you like to bring in?"

"All of them."

Amber shifted slightly, though remained at attention. "All of them, sir?"

"I'll explain to the defense board that I wish to test SIERA's response time. With everything happening on Celhara, they should let it pass. I'll leave it to your creativity to keep our unit here as long as possible. And check on the upcoming call-ins for the regular military reserves. Whatever was schedule for the next nahm I want in here now."

"Yes, sir."

"Hopefully I can convince the board to put the rest of the military at least on alert stand-by."

Amber gave a terse nod. "Let's hope so, sir."

"De'oolay, stay on those channels to Celhara."
Riechet turned on his heels to head for the door. "I
expect regular reports and should there be any
change, no matter how insignificant it appears, I want
to know."

"Yes, sir."

David lingered on a bench across from
Melina's gravesite. His left arm rested in a sling, but
he remained numb to his shoulder's pain. Though the
sky only now began to show the soft reddening of an
evening sun, to David the world lay black around
him. Three days had past since that tragic night.
Medics worked fast to heal David's injuries but there
was nothing they could do for Melina. The only
assistance anyone could provide her was a proper
burial.

Keven stood over his sister's grave, consoling
his parents as best he could. David had spoken very
little to his friend since leaving the hospital. He found
it difficult to look Keven in the eye. He hated the
grief he saw in him. More so he feared the questions
that lay in his friend's gaze. Though he suffered
through the retelling of the entire event for the
records, David found it impossible to speak of the
guilt he felt. The night played over and over in his
mind. He saw it every day. He lived it every night.
And each time it maliciously replayed itself, he
questioned the choices that ultimately cost him what
he loved the most. He had failed, and she paid the
price.

Keven slowly made his way past David's
bench.

"Keven," David choked as he rose.

A raised hand stopped him from approaching. David could feel the tightness in his chest.

"I…"

"Please," Keven said, his emotions causing the words to come out in a raspy whisper. "Please, not now. Just… not now."

Heartbroken and alone, David watched his best friend turn his back and walk away.

"I loved her, too," he managed to say, though it was only to himself.

Forcing back tears, David turned to the gravesite. His body tensed. A large, black Candonian stood over the grave. What was a Candonian doing here? Melina never mentioned knowing any. What possible business could he have with her? This creature held no connection to her in any way. The Candonian appeared to sense David's suspicious stare for he tossed his head to lock eyes with the young man, causing David to take a step back. Who was this great creature really looking for?

That night David locked himself in his family's estate to do something he usually avoided – get drunk. It was a trait David associated with his overbearing father, Benjamin Malard, who had been a wealthy, successful businessman in his time. He garnished great respect within the community and built a comfortable life for he and his wife and son. Many of his peers admitted being envious of him. He never lacked the physical comforts a well-situated life offered. Both David's mother and father proved successful in their professions, his mother being an interior designer and artist. Together she and Benjamin carefully designed and built their dream home atop the western hill known as Scout Ridge that overlooked the sparkling jewel of San Terres. They shared a passion for all things Earth, which drove them to build a home based on the known models shown in surviving pictures brought from the home world.

Theirs was not a unique fascination. Love for Earth was a common emotion among the Humans on Telamier. Two hundred years earlier, one hundred forty-one Humans from every reach of the home planet found themselves guided through one of the mysterious gateways to Telamier. Unfortunately, upon arriving, they became trapped, the secrets of the gateways vanishing into distant legend with the extinction of the gatekeepers. Ever since that time, Humans looked to Earth with wonder. It was their home world, though no living Telamierian Human had ever seen it beyond a few faded pictures. It was an agonizing concept to know that Telamier's own sister planet, separated only by the folds of space and accessed by enigmatic gates, was the home of their ancestry.

And so the Malards chose to build their home as a testament to their Earth heritage. A grand staircase graced the main hall. A ballroom and formal dining hall acted as a meeting place for important dignitaries Benjamin Malard often entertained. Even a grand piano, one built after years of research and countless payments, adorned the great room where David grudgingly played to the delight of guests. To the right of the entry lay the more intimate family room with a traditional fireplace and plush furniture. Around the edges numerous reproductions and a few actual Earth artifacts boasted the wealth of the Malards.

But all the wealth proved inadequate to save the Malards' marriage. At the age of fourteen David witnessed his mother leave without a word. He never saw her again. The breakup destroyed his father. David watched as Benjamin drugged himself further into despair. The habit finally claimed his life, leaving everything to David. The inheritance did little to stem the bitterness David felt. Though he often argued with himself that he held no responsibility to the Malards' downfall, he never fully believed his own words. Now the most unimaginable act crushed his spirit. He had failed to protect the one person he truly loved.

The lights remained off. David didn't need them to know his way around. He wanted the darkness. He needed the darkness. Clenched in his fist were a handful of alcohol pills, which he swallowed at regular intervals. He staggered as his leg bumped against the couch. Reaching out to catch himself against the fireplace, his eyes locked with a framed picture of his father.

"You knew, huh?" he said, imitating his father in a slow drawl. "What you hope to gain by the CLE, boy?" David's face flushed with rage. "Obviously nothing," he shouted, flinging the picture across the room.

After a moment he stumbled toward the sputtering image.

"You laughing, aren't you? Always knew better."

He gave the dying image a kick, nearly falling in the process. His left shoulder struck the wall. A burning pain shot along his back and neck. Oddly it felt almost good. David was unsure if it came from the alcohol or some deep need to feel something physical, something stronger than the emotional pain. With a moan he rolled against the wall to press his back against its cold surface. His mind swam with thoughts, but none would hold long enough for him to make any sense of them. Glancing to his right, he staggered through an arched doorframe into the slightly smaller sitting room.

Large picture windows made up one half of the room. Beyond, the world was black. David relished it. He stepped up to the dark green sofa, using it for balance as he faced another fireplace. Above it hung a beautifully fashioned sword. David's eyes narrowed.

"Jonathan Alsen."

After he convinced himself he was steady enough on his feet, he approached to remove the sword from its plaque. It felt good and solid in his hand – an old friend. Growing up he spent hours pretending he was the famous Earthenian hero, sneaking the sword from its place above the mantle much to his father's disapproval.

"A hero?" He spoke the words he so often heard in his youth. "You? The hawk?"

David drew his attention from the sword to a family portrait displayed on the nearby wall. Leaning in close, he spoke directly to the image of his father.

"I never understand you."

In a sudden fit of rage, David spun, swinging the blade wildly to cut through the wall. Anger enveloped him. The sword sang through the air, smashing into anything David managed to swing at. He felt detached from himself, like a spectator to his own movements. There was no control any more. Only rage – violent, pent up rage.

"Worthless," he shouted. "Coward. Failed."

He swung around, nearly falling over as he found his move blocked by another sword. Colonel Amber Riechet stood calmly before him. With a simple twist of her wrist she deflected his blade.

"Someday I'll teach you how to use that," she said.

The shock of seeing her appear so suddenly melted back into anger. What was this apparition? Why did she come to mock him? David lunged. Amber remained undeterred, easily sidestepping out of his path. With a simple move, she disarmed him and pushed him down onto the couch. David blinked, slowly realizing the woman was real.

"How'd you get in?"

"Not your concern."

Amber sheathed her sword before raising David's for a quick examination. It was etched near the hilt with the image of a crown, sword and stone. She gave an approving nod.

"Nice replica but still not a Blade of Norian." She paused to study David. "Alsen fan?"

"Get outta my house."

"You want to be like him?"

David gritted his teeth. He was not in the mood to tolerate intruders. Slowly he reached for a concealed gun that lay under his rumpled jacket. Amber didn't flinch. Still looking at the sword, she drew a gun of her own and pointed it at David.

"Don't try it," she warned in a smooth, calm tone.

David released his hold on the grip. Drunk as he was, he was no fool. To his surprise, the same Candonian he observed standing at the gravesite, suddenly appeared out of the shadows to reach over the back of the couch with his head. Taking the gun in his teeth, he pulled it from its holster and dropped it out of reach. David made no move to stop him. He was too shocked to respond. How did he miss the entrance of not only this strange woman but a Candonian as well? Was he really that drunk? Furthermore, how did they manage to slip past the house's security?

"Fia! Who are you guys?"

"Colonel Amber Riechet, Strategic Intelligence and Enforcement Regional Agency. Our Candonian liaison, Darkracer."

David had heard enough. "Get out." Amber remained where she was. "What do you want?"

"You."

"Sorry, not my type."

Amber refused to be rattled by David's remark. Instead she watched without emotion as David reached into his pocket to pull out another handful of alcohol pills. Before he could take any, Darkracer swung his head to strike David's hand. The pills scattered across the carpet.

"Fia!"

David tried to rise, but the tip of his sword pressed against his chest in response. Angrily he looked between the blade and Amber.

"Who you think you are? Natchua?"

"Do you want to find out?"

Was she serious? David couldn't be sure.

"Thought you were SIERA," he quipped.

"I am. We want you to join."

"No."

"Well, the CLE doesn't seem to hold any interest for you anymore."

The words cut deep and David found his temper rising.

"No."

"Really? And there's no convincing you otherwise?"

"No."

"You plan on wasting away in here?"

"Maybe."

Amber's eyes burned into him. "I doubt that. I think you want to be something more than…" she gave a disapproving wave across David's slouching form, "this. Am I right?"

"No."

"That's not the way I heard it."

"Not my fault."

"You come highly recommended."

"Not interested."

"I see." Amber turned away, resting the blade on her shoulder as she pondered David's predicament. "You're going to waste your life," she looked him over again, "or what's left of it, as a filthy drunkard. You're going to forget all the hard work, the struggles, the challenges you overcame. And obviously you don't care about the memory of those who fought to help you get there. If you can't be perfect, you can't be anything. Is that it?"

David winced under Amber's sharp words and penetrating stare.

"Maybe you really didn't love her."

David clenched his fists, his face flushing. "You pissin' sob!"

In a sudden burst of rage, David lunged forward. Amber easily sidestepped his attack. Grabbing hold of his good arm, she twisted it behind his back and spun him around. In a single, swift move she caught his leg with her foot and threw him off his feet. Almost as quickly as he had risen, David found himself seated back on the couch. Amber stood threateningly over him, her knee pressing into his thigh, her hands firm against his shoulders.

"Now you listen to me," she snarled as she leaned in to his face. "I really don't care about your little pity party. You think you're the only one who's had to deal with loss? Well you're not, so you've got a choice. You can join the group that curls up in a sniveling wreck of their former selves or you can fight back. It's up to you, but if you choose to quit it will be a spit upon her grave. I'm giving you the chance to prove you're not the sob you look like right now. There's a situation that needs dealing with and I believe you have what it takes to prove you're better than this."

David sat dumbfounded as Amber reached across to Darkracer's saddle to pull another blade from its sheath. She dropped it into David's lap and stepped away.

"That's not a replica."

With that she and Darkracer left the room.

Darkracer gave a snort as he waited with Amber in the front entry.

"I can't believe you gave him *Legacy*," he said in a hushed voice.

Amber shrugged. "You want the guy? He'll bring it back." As she spoke, David stepped slowly around the corner, holding the sword in both hands. "See?"

David looked between the Candonian and woman, the anger having been replaced by curiosity and emotional fatigue.

"What kind of situation?"

CHAPTER FIVE

David found himself turning in circles as he took in the activity surrounding him within the SIERA's main holding bay at Valor Peak. Transports were in various stages of loading. A few skiffs sat heaped with supplies being checked by an Airisun and Human corporal. A crane swung over their heads as it lifted another skiff to a new location. Everywhere newly arrived members of SIERA and other military units were hurrying to get to their respective places within headquarters.

Amber's step was proud and authoritative. As she went, people hurried out of her way, saluting as she passed. David felt a bit awkward. He dropped his gaze to the floor and pulled his pack higher onto his shoulder. Amber could not be any older than he but had risen to a very high-ranking position, one he managed to embarrass himself in front of the night before. His head still throbbed from the pills. The echoing bang of metal on metal made him cringe. Hot, pulsing pain through his shoulder left his arm limp within its sling.

What was he doing here? It was a question he repeatedly asked himself ever since he agreed to meet with General Riechet. It would have been so easy to stay at home. He did not really need a job – certainly not for some time. His inheritance could last him years.

"Sergeant."

David jumped at the sound of Amber's shout. Slowing, he watched as the colonel jogged over to a crate being unloaded. The sergeant and corporal stopped their work to salute. Amber immediately reached past them to pull out a rifle.

"Is this the new line?"

"Yes, ma'am," the sergeant replied. "J-Class sniper."

Amber gave an approving nod. "Excellent."

Slinging the rifle over her shoulder, she continued on her original course, not acknowledging David as she passed. He knew to follow and hastened into step at her shoulder. From across the hangar he watched as a man in a flight jacket jogged toward them.

"Commander," Amber acknowledged.

Mikander Soerin gave a quick salute. "Colonel." Falling into step, he gave a sweeping gaze of the holding bay. "I haven't seen it this busy since the Heedaran terrorist strike."

"How's our response time?"

"SIERA's spurred but the rest could kick it up," Mike replied. "They're not doing badly, though, all considering. Most of the non-SIERA members were newly recruited, just in for mental training. Some haven't even seen Eenosha's physical courses yet. There are a lot of questions over what they're expected to do next."

"Whatever they're ordered to do," Amber answered curtly.

Mike eyed David carefully. "So this is the new recruit. We could use a few more, you know."

Amber didn't comment as she instead listened to an incoming private call.

"On my way, sir," she answered.

Mike took the time to slip behind Amber to come alongside David.

"What's your name?"

"David Malard."

"Mikander Soerin."

David returned the pilot's sweeping gaze with one of his own. "Flight?"

"Mhmm. One of the only fighter pilots in the division. Pity, huh?"

"I don't know."

Mike gave a weary chuckle. "You've got a lot to learn."

David continued to follow Amber out into the main corridor. He was surprised to see the activity dissipate once they emerged from the holding bay. Those he met in the corridor expressed a decidedly more relaxed state, moving about in normal military base fashion, coming to attention as Amber passed, before resuming their own quiet business. She led the way past a workout center and shooting gallery, those training inside causing David to slow a couple steps to observe the soldiers' abilities. The exercises were nothing new to him although he felt inadequate to tackle such courses at present. He must be mad to be here.

Within a few minutes, David found himself standing in a small office before General Riechet. Amber quietly exited, leaving the two men alone.

"David Malard."

David set his pack at his feet and stood at attention. Though he never trained directly in the military, the CLE demanded a great deal of the same protocol. He could sense Riechet's approval.

"I see my daughter has convinced you to come in. She can be very persuasive."

"Yes, sir."

"You come highly recommended. Unbeknownst to you, we've been watching your progress in the CLE. Your skills are exceptional. I heard talk that your name was being placed in upcoming promotion lists."

David allowed his gaze to drift from the general to the far wall. All that lay behind him now.

"I…"

"You may speak freely."

Something in Riechet's voice calmed David. The general was a powerful man, one whose reputation made him known even within the CLE. Standing before him now, David observed that as commanding as his reputation was, the general was not unapproachable. David found himself growing confident before Riechet, though he chose his words carefully nonetheless.

"I suppose that's not possible now, sir."

"Why not?"

David struggled to find the words. "I… if… I chose to go the route I did. I led Mel… Agent Arzen into the ambush. I couldn't protect her."

"You did what you felt was right. Under the circumstances, there were few choices before you. Reviewing the reports I find no blatant irresponsibility on your part. Much of what you feel is personal grief. It's all too common for us to wonder if we could have done things differently. The problem is, none of us know what the outcome will be, even with our best efforts."

"Yes, sir. I…"

David's words trailed off and he tightened his mouth less he say something regrettable.

"Go ahead."

A tentative glance at the general warned David not to refuse. "With everything that's happened, I don't know if I can do… I don't feel like I…" David took a deep breath and forged ahead. "I failed. Reports or not, I couldn't stop her from dying."

"Was it in your power to have it otherwise?"

The question caught David off guard. Taking a deep breath he let his gaze drop to the floor.

"Sir, I don't know."

"A wise man admits to mistakes." David refused to look up. "Your desire to protect the one you love is very honorable. Sadly, though we may wish to keep our loved ones safe, our best efforts can fall short. Some things are beyond us." David slowly looked up. Was the general still speaking to him? Riechet stood half-turned with his hands clasped behind his back. "If it means anything, I am truly sorry for your loss, and though it will sound meaningless at this time, I understand how you feel. I'm afraid you will always carry the scars, but you strike me as one who will bear them well."

"I hope so, sir."

A hand gripped his right shoulder. "The past is not the full measure of the man. Perhaps here you will have the opportunity to learn that."

David drew his gaze back to the general. He had spoken with superiors many times in the past. This did not feel like any of those times. Instead, he felt surprisingly at ease due to the notable compassion in the older man's voice. There lay an earnest respect in him that demanded the same respect back. David wondered if this was what a conversation with a father should feel like, for he found himself looking upon not a superior officer, but an honorable leader.

"If I may," Riechet continued. "You found the courage to come here. That says a lot about a man. But why did you? What possessed you to come to me? As persuasive as the colonel is, she did not force you at gunpoint."

A heavy weight of uncertainty fell upon David's shoulders. It was the very question that he struggled with ever since he stepped aboard the transport that flew him from San Terres to Karnoss. By the time he followed Amber into the military craft that provided them a short flight to Valor Peak, he felt physically exhausted with the question. Unfortunately he still found it impossible to come up with a reasonable answer.

"Perhaps," he said slowly, "I just can't sit still for very long."

"You're a fighter," Riechet answered with such confidence that David wondered if he had really needed to ask the question in the first place. "You don't give up easily, and I'd hate for you to start now. Fights must be fought on many different battlefields, but you, David, have what it takes to face them. Otherwise you would not be standing here now."

A wave of energy flowed through David. Through the grief and pain he felt the subtle twinge of fierce determination, the same feeling that saw him through countless days of family quarrels and disintegration. It always drove him to levels he never knew he could achieve. Would it now be enough to carry him through this new 'battle' as the general so eloquently put it? He could not tell for sure, but at least here, with this man, he felt he might have a chance. Deep down, he still wanted that. Looking General Riechet squarely in the eyes, David straightened.

"Sir, what are your orders?"

A smile creased the lines around the general's warm eyes. "I'll have Commander Soerin show you to the officer's bunks. You'll retain your rank of First Lieutenant and join the Special Forces branch. Settle in quickly. There's much to do. Your information will be processed immediately." He stepped back to salute David. "Welcome to SIERA, Lieutenant Malard."

David returned the salute, heart pounding madly. What had he done?

"It might not be much," Mike confessed as he and David stood in the male officer's quarters a few minutes later, "but believe me, I've seen worse."

David took a careful look around him. He was standing in a T-shaped room, spacious, but not overly so. The main part in front of him was set sparsely with a few tables and chairs. To his left, the room stretched back with a long row of bunks stacked three high lining both sides. Lockers separated each stack.

"So which bunk's mine?"

"Whichever's not taken," Mike said, going to one of the lockers to pull out a stack of blankets and a pillow. Handing them to David, he pointed to an empty lower bunk.

"So," David began, fishing for some form of casual conversation, "you're a fighter pilot?"

"That's right." Mike leaned back against the lockers. "Served nine years in the Earthenian Air Force before coming here."

"Any particular reason for the change?"

Mike waved off the question. A long uncomfortable silence followed.

"You're one of the only pilots?" David ventured.

"*Fighter* pilot. Enough know how to fly air transports and such."

David smoothed the blankets on the bunk. "Why is that? You being the only one?"

"Not enough ships. My co, Lash, has his Max-180, and I've got the *Predator*. That's it."

"*Predator*?"

"CAF-47. Great ship. Ever flown in one?"

David had to admit that he had not. He knew about them, though. Despite his decision to join the CLE, David studied the Earthenian military with great admiration for as long as he could remember. It remained separate from the Coalition as each region constitutionally maintained complete control over its own military operations.

The Cross Atmospheric Fighter was a popular ship within Earthenia's arsenal. Capable of atmospheric speeds of over 2,500 kilometers an hour, it was the largest fighter craft in the Air Force with a wingspan of twenty-seven meters. With the ability to perform equally outside an atmosphere as within, the CAF often carried strike teams or supplies, its fuselage being able to hold up to ten passengers with gear. Despite its size, the ship was extremely agile, able to maneuver as easily as smaller ships while providing a great deal of firepower.

"It wasn't easy getting her transferred to this division," Mike continued. "Luckily the general can be very persuasive."

"So can his daughter."

"What?"

"Nothing. You'd think the government would supply SIERA with a few more ships."

Mike shrugged. "Funding isn't always the greatest. I guess the government wants to be sure the Air Force has what they need first."

"I always thought SIERA was important."

Mike gave a laugh. "Ah, who knows what they're thinking. And now with the Celehi taking off for Celhara, the ships we were hoping for have been rerouted."

"Wonderful."

CHAPTER SIX

The stairway shifted as David twisted to the right, narrowly avoiding the swinging arm meant to knock him from his place. After a second to steady himself, he climbed the rest of the way to the platform, ignoring the continued movement of the stairs. Reaching his destination he took a moment to catch his breath and survey his surroundings once again. Four days had past since his arrival at Valor Peak. Every day he worked the repaired muscles of his shoulder a little more, impressed with the rate of healing. For the time being, the training center remained empty, providing him with a nice opportunity to test his physical stamina away from watchful eyes. Taking a deep breath, David turned his attention to the second part of the course.

Ahead stretched a narrow beam that led to another platform. From there he would have to jump, catch a rope and swing to the opposite side. Having already mastered the climbing wall, tunnel and nets, this last bit appeared relatively simple. David jogged confidently out onto the beam. Usually the training included targets to shoot as the trainee made the run, but for the time being, David left that out. He neared the platform, feeling that the most difficult section lay behind him.

His foot struck the ledge and the world changed around him. The same feelings, thoughts, even images of that fateful night shot through his brain. Once again he stood on the edge of the service platform, ready to make the jump for the rooftop. The rooftop – why there? Why had he led her there? He could see her make the jump and through impulse alone he followed.

Only as the ground dropped out from under him did the reality of his move become apparent. Surprised to see the rope suddenly before him, David made a grab for it. Too late. His hand brushed the lifeline for only a second as he fell, his back smacking the mats. Though they cushioned his fall, he still managed to get the air knocked from him. As a result, he chose to stay sprawled on the floor a minute longer before struggling to his feet. His body shook and he felt light, as if he had somehow become disconnected from his physical form. The memories remained vivid, confusing his senses and threatening to break him. Enough was enough. With a grunt of defeat, he stepped off the mats and headed for the door.

David leaped back as he suddenly saw General Riechet blocking his path. He was surprised by his presence, as he neither saw nor heard the general enter. The surprise melted quickly into embarrassment at being caught off guard. Riechet stood quietly, his look passive, calm, yet strong. David hurriedly drew himself to attention, keeping his gaze on the floor in front of him. He could not bear to look into those deep, powerful eyes. Step by deliberate step, Riechet approached until he stood so close David could make out the threading of the general's uniform. Riechet said nothing, any thought well masked behind a persona of apathy. Quietly he studied the platform and rope before looking back at the man before him.

"Do it again," he said softly.

David winced at the words. He had hoped to slip unnoticed from the training center and return to his bunk in defeat to agonize in silence over his grief. He did not possess the mental energy to try anymore. However, he knew the danger in refusing the orders of a general. His voice barely escaped his tightened throat.

"Yes, sir."

Per Riechet's instruction, David bypassed the bulk of the course to instead climb a side ladder to the platform from which he fell moments earlier. The rope seemed to taunt him as it hung three meters from where he stood. He didn't want to do this right now. He couldn't handle it. Rotating his shoulder to be sure all was working properly, he took a deep breath, stepped back and made the leap. Though his hands caught hold of the rope, his grip failed and he slipped downward, the momentum of his swing coming up short of the second platform. Unable to hang on, David allowed himself to half slide, half fall from the rope to the mats. Breathing unnaturally heavy, he rose to find the general standing before him.

"Again."

David felt his stomach drop at the word. Reluctantly he climbed once more to the platform. This time, instead of carefully studying the distance he lunged out angrily. Catching the rope, he swung toward the far platform, but as his feet touched the edge, his grip slipped and he found himself once more on the mats. A sharp stab of pain coursed through his injured shoulder. He winced as he got to his feet, disheartened even more by the general's presence.

"Again."

David grimaced, feeling as if icy needles jabbed his flesh. For a brief moment he wondered what would happen to him if he refused an order. However, though General Riechet had yet to express any harsh manners toward him, David felt incapable of deliberately making him angry - not out of fear but out of respect. With a terse nod, he once again did as asked and once again found himself failing. Still, Riechet would not yield.

"Sir," David said, his voice cracking under a mix of emotion and fatigue. "I'm afraid I haven't quite healed yet."

Riechet reached out to take David's left arm. He ran his hand along it, examining the shoulder as David slowly rotated it. Calmly he gave a nod.

"Yes, you are still healing, but your shoulder is fine."

David stood trembling from the exertion, knowing what the general would say next, but not wanting to move until it was imperative.

"Again."

Slowly David returned to the platform. For a long moment he stared at the rope. What was he doing here? Why had he chosen to come? He was a fool. He could not do this. A moment later he picked himself up from the mats. Anger boiled up in him. This was stupid. He could not even complete a simple exercise – one he had successfully mastered numerous times in the past. How could he let this be the impression he left the general? It was embarrassing. It was wrong. He had to be better than this. Without waiting for the general to speak, David turned on his heels and climbed the platform once again.

General Riechet gave only the slightest smile as he watched.

"Well done," he said too softly for David to hear. "Well done."

With that he quietly left the room.

It was getting late the following evening and the officer's mess was only dimly lit when David entered. Quickly he sought out a secluded place in the corner. He held no desire to mingle. It had been a long day of physical evaluations and personal training with the general. Now, after pouring himself a hot drink, he wanted nothing more than a quiet corner to settle into in order to study his files on Vairdec attack strategies. He had not gotten very far before voices and footsteps drew his attention to where Mike and Lash, entered at the far end. With a disappointed sigh he shifted deeper into the shadows. The one problem with military bases was the lack of privacy. Keeping their voices low, the pilots went to the main counter to grab a couple drinks and a few snack foods that remained out for those working late. As they turned to

75

leave, Lash paused to stare intently at David who pretended not to notice.

"Do you mind if we're here?" Mike asked.

David glanced up. "Not really," he lied.

Lash's red eyes narrowed. "The new one?"

"Oh, yeah." Mike stepped forward and David relinquished his solitude by shoving the pad aside and leaning back in his chair. "Um, David, right?"

David gave a nod. "Malard."

"That's right. David Malard, Prysadeon-Marsoenian Alimar-Torsmod, call sign Lash – which is what we all call him around here."

For obvious reasons I'm sure, David thought. Out of respect, he kept his comment to himself and half rose from his chair to place his flat palm atop Lash's in a typical Teshian greeting. "Nice to meet you."

Mike pointed to the table. "Do you mind?"

With a shrug, David motioned for them to sit across from him. At least they appeared polite company. He supposed he could suffer their presence for a while.

"Now you were in the CLE, is that right?" Mike asked as he took a bite from one of the bread sticks.

"I was," David answered flatly, shaking his head when the food was offered to him.

Lash's eyes glimmered over the rim of his glass. "More interesting with military life?"

David refused to look at him. "At this time."

An awkward silence followed. Mike could sense a nerve had been struck with David. He was curious to know what was holding the new SIERA officer back, for it did not seem his usual nature. However, Mike was sensitive enough to know when not to say anything on the subject.

"Where are you from?" he asked instead.

"San Terres."

"Ah, nice. Lived there for a while. Most of my life has been in the Air Force, so I get around."

"I see."

"You wouldn't happen to be related to the Malards up on Scout Ridge, would you?"

"My father."

"Really." Mike leaned back to study David with renewed interest. "Heard he's some rich business tycoon."

"Was."

Mike dropped his gaze to the table. "I see. I'm sorry. I didn't…"

"We were never close."

Another silence. Pangs of guilt rose through David. The pilots only wished to be friendly. He admitted it felt good to be welcomed into the unit. If only he didn't have so much weighing on him. With an effort, he tried to be more cordial.

"What of you, Lash?" he asked. "What brings you to Earthenia?"

The Teshian bared his teeth in a crafty smile. "A change."

"Lash and I've worked together for years, so we're real co's now," Mike explained.

David glanced between the two. Yes, they certainly shared an air of close camaraderie, true friends as Mike so proudly pointed out.

"We were part of an international squadron linked in part to the Earthenian Air Force," Mike continued. "I couldn't ask for a better wingman."

"Events make SIERA an interest to me," Lash added. "Humans study Vairdec well. I wish the same to be on Hardiban. Teshians also like little of Vairdec."

"Do you really think the Vairdec are a threat right now?"

Both pilots shifted uneasily. Mike could not be sure how much General Riechet had already told David. It was best to word the answer carefully. Reaching across the table he pushed the datapad toward David.

"Let's just say the more you study the better."

CHAPTER SEVEN

Deep within the holds of space the Celehi convoy from Telamier had joined with its other reserves from various colonies across the super system. Numerous battle cruisers, heavy transports, freighters, command ships and shuttles banded together in an ever-expanding army. Once again two of the galaxy's super powers would clash.

A brooding tension settled quickly over the battleship *Troby's* bridge. Its admiral, Sladoe De'lia Nalor, stood at his post, reluctant to stand down and rest though several days remained before the gleam of Celhara would become visible out the main view port. His knowledge of his enemy made it difficult for him to relax. Not many aboard his vessel had seen a Vairdec in person. He had, serving long years along the borders of the super system - a place the Vairdec regularly tested the vigilance of their enemies by slipping in and out of forbidden zones. They were a formidable force, even in small numbers.

"Eirab-nia," he muttered.

He cared little for an answer. He knew the number of days it took to reach his home world. The words escaped his lips more for his own sake as he considered the long, impatient wait before the storm of war. His eyes narrowed as he fingered a knife at his side. It once belonged to a Vairdec warrior, one he slew many years ago when he stole the blade and used it against its owner. He intended to use it again. His first officer, Captain Ry'Gia, stepped closer to keep his words from being overheard by others on the bridge. He had heard many rumors since leaving Telamier as to the size of the Vairdec army. Now that he was well on his way to war, he wished to know the truth of the number of factions. If word proved true and they were headed toward two instead of one, driving the Vairdec off could prove more difficult, and more deadly.

"Rye agnileet deekat nakrone?"

"Mol."

The captain gave a slight shudder, trying to hide the ripple of yellow in his skin. The concern over two factions melted away. Things were far worse with three.

"Co ultit Vairdec."

Admiral Nalor nodded, his skin and expression remaining unchanged. Regardless of the fact that over a million warmongering invaders awaited them, he refused to show fear.

"Kit quantet reflet gin coeshait," Nolar said, reminding Ry'Gia of the first war, which they won. "Nu darquev deekat amion'el. Deekat jap yark."

Yes, he restated in his mind to reassure himself, they would win again.

Nalor found it far more difficult to hide his feelings. Despite the encouraging words, he knew the battle would not be so easily won. The Vairdec had learned much about the Celehi since the war for Telamier. They continually strove to perfect their tactics and killer precision. Meanwhile, the long span of peace within the Celharan nations left the vast majority of Celehi soft and unprepared for such an assault. In matters of war, the Vairdec held the advantage. But where the Celehi lacked viciousness, they made up for in pride. The pride they held for their species and homeland provided a strong motivation to stand firm.

"Lattonleet," the helmsman called, alerting the admiral. "Yenit rea gross wygrin-auh."

Nalor remained unmoved. Reading ships on the sensors held many explanations. Panic would not be tolerated.

"Nia toaf?"

The helmsman shook his head, unable to draw up an accurate count of the approaching ships' numbers. "Naket. Ordinal rysh."

A petty officer quickly took up a new station behind the helmsman. Captain Ry'Gia pressed closer to Nalor. Scrambled signals came as a bad omen.

"Eing yenit trose?"

"Dee holepet…" The helmsman struggled to find an answer to the types of ships on approach. A sheen of yellow suddenly rippled across both his face and the petty officer's, who turned sharply to her commanding officers.

"Taun, yencoeshait."

Identifying battle cruisers made even Nalor tense. Captain Ry'Gia tried to remain hopeful that the cruisers belonged to another Celehi convoy.

"Deekat?"

The helmsman, unable to get a lock, could not be sure. "Naket. Dee ouse'ed-et katoe."

"Nia toaf?"

The crew on the bridge glanced back at the stern features of Admiral Nalor, still unable to discern any change in his color. The petty officer straightened, trying to follow his example.

"Yeerye. Quant shlida."

Captain Ry'Gia glanced questioningly at the admiral. One battle cruiser moving toward them with scrambled signals proved suspicious enough, but over twenty of them? Perhaps they were Teshian class coming from Hardiban. This he put to Nalor, but the admiral was not convinced. If that were so, why were they moving in the opposite direction of Celhara?

"Ordar katoe," he ordered.

The communications officer responded, sending the hail. A moment later he glanced back in defeat.

"Holepet."

"Lattonleet!" The helmsman nearly stood as he spun to face Nalor. "Vairdec!"

Just off the starboard side of the *Troby*, the battleship *Shendron* also discovered the same horrifying truth - an ambush. With orders from Nalor, the multiple pilots on the bridge hurriedly changed course to bring the two battleships to bear on the enemy. Ahead and closing fast, ships enough to carry three factions of Vairdec spanned across vast reaches of empty space. They appeared from nowhere, dropping through long-range vis-shields that had gone before them with an empty image of space, able to confuse the naked eye and sensors alike. Battle cruisers, Concussioners, fighters, transports, Bloodrunners – all heavily armed with cannons, missiles and giant gun ports - bore down upon the unsuspecting convoy.

Upon orders of the *Shendron's* captain, pilots frantically raced for their fighter crafts that hung in wait for battle within the hold of the main ship. Lights flashed. Alarms wailed. As the outer doors of the hold ground open a missile ripped through the inner doors, detonating upon exposure to the oxygen filled room.

Admiral Nalor watched from the bridge of the *Troby* as a flash of blinding light flared for a fraction of a second from the *Shendron's* hangar. One of their largest ships lay crippled and the battle had only just begun. His fingers tightened around his knife's hilt. With great effort he controlled his emotions, focusing on the task at hand. Beside him stood Captain Ry'Gia who found courage in the admiral's strength of character. Together they called out orders to intensify firepower on given ships, focus on specific weak points in the Vairdec defense and try moving out of the pack to keep from being surrounded. Admiral Nalor was aware the orders were the best they could give, but secretly knew it was in vain. Their ships were being ripped apart with vicious accuracy.

"Coeshyen-deekat lyndet yenpreed," Ry'Gia informed.

Nalor knew their fighters were useless. The Vairdec planned the ambush perfectly, focusing a great deal of effort on keeping the larger ships from opening their hangar doors. Smaller ships burst apart as missiles sliced their hulls and larger enemy ships, well protected with armored plating, ripped through their ranks. Little hope remained for the Celehi against such intense opposition. Word must be sent before all was lost. He knew trying to direct the mayday to Celhara would be pointless. The Vairdec surely saw to a block in communications. An "all hail", sent generically to any allies within range, had to be sent.

"Broust ordanalamo."

It was the last order Admiral Nalor ever made.

CHAPTER EIGHT

A flash of bright light lit up the training room, the nerve-grinding buzz of the alarm replacing the earlier sounds of battle.

"Freeze program."

At Darkracer's command, the holographic images of Vairdec soldiers froze in their various attack positions. The Candonian stepped up to one who held a large, wide-barreled weapon. He glanced from it to his pupil.

"You're toast."

David angrily kicked a low training wall in frustration. "Well aware of that."

"Flamethrowers – one of the ugliest weapons in the Vairdec arsenal, which makes them an instant favorite. They will always stay on the same trajectory and always lose power after seven meters. Best way to avoid them is to duck. And don't worry about being hit while getting up. Once fired, flamethrowers need time to recharge. Personally I would make a point on killing any Vairdec I see carrying one."

David begrudgingly listened to the lecture, already aware of the weapon's deadly capabilities. His problem came not from inexperience with the weapon, but a deep apathy for any current activity. The last two days dragged by for him, proving emotionally trying. He could not be sure why now as opposed to the days directly after Melina's death. Upon entering SIERA he had hoped the activity would keep his mind off his grief. Unfortunately that was not the case. Most of the time he felt numb and irritable, which only made him feel worse, for he truly longed to feel differently. But how? Slowly he allowed himself to sink to the floor, resting his back against the wall.

"I can't do this."

"That's the attitude," Darkracer retorted. "Go again."

David refused to move. "This is crazy."

"Funny, that's what I would say about your attitude."

David glared up at Darkracer only to receive flattened ears and squinting eyes. He knew Riechet personally placed the Candonian in charge of his training but found it easy to forget protocol in the creature's presence, as Darkracer held no military rank.

"You've come through adversity before," Darkracer continued.

"What would you know?"

"Comes from you living in my backyard."

"Didn't think Candonians had backyards. Besides, I live on the edge of the woods. You live in my backyard."

"That's a matter of perspective."

Realizing the ridiculous nature of the argument, David stood with a growl. All he really wanted was to find a dark corner and crawl into it for a while. Having to do anything else put him in a foul mood. However, he knew no matter how much he complained he would not be getting out of the training exercise.

"Just start," he snapped.

Darkracer ignored David's rudeness. "Activation 213. Program 4."

The room dimmed as the Vairdec sprang to life and immediately engaged in the new program sequence. David angrily tried to focus on each target, missing several shots in the process and narrowly getting hit as he took cover behind the low wall.

"Don't shoot in anger," Darkracer instructed. "Control. Focus." They were instructions far easier to listen to than to put into practice. "The right is open. Take the advantage."

David remained where he was, his back pressed against the wall.

He has the advantage, Melina's voice echoed in his head. *Let's go back.*

It's two against one. We just have to hold him a while.

We don't have backup.

Squeezing his eyes shut, David suddenly jumped forward and fired. A laser swept past his head, jolting him from his thoughts. He staggered back, stumbling over a low barrier. Darkracer stepped in to shove him behind another wall.

"Kick it up. And focus."

David trembled as he tried to assess the situation. Shots sailed past the wall. All David could see were the shots that Melina dodged as she tried to escape the Assassin's attack. The crime lord's hold around David's neck felt unnaturally strong. He could do nothing to help her. Fighting to breathe through a tightening throat, he twisted away from the wall's protection.

The holographic flamethrower caught David's eye. A second later a blast of energy surged toward him. David dropped to the floor, shaking as he pushed himself back up. Blood began to form on his lower lip. Why couldn't he get control of himself? Why was this so difficult? This should be an easy exercise. If only he could push back the memories.

Melina's face turned to one of agony as the spike drove deep into her chest. David watched it as clearly as if he stood on that hellish rooftop once more. Turning in circles, he tried to draw his focus back on the holographs closing in around him. They swirled, losing shape, losing purpose. Where was he?

Darkracer jumped in, giving David a push with his head. The impact threw David off his trembling legs. He lay there, seeing Melina on the ground, struggling to reach him as her life painfully ebbed away. David pushed himself to his knees, longing to hold her.

"Take the shot," Darkracer's voice broke in. "Malard, take the shot!"

David blindly did as told, missing completely. The flamethrower's shot ended the exercise. As the room quieted, David struggled to his feet. Confusion and grief melted away into anger. He wasn't angry with Darkracer or the exercise. He was angry with himself. In a fit of sudden rage, he threw his gun toward the wall, narrowly avoiding striking Riechet in the head as the general entered.

"Not exactly the way to greet an officer," Riechet observed quietly.

"Though the way he's been shooting, it's probably the most effective tactic he has against Vairdec," Darkracer grumbled.

David hurriedly straightened to attention. It was one thing to relax around a Candonian, it was quite another to be so abrupt around his commanding officer. His pulse quickened. The general held every right to force him to listen to a screaming discipline followed by a grueling physical activity as punishment. To his surprise, Riechet stepped up to study him in silence. The firm, yet disappointed look, came as a harsh enough punishment.

"Go clean up," he ordered quietly.

David said nothing. With a quick salute he hurried from the room lest the general change his mind about further disciplinary action.

"What happened?" Riechet asked once David was gone.

"He's not taking charge," Darkracer commented in frustration. "It's a complete fold out. He refuses to focus."

"I wouldn't say 'refuses'. Lacks the current ability, perhaps, but I can see it in his eyes. He wants to do better."

"That may be, but can we trust him as a lieutenant? He's under too much emotional strain. I'd hate for him to falter on the battlefield."

Riechet nodded as he thought. "True, but I'm not putting him on a battlefield just yet. And, speaking of which, let's pray there is no battle to be fought in the first place."

"I thought you were leaning toward a Vairdec invasion coming to Telamier."

"Yes, but I could be wrong. There are possible other explanations for the activity around Celhara. Plan for the worse, hope for the best. As for Malard, having him here allows me to keep an eye on him – help him through."

Darkracer dipped his head low to eye the general with a scrutiny that few Humans would dare give.

"Aren't you being a bit soft on Malard? This is SIERA after all."

Riechet gave a huff. "Perhaps I am soft, but right now he's on the edge. It won't take much for him to walk away. If I come off too harsh I'll lose him."

"That may be for the best."

Riechet returned the Candonian's scrutinizing gaze. "I thought you had faith in him. After all, it was you who first pointed him out."

"True, but that was before seeing his performance now. He's not what he use to be."

The general grew quiet, staring at the door through which David had exited. Darkracer understood the look and averted his gaze.

"That may be," Riechet continued softly, "but I can see what this young man is capable of. Even the best of us struggle with traumas. He will heal. As you said, he's good. In time I believe he will be a great asset to our Special Forces unit."

"Yes, but in time."

"Unfortunately we Humans don't have the luxury of being picky. Our numbers are too small for that. When I find someone I know can become a valuable SIERA operative, I must act. We just don't have enough people."

Darkracer's ears turned in Riechet's direction to pick up his hushed last statement. With no comment to counter the general's words he watched in silence as Riechet headed for the door.

David sat on a bench in the men's shower room, his shirt in hand. He felt numb, unable to feel any particular emotion whether for good or ill. No single thought stayed with him for any length of time. Melina was gone. What else mattered? Melina was gone. Who was he now, knowing what he had done, what he lost? He gave a groan and lowered his head. Yes, Melina was gone, and if he had been stronger perhaps she would be at his side right now. Lost in listless thoughts, David never heard the general enter, nor did he respond when Riechet sat down beside him.

Riechet allowed David his time for a minute longer. Looking at the young man he saw clearly another individual, knowing all too well the feelings raging within. His gaze fell upon the still healing wound on David's left shoulder. It was a poignant reminder of the inner scars.

"It's healing nicely," he said, making David jump at his voice. Riechet lifted a hand to reassure David that all was well and he could remain where he was. "It's unfortunate that inner wounds don't heal as quickly."

"I don't know if I can do this."

"So you're quitting?"

David winced at the word. "No, sir, not... I... maybe I'm just questioning my capabilities. Perhaps I shouldn't..."

"Give it time. It's been less than a nahm, after all."

David turned away with a slight shiver. "All I could see was that night – her. She knew. She knew to turn back, but I thought I could do it." With a shake of his head, he dropped his gaze to the floor. "I thought I could, but I couldn't stop him. One guy..."

"Looking back we find a lot of errors with our lives. The challenge is to look ahead." He paused, allowing his words to reach David's troubled mind. "For now, the colonel has agreed to assist in the security detail for tonight's festivities. I want you to go with her."

David only nodded. Any words stuck in his throat. Riechet showed no disapproval for the lack of verbal confirmation to his order. Instead he simply placed a hand on David's shoulder as he rose, then silently exiting the room.

A few hours later, in dress uniform, David stood in the holding bay staring blankly at the *Predator*. He was still trying to figure out how he managed to get himself assigned to the Rew'cha Festival taking place in the heart of Karnoss. Under normal circumstances he might actually have enjoyed the night as in past years, but now? The thought of crowds, noise and overly enthusiastic people surrounding him filled David with a distasteful feeling.

Rew'cha, the "Day Night", occurred once a year when Telamier's three moons converged in a close configuration, creating enough moonlight to change night to day. How the festival started, David never fully figured out, though records showed it already maintained a strong following when Humans first arrived on Telamier. True to form, Humans quickly joined in, not about to pass up an excuse to flood the streets for an all-night celebration of festivity and drinking.

David knew that despite the early evening hour, Rew'cha had already begun, partygoers having spent much of the day carousing about shops and taverns as they meandered toward the large central avenue where the main party would commence later that night. Many others would be huddled around gambling blocks within the large hotels that lined the Avenue, waiting for fortune or financial drain to finally convince them to join the rest outside. David witnessed Rew'cha in Karnoss only once before, right after he graduated the Academy. He doubted much had changed since then, which made him uneasy now. The level of insanity that the partying usually reached did not bode well for his current mood, and he wondered if it was for this reason Riechet chose him for the detail.

Darkracer and Phantom stood beside the *Predator* with saddles on their backs and protective masks over their faces. While many Candonians detested the idea of Humans taking advantage of them

93

as a mode of transportation, those working directly with Humans found it a common part of the alliance. Humans were naturally slower and clumsier. Providing the smaller species with the advantage of more sufficient mobility proved beneficial for Candonians, who were not known for patience. The first to work with Humans also found the use of hands a major bonus in the effort to drive the Vairdec off. During the war, Candonians provided the speed and strength while Humans provided the firepower. The symbiotic relationship remained a tradition ever since, if only for a few individuals.

Saddles were allowed. Some Candonians over the years even preferred it to having a Human directly on their backs. Saddles provided better security for the Humans as well as a place to store weapons and supplies. They also doubled as armor. During the war, heavy blankets, breast collars, leg guards and facemasks added to the saddles to make the Candonian a formidable war machine. Over time, technology added comlinks that fit their larger necks and behind their swiveling ears to keep them in constant connection with their Human partners. One piece of tack, though, that never nor ever would be accepted was the bridle. Humans found themselves forced to learn to work with their Candonian mounts, not control them. As willing as they may be to allow Humans to ride, theirs was a proud and noble species. Never would they allow themselves to be viewed as simple beasts of burden.

Phantom eyed David with brilliant blue eyes, studying him as if to be sure the man lived up to what he had so far heard. David eyed Phantom right back.

The Candonian was as tall as Darkracer but not as muscled. His lankier form spoke of his younger age. He sported the same black coat as his elder, though his mane and tail held a distinctive reddish highlight. Amber peered under Phantom's neck to watch David's hesitant approach. With a jab of her thumb she motioned to where Darkracer stood quietly, appearing to be half asleep.

"You're with Racer. Ever done festival security?"

David's eyes locked on the saddle. "Yes, ma'am."

"Good. I don't want to baby-sit you out there."

As David stepped alongside Darkracer, the Candonian's eyes suddenly opened wide to study the Human's uneasy stance.

"Never ridden, have you?"

"No." David cleared his throat. "No, sir. I've never been on the back of any living thing."

"Ah, does this mean I can't spread rumors about you and the ladies?"

"Commander Soerin!" Amber snapped.

Mike straightened and gave a hasty salute.

"Sorry, ma'am." He suppressed a chuckle as he walked down the gangplank of his ship. "The *Predator's* ready, Colonel."

Without a word, Amber strode up into the ship, followed by Phantom. Darkracer looked David up and down before giving a shake of the head.

"Just hold on," he instructed. "You won't have to do any hard riding tonight."

"Be thankful for the ride," Mike said. "With those crowds it's good to have a bit of height."

David stepped around the pilot without making eye contact. "I suppose."

Inside, the *Predator* was open to allow maximum cargo space. Storage racks and cases dominated the tail end while utilitarian seats lined the fuselage wall. David took a seat next to Amber while the Candonians lay down in the center. After securing the door, Mike stepped around those on the floor to take his place in the small, two-man cockpit.

"Will you be staying for the festival?" David asked as the pilot passed.

"Of course. It's my one night of R and R. Besides, I'm not interested in making two round trips to the city when I can do one."

"Just don't show up in the morning inebriated," Amber warned.

"No, ma'am."

A moment later the *Predator* slid gracefully from her hanger into the evening Tralex air. The trip would be a very short one as there were only ten kilometers between Valor Peak and the Karnoss Plateau. David never bothered to get comfortable or even look out one of the windows at his back. He knew the area. The juts of red rock and endless miles of desert afforded little in the way of visual interest.

"It looks like maintenance is working in our favor, Colonel," Mike's voice came in over the speaker.

"How so?"

"They want to divert us to South Ridge, west side. Looks like Pole Dock is jammed with supply vessels and two of their hangars are down. I guess we won't need to make a trip across the city."

"Fine by me," Amber said, her voice devoid of any personal feelings on the matter.

The *Predator* dipped low over the southern canyon that cut a path from Valor Peak's mountain range to the south edge of the plateau. Coming up on the lee side, they avoided the heavy desert winds to enter the air traffic headed for the large main airfield of the city. It consisted of an array of hangars, multi-level landing pads, transit docks and resource centers all overlooked by two glittering towers that welcomed visitors to Earthenia's tourist playground. Flashing lights and vis-ads kept everyone well informed of the events and amenities available within the city, creating a colorfully busy look to an already busy port.

Several large cruise liners were docked on upper levels with direct access to the towers while smaller commercial vessels and private transports filled in available space. David took the time to look out the window and note the make of several of these ships. Evidentially many Celehi and Teschian travelers had chosen Karnoss for Rew'cha. An off world liner, probably from Airisus, added to the multi-cultural flair, along with a couple Oxyran transports from Telamier's neighboring planet. He was even surprised to see the Faxons present. They usually preferred to stay to themselves as their numbers on Telamier remained few, though it was not unheard of for them to slip in among crowds during large festivals, especially when wild nights of drinking were involved. David made note to keep an eye out for troublemakers.

Avoiding the main hub, Mike guided the *Predator* to a quieter section where VIP and government transports were docked. As they disembarked, two CLE agents stepped forward to greet them.

"Colonel, Agent Gevlick," one introduced as she gave a salute. "We appreciate your assistance. We expect upwards of eight thousand extra civilians over last year's count."

Darkracer gave a snort. "I never thought Karnoss would be so favored."

"After the riots at Miersaldo, their celebrations scaled back significantly. Festival-goers have been looking elsewhere. This city did a lot to be among the top ten for Rew'cha."

"And I don't plan on missing it," Mike said. "Colonel, if I may take my leave."

Amber gave a nod. "Enjoy your R & R, Commander."

David found himself actually envying the pilot as he hurried down a side passage that would lead to the main transit system.

"If you wish," Agent Gevlick continued, "we have transports that can take you to the Ave."

"I'd prefer the exercise," Darkracer cut in before Amber could speak.

"It may be for the best if we walk," Amber concurred. "Those not yet at the Ave can see a military presence at hand."

"As you wish," Agent Gevlick replied. She led the way down a corridor to the exit. "We'll be rejoining our unit and meet you there."

"Very well."

As the agents left, Amber swung onto Phantom's back, glancing at David to indicate he should do the same. David gave Darkracer a cautious look. The Candonian stared back.

"Well?"

"Put your left foot in the stirrup," Amber instructed. "Hold the saddle and pull yourself up."

David did his best to comply, pulling at just the right angle to send a jolt of electrifying pain through his healing shoulder. He struggled to compensate with his right arm while trying to maintain a shred of dignity in front of his commanding officer. Darkracer lowered himself to one knee, giving David enough help to get himself seated. He glanced at Amber with dreaded curiosity over what her expression would be. To his relief she seemed neither annoyed nor amused.

"Use your knees to grip Darkracer's sides," she said. "Feel free to hold onto the saddle, but not too tightly. We don't want people thinking you're uneasy with your position. Sit up straight, heels down. Let's go."

It came as a pleasant coincidence that they avoided all crowds for the first couple of minutes, which gave David a chance to get a feel for sitting on a Candonian's back. The motion was smooth and comfortable, and soon David was relaxing. Entering the main walks, they skirted the edge of the crowds. With the extra height, David felt an added sense of power and importance. He wondered if this was how Jonathan Alsen felt when sitting upon his Candonian partner, Poseidon. Glancing down, he studied those they passed. Numerous species jostled one another, dressed in an eclectic assortment of attires, from the elegant to the gaudy. There was plenty of color accessorized with bits of glowing material to add to the spectacle of the all night party. Some glanced up at him, but most remained focused on their own enjoyments.

Keeping it slow to allow their riders a chance to watch the crowds, over a half hour passed before the Candonians reached their destination. David could actually feel the celebration before entering the main festival center. The heavy beat of music sent concussions through the walkway and surrounding buildings that took on a surreal glow from the many floodlights. Flickers of colored laser and other dancing lights, coupled with the occasional waft of festival food beckoned the masses inward. Rounding the bend, the splendor of the gala became fully revealed. Nearly a full kilometer of wild, carefree glamour lined the already spectacular stretch of walk called simply the Avenue.

It was one of the signature features of Karnoss, having become the central hub of tourism within the city. Running north to south along the western edge of the plateau, it stretched between lines of high-end resorts and shopping venues, drawing people down its length with the intrigue of being a warm, protected outdoor attraction. Heated walkways and overhead heat lamps warded off the usual arctic nature of the environment. Sculpted plants, works of art and fountains of iridescent liquids added to the style and class. Eateries competed with the retail establishments for every bit of currency flowing through the tourists' hands. And tonight the usual activity escalated tenfold.

Towers glinted in the varied lights, erected in a staggered line to provide hired dancers the elevation needed to stay away from the ever-growing masses. In their flashy attire they goaded those below to join the jovial dances many were making up as they went. Smaller platforms allowed other performers access to the crowds where hapless visitors were randomly dragged up to entertain their enthusiastic friends. Huddled near these islands, vendors sold their variety of food and simple party wares that would more than likely litter the walk in the morning. Along the sides other islands provided oases where myriads of colored drinks were already flowing freely.

David made note of these outdoor taverns, assessing both their location and clientele. He could sense they would be a loud, boisterous bunch, but luckily appeared harmless enough. Species mingled together, dropping racial issues and rank for the occasion. A small group of men were laughing over some joke, glowing glasses in their hands and voluptuous women at their sides. Their flashy leather attire was adorned with metal studs, strips of glowing threads and multiple jewels. One glanced up from under his brimmed hat to raise his glass to the passing Candonians and riders. David nodded silently in response.

"Colonel," he said after a moment's thought. "May I ask you something?"

"You may speak freely."

David paused to study Amber. Having grown up in the military she held strictly to protocol whenever required. However, he sensed the influence of her father. She was not unfeeling toward others.

"Do you ever wish to be one of them?" He motioned toward the crowd. "Naïve to problems abroad?"

Amber sat back in the saddle with a sigh. "I never gave it much thought. You?"

"Haven't decided."

Back at SIERA Headquarters De'oolay sat tensely before the control room's main computer. Riechet entered. He, too, was tense, his motions precise, his steps brisk.

"What is it?"

"A signal from deep space, sir. Possibly the convoy."

"And?"

"Very distorted. The computers have trouble translating. It reads of Vairdec, but I cannot decipher what context."

"They left on Getch 8, did they not?"

"You are correct, sir," De'oolay confirmed.

"That was ten days ago. They should be nearing the Jysah system by now. How old is the message?"

"The signal appears eighty hours old. Maybe one hundred five."

Jylin entered to immediately make his way to Riechet's side as the general pulled up a map of the super system.

"Four days," Riechet muttered as he plotted the convoy's course.

"That places them beyond Hardiban's solar system," Jylin observed. "There appears to be at least a day of open space from any system."

"Yes," Riechet answered slowly, "and yet too close to be speaking of Vairdec as far as I'm concerned. Was the signal directed to Telamier or Celhara?"

"None," De'oolay answered. "It is an all hail."

Jylin stepped up behind her. "About?"

"I do not know. Everything is messed."

"Celehi do not send disorganized messages."

De'oolay shook her head. "Communications prove difficult. I had to focus Spynix to reach the signal. Everything is moving slower."

"Any known reasons?"

"None, sir."

Riechet was already headed for another consol to speak with the Earthenian government.

"See who else is responding," he ordered over his shoulder.

Night had reached its darkest hours though it went largely unnoticed due to the amount of light on the Avenue. Before long the glow of the three moons would be seen over the distant southern mountain range. David glanced up. It was a clear night. The view of the moons would be spectacular, though only those on the north end of the Avenue would be able to see them fully. He wondered how many really cared. The activity on the streets always proved more exciting than any annual celestial event.

Already a large portion of the crowd was gathering at the main stage situated on the north end where the spectacular rays of moonlight would usher in singer Lameena Nahreen. Her elegant looks, melodic voice and intense style caused her fame to grow over the past couple of years and her faithful fans turned out in droves. A preliminary band was already in full swing to work the crowd into a frenzy.

"Is Bryson Knight here?" David asked, thankful that their comlinks made speaking to one another doable over the noise.

"No," Amber said, her eyes on a ragged youth ducking suspiciously away.

"You a fan?" Darkracer asked, glancing over his shoulder.

David shrugged. "Not particularly. Just didn't know how much security was needed for them."

It was a well-known fact that Lameena Narheen's fame came in large part from her highly popular actor husband. If both chose to show in Karnoss, the strain on security would prove nightmarish. Though David refrained from complete honesty over his feelings toward Bryson Knight, he was glad for the sake of the CLE that the celebrity remained at home. However, it also made him wonder just how much good he was doing this night. Surely enough security was in place. After all, not only were the CLE out in full, Karnoss had received a number of military personnel called up from their reserve status in various other Earthenian cities. Having SIERA present was nothing more than a formality.

He watched as lightweight balls of swirling colors and lights were batted back and forth above the

104

crowd's heads. One floated lazily toward him, too high for a laughing group of teenagers to reach. From his vantage point, David reached forward to bounce it back to them. They cheered and clapped approvingly. One girl tossed him a flashing streamer, which he took with a gracious smile. Perhaps tonight wasn't going to be all bad.

Darkracer turned away from the crowd, following Phantom to a slightly higher point of the walk to watch the activity. After receiving no order to be rid of the teen's gift, David tied the streamer to the saddle and sat back to let his mind wander for a moment. He stared down the Avenue to where the moons would rise. Though it was impossible to see the distant mountain range for all the buildings, a projection at the south end gave a real-time view of what was happening across the desert. At the moment, all was dark.

"Alsen was married under the three moons," he muttered, not intending to start a conversation.

"You really like him, don't you?" Amber said. David glanced over at the colonel to see her looking up at the projection as well. "I bet you've read all of Alsen's journals."

David had, though he still struggled with what to say on the matter.

"How about you?" he finally returned. "How many have you read?"

"All of them," Amber answered casually. "He was a good man. Interesting," she twisted in the saddle to look David in the eye, "in a small way you remind me of him."

David gave a disbelieving laugh. Alsen was a national hero. He was just David.

"I lost now Delta Mirano and Scout 42," De'oolay announced, her puzzlement quickly growing to concern.

Riechet turned from his work to be at her side in an instant. "Reason?"

"Unknown. Ships just disappear from the reading."

"Anything on the all hail?"

"None, sir."

Jylin looked up from his own investigations. "No one appears to know. Regions have lost contact with Celhara."

A signal drove their attention to the main computer.

"Sir," De'oolay said, "I now lost contact with one of our Scout Control Modules."

"Which one?"

"H-5."

"That is very close," Jylin observed.

"Too close," Riechet agreed.

"There was a mention of Faxons before the signal was lost."

Riechet turned to De'oolay in surprise. "Faxons?"

Behind them Lash entered, a grimacing snarl on his lips from De'oolay's announcement.

"Military Deep Space Divisions are increasing activity," Jylin said.

"Why not they speak to us?" Lash asked.

Riechet only gave him a sideward glance. "We're not Deep Space. Any detection of Vairdec vessels?"

The room grew silent a moment with the heavy tension.

"No mention," De'oolay announced after her hurried check, "only Faxons."

Jylin's gaze followed Riechet as the general hurried over to answer an incoming message from the Earthenian government. "What would Faxons want with us?"

A slightly tipsy party-goer backed into Darkracer's shoulder as his attention remained on the beautiful young woman at his side. He jumped in surprise, nearly spilling his drink as the Candonian gave an indignant snort. The woman only laughed as the two hurried away lest the riders decide to remove them from the festival. Amber only shook her head.

"It's strange how a festival atmosphere can make people act so carelessly," she observed.

David studied her expressionless face a moment. "Haven't you ever loosened at a party?" he asked, finding it difficult to visualize.

The slightest twinkle shone briefly in her eye before she suppressed it. She opened her mouth to speak, but was cut off by the sudden call of her father.

"Colonel, you and your team return to headquarters."

"Yes, sir."

The Candonians turned south to begin trotting as quickly as they could through the throngs of people. A moment later a roar of engines sounded from the western edge of the plateau.

CHAPTER NINE

Mike also heard the order from where he sat relaxing in a posh resort with several other pilots. Cursing under his breath, he slammed his drink onto the table and rushed for the door, leaving his companions in a state of bewilderment. He normally did not react so strongly, but something in the general's voice spoke of the great urgency needed. He was thankful for his choice not to join the masses on the Avenue. It would have taken a lot longer to get back to his ship if he had. As it was, the main corridor of the resort was clear, allowing him to sprint for the shuttle bay that would take him to the airfield.

The sound of engines did little to change the atmosphere along the Avenue. A few turned their heads in acknowledgement of the passing aircrafts but did nothing more. It was likely part of the celebration. At worse, a couple cocky pilots figured a fly-by would add to the festivities and would already have the CLE's watchful security in pursuit. Only the Candonians and their riders responded differently. No doubt the order back to headquarters was linked to what they just heard.

"Clear the way," David shouted.

Startled citizens jumped back, some cursing as the larger creatures bumped them out of the way. Tucking in alongside a stretch of buildings, they lengthened their strides. Before David could speak up about the sudden turn of events, new voices squawked over his comlink. This time it was the CLE. A jumbled mess of reports filtered through with news that Pole Dock was ablaze from some unknown explosion. From the sound of it, David and the team had met with good fortune when turned away from the northern airfield. Now he hoped their luck would hold.

Already security was evacuating the main stage, leaving the audience muttering in confusion. A few citizens began to somber as family and friends residing on the outskirts of the plateau started calling in to their loved ones with eye witness accounts of possible explosions. Under the throb of music, the distant roll of explosive concussions sounded. The Candonians' ears flicked with agitation. The situation was growing more serious by the second. David clung tightly to the saddle, fearing what would happen if he fell off. The south end of the Avenue seemed to be getting closer at a painfully slow pace. His mouth ran dry as the frantic words washed through his earpiece.

"Evacuate the Ave. Evacuate. Evacuate."

Darkracer and Phantom leaped a low barrier and broke from the Avenue just as the roar of an aircraft swept down its length. The Candonians nearly buckled under the concussion of its passing. David fell forward against Darkracer's neck and clung tightly. There was no need to look up to know that the craft had actually flown between the buildings. It was followed by the sound of two more ships.

Mike broke out of the shuttle bay in front of the VIP hangars. As he hurried toward them, an explosive wave of heat slammed into his chest. He flung himself back against a side pillar to watch part of the west tower burst into flames under what could only be a missile hit. There was no time to make sense of the destruction. Another explosion rocked the ground. He had to get to his ship and away from the hangars before they all collapsed. Pushing off from the pillar, he raced for the hangar, instinctively ducking as the signature scream of fighter engines swept over him.

"We're under attack." Mike's voice cut through the rest of the chatter.

"... get out..." the voice was breaking up. *"... airfield under attack... stay away."*

Phantom and Darkracer pulled up short. David shakily pushed himself back into the saddle to join Amber in watching the glowing blazes from the commercial airfield.

"General," Amber called, "we can't make it to the *Predator*. Doubling back. Will assess options."

"Head underground," Riechet ordered.

They turned back to look toward the Avenue. Lights flicked unsteadily.

"They must've hit the power generators," Amber said.

Phantom shuddered. "It's an attack on the city."

"You think?" Darkracer snorted.

A craft screamed past. Amber glanced up, briefly catching sight of it before it disappeared behind the buildings.

"That's a Faxon ship."

"Guess Vairdec aren't the only ones who want us dead," Darkracer growled as he and Phantom lengthened their strides back toward the Avenue.

"But there's no reason," Amber argued.

"Do they need one?"

"Usually."

De'oolay's skin turned a nearly perfect white as she scrambled to keep up with the incoming information. Bypassing the normal communications network, which was now nothing more than a bank of blank screens, was a daunting task. Military lines flickered, their systems also severely compromised. Behind her Riechet stood rigid and stoic, his eyes narrow, his arms crossed.

"I lost the Military Board," she announced shakily. "The attack proves well-planned. Communications are lost. I cannot connect to CLE Headquarters. Faxons are taking control of the city."

Jylin turned from his consol, his skin a mixture of white and yellow as he fought back his inner feelings. "Pole Dock is gone. Their units cannot take off."

"Contact San Terres." Riechet's tone remained surprisingly calm. "Alimar, get ready to fly. Py'guela prepare the Bravo Unit. I want them in Karnoss in ten."

Lash and Jylin were already jogging to the door.

"Yes, sir."

When the fighter swept down the middle of the Avenue, it brought with it a mixture of alarm and exuberant cheers from the crowd. Though the CLE immediately began to usher people out of the area, few understood or obeyed. Not until the lights began to flicker and dim did people begin to take notice. The heavy blasts from the exploding airfield finally brought the gravity of the situation to light, creating a panic that swept up the Avenue like a wave.

Power generators, mangled by earlier hits, finally gave out, plunging the city of Karnoss into darkness. Again a fighter dipped low, ripping down the Avenue between buildings, its high speeds shattering windows. Citizens screamed in terror as shards of glass rained down. Following the first craft, a second suddenly opened fire. The red-hot flames erupting from missiles and lasers replaced the extinguished lights of the festival.

Darkracer and Phantom nearly sat down as they slid to a halt. David found himself unseated and gripped his mount's neck as he flipped from the saddle. Keeping a hold of the Candonian, David managed to stay on his feet. With adrenaline running high, he easily swung himself back into place as the first wave of panicked civilians swept around them. Ahead they could hear the weapons and see the glow of fires coming from the Avenue. A sickening acrid smell of smoke and super-heated flesh wafted past. Amber leaned over Phantom's neck.

"Nearest transit's at the Artisan."

Without a word Phantom and Darkracer wheeled around and raced for a tall shopping complex.

Mike found himself choked by the waves of smoke. Heat stung his eyes and burned his lungs, but so far the side hangar remained unscathed. He could still hear enemy crafts sweeping around the plateau. Precious little time remained before the hangar was obliterated. Two other pilots scrambled down the corridor, trying to escape the building before it collapsed. Mike doubted any held the desire to save their ships. With fighters in the air, any ship taking off risked being shot down. He knew it was a risk he would have to take. Luckily, unlike the rest, his craft equaled those of the attackers. If only he could reach it in time.

He slammed himself against the door leading to the *Predator*, rocked by a horrific explosion. Out of the corner of his eye he saw a blanket of flame racing across the ceiling. The far end of the hangar must have been hit. Falling through the open door, he kept his head low as the flames lashed out after him. The *Predator* glowed in the reflection of the fire. Mike held no fear of the flames damaging his ship. The outer skin was strong enough to withstand far hotter temperatures. The collapsing building worried him more. Fighting to stay on his feet as the floor lurched, he staggered toward his ship.

"Command. Beta two five echo," he called out.

The hatch opened instantly in response to his words.

It was a relief to leave the smoke, heat and noise behind, but the rocking under his feet refused to cease as Mike locked the hatch. Stumbling into the cockpit, he looked anxiously out the open hangar door. Nothing could be seen beyond a reddish wall of smoke. Firing up the engines, he did a quick sensor scan to find that no solid object blocked his path. The ship dipped to the right as a piece of the ceiling clipped its unfolding wing. Mike grabbed at the controls. There was no time for pre-flight preparations. Gunning the engines he headed for the opening.

Another shudder of the ship signified the crumpling of the ceiling behind him. The *Predator* pitched forward, dropping from the hangar with the force of the building's collapse. With skill and focus, Mike pulled his ship up, scraping the ground for a second before gaining altitude. A spout of flame shot skyward. Mike banked to the left, narrowly avoiding the remains of a control tower before ducking from the city and out across Tralex.

"Cruiser reporting in," he said, using his call sign to signify he was airborne. "The south airfield is heavily compromised."

"What is your current status?" General Riechet's voice spoke over the *Predator's* speaker.

"Three clicks over Tralex. Assessing situation."

"Circle back to the Peak. Provide air cover for departing Bravo transport."

"Affirmative."

"Phantom," Amber called, "take the main ramp."

She, David and the Candonians had made it into the Artisan, a large specialty-shopping complex that housed artists who created and sold their wares right in view of the buying public. Passing through the decadently constructed entry hall, they stepped out into the expansive center of a giant cylinder, hollow through the middle and lined with art centers that ran nine stories high. Center lifts were being abandoned in favor of the spiraling ramp. Around them the building rumbled and groaned from the outside attacks. David was grateful the building was being passed over as a target.

Around the Candonians, citizens crowded toward the ramp. They groped about in the dark, many weeping as they staggered toward the lower levels. Some managed to procure portable lights and led the way. The Candonians joined the crowd, allowing themselves to be swept along. There were four levels to go as their escape path forced them up to a higher walkway to get into the building. The damage caused by falling debris blocked the lower levels.

A nearby woman staggered and fell. She refused to heed a younger lady who grabbed her wrist and attempted to pull the stricken woman up. David knew he could not ignore the needs around him. He slid to the ground and struggled on shaky legs to where she sat trembling in terror and pain.

"Malard," Amber called as Phantom halted.

David forced the woman to her feet and dragged her to Darkracer's side. Amber dismounted to assist in getting the woman onto Darkracer's back. Turning to a disoriented Celehi man, she grabbed his arm and turned him back toward the ramp.

"Transit levels," she called out. "Go!"

Helping the wounded onto the Candonians, they began to drive the terrified crowd down with greater urgency. David found the progress frustratingly slow as they struggled through the dark. Untying the still flashing streamer from Darkracer's saddle, David handed it off as a rope to keep a group of children together. They clung to it tightly, finding comfort in the light. Hesitantly David chanced a look at the ceiling far overhead. Hanging as a decorative centerpiece swung a giant art sculpture, barely visible against the night sky. It swayed menacingly, flickering bits of starlight that penetrated through the waves of smoke. For a brief moment David found himself hypnotized by its motion. A fighter passed outside, the concussion sending a jolt through the structure. A snap signaled its demise.

"Out of the way! Against the walls!"

Glass and metal crashed past the lifts, bouncing erratically down the open center. Bits were sheered from the sculpture as it fell, becoming missiles to those along the ramp. It was impossible to see everything coming. The deafening noise of the crash sent jolts of hot adrenaline through David who jumped against the wall in time to avoid a piece of glass that speared the floor at his feet. Another shard glanced off a sign above his head. Those unfortunate to be on the ground floor were crushed by hundreds of pounds of metal and glass. There was no time to contemplate the devastation. Amber was already pressing the group downward.

"On your wing," Mike announced as he guided the *Predator* alongside the SIERA transport.
Aboard was the first wave of military relief for the stricken city. Two Faxon fighters swept in, both firing. One took a position left and low while the other dove in from the right. Mike fought the controls of his ship as the lasers deflected off the protective shielding. Too many direct hits like that and the *Predator* would be done for.
"Holy…" he gasped. "Fia! That is not a Faxon tactic. Sir," he called, "they're attacking fast."
Already the fighters had banked and come in for another pass. They gave Mike little time to readjust his own tactics.

Riechet leaned over the control consol, his eyes narrowing with Mike's words.
"These Faxons are not fighting like Faxons. I'm getting hammered."

Mike dipped under the transport to shake off one fighter. Instantly he was back around, pulling up to fire on the oncoming craft. A sudden burst of heavy shots ripped through the air. They slammed down through the transport, driving it into the side of the plateau. Mike banked hard to avoid the explosion.

"Fia!"

Pulling up, Mike turned his ship to look skyward. A landing vessel rimmed with cannons appeared as a black void against the night sky. A smaller ship broke away to head for the city.

"Command. Command. We've got hostile cruisers. These are off planet. I repeat, off planet."

"Get out of the air," Riechet order. *"South bunker."*

Mike didn't need any persuading. "Yes, sir."

Using the mountain range, he shook his pursuers and retreated for a secure bunker in the side of the plateau.

Riechet slammed his fist against the counter. It was the first real emotion he allowed himself to show since the attack began. Jylin and De'oolay watched him in tense silence, awaiting their next order. Composing himself, Riechet turned to Jylin.

"Prepare all units. We're moving into Karnoss."

"Under what call?"

"War."

"Was there a declaration?"

Riechet was already heading purposefully to the door. "When you want to catch your enemy off guard, you don't send one."

"But sir," De'oolay called after him, "why Faxons? We are not enemies."

"It's not the Faxons."

CHAPTER TEN

Down on the transit station floor, people pressed in ever increasing numbers to get to the system that would take them further underground. Entering, David pressed himself against Darkracer's shoulder to avoid being separated and trampled by the crazed mob. They came not only from the Artisan but from the streets and other buildings that connected to this central transit hub. It sat just under a plaza on the plateau's surface. Glancing up at the transparent ceiling, he could see little of the sky beyond. The buildings crowded out any starlight and the moons had not yet risen over the city. With only the few portable lights and the glow of outfit adornments, the black station resembled a surreal tomb filled with psychedelic insanity.

The authoritative shouts of CLE agents turned his attention to the far end where directions were being given to get people on board the long, sleek vessels. The transit system was the main line of transportation within Karnoss and ran through kilometers of tunnels that burrowed as low as four stories below the surface. It was a necessary system for a city that lay in freezing temperatures a good portion of the year. The CLE knew the specific codes needed to reroute the transits to stop near secret shafts that dropped into the deep, underground bunkers. They just needed to get everyone on board.

As David moved slowly toward the transits, he found himself thinking of San Terres. What was happening at that moment in his home city? Was it under attack, too? If so, its citizens didn't have the benefit of protective bunkers, and he worried they would find few safe places to go. His thoughts turned to those he knew still living in the southlands. Would any of them escape?

"You, help her up."

Amber's authoritative tone snapped David back to his own predicament in which the colonel was directing a young man toward a wounded girl. Seconds later she reached under Darkracer's neck to grab David by the arm.

"We've got to get to the field station."

"Not the bunkers?" Darkracer asked. It seemed like the best place to go at the given time.

"We've got to get to Captain Gilpar."

Amber began pushing her way through the crowd toward an exit.

"The general ordered us underground," Phantom argued.

"We will be," Amber answered.

"Get those doors open," a CLE officer ordered as a second shuttle took the place of one filled to capacity.

David admitted he sided with the Candonians' sentiment. He preferred to head for the bunkers. However, as a soldier he must act like one. Quietly he helped the terrified woman off Darkracer's back and directed her toward the waiting shuttle. Amber snatched the youngest of three children from her path and shoved him into a nearby Celehi's hands.

"Take him."

As people crowded onto the waiting shuttle it became easier to make for the exit. David took the opportunity to climb into the saddle again. A low hum rumbled through the floor and caused the walls to vibrate. Hating to do so, David glanced up at the ceiling. He could barely make out the movement of something very large passing overhead. Amber saw it too and swung onto Phantom's back.

"Get out of here!"

Phantom and Darkracer leaped forward. They raced for the exit, crashing through a partially opened door to make it to the surface. Behind them the ship fired. There was no major operative need to do so, but the mass of civilians in the transit station was too tempting a target. The missile dropped straight down, striking the transparent ceiling like a massive bullet. A blanket of flame spread across the surface on impact. Terrified screams mixed for a second with the roar of the explosion. For a brief second the ceiling held. A part of the missile continued through the point of impact, slamming into the floor to cause a smaller, secondary explosion. It was enough of a concussion to shake the weakened ceiling loose. Tons of flaming debris poured into the station floor.

The Candonians slid around a corner of the street as a burst of flame shot up from the tunnel exit. Slowing their pace, they retreated further from the building while the fire died down. They would need to be cautious. There was no telling how many enemy crafts were in the air or soldiers on the ground. David found himself unable to hold back the curse that formed on his lips. All those people he was just with were suddenly gone. He pulled his gun, feeling slightly comforted by the solid weight in his hand. Amber, too, drew her weapon. All four were shaken though they fought to stay in control. The smell of smoke and burning debris wafted through the air. Screams, sounds of vessels and, most disturbing, the sound of gunfire, echoed among the buildings from deeper in the city.

David's training tugged at him to go toward the sounds in order help. Logic warned him of the futility. They would be running blind into an unknown number of enemy fighters with weaponry already proven superior. Amber obviously already had a plan, and it would not be to run and hide. Relinquishing himself to his current situation, David turned away from the noise of the city center. A few civilians rushed by, disappearing into the lobby of a hotel. Darkracer glanced back over his shoulder, watching the clouds of smoke from the shopping complex.

"That was not Faxon," he said with a shudder.

Amber's eyes darted back and forth as she continually scanned the streets. "Well aware of that."

Phantom was matching her steady search. "How many do you think are out there?"

"Enough to be cautious," Darkracer answered.

"Are you sure the two of you are safe up here?" David asked. "No offense, but you're rather large targets."

"They're faster than we are," Amber replied without turning around. "You want to foot it across this city?"

"Not really," Darkracer grumbled.

"But if we avoid detection..."

"Mechanical devices and tactical buildings are the first targets in initial sweeps," Amber cut in. "It's logical to bypass individual biological forms."

"We often don't even read on scanners," Phantom explained.

Darkracer glanced over his shoulder. "Didn't read that chapter, did you?"

David remained silent as they galloped northward.

Undeterred by the wars waged between civilizations, the three moons of Telamier rose as they had always done since the dawn of creation. They looked without feeling upon the world with the same glow whether celebration or chaos ensued. Kelapore, Brakni and Nactar had seen it all and now set their white faces upon the ruins of the once magnificent city of Karnoss.

Darkness was replaced by the "Day Night" as the three moons worked as one to illuminate the silent Avenue. Fires still crackled in pockets where fuel had not been completely spent. Bits of fabric and ashen debris fluttered in the arctic breeze that pushed its way among the solemn buildings. Bathed in the cold light lay the countless remains of a crowd that an hour earlier enjoyed the fullness of life. Now there was nothing but silence – and blood. The light of the moons that first drew them to celebrate now became their death shroud.

Further north, remnants of life remained. Four figures pressed themselves against the icy wall of a tower, melting into the deep shadows. Amber and David huddled beneath the necks of their chargers, guns held at ready, though at the moment they hoped not to use them. They barely dared to breathe. Though still unseen, they could hear the heavy footfalls of an approaching column of soldiers. It would be fatal to engage them and there was no time to try and run. All they could do was wait, hoping the shadows would conceal them. The rhythmic pounding of feet drummed loudly in David's head. The world slowed around him. His heart throbbed with the same rhythm as the steps. Tightening his grip on his gun, he shifted his head slightly to catch an angle of the street.

With the help of the intense moonlight, he could clearly see the troops as they passed nearby. They were a good six to seven feet in height, powerfully muscled with thick limbs and broad shoulders. Their entire bodies were covered in heavy black armor whose design made it possible for each soldier to carry a multitude of weapons including high-powered assault rifles, battle-axes and flamethrowers. Not much of their soft, gray-green skin could be seen beneath their armor and brown uniforms. Even their faces were covered with war masks designed to designate rank, faction and family.

Many took on shapes of fierce creatures, fanged skulls and grinning demons, each framed by a naturally growing black mane.

David felt the prickle of anxiety crawl across his skin at the sight of eagerly sniffing larkrae perched upon the shoulders of their handlers. They stood roughly half a meter in height upon stubby, one-toed feet adorned with a single oversized claw on each. Their serpentine middle allowed them to stretch over a meter in length and provided for uncanny flexibility. With olfactory senses to rival any predator and the tenacity for aggression, they were favored as hunters. Trained to ride on a handler's shoulder, they would leap after targets either smelled or seen, attacking with claws and serrated teeth. By nature, they would go for the face and throat, falling into horrifying frenzies at the smell of fresh blood. Able to glide using flaps of skin attached to their legs, escaping their detection would prove challenging. Luckily a wave of smoke from further down the alley, wafted between them to mask any scent. Eventually the soldiers disappeared from sight.

David and Amber exhaled slowly, listening to the retreating footsteps.

"Well," Amber whispered, "now you've seen the Vairdec."

A thin, wiry figure nearly shot past them. He was an energetic young teenager whose bony fingers were wrapped tightly around a modified high-impact shotgun. His eyes were alight with a fiery hatred behind strands of long, stringy black hair. By the rumpled nature of his clothes and the smell of his body, David could tell his dirt had been with him longer than that night. Seeing the boy's direction, he quickly caught him around the middle and pulled him back. Amber was practically snarling as she glared at the teen.

"Are you out of your mind?" she hissed in as loud a tone as she dared. "The Vairdec are that way."

"I know," he answered, just a bit too loud.

David slapped a hand over his mouth and dragged him further down the alley. To his surprise, the teenager did not approve of the rescue attempt.

"Let go of me," he mumbled through David's hand.

"You'll get us killed," Amber snapped back as she ripped the shotgun from his grasp.

Assured that they were far enough from harm, David relaxed his hold, thankful that the teenager relaxed as well.

"I'll kill them," he said, turning toward the main street.

David grabbed him by the back of the neck to turn him away again. "You're outnumbered."

"I can take them."

"Sure you can." David looked over the slender form skeptically.

"They killed Eric."

"What?"

"My brother. They killed my brother. I'll kill them."

Again he tried to make for the main street only to be blocked by both Candonians. David grabbed the teen once more, holding back his hands as they groped for the side arm hanging on David's hip.

Phantom glanced in the direction of the main street, listening intently.

"We need to get out of here," he warned.

Amber pressed in between the teenager and the Candonians to shove the boy back. Her gun leveled with his face. She didn't need to speak for him to understand her meaning.

"Racer, Phantom," she said, her eyes never straying from the boy, "outta here."

The Candonians slipped into the shadows to disappear down a side street. Giving the boy a shove, Amber motioned him forward and together with David they hurried away.

In SIERA's control room, Lash joined De'oolay, Jylin and the general to get the latest news on the situation. De'oolay continued struggling to gather what scraps of information she could from the broken lines of communication that appeared to be planet-wide. As she spoke, Riechet listened in tense silence, pacing the room deep in thought.

"CLE, airfields, communications – they all look to be gone or damaged severely. All major industrial areas of the planet look the same. I at this time cannot confirm. Central cities hold small control with most defenses gone. The Vairdec understand destroying CLE headquarters first."

"It disturbs that they knew where to aim," Lash commented.

"We spy on them, they spy on us," Riechet muttered. "Unfortunately their infiltration techniques are still surprising us. They must be operating with a rogue band of Faxons. It would explain the use of their ships. Who knows who else they bought off."

"An intelligent ploy," Jylin admitted. "They entered right through our sensors."

Riechet smacked his fist into his open palm. "I warned the government to inspect the Faxon ships. It never settled well with me that they allowed such fighter crafts near our city to begin with. I should have fought harder when they turned down the idea of thorough inspections."

"But with Faxon high officials here for Rew'cha, their presence is understandable," Jylin argued. "Do not blame yourself. No matter how hard you fought to remove the fighters, no government would risk bad diplomacy by singling out the Faxons."

"Mm." Riechet stopped his pacing to look at the main computer's readout. "Regardless of how they arrived, the Vairdec are here. Lack of communications and resources will limit us on the plateau. We don't have enough for me to split SIERA around the region. Our focus is Karnoss. Let's hope the other cities can hold their own for now."

"What about Earthenia's other military branches? What expectations do we have from them?"

Riechet turned to the screens, though he didn't need to read the information from them. He knew what the military had in place.

"Eanoshia had five active platoons and was calling up two extra recertification units ahead of schedule. Air Force only activated two squads, but a third was stationed on Kelapore. Their reserves were on alert stand-by, so hopefully they made it to their ships in time. The rest of the military reserves will fight where and how they can. I'm sure they've moved to the nearest bases. As for our ECO agents, they were on other missions. At this time they'll only be able to assist from where they are."

Jylin shook his head in slow defeat. "It is the best we can hope for, although it sounds like it will not be enough. I would be happy with some ECO agents here."

"There are those in Special Forces with covert training."

"It is time to see if the training was worth it," Jylin said.

"Intelligence gathering is over. It's time to pull out the heavy artillery. We're no good to anyone if we stay cloistered in Valor Peak. I want every able body ready to move. De'oolay, see if you can get us a status on Vairdec positioning, and try to get through to the colonel. Py'guela, Alimar, prepare the units. We don't have enough defenses to transport by air. We'll have to take the canyon route." He paused to look between his officers. They could see the remorse buried deep in the expression, though the general fought it off with a fierce glare of determination. "I know this isn't exactly the way we would have wanted to face the Vairdec, but there's not much we can do about that now. Yes, I underestimated their abilities. It will not happen again."

CHAPTER ELEVEN

Forced to duck enemy regiments and stay to the deeper shadows, it took Amber and her team nearly three hours to make it to the military's field station on the northern end of Karnoss. It was a short, sturdy building, stark and unadorned, with only one apparent entrance. Most of the time, like other stations around Earthenia, it was used for recruitment and evaluation. Public relations seminars and military exhibitions also found use for the buildings. SIERA used it in conjunction with the CLE to conduct joint classroom training, since CLE was outside Earthenian military jurisdiction and was not allowed into the nearby base holding Special Forces and covert operatives. David was familiar with the field stations and their agents. As a CLE officer, his duty included attending several classes focused on understanding the Earthenian military as well as various topics concerning the Vairdec. Those all seemed so distant and irrelevant now that it was actually happening.

Inside, the group found themselves in a clean, spacious, yet very deserted lobby. The hazy blue flooring gave softly underfoot. An ornamental chime spun lazily in a corner, refracting bits of moonlight as it tinkled like soft rain. A couple of stately Human statues stretched their arms on either side of a rippling waterfall that trickled down the wall while a flowering plant opposite it glowed in the dark. After everything David endured that night, this had transformed from an average lobby to a virtual paradise. He secretly wished it were possible to stay there and forget the whole invasion.

"Doesn't look like anyone's here," the teen said as he peered into an empty lecture hall.

Amber ignored him and walked over to the waterfall. With her foot she tapped a sequence on the stone base. Accepting her code, the center stone rose slowly to form a canopy, the water spilling down either side. David peered through the opening to a stairwell. He couldn't see far beyond the bottom of the stairs, but figured there was nothing to be concerned with as Amber started down.

Unbeknownst to David, while the upper building housed nothing more than a series of classrooms and offices, underneath lay a vast weapons cache along with numerous pieces of surveillance, communications and espionage equipment. Always one to prepare, General Riechet and a few private investors, chose to personally stock pile much of it when the military downsized a couple years before. He always sensed the need for arms would eventually come, and he was not one to trust the government to supply him when such need arose. His field agents joined in the stock piling and took on the task of maintaining the stores below while providing the public service of education to the military and CLE topside.

At the bottom of the stairs, the group found themselves in a long, narrow, bunker-style passageway. It was dimly lit, having to rely on backup generators for the time being. David looked cautiously around, refusing to holster his weapon despite Amber leaving her handgun on her hip and resting the confiscated shotgun casually against her shoulder. A streak of motion from a dark figure was enough to make David bring his weapon to bear. Before them a Manogonite hovered with rifle poised and ready. Amber remained unmoved.

"A little edgy, aren't we, Toodat?"

Recognizing the colonel, the Manogonite dropped to the floor. His beady eyes glared up at Amber. An electronic voice answered from a translator collar that picked up the strange language of clicks and hisses.

"Can you give me reason not to be?"

"No," Amber admitted as she stepped around the creature to turn a corner and down the passage. "Where's Gilpar?"

"Control room."

He followed at her heels, walking on his back feet and wing tips to allow him to keep hold of his rifle. David and the teenager kept a few paces behind him.

"Any others make it in?" Amber asked.

"Just a couple of gents."

"Well CLE's better than nothing."

Amber glanced back at David who gave her a double take, wondering if he really had seen a playful glint in her eye. The attempt at levity seemed out of place under the current circumstances. However, David knew Amber was wise to keep the tension as low as possible. Toodat followed her gaze. He studied David a moment with narrowed eyes. Manogonites had always been difficult to read, and David could not tell whether this one approved of him or not. At the end of the passage a young woman stood rigidly in wait for them to approach.

She looked about the same age as Amber, though stood several inches shorter. Her long, black hair was braided down her back. There was a fierce, somewhat cocky light in her dark eyes that clearly stated that despite her size, she would not back down from a fight, especially now.

Amber stopped in front of her and accepted her salute. "Captain Gilpar."

"Colonel."

The captain's voice remained steady, but David could tell she, like the rest of them, was shaken by the sudden invasion. Amber stepped to the side.

"First Lieutenant David Malard. He's with SIERA, ESF Division. Malard, Captain Kailyn Gilpar."

He and the captain exchanged salutes.

"The kid we dragged off the streets," Amber added harshly.

"Nathan," he replied indignantly. "Nathaniel Darson."

"Fine." Amber never looked his direction. "We need weapons. Supplies."

"Soldiers?"

"SIERA's on the way."

"Good," Kailyn turned back to head for the control room, "because I can't help you there. There was little chance for any to make it in. Perhaps more will show, though I have a feeling they headed for the bunkers."

"We just need the weapons."

"Help yourself."

Amber turned to David and motioned back down the passage to the left. "Get outfitted."

Acknowledging her with a nod, David headed in the direction indicated. Nathan stayed close at his heels to enter, much to their surprise, a large storeroom. Racks of every firearm imaginable lined the walls. Various tools and miscellaneous weapons sat on table-topped shelves down the middle of the room. With an excited laugh, Nathan reached for the nearest gun. David hurriedly grabbed the teen's wrist, giving him an angry glare.

"David?"

The familiar voice caused David to draw back in shock. "Keven?"

Keven Arzen jogged up to grab David by the shoulders. "David! What are you doing here?"

"What of me? What of you?"

"Transferred. I just couldn't stay in San Terres."

The initial excitement over seeing his best friend died. David found himself suddenly unable to look Keven in the eye. He let his gaze travel along the racks of weapons.

"I'm with SIERA."

"SIERA? What branch?"

"ESF."

"I guess that makes sense. You're more special forces than covert ops." Keven paused enough to give David a smirk. "Though you've proven yourself pretty good at espionage, if I remember correctly."

"If I remember, I was not alone in that little dorm raid."

Keven grew silent, his gaze trailing from David to follow Nathan who pushed his way between them to pick a sniper rifle off the rack.

"And this is?" Keven asked.

David snatched the rifle away, not noticing the handgun already slipped into the teenager's belt. "A civilian."

"A recruit," Nathan retorted angrily. Defiantly he snatched another rifle.

In the control room Kailyn was transferring information onto the intel-band strapped to Amber's wrist.

"It's the most accurate information I've got on the city's status," she said. "Information is still being gathered. It looks as if they've landed the Faxon fighters in the city, but they're spread out – not easily sabotaged."

"That's the least of our worries," Amber said. "Can you manage here?"

"There's enough supplies to hold us for a couple nahms."

"Good. Keep gathering intel and stay on coded channels."

Walking to the weapons cache, Amber leaned into the room. "Let's move, gentlemen. The Candonians are waiting north side. Load them up."

David hefted a bag of guns.

"Are we headed for the bunkers?" Keven asked as he slung a bag over his shoulder.

"Looks that way," David replied.

Keven gave a shake of his head. "Never thought they'd ever get to use them."

David said nothing despite thinking similarly to Keven. Most gave the inner workings of Karnoss's plateau little thought despite its importance to the city. From its humble beginnings, Karnoss was a mining town. Rich deposits of karnocite, a lightweight yet extremely strong metal after which the city was named, served as the catalyst for the city's growth. As the mines dried up, the city's inhabitants turned to the latest discovery of numerous mineral springs whose health properties drew a new clientele interested in posh resorts and healing centers. The empty mines served as underground storage, transit systems and, deeper still, fortified bunkers. David hoped the city's inhabitants still remembered enough about the bunkers to head in the right direction.

As they began packing their loads onto the Candonians' backs, Keven turned to David.

"Why do you think they're here?"

"Hard to say. They're probably still mad about the first war."

"I suppose that makes sense. Think we have a chance?"

For the first time that night David paused to consider the possibilities. He wanted to jump in with a quick and easy phrase of encouragement. Unfortunately the words caught in his throat. The fact was, he did not feel very optimistic. In a matter of a few short hours he witnessed more death and destruction than he ever saw throughout his entire life, and there was nothing he could do to change any of it. The Vairdec were strong. Should he dare to hope to make it through the invasion alive? Should any of them?

"I don't know," David finally managed.

The vicious grind of massive metal doors fell silent in the cold emptiness of space. All around the activity seemed to slow in watch, waiting for the next phase of this new and deadly takeover. Three giant battle stations orbited in strategic positions around Telamier. Around them countless transports, fighter jets and battle ships came and went, swarming the upper atmosphere and dipping to and from their new terrestrial claim. The surprise attack had been executed perfectly – the takeover far smoother than Arct-Ieya originally hoped.

She stood aboard her command ship, gazing at the soft green and blue jewel of the planet before her. Two hundred years she patiently waited for this very moment. Two hundred years she perfected her revenge. Calmly she slipped her hand to her side to stroke the nose of her pet seslarn. It was a Telamierian creature – a predator the Vairdec quickly grew attached to and trained during the glory days of their colony's reign. Over the long years she carefully bred and maintained the selsarns' descendents. To her it was a show of her continued claim of the planet. She wanted Telamier, not for its bountiful natural riches or strategic placement within the galaxy but for a show of power. She and her people endured horrible humiliation, their claims on the planet being torn from them. Their place within the super system was destroyed. Now the Celehi, with their god-like superiority, would know they were not as powerful as they liked to believe. This planet was hers, and no one would take it from her. They would all die before she gave it up.

Her rich, black eyes narrowed with silent glee as the doors of the stations opened fully to jettison mountain-sized pulse shield generators into orbit around the planet. Once in place they would activate an invisible net that would encompass Telamier. Her own ships were immune to the defense, which would recognize their unique signatures. However, any unauthorized ship foolish enough to pass through would lose power, thus falling easy prey to the battle ships lying in wait or to the gravity of the planet. All was perfect – all except Kelapore.

Arct-Ieya's fist clenched around the seslarn's nose horn, causing it to growl as if to voice its owner's feelings. The Vairdec's eyes turned in the direction of Telamier's moons. Since the last war, Kelapore had been converted into a fortified battle station. Its defenses proved stronger than expected, but the speed and strength in which she attacked left them unable to provide much protection for the planet. However, her ships were having trouble getting close to its deadly cannons. More disturbing, the shield generators would not be able to get within one hundred kilometers of Kalapore's long-range guns. That would leave a patch of unprotected atmosphere near the moon. Enemy ships could come and go through that small opening. Quite small, she tried to remind herself. No real threat. But she hated it just the same. It was a weak point in her armor, and Arct-Ieya would not tolerate weakness.

The ringing of feet and hooves sounded deafening to David though he with Amber, Keven, Nathan and the Candonians were moving with great care through the underground transit center. There was no telling where the Vairdec were, so stealth was key. Every slight sound was rubbing on David's already raw nerves. After all, Vairdec hearing was apparently far better than Humans. Were they listening right now? So far no evidence showed enemy troops venturing into the underground network below Karnoss's towering skyscrapers. Trained to be cautious, David still found himself carefully scanning the windows to every wait station they passed. A couple blinking vis-ads made him tense, his weapon coming to bear.

The transit center, usually a round-the-clock example of organized chaos, stretched on as a meandering network of empty halls and hastily abandoned loading docks. Packages and bags lay strewn about the stone floor where their owners abandoned them in terror, a temptation that proved too strong for Nathan who grabbed a couple packs that looked promising. A distant vibration of shuttles from other parts of the city echoed through the track lines.

David knew that a couple thousand citizens would be crowding into those units in hopes of escaping the exposure of the upper city. At the moment, he and the team were moving under the hard-hit center of Karnoss. There were few citizens left in this area to make an attempt for the bunkers. The slight whir of approaching engines sounded like a scream that whipped them around in time to watch one of the sleek, elongated shuttles streak past their location inside its protective transparent tube. David could not tell how many had made it safely aboard. Seconds later all was silent.

Keven held close to David's shoulder. It felt good to have someone he knew and trusted at his side. Times were trying enough without worrying about the capabilities of your fellow soldiers. Up ahead, David could tell Amber was just as tense as he, though she hid it well. Her features were hard set. Her focus constantly jumped from one side of the walk to the other. David was glad to be with her. She made for good company under the circumstances. So did the Candonians. Their ears remained in constant motion. Vairdec weren't the only ones with excellent hearing. Coupled with an amazing sense of smell, the Candonians would easily pinpoint a threat before an ambush could be made.

After a long trek down through a series of passages and stairways, Amber halted the group outside one of the secure bunker doors. They were now nearly three hundred meters below the surface, buried deep within the lower portions of the plateau. David figured it best not to contemplate the amount of rock above him for very long. With Amber's code, a smaller side door groaned on its metal track, signifying the long years of disuse. Beyond it was yet another tunnel that sloped downward through the darkness. A soft, orange light glowed at its end.

Though dim, David found himself blinking as his eyes adjusted from the darker tunnel he stepped from. Around him stretched a wide, domed room nearly seventeen meters in diameter, carved right out of the bedrock and supported by massive steel beams. It was filled with various crates and electrical equipment, but to David's disappointment, not filled with many survivors. A few small groups huddled along the edges while a couple uniformed military personnel had begun to open the crates and assess their contents. Amber ignored them to lead the way to one of the smaller chambers that rimmed the perimeter.

"Secure this room," she ordered. "No unauthorized personnel."

David gave Nathan a shove toward the door. "Join the civilians," he said.

Nathan squirmed at his touch. "I'm personnel. I'm fighting."

"Leave kid."

"I'm no kid," he argued. "I know how to fight."

Amber eyed the quarrel with a touch of disdain in her eyes. "We'll call if we need you."

Nathan planted his feet and glared at her. There was no fear in him over repercussions. Military rank meant nothing and he was not about to let this hot-tempered woman order him around.

"You're making a mistake. Let me stay. What am I to do with a bunch of scared mothers and children? You wanna fight these things alone?"

"Don't get bright with me," Amber snapped back. "You don't belong here."

In the blink of an eye Nathan's newly acquired handgun was out of its holster and in his hand. David and Keven jumped into action, reaching for their own weapons, but Nathan had already fired. The shot passed close by Amber's head. She remained motionless, expressing neither fear nor anger. Slowly she turned to look at where the shot had struck the far wall. An unfinished piece of it had long ago cracked to create a cross mark that now sported a perfect blast point at its center. Contemplating the matter, she stepped close to stare Nathan down.

"Can you hit moving targets?"

"Point one out and I'll show you."

A touch of amusement played quickly across her face. Giving it a few more seconds thought, she walked away.

"Okay, you're steely. I like that. Guard the door."

David found himself a bit exasperated by the decision. The colonel was actually going to let that belligerent youth stay? He knew better than argue, but gave Keven a glance that expressed his dislike. A shrug answered his unspoken concern. It was logical to keep good fighters close at hand as there would be plenty of fighting. The fact did little to appease David. Nathan proved masterful at rubbing on his already raw nerves.

Steady, he told himself. *This is war. Nothing's right. Deal with it.*

Though Nathan preferred to assist in unloading the Candonians' packs, he accepted his position at the door as opposed to the alternative of staying with the other refugees. Amber grabbed a portable tactical comp-unit and headed away from the group. David eyed her as she seated herself in a corner to begin assessing their situation in more detail. He knew it would be a grave assessment indeed.

"What next, I wonder," he voiced aloud.

"I'll wait for the general's orders," Darkracer answered, glancing over his shoulder to watch David slide packs of guns from his back.

"General?" Keven asked.

It was the first time David considered the fact that Keven was unaware of the inner workings of SIERA and only followed along out of necessity. As they unpacked, David quietly filled him in on who was who. His friend listened without comment, studying David carefully as he finished speaking.

"Sounds like you're managing," he finally said.

David refused to look at Keven. Instead he continued to busy himself with the sorting of weapons.

"I do what I have to," he answered softly, "but it's not always easy."

Keven nodded, saying nothing. They completed their work in silence, allowing the Candonians to stretch then settle down to sleep. With nothing to do, David and Keven followed suit, settling themselves on opposite sides of the weapons cache. It was hard to get comfortable against the cold stone wall, but David found the moment of rest rewarding nonetheless. He was grateful for the dark – no one would notice the shaking that had seized his body. The adrenaline had worn off, leaving him weak.

Tightening his fists, he forced himself to settle. He must focus and stay in control. With a sigh he lay his head back against the wall and shut his eyes, unable to escape the images he had endured earlier that night.

With a jerk, David woke. He pressed his back against the wall, taking a moment to calm his breathing. It took a couple minutes more for him to remember what brought about the rude awakening. It had been a Vairdec, whose war mask had come to life, contorting and frothing as the alien rushed him. David responded defensively, trying to raise a gun he did not possess.

Brushing the sweaty strands of hair from his face, he glanced at his wrist for the time. Barely an hour had passed. With a groan he rubbed his face, shaking off the uncomfortable knotting of his stomach. Shifting his position a fiery jolt of pain from his complaining muscles raced up his back. As well conditioned as he was, David's unusually sore body reflected the stress of the events and strained activity of riding. He forced himself to sit up and work out the stiffness, refusing to accept his weakened state.

The room around him was quiet. Darkracer lay nearby, leaning against the wall with his legs folded beneath him. Phantom stood near the door, his nose nearly touching the floor, his body twitching in spasms from a fitful dream. Keven, too, was not sleeping peacefully, and shifted with a groan. The only one that appeared unscathed was Nathan, who lay stretched across the doorway, cradling his rifle like a pillow. David shook his head. He had yet to decide what to make of the youth. In the far corner,

Amber still sat in front of the computer. Her arms were wrapped around her legs with her head on her knees. Unable to tell if she was asleep or not, David decided to take the chance and approach. She slowly lifted her head to watch him slip through the dark to kneel beside her.

"Trouble sleeping?"

"Yes, ma'am."

"I'm afraid you'll have to get use to the conditions."

"Yes, ma'am."

Amber eyed him with what appeared to David as a cross between approval and amusement. He wished he could read her better. She was a growing enigma with him. At times he felt relaxed enough to allow informalities, and yet there was always a sense of apprehension for any such behavior. Figuring it best to stay silent, David settled nearby and averted his gaze. He could feel Amber's eyes on him. She was studying him. It was an unpleasant feeling, especially not knowing what conclusions she was drawing. He refused to betray his thoughts on the matter so remained still.

"Take care of that."

The order caught him off guard and he stared dumbfounded at her. She gave a motion with her head. Following her motion David found his right arm soaked in blood. The realization of his injury surprised him, as he never felt any pain from it. Carefully he rolled up his stained sleeve to reveal a gash across his forearm that fortunately looked far worse than it really was.

"Medic kits are in the main chamber. Bring one back here, we could use it on hand."

Nodding, David rose to do as asked. Nathan never stirred as he stepped over, causing David to wonder how good a sentry he actually was. However, after assessing the chamber beyond, he could see no reason to guard the door at all. Amber's order had been nothing more than a wise way to quiet the youth quickly.

Near a stack of crates stood two Human military enlistees and a Celehi CLE agent. They spoke in low voices, keeping a watchful eye on the small civilian groups that huddled some distance away. David gravitated toward the threesome and they let him into their circle without complaint. They smiled and nodded in greeting, going no further with formal introductions. David could sense their stress. He had heard their soft conversation mentioning the doubt of other survivors since news of Karnoss's CLE headquarters being bombed had become official. Part of him wanted to ask for more information, but he refrained, figuring he would learn more than he cared to in due time. Instead he graced the group with a change of subject.

"Medic kits?"

One of the Humans nodded and turned his attention to the crates. The other two looked him over silently.

"Army?" the Celehi finally asked.

"SIERA."

"Are they coming?"

David hesitated. He knew it would be the likely scenario, but felt uneasy giving too much information, especially since he had not been given official word from the colonel.

"Probably," he answered simply.

"And Earthenian army knows how to kill the krashka, right?"

A smile tugged at David's lips at the insulting description the Celehi so readily used to describe their old enemies. "Let's hope so."

The soldier returned with a medic kit in hand. His eyes narrowed as he handed it off.

"It doesn't sound like you're very confident," he observed.

David sucked in his breath uncomfortably, letting his gaze wander to the far wall. He had not intended to sound so pessimistic. The division was well trained and boasted two strong leaders in the Riechets. It was not his place to doubt their success. Everything was just so overwhelming right now. He was still taking in the number of lives lost in those first short hours.

"Where're all the survivors?" he asked, turning to look out at the empty chamber.

"All?" the Celehi scoffed.

"Not many made it in, though more are coming. Most went to the north and east sides. That's where citizens are trained to go. This is meant for military or overflow."

"I doubt we'll see overflow," the younger of the two soldiers muttered.

"But everyone knows about these bunkers, right?" David asked.

He hated the thought of people huddled in unprotected buildings, unaware of the safety below their feet.

"Not everyone knows. That's why it's taking a while. Citizens are drilled to head for secure shelters and await instruction from authorized personnel. If it's felt that going to the bunkers is necessary, special transports move them down."

"It's necessary," David said.

Taking the medic kit, he headed back to the side room. Amber was leaning against the wall next to her computer, looking for the first time very worn. David glanced about for a place he could sit and work on his injury when Amber slowly raised her hand to wave him over.

"Over here," she said softly.

David obeyed, though felt a bit of discomfort settle in his stomach for doing so. He truly hated not knowing how to act from one moment to the next around her. Taking the kit from him, Amber motioned him to be seated. David had to tell himself not to squirm as she started her work on the cut. It was not the pain that bothered him as much as the feeling of incapacity. He much preferred doing things for himself. If Amber was aware of his discomfort, she never let on.

David was ready to pull away when the cleaning and dressing was done, but Amber kept a firm grip on his arm. He shifted uncomfortably as she examined the tattoo on the inner part of his wrist. It was the image of a hawk, meticulously recreated from the few surviving images from Earth. Talon-tipped feet stretched toward David's palm, as a silent scream

149

seemed to emanate from the hooked beak. Its golden wings stretched outward to wrap around David's wrist.

"Interesting choice," Amber commented softly. "Any particular reason?"

David yanked his hand free and looked away. "Maybe I just like it."

He didn't care if he was impertinent. All he wanted was to be left alone. Amber said nothing as he stood and returned to his place at the wall.

General Riechet knew he should get some sleep. Unfortunately the events left him unable to relax enough to get a few hours rest. The Vairdec were in his own backyard. He spent a lifetime preparing for catastrophic events though secretly never imagined any such atrocity would ever happen. At least not in his lifetime. It left him drained and agitated. However, he knew what must be done and would not let his emotions get the better of him. He had not risen to his position by any trifle means. It was time to set all his years of training into action. But there was his daughter. It played more heavily on him than he liked. For all the troubles facing him now, where she was and what she faced was the most difficult for him to stomach.

He paced his room, deep in thought, weighing every scenario, every outcome. There was his duty to his division and to the city of Karnoss. He needed to get his soldiers onto the plateau where they would be most beneficial to the war effort. But in doing so, he would have to ask his daughter to place herself in harms way. The thought came as a terrible burden. He had ordered soldiers into battle before, knowing the price they might pay. It never came as a simple task and he always took such orders very seriously. But his own daughter?

Riechet sank wearily into a chair. If only they could be together. Somehow he felt the decision would be easier if Amber's hardened tenacity could argue against his paternal instinct. She was a fighter – a good one. He trained her himself. Time and again she proved capable of a great many things. Already she had faced more action than he in this war and was holding her own. And she was not alone. Darkracer and Phantom were with her. Both had grown up alongside his daughter and would defend her with their lives if the need arose. Commander Soerin was near, having stayed with the *Predator* to receive instructions through the CAF-47's secure channels. He remained one of SIERA's best, and like the Candonians, was devoted to his daughter's protection. And then there was Malard.

Rubbing his hand across his careworn features, Riechet lay back in the chair and closed his eyes. David was strong and intelligent, a man of deep thought and deeper emotions. The war would be the ultimate testing ground. A wave of sympathy for the young man gripped the general. He held an understanding for David's struggle that he rarely voiced to others. The inevitable events to come would either shape or destroy him. Riechet hoped that, like himself, David would find the strength to overcome, but it was still too early to tell. An icy sting of fear stabbed at the general. Yes, he, Kyler Riechet, overcame in the past, though a piece of him had forever been lost. Could he suffer it again with his daughter?

CHAPTER TWELVE

David woke to soft voices across the room. Nathan stood in the doorway having to be reassured that Mikander Soerin was authorized to enter. The conversation roused Darkracer who gave a pleasant huff and got to his feet to join. David, too, stood to step alongside the commander. Mike gave him a tired smile.

"Good to see you, Malard."

"And you."

"Commander Soerin has orders from the general," Amber announced. "We'll need to review them and prepare. Malard, wake the others."

David gave a nod. "Yes, ma'am."

Keven rose quickly, but Phantom proved difficult and ornery. David had to move quickly to avoid a disapproving nip in the side. Once assembled, Mike leaned back against the wall to look them over.

"Looks like air transportation is out of the question," he began. "We already lost one transport in the attempt."

Amber growled her frustration. Losing comrades was hard enough, but when soldiers were in high demand, the loss was even greater. Mike shared her sentiment.

"Fourteen lost. Knew a lot personally." He fell silent a moment, shaking his head in disgust. "The canyon's the best option - if they can make it through undetected."

"That's the real challenge," Darkracer said. "Mobilizing the entire division will draw attention."

Phantom glanced between Darkracer and Mike. "But is it the entire division?"

"Most of it," Mike answered. "The general knows the risk, but there's not much that can be done about it. If they move small groups at a time and are discovered, our only way will be cut off before everyone's in."

"Diversion."

Mike pointed at Amber. "You two think alike. That's the plan. The Vairdec don't know about the canyon's access to the plateau. They've made North Slope an item for themselves. There're lots of transports stationed at the base of it. Guess they figured we'd sabotage their crafts if they landed in the city."

Darkracer gave a nickering chuckle. "They figured right."

"Too bad for us," David muttered.

"I don't know," Amber returned. "It places them opposite the canyon. SIERA has a better chance of making it in."

"What's up with Karnoss anyway," Nathan blurted, tired of being left out of the conversation.

"They like the resorts or something? I thought they hated the Celehi. What do they got against us Humans?"

"Who don't they hate?" Phantom replied.

"They'll kill anyone in their way," Amber said. "If we stay out of their way, they won't openly kill us immediately, but they'll take what they want. Karnoss is a strategic point on the globe. That's what they're after."

"Strategic?" Nathan shook his head in disbelief. "We're in the middle of a pissin' desert."

"Exactly. From here they can see anything coming long before a strike can be made. There are no woodlands or mountains to aid in an ambush. They can also quickly launch attacks anywhere in the northern hemisphere. The only resistance they'll have to face is what's already here – a resistance that is cut off from the aid of the region."

"Then we're fortunate that they don't know who they're dealing with," Mike said.

Amber gave him a tense stare. "They soon will. What are the general's plans on the diversion?"

"We attack North Slope. Hopefully the Vairdec will consider it the most logical defense move for a resistance. They'll keep their focus on our efforts there long enough for the general to move everyone through the canyon. We'll have to be convincing, but he wants to keep the numbers low, hopefully for fewer casualties. Basically, hit them with a lot of chaos and noise. We have to stay focused. Once the order is given to retreat, we do. Right now the general doesn't want to lose a lot in such an open strike. He'll give the order to pull back once they're in. However, the retreat will have to look scattered. If the Vairdec catch on too quickly to how organized we are they'll be on high alert."

"What about air cover?" David asked.

Keven nodded in agreement. "If they have crafts attacking from above, it'll be suicide. We're too exposed on the north end."

"I'll be up there," Mike reassured. "So will Lash."

"Will that be enough?"

Mike glared at Keven. "The Vairdec don't know the kind of pilots they're dealing with."

"But this is suppose to look unprofessional," Keven argued, "right?"

"On the ground, yes," Amber answered, "but the Vairdec are already aware of a military presence here. They just don't know how big. We don't have much choice when it comes to air battles, but we can keep them guessing about the full extent of our firepower on the ground."

Keven crossed his arms as he shook his head. "I'm still not convinced that we'll be able to survive any aerial attack. No offense, I'm sure you're good, but you'll be outnumbered."

For the first time Mike let his confident façade drop. "Don't remind me."

David shifted slightly. He had been deep in thought, working through everything said in his own quiet manner. Finally he spoke up, choosing his words carefully.

"If I may, has the experimental shielding been considered yet?"

All eyes turned to him.

"Continue," Amber said.

"Can we confirm if the towers are still operational?"

"They are," Mike answered, "but the power grid is down."

David motioned to the lighting in the room. "Not backup generators. We'd be without power down here for a while but it should be enough to send at least one burst across the skyline."

Darkracer flicked his ears at the thought. "But if the power grid is down, the boards would be destroyed."

"CLE took control last year. The operations were moved."

"CLE's destroyed," Phantom reminded.

"Headquarters was one of the first things the Vairdec hit," Keven confirmed.

David nodded his understanding but pressed on with his plan. "There was a reshuffling with the operations' location. It went to Government Hall, military wing. I overheard Captain Gilpar say the Hall was overlooked – correct?"

Amber nodded.

"This EMP shielding is a new technology. It's likely the Vairdec aren't aware of its existence."

"Soerin," Amber said, "do you think you can avoid the blast?"

"Just tell me when you fire. I'm not fond of crashing."

"We need to get this to the general."

Mike gave Amber a concerned look. "Communication is temporarily down. I'm not expecting to be able to contact headquarters until almost the time of the attack."

"It won't do. For this to work we need someone to operate the shield. I refuse to rely on its usual non-military personnel that may not even be alive anymore. We need De'oolay."

"We need to be in position at five-o tomorrow," Mike warned.

Amber checked the time. "That gives us sixteen hours to make this happen."

David eyed the Candonians, still running silent plans in his head.

"How fast can you run?" he asked Darkracer.

The Candonian grunted. "It's a ten-kilo run, maybe more."

"You're the faster," Amber said.

Phantom gave a chuckle. "I don't know. He's getting a bit old."

Darkracer squinted at his companion with ears pinned back. "Give me two hours," he answered. "Three if I have to skirt the south end."

"Fine, get going. Bring De'oolay back as quickly as possible." Amber turned to the four men. "Sergeant Arzen, do you think you can find other CLE agents? I'd like to have people I can rely on out there. Look for military as well. We'll need them stationed here. While you're out, see what we can get in civilian recruits. Malard, we need to prepare the weapons for distribution."

"Got it," Nathan jumped in, intent on heading for the weapons cache.

David caught him up by the jacket collar. "She said Malard."

"Soerin," Amber continued without acknowledging Nathan, "go get some sleep. I doubt you've had any and you'll need to be alert up there."

"I'll bunk in the *Predator*."

"I can take you as far as the S9 tunnel," Darkracer offered.

Mike obliged and climbed onto the Candonian's back. As they exited the room, the rest began their tasks in silence.

By early evening a group of willing recruits milled quietly within the main chamber. Amber spent much of her time assessing their skills and deciding where best to use them in the coming strike. David leaned against the wall with arms crossed, looking them over while silently analyzing each in turn. Many proved eager enough to fight, most having lost friends and family to the first attack. However, he knew they were completely unprepared for what was to come. The knowledge brought with it the agonizing realization that many may not return. Wisely he kept his thoughts to himself. To bring down morale could have far worse consequences. In the end, he found it best to stay to himself and not look anyone directly in the eye. He sensed that Amber, too, struggled with her position as recruiter. Knowing she was not unfeeling toward those around her made her a strong leader in David's eyes; one he willingly followed.

Keven stepped through the milling crowd to lean against the wall next to his friend.

"It appears more CLE survived than first thought."

"Good," David answered simply, not looking his direction.

"Rew'cha had a benefiting twist – most units were on the streets." He gave a wave of his hand. "Are all these people going?"

"The colonel will let us know shortly."

"I'd hate to trust my life to a lot of these."

"Mmm."

"Don't think we're assigned together." Keven dropped his voice. "Pity."

David turned his eyes toward his friend. "You sure you want to trust your life to me?"

Keven grew silent, staring a long moment at the floor.

"Yes," he finally said. "Yes, I would."

David said nothing. He did not like the thought of being responsible for anyone. A crash of a large satchel being dropped at his feet made him jump, snapping him from his contemplations. Nathan stood at his side with a smug look on his face. David rolled his eyes. He had noticed the disappearance of the youth earlier that day and hoped that he would not return. While there was nothing particularly wrong with the young man, David found he just could not muster enough patience for him.

"What's in the bag?" Keven asked.

Nathan pulled it open to reveal a large contingence of guns and ammunition. The apathy David felt turned to shock.

"Where did you…"

"Didn't think I could?" Nathan cut in sharply. "Told you you needed me."

160

"Right," Keven replied skeptically as he reached for a CLE issue LB-42.

Nathan gave the bag a gentle kick. "Got two more like this."

"Where did you get them?" David repeated slowly and deliberately.

Nathan snatched a power clip and pocketed it before Keven could pull the bag away. "I got my sources. What do you care? Thought we were on the same side now."

"Now?" Keven looked up from the bag to eye him suspiciously.

Nathan kept his eyes on David. "Want them or not?"

"Get the other two over to the colonel," he ordered.

Nathan scowled as he walked away. "Thanks would be nice."

Keven tossed the LB-42 to David. "What's a civilian – an under aged civilian – doing with this?"

Turning the gun over in his hands, David gave a shrug. "He is right about one thing, we are all on the same side."

He glanced up to watch the colonel's approach. She was visibly stressed, though was doing what she could to hide it. David could guess any number of reasons for it.

"Darkracer not back yet?"

"No," she growled. "And communications are still blocked."

"He'll be back."

Amber forced herself to relax. "Of course. As for these," she pushed the bag of weapons with the toe of her boot, "let's get them handed out. Be sure to instruct in their use. I've got a roster."

She tossed David a list then hurried away. Keven shook his head as he watched her go.

"She's a colonel?"

To his surprise, a sudden need to defend her washed through David.

"I couldn't ask for better leaders. The Riechets are among the finest."

Keven raised his hands. "Ease it all, co. I'm impressed. Just think it's interesting that she's the same age as we are. Makes one feel a bit under achieved, doesn't it?"

David refused to answer. He had thought about it before. He just didn't see the need to dwell too deeply on the matter. Too many other issues took precedence.

"Though I must admit," Keven continued as he shouldered the pack, "she's the best looking colonel I've ever seen."

David remained rooted in his place as Keven walked away, trying to assess whether he really heard what he thought he heard. He always knew Keven to have a playfully flirtatious side, but the idea of his best friend expressing attraction toward his commanding officer made him wince. In fact, the thought of any attractions between men and women caused a queasiness to settle in the pit of his stomach. It reminded him too much of… The war, yes, odd as it was, it was a welcome distraction. Shaking his head to clear his mind, David joined the rest of the officers in charge of distributing weapons.

Over the next two hours David tried his best to avoid eye contact with those quietly stepping up to receive their weapons. Their eagerness in taking up arms was one he did not wish to quell with the somber reality of war. Amber did what she could to choose out those with at least some working knowledge of firearms, which freed David from having to play the undesired role of instructor. Beside him Nathan busied himself with the inner workings of a sniper rifle.

"What are you doing?" David finally asked.

"Maximizing distancing. Remove the secondary sensors and you can get a higher caliber power cell into these things."

Keven gave a huff from where he stood nearby. Nathan returned it with an angry glare.

"What? They don't teach you that in the CLE?"

"You have something against CLE?" Keven returned.

"Just those in it."

"You've got a pretty big mouth, kid."

"Counters your small brain."

David found himself caught between the two as Keven moved threateningly toward the teenager. Nathan stood his ground, goading the agent on.

"Oh sure. Real BA snapper. Think that's what you are, gent?"

"You sorry excuse for a bardroe sob!"

"Easy, easy!" David snapped, pushing his shoulder against Keven while holding his right hand to Nathan's chest. "We're all uptight. Save it for the battlefield."

With a growl, Keven turned away. Nathan gave him a smug glare as he shouldered the rifle. "Probably won't last the first hour."

David, too, wanted to strike the youth but held himself in check through sheer strength of will. He would not be responsible for starting a row. Taking a deep breath he finished his work in silence then retreated to a corner to begin reviewing his role in the upcoming offensive.

The clatter of hooves sent a jolt of adrenaline through David's body. He pulled himself away from the map of North Slope he was carefully studying, thankful for the distraction. Darkracer had returned and stood near the entrance, breathing heavily. Carefully De'oolay slid from his back to face Amber. Seeing the activity, David jumped up and hurried to join.

"The general wishes to use the shield," the Celehi woman said. "He believes this plan can work."

"I'll have Captain Gilpar go with you to Government Hall." Amber checked the time. "We've got three hours before departure. Racer, rest up. De'oolay, I'd like a more secure com-line with the field station. See what you can do." She glanced over to where David stood a short distance away. "Is our army ready?"

David stepped forward so no one else would overhear. "As ready as possible. CLE and military personnel have been running them through target training. There's no way to prepare them mentally for what will be out there, though."

"I'm afraid what we have is all we can hope for." She fell silent as if trying to decide how best to proceed. "Are you ready?"

Finding himself unable to think of any words, David breathed deeply to clear his head and gave a quick nod. Amber asked for nothing more. As she left, he checked his LB-49 and the new backup piece he chose from the stack of weapons earlier. Three hours would come and go quickly enough.

CHAPTER THIRTEEN

It was still several hours before dawn when David pulled himself onto Darkracer's back once again. He gripped the saddle tightly as he remembered the harrowing ride from the other night. Beneath him the Candonian remained surprisingly calm. Leaning over, David touched the warm, black neck.

"How are you after that run?"

A heavy snort answered him. "Don't underestimate a Candonian." His ears twitched in thought. "Just don't fall off," he added as a side.

A slight smile tugged at David's lips. He never really knew any Candonians while growing up but found himself liking Darkracer despite the creature's somewhat forward attitude. Phantom trotted up with Amber in the saddle. She glanced back at the groups of men and women clustered around their respective officers and gave a slight hiss through her teeth.

"Do what you can to keep as many alive," she muttered.

Peering over his shoulder, David caught the gazes of their renegade army. He sensed their anxiety though they masked it well, using their hatred of the Vairdec and their determination to drive the enemy away as a front. They had a lot to fight for. Many were leaving families behind. What did he, David Malard, have to fight for? He supposed the survival of his entire nation counted as a good enough cause. It still felt empty, even cold as he realized that no specific loved one remained for him to stand up for – not anymore. Squeezing his eyes shut a brief second he focused his mind on the task ahead.

An endless dull rhythm of marching feet followed David through the dim passageway as the army journeyed through the chambers of Karnoss's foundation. They would stay underground as long as possible to avoid detection. The comfort generated by the relative safety of the deep tunnel system was indeed welcome even if David could not dispel the concern from not knowing the activity above. There was no way to predict the numbers they would face once they moved to the surface, nor could they account for the defense systems that may already be in place. It would be a blind attack and the surprise they hoped to gain could very well be turned back on them.

The black walls felt oppressively close as he thought of the grim reality ahead. With nothing to do but dwell on these thoughts, David found himself coming to the realization that he possessed no fear of dying. Despite the pressure he felt, it was not for his demise, but for those around him that he feared. The

167

thought of facing the horrid emotions caused by witnessing tragic death came as a greater burden than to think of not personally returning at the end of the day. If he died, he would be free of any lingering grief. That pain was for the living.

A sudden jolt forward jarred David as Darkracer began to climb. Throwing himself forward, David gripped the saddle to stay aboard. He could feel himself slide back from the incline.

"Grip with your knees," Darkracer directed. "I'm not waiting for you to climb aboard again."

"Why can't I just walk?" David whispered.

"Don't question instructions."

Pulling himself forward, and using the stirrups for balance, David did as told. A growl sounded beneath him.

"Your knees, boy, knees. Not your heels."

Correcting his position, David managed to hold on as the climb to the top continued. The ramp they took cut straight through several levels of the plateau's infrastructure, passing through barriers that slid aside as they approached. Turning his attention to Amber, David observed that she was responsible for the opening passages, triggering the barriers by sending codes through her comlink. Her control within the city was truly far reaching.

After a couple of jarring minutes, the ground leveled out to a flat expanse. David leaned forward across Darkracer's neck to keep his head from striking the ceiling. Though no expert in the design of the Karnoss Plateau, David deduced that they had made it to a space between the lower bunker network and the upper, public access transits. The ragtag army filed in behind them, filling in all available space as best they could. The leaders of each squadron pushed their way forward to gather around Amber. Keven gave David a quick glance but said nothing.

"Above us is the city's main transit tunnels," Amber explained.

The room grew heavy with the silence. Everyone had refrained from speaking throughout the entire journey, but now even the shuffle of feet or rustling of fabric could not be heard. Barely a breath was dare drawn. If the Vairdec had ventured below the street level, they could easily be patrolling just overhead. It was a prospect that drove the reality of their peril into stark view.

"Arzen, Gry'toena, McTavish, you know your positions. Go."

Each one raised a hand to signal their assigned squads to follow as they slipped as silently as they could through various passageways. The remaining group clustered around the Candonians. David spotted Nathan fingering his rifle with anticipation. He hoped the boy would retain enough sense to pick his targets and not begin firing randomly. Though he held no fear of dying, David felt slightly ill at the thought of his life ending by the teenager's hands.

"Fia," he said under his breath at the thought.

Darkracer flicked an ear. "Steady," he muttered.

David straightened as best he could in the tight space and said no more. He had not intended to speak aloud and chanced a look in Amber's direction. Luckily she and Phantom were already heading toward one of the passages. Climbing into the dark transit lines, David found that the earlier fears of Vairdec patrolling just above were fortunately unfounded. After a bio-scan, the announcement came that the tunnels were clear. A deep sigh of relief echoed softly through the black void.

Winding through a network of service passageways, they came at last to a station just a couple stories below the towering buildings on Karnoss's surface. Unlike the Artisan's main station, this one was small and relatively unadorned. No transparent ceiling existed to expose them to the dangers above. Even so, David glanced up, half expecting to see a missile drop through the ceiling's center. The chilling memory of the slaughter set his resolve for the task ahead. Drawing his weapon, David focused on the exit Darkracer headed for.

David found himself in yet another long passageway. Slowly he lowered his gun and twisted in the saddle to look back down a hall that went well past the door the squad was still filing through. Darkracer sensed David's curiosity and spoke before his rider could question.

"We're in a passage between the courthouse and the lockup."

"That means we're underneath CLE headquarters."

"Correct."

"I thought it was destroyed."

"Correct again. These tunnels are quite strong."

David wanted to question their route further but wondered how long the Candonian's patience would last. Knowing Darkracer, he figured not long enough.

Amber jumped to the ground. "Malard."

Dismounting less nimbly, David stepped alongside the colonel.

"Take Sergeant Mertrie into the lockup." She pointed to a side door with her gun. "Pull any survivors." Catching sight of David's questioning eyes, she explained. "If there're agents or prisoners who can fight, we need them right now."

Giving a silent nod, David took up position as Amber's cover as she opened the door. A reek of melted metals and charred debris swept past them from the darkness beyond. Cautiously David entered what had once been a lift. A beam of light from his weapon exposed the twisted wires and bombed out center of the shaft. Pulling a cable from his belt, he secured the end one level up.

"Hopefully the shaft is the only thing severely damaged," he said softly as he gauged the climb.

Taking hold of the cable, he led the way up to the next level, waiting on the edge for the sergeant to join and add the extra strength needed to push the wreckage aside. They squeezed through the narrow opening to emerge into the hall of the CLE's basement lockup. David was all too familiar with the system. Being a small nation, Earthenia did not rely on any maximum-security prison. For that they cooperated with the Celehi's neighboring region of Pokonia. For troublesome individuals that needed to be contained within Earthenia for shorter periods, each city's CLE headquarters held a lockup in basement levels. While the criminals held there were for the most part petty thieves and troublemakers, David knew the wisdom in remaining cautious.

Ahead, a shadow moved, drawing David's weapon to bear on the stranger. He sighted down his gun, using its light to illuminate the other's face. With a sigh, everyone relaxed. A CLE agent, equally as alarmed, lowered his weapon.

"Didn't expect to see the army," he replied.

"Are you alone?" David asked.

The agent nodded. "I was checking prisoners when the place blew. Communication's sketchy. What's happening? Is the city under attack?"

"Vairdec invasion," David answered flatly.

"Fia. Just Earthenia?"

"Planetary most likely."

Though he had yet to receive any official word, David could not imagine the Vairdec making such an effort for something as galactically insignificant as Earthenia.

The agent cursed again and followed to the lockup's central office. "How can I help?"

David headed straight for the weapon's case, yanking out rifles and prison riot gear and tossing them back to the two waiting men.

"How many prisoners?" He asked over his shoulder.

"Eleven," the agent replied, "though two were injured in the blast."

"How badly?"

"Well," the agent hesitated.

"Can they walk?"

"I suppose. You're releasing the prisoners?"

David turned to face the agent. "We have a

common enemy. We need all available fighters." He returned to his work. "Sergeant, release the prisoners. Bring them to me. Is there a way up from here?"

"Not that I've found."

"We'll take them down and around. Go."

As Sergeant Mertrie hurried off, the agent slipped up alongside David to silently sort through the weapons.

"We're fighting Vairdec now, huh?"

"We're headed for North Slope. We need to hold them there in order to allow SIERA a chance to make it to the plateau."

"So SIERA is still operational?"

David nodded.

"At least we have one piece of good news," the agent said with a huff.

A smile tugged at the corner of David's mouth. It was nice to hear a touch of optimism.

"Lieutenant."

David turned to see the sergeant standing behind them, looking rather sheepish.

"Yes?" David asked.

"One of the prisoners that was injured. Well, I don't think she's fit to fight."

"How bad are the injuries?"

"Oh, those are minor. It's just," he glanced over his shoulder. "It's not like she's wearing much, and I don't think fighting would be her style."

The CLE agent stepped forward with more detail. "She was brought in for advertising on the wrong end the street, as it were."

David gave a frustrated growl. He would have to concede to losing a couple possible fighters. It was probably for the better, though. A prostitute on the front lines of battle wouldn't last long. Instructing the sergeant to have her and the other injured prisoner prepare to head for the bunkers, he grabbed the rest of the gear and proceeded to the office.

It took only a couple minutes for the rest of the prisoners to be assembled and armed. David studied them carefully. As expected they were a misfit gang of low-end criminals and now sober miscreants from the Rew'cha festival. He averted his gaze from a twitching young female Faxon, never caring for the hollow stare of the species' pinkish eyes. A pair of Oxyran's clacked their broad teeth in agitation, their short fur bristling as David explained the situation. All quickly agreed to join, eager to be out of their cages and back in action. Reluctantly the CLE agent handed out weapons and comlinks to his former prisoners before following the group back to the lift.

At the bottom, the waiting squadron gave the newcomers as wide a berth as they could, especially the Faxon who growled as she jostled a couple Celehi aside for a position near the front. David waited at the bottom of the lift for each to descend, having to assist the two injured members safely to the floor. The prostitute proved an awkward task. He wasn't sure where to properly place his hands on her near naked body in order to lift her down. After embarrassingly catching himself focusing on her chest, he finished by keeping his eyes fixed on the far wall, not noticing the fear on her face as she was finally brought down among the rest of the group.

He hurriedly took his place back by the Candonians, ignoring the woman's stare as she and the other injured prisoner along with a teenager Amber felt unfit for battle were ushered to where they could make it down toward the bunkers. Reassured that someone would be meeting them along the way, they disappeared down a side passage. At least three were guaranteed to survive today, David thought. With the team trailing behind, they moved away from the lockup and back toward the station they had first entered. Passing it, they walked a short distance to where the hall took a sharp bend to the right.

"We go up from here," Amber told David. She pointed to the double doors in front of them. "The emergency stairs will lead up to the courthouse's lobby."

She opened the door and led the way to the winding staircase. David signaled back to the rest to remain as silent as possible as they carefully maneuvered through the dark. They took each stair one soft step at a time to avoid creating an echo on the metal rungs. At last David and Amber stood with nothing but a single door between them and the unknown perils of the city's surface.

General Kyler Riechet stood atop a low ridge at Valor Peak's entrance. Below him snaked the narrow canyon running to the plateau that towered before him. Using field glasses he trained his sites on the northwestern edge of the plateau. From this distance he managed to just make out the supply line the Vairdec had set up at North Slope. Their landing vessels sat hunkered near the plateau wall for security from the desert winds that buffeted them from the east. It made it difficult to tell how many were stationed on the far end, and Riechet spent little time trying to figure the number. At this point it was inevitable. One transport or a hundred, his objective remained the same.

Turning his attention back to the canyon, Riechet watched the line of SIERA troops moving cautiously yet quickly along the protective floor. Everything needed to be timed perfectly. The Vairdec had set up regular patrols to circle the plateau, leaving Riechet's army unable to slip in without a diversion. He hated the thought of sending his daughter out with a hastily recruited militia to do nothing more than distract their enemy, but no other choice remained. At least he was able to take advantage of the gap in the Vairdec's patrolling sweep to start moving before the strike was scheduled to begin. They had laid in wait until the last patrol passed, knowing it would likely be a while before any patrols returned. Riechet willingly took every minute presented to him in order to spare those on the plateau from fighting longer than necessary.

But fight they must. Already the sun was warming the peaks, spreading its rays toward the plateau and desolate city. It would not be long now. As a general he kept his thoughts on his task with cold indifference. As a father, he allowed himself one last look north and muttered a silent prayer for his daughter's safety.

Amber placed her back against the door to look at those on the stairs below. Their hard-set features glowed eerily in the dim lights they carried.

"This is it," she said softly, allowing her comlink to carry her voice through the squadron. "Once on the surface we keep moving until we hit North Slope. Engage any enemy you see along the way but do not get separated. We've got about three blocks before open ground. Do not pass into that zone. Stay against the buildings. Stay with your leaders and watch each other's backs. And above all, listen for the call to retreat. You have your instructions so stick with them. And don't let any Vairdec follow you into the lower tunnels. Stay to the transits until given the clear."

She took a deep breath as she turned back to face the door. David stood ready at her side.

"Here we go," she told him.

The door swung open and they leaped forward. The battle had begun.

CHAPTER FOURTEEN

Miraculously intact, the courthouse lobby stretched into shadow in front of David. The high ceiling echoed the soldiers' steps as they navigated the spiraling pillars carved with Earthenia's laws. No enemy awaited, but David held his gun at ready, his eyes darting back and forth between every shadow. Phantom, already carrying Amber again, held the pace at the front, keeping the team moving at a steady, purposeful jog. There was no point running headlong to the doors that swung aside at Amber's command. With nerves on edge, those behind could easily forget to watch for signs of danger. It was a simple yet brilliant example of leadership David admired in the Riechets.

Stepping onto the street, David noticed more of the genius behind the battle plan. Around them lay the ruins of CLE Headquarters. Though grisly, the charred remains provided cover along the street. David figured the Vairdec would not expect an opposing force to emerge from the damaged building, giving the squad precious seconds of safety.

Darkracer nudged David's shoulder.

"Get on," he ordered softly.

David hesitated. He felt inept at climbing in and out of the saddle and hated to turn his back on any potential threat. Unwilling to argue, Darkracer circled tight to his rider, using his head to slam David in the back.

"Now," he snapped.

Grabbing the saddle David pulled himself up, ignoring the stinging of his left shoulder as he did. Amber signaled the squad to split, half following her and half following David. From astride the Candonians, there would be no confusion over whom to follow. Darkracer knew the way, giving David the opportunity to keep a lookout for danger.

To the east the glow of morning pushed back the concealing shadows. Having dipped only shallowly below the horizon, the sun now swiftly swept its light uninhibited across the open desert. Like a curtain drawn up to begin the show, the darkness along North Slope lifted as Darkracer led the charge onto the battlefield.

David glimpsed the wide-open ground ahead for only a brief second before his world spun out of control. His right side slammed the pavement, blurring his vision. He could feel his leg pinned down by the Candonian's weight. Darkracer had fallen. Before David could contemplate more, a searing blast of superheated air swept overhead. It wiped clean all images, leaving nothing more than bright emptiness and a burning agony behind his eyes. The only thought was of dying until the world suddenly flashed back to life and David found himself back on the pavement with the rest of the squadron who scrambled for cover around him. He struggled to clear his head, groaning with nausea as he became aware of the smell of melted flesh.

"With me?"

The sound of Darkracer's voice jarred David. He reached forward to grab the saddle as the Candonian rose quickly. The momentum yanked David up to his feet. Keeping hold of the saddle, David shakily jogged alongside Darkracer to a protective building alcove.

"Shake it off," the Candonian ordered as he pressed David against the wall.

Giving a forceful shake of his head, David was back in the fight.

"They're using flamethrowers," Darkracer explained. "Target them."

Allowing his training to kick in, David took a deep breath as he made a quick assessment of the situation. Keven joined the fight along the eastern edge while the other two units rushed in on two points west of David. Amber lay on the front line, her back pressed against a barrier with a civilian soldier at her side. She continually barked orders despite the growing intensity of firepower.

"Alternate attacks. Keep them guessing."

Along the open space near the edge of the slope, the Vairdec scrambled to set up a proper counterattack while attempting to avoid the crossfire. So far the militia held the advantage, but David knew not to get cocky. The advantage could easily shift. A roar of engines reverberated through David's gut as a fighter craft sailed overhead. Before it could turn back to fire upon his team, another, deeper roar shook the surrounding buildings. The *Predator* dove in to engage.

Instantly the confiscated Faxon fighter peeled off across the desert in an attempt to lead the CAF-47 away from the slope. However, Mike's operative was to protect his people engaged below. Pivoting tightly on a wing, he brought his ship in line to fire upon the slope itself. Even before the missile slammed against the heavy rock of the plateau, crumbling part of the slope beneath an enemy transport, Mike was pulling into a steep climb to avoid another missile launched at him. A second Faxon ship swept around to cut him off.

"Lash," he called.

He was answered by his partner's Max-180 appearing from its hiding place in the sunlight to dive the enemy ships, slicing the air with rapid laser fire.

"Cruiser," the Teshian's voice crackled over the speakers, *"head up. Eight-oh."*

Mike flipped his ship to get a visual on Lash's warning. A squad of four VY-Crafts screamed across the desert to join the two Faxon fighters.

"Fia. Keep sharp. Draw them north."

Years earlier, SIERA's spies discovered the specifics about the Vairdec's notorious one-manned fighters. VY-Crafts were fast and deadly with their swept-back wings and sleek, tear-shaped design. Though not the crafts' official name, with no cooperating Vairdec to give their actual title, the small crafts became known as Vass Yardah

Coesanica, translating from Celharan to "small, fast fighter ship". Their capability of maneuvering through numerous terrains with incredible speed and agility made the name most fitting. Knowing their abilities provided SIERA and their allies with counter-defensive measures Mike was thankful to have learned, especially facing them now. No doubt without the training he would already be dead. The *Predator* shuddered under a glancing blow.

"Two-oh," Lash warned. "Watch it."

Mike gritted his teeth as he banked hard. A second craft barely missed as it swept by.

"Warn faster," he said as he fell into pursuit of the second craft.

Captain Kailyn Gilpar kept her gun up and ready as she hurried down the main hall of the government building's military wing. A rush of air signaled Toodat's passing as the Manogonite took the lead, sailing smoothly just inches from the ceiling. Behind Kailyn, De'oolay and three other soldiers kept pace, fingers on triggers, eyes scrutinizing every dark corner. It was highly unlikely to find Vairdec in the building. Right now most were focused on North Slope. However, training forbade the team to drop their guard.

Near the end they came to a door on the left, its sophisticated panel indicating tighter security. Without hesitating, De'oolay overrode the system and the door swung open. All was silent. The post had been abandoned. The last to leave had shut the system down. De'oolay could not be angry at the decision, as it was what operators were trained to do, but she made no effort to hide the ripple of frustration. It would take a couple minutes to reboot the system – minutes she wondered if she had.

"Hold this position," David shouted back to those around him. "You two," he indicated his choices with only a quick glance, "follow me."

David raced from cover and leaped over a low rail. The ground sloped away beneath his feet. Ignoring the shots pelting the pavement around him he slid on his hip to a lower vantage point along a walkway. He brought himself to a halt with his foot against the walkway's barrier. It was only a low wall of thin metal but it would have to do. Luckily it continued to hold against the shots that bounced off its surface. Keeping low, David chanced a quick glance back at the two hesitating soldiers.

"Get down here," he snapped.

One obeyed, making it down with the assistance of David's cover fire. The second hesitated a little too long, dropping without a cry as a well-placed shot found its mark. David took no time to contemplate the death. The Vairdec's firepower was steadily increasing. From his vantage point he managed to see further to the west.

"Cannon going hot. West flank, move up. Take it out. Gry'toena, on your left. Don't let them get behind you."

Mike's voice broke through the stream of orders. *"Heads up down there. Enemy crafts comin' hot."*

The bone-jarring explosion erupted before Mike finished speaking. A shower of hot debris pelted the troops below. Nearby a building crackled from the hit. David pressed himself into the depression made by the slope and railing, feeling the heat of debris at his back.

"No kidding," he growled to himself.

Making sure no other projectiles were headed in his direction, he rose to a knee and fired on a line of Vairdec rushing through the smoke. Beside him his newly recruited partner at the rail cried out in fear of the sight.

"One at a time," David told him.

The man began to lower his gun. David reached over to push it up.

"Don't look at all of them – just one at a time." He could sense he wasn't getting through. "What's your name?"

"Hethron."

"Okay, Hethron. I'm David. We're partners now, got it? I'm watching your back. Just focus on one and shoot. Then take another. I'm beside you. Partners."

Hethron nodded nervously and began focusing as told. A line of superheated bullets sprayed the road overhead, forcing everyone to dive for cover. Two didn't make it. The concussion from a shock bomb struck the walkway, causing Hethron to fall into David with a cry. Keeping his eyes on the recovering Vairdec, David shoved the soldier back into place. It was going to be a long day.

Across the way, Amber continued to bark her own orders from where she held position against the low barrier.

"Stay low. Arzen, get your unit north. Hold Roxen. Malard, keep that east flank back. Gilpar, get those fighters off us."

Kailyn gritted her teeth. She knew as the commanding officer the orders would be directed at her, but at the moment she had no control over the mission. All hope of bringing the shield up lay upon De'oolay whose fingers flew over the controls. Glancing down the hall she was grateful to find they were still alone.

"We're working on it," she replied to Amber's call.

A spout of fire erupted against the wall of an eastern building. Amber shielded herself as bits of rubble pelted her barrier.

"Cruiser!"

"I can't stop them all," Mike argued, whipping around a tower to cut the fighter off from attacking the ground troops again. "Where's the shield?"

"Working it," De'oolay snapped as she watched the screens impatiently.

Mike dropped low, firing rapidly into the Faxon fighter's engines before pulling up hard to send his ship into a vertical climb only meters from a thirty-story building. Even the durable Celharan glass shattered from the power of the *Predator's* passing. A glittering rain of sharp shards cascaded to the streets, scattering a Vairdec platoon that had slipped through the perimeter defense.

David grimaced as the Faxon fighter struck the top of the nearest building and toppled to the street beyond. He hoped his own people had not been in its path. The concussion rippled under his feet. Two VY-Crafts screamed overhead, targeting the *Predator* as the ship circled around.

"Where are you, Lash?" Mike called as he evaded incoming shots.
"Two clicks east. Busy."
"Bring 'em to me, co. How much time, captain?"
"Not long. One minute – maybe less."
Mike accelerated toward Lash's position, quickly spotting the three VY's swarming the Teshian's Max-180. The second Faxon fighter was heading to the scene as well. The *Predator* roared into the swarm, thwarting a VY-Craft's kill shot and bringing Lash alongside his port wing.
"Grateful," the Teshian replied. *"I was getting beaten."*
"Yeah, what made you so popular? Break high."
Lash pulled his ship skyward as Mike dipped toward the desert floor. It was a tactic they had perfected over years of teamwork and there was no need for further communication. As their pursuers worked to split their ranks and follow, Mike and Lash angled back to open fire on the Vairdec. The Faxon fighter dipped to the side only to be clipped by a VY-

Craft. They spiraled downward while a second VY struggled from a crippling shot. The three remaining crafts fell into pursuit as Mike and Lash headed for the city.

"Once they're in, pull out fast," Mike instructed.

"What of you?"

"Just do it."

David struggled to hold his team together. They were no longer listening to his orders and every time David tried to make his way back up to the street, he was fired upon. Hethron's nerve was breaking down, making him unreliable in providing cover. Vairdec troops streamed through the broken northeastern line and were now driving David's team along the street. Keven held the street above as his squadron joined David's, many of them fanning in undisciplined lines or simply breaking to make a run for it. Darkracer and Phantom galloped along the perimeter, driving as many as they could back into the fight while doing everything possible to organize a more tactical retreat.

A hit brought Keven tumbling down the slope to where David and Hethron had managed to hold off any advancement along their line of sight. David dared a quick check of his friend who struggled to his knees. Blood ran down his left leg.

"I'll live," he said as he checked the injury. "Watch out!"

The shadow of Mike and Lash's ships preceded the roar of their engines. Right behind them came three VY-Crafts, two of which fired on ground troops while passing. The walkway's remaining canopy buckled under a hit, flipping skyward before toppling down around the walk. David flattened himself against the railing, shielding Keven as bits of rubble pummeled them. Hethron panicked, leaping the rail to run across the walkway. David had no time to cover him before a flamethrower seared the man's flesh from his bones. Though angry and frustrated, David tried to focus on the advantage of having the flamethrower temporarily out of commission.

"Stay here," David said. "Cover me."

Keven obliged as David took a running leap and scrambled up to the street above. He lay flat against the ground as bullets and lasers criss-crossed the air above him. Spying his team drawing ever further south he began to crawl toward an abandoned vehicle to gain the cover he needed to make a dash for their position. Suddenly the fire pattern above him changed. The Vairdec ceased momentarily. Chaotic shouts drew his attention east to where the rest of Keven's team had rallied behind Phantom and Darkracer. David knew their only hope lay in his team turning to the offensive at the same time to catch their enemy in a crossfire. Pushing himself to his feet, David raced to the slowly backing line.

"Advance! Advance!"

A shot struck the nearby vehicle, causing David to throw himself backward to avoid the spray of projectiles that coursed through the space he occupied a second earlier. His back struck the ground and he twisted to fire. A Vairdec soldier rushed forward. Before David could shoot, Darkracer appeared from behind. He struck the Vairdec in the back, his strength flinging the alien into the air. The soldier landed heavily in front of the galloping Candonian, the churning hooves crushing his spine and skull. Darkracer didn't slow. Making it to David's side, he pivoted around the vehicle to avoid more shots.

"Colonel says to fall back to Rester Street," Darkracer announced.

"I didn't hear anything."

"Communication's spotty. The Vairdec are interfering with our equipment."

"Get them back," David told the Candonian as he pointed toward the remaining troops.

"You?"

"Not leaving anyone behind."

"This is an awfully long minute," Mike's voice snapped over Kailyn's comlink. *"Where's that shield, Gilpar?"*

"It's coming," she snapped back. "Talk to Soe."

Allowing Toodat to continue guarding the door, Kailyn stormed over to where De'oolay worked.

"This is not a powering of simple lights," the Celehi woman argued. "The shields must take power from back up generators. The charge time increases. The generators have not been charged in a long time. Processing is taking place."

"Do it," Mike cut in, *"don't explain it!"*

By now Mike could not be sure if he was that skilled or just incredibly lucky. He continued to evade the VY-Crafts with only minor hits by proceeding in a weaving path among Karnoss's higher buildings at suicidal speeds. Lash had slipped away, heading back out over the desert in anticipation of the shield's use.

"Ten seconds."

"Thank you."

The warning was just what he wanted to hear.

"Cruiser," Lash's worried voice broke in, *"no time left. Go vertical!"*

"Negative."

Mike narrowed his eyes on the navigation system. He knew where he was going. Ten seconds was all he needed. Though his plan was risky, he knew if he retreated the VY-Crafts might make it safely out of the city as well. Dropping low he cut his speed, pivoting around a resort's tower as his pursuers whipped past. It would take only seconds for them to readjust. Mike raced over his ship's controls, cutting the rest of the *Predator's* main power and gliding her down under a low bridge. It was a tight fit, but he knew his ship's abilities. The CAF-47's break thrusters pulled it up short and Mike landed with no time to spare. Instantly he shut off all power.

Around the plateau's edge, giant towers began to hum with a surge of power. The hum grew rapidly to a screaming pitch as all accessible energy within the city reached the spires. An electro-magnetic blast suddenly ripped across the Karnoss skyline to envelope the city. The three VY-Crafts wobbled unsteadily as they lost power. A wing clipped the side of a building, flipping the small fighter and sending it to a fiery end on the streets below. The other two glided momentarily, though had been going too fast to maintain any amount of control. One embedded itself into the side of a tower as the third skimmed the *Predator's* protective bridge to break apart just beyond.

Mike winced at how close the crash came to his position.

"Better you than me," he muttered.

Riechet silently calculated the time needed to see the rest of his soldiers safely into Karnoss. If they hurried, another five minutes would be enough, but looking south across the desert, he knew it would be five minutes too long.

"We've got incoming," he told his pilots.

Mike growled at the flickering lights before him. The *Predator's* board was sluggish.

"Lash," he called. "I hope you're airborne, 'cause that call's for you."

Despite the shield's pulse crippling the ships above, little was felt on the streets of North Slope. David had just begun his run back to Keven when it struck, announcing itself in nothing but a low subsonic boom. A Vairdec emerged from the shadows to David's right. He snapped around to fire, sensing the Vairdec already managed to get off a shot. How did he let himself run into the open without checking? He tensed for the impact. Surprisingly, the shot never hit. As David fired again, he understood why. The laser systems had been disabled by the blast. With subconscious dexterity, David switched his weapon to bullets and tried once more, leaping over the side of the street to slide down to the walkway.

"Welcome back," Keven said.

David hurried to his side and caught him up under the arm. "Time to go."

Keven yanked himself up with the help of the walk's railing, firing toward the street as he did. The Vairdec above stumbled back.

"By all means," he groaned.

They made their way along the walkway's railing, coming at last to the stairs. Thankfully the battle had swung west and their path remained uninhibited. As David began to help Keven up to the street a movement caught his eye. He spun on the Vairdec who lunged toward him. David braced for the impact as Keven brought his weapon around. Without a sound the Vairdec lurched back and collapsed in a dead heap, a shot embedded through his mask. Following the projectile's path, David spotted Nathan atop a balcony. The kid remained calm and poised, killing any Vairdec that blundered into his sights.

Laser fire sprayed the canyon floor as the incoming VY-Craft spotted the line of soldiers. Riechet ducked among the rocks, waiting for the ship to pass.

"Stay against the rocks," he ordered. "Move."

The already hurrying army doubled their efforts, pressing themselves against the shelter of the cliff. A switchback path wound its way to an entry point halfway up the plateau. The last of Riechet's army was heading up this trail, uncomfortably exposed along the cliff face. The shadow of the VY-

Craft enveloped the troops as it swooped back to take aim. Luckily SIERA was not without defense. Per Riechet's order, a mobile anti-aircraft missile launcher sat at the entrance of the plateau. As the hostile ship came into view they opened fire. The VY's pilot took evasive measures, his own missile missing its mark to slam into the plateau's upper ridge. Rock rained down along the trail.

"Get inside," Riechet ordered. "Leave the trans."

He hated leaving the last transports and their supplies, but his soldiers took precedence. Fortunately the remaining transports consisted of extra uniforms and housing supplies, low priority though sorely missed. His military prowess led him to spread the transports throughout the line of troops, placing the top priority supplies near the front. If they were attacked, it would be, as proven, further into their run. At least weapons and combat equipment were safe. Now all he had to do was protect his people.

Shots lit up the sky as the Max-180 raced in from the northern side of Karnoss. Thwarting SIERA's attacker, Lash retreated down the canyon with four newly arrived VY-Crafts in hot pursuit.

"Cruiser! Cruiser, where are you?"

Mike kicked the *Predator's* consol angrily. He could not bear the thought of listening to his friend's desperation without being able to help.

"Come on!" he yelled at the ship.

One of the VY's broke off to return to SIERA's line. Riechet held his ground as bullets and lasers simultaneously pelted the cliff face. A couple of his soldiers failed to elude the attack. Forced to ignore the losses, Riechet rushed along the line, driving everyone forward with great urgency. By now the Vairdec would have seen and understood the opening into the plateau. Another anti-aircraft missile shot from its station next to the plateau entrance. The first attack caused broken rocks to nearly knock it from its rocky perch, leaving the team scrambling to reestablish it as a defense for SIERA. The shot drove the VY-Craft back, but Riechet knew they could not hold off the Vairdec forever, especially with the convergence of more hostiles overhead. He could see two breaking away from their attack on Lash to head back for the canyon.

"Be ready to fire," he instructed his soldiers. "Lash, we need you at the plateau."

"Trying, sir," he responded with a snarl.

His ship rocked from the shots. He quickly checked his status, thankful that the blow had been a glancing one. However, Lash knew it would only take a couple more shots like that to fatally slow his ship. His only defense was his superior knowledge of the canyon's layout. Skirting the southern edge, he circled back to the plateau.

Two of the VY's were racing down the length of the canyon, their missiles going hot. Lash forced his ship to greater speed despite its shuddering complaint from another hit.

Riechet could see the crafts' fast approach. A third suddenly swept into view from around the southern tip of the plateau. It immediately aimed at SIERA's defensive missiles whose shooters managed only a single shot before succumbing to the attack.

"Everybody down!" Riechet shouted.

A shadow blanketed them as a mass of firepower erupted from overhead. The *Predator* roared past, its shots clipping the lead VY whose attention was on the firepower from the plateau. Caught by surprise, the Vairdec was slow to evade. The craft spun once, clipping its wingman and sending him into the side of the canyon. Unable to regain altitude, the first craft followed to the rocky floor. Mike fought to keep his sluggish ship from joining. Full power was still being restored, and most of the available power was being routed to weapons. The third VY-Craft fell into pursuit.

Lash turned down the canyon to face the oncoming *Predator* with his own pursuer preparing to lock missiles onto him.

"Eye up," Lash called. "Double pursuit."

Mike instantly caught on and pulled up hard, flipping his ship over the top of his pursuer. Lash unleashed a barrage of firepower the VY-Craft could not dodge in the canyon's confines. As it succumbed, the *Predator* was on its own attack run, firing down on the Max-180's pursuer as it passed underneath. Shortly thereafter both Lash and Mike were headed back across the desert, watching for any more incoming crafts from the southern mountain range.

"You're clear, general," Mike announced.

Riechet continued to urge his troops on from his position at the plateau entrance. "Good work, we're just about in. Head for EAF hangars. Colonel."

Amber jogged along the side of a building with seven of her team. Everyone was regrouping along Rester. The Vairdec were beginning to map out their movement so she hoped they wouldn't have to hold the street for long.

"General," Amber acknowledged through her labored breath.

"Fall back."

"Yes, sir."

With a gasping sigh of relief she signaled the rest of the soldiers. "Fall back. Head for assigned routes. Move it!"

She slid to a stop at the corner as a larkrae scrambled along the wall toward her, its massive claws holding it to the wall's narrow ledge. Spying her it gave a screeching yell and leaped into the air. Amber was ready and dropped the animal as it reach for her face. With a firm motion of her hand, she signaled those behind to make for the opposite street. The larkrae's handler would not be far behind.

As the team hurried to safety, Amber flattened herself against the wall. Just as she predicted, a bulky Vairdec in a snarling war mask fired around the corner. She fired back, holding the alien at bay. A stream of bullets joined hers as David and Keven came up alongside. With the added firepower she kept the larkrae's handler tucked behind the building's corner as she, David and Keven backed across the street and made a run for it.

196

The Earthenian Air Force's Deep Hangars lay on the southeastern side of the plateau. A natural jut in the cliff protected the opening from high desert winds, though the run remained a challenging one to maneuver. The opening, hidden behind a camo-net, was large enough for the CAF-47 and Max-180 to fly in together, but both pilots agreed the risk was too high with their ships sluggish from the damage they sustained during battle.

"Head in," Mike told Lash as he zeroed his navigation onto the entrance.

"Affirmative."

The ships dove for the cliff face.

"Cruiser, Concussioner!"

Mike hated the sound of the word. He had already spotted the bulky craft slowly making its way around the far rim of the plateau. Though not very maneuverable, Concussioners packed a serious punch. Their concentrated shots of electro-magnetic pulses could render any ship inoperable and send it plummeting to the ground.

"Can you make it with the net up?"

"The Max will control it."

Pilots held the ability to lower the camo-net upon entry. It was advisable as the electrical current that made the net possible often scrambled navigations and onboard computers. However, lowering it now would give the Vairdec a clear view of what Mike and Lash were aiming for.

Mike circled wide to give Lash time. He fired on the Concussioner in hopes of drawing it after him. The tough armor made his efforts appear petty, but it was enough to bring the ship around. Two VY-Crafts darted out from behind.

"Really?" Mike gasped.

In the *Predator's* current state, there would be no outrunning the VYs by going around the plateau. Only one option remained – going straight into the hangar at full speed and hope for the best. Without the proper navigation system, it would take the enemy a while to map out the entrance. Mike hoped it would be enough time to lower the emergency doors.

"Lash," he called, "I hope you're out of the way 'cause I'm comin' in hot."

As the VY-Crafts raced toward him he broke through their formation and headed straight for the plateau. The Concussioner followed his movement as it lined up for a shot.

"Not good," Mike groaned.

The cliff filled the view port. Seconds later half a dozen alarms began screaming inside the cockpit. The *Predator* struck the camo-net at the same instant the Concussioner fired. Though the electro-magnetic pulse only clipped the ship, it was enough to cause its engines to sputter. Mike scrambled to cut main thrusters and slow his ship as it hurtled down the long, tunnel runway. Unable to stay aloft, it slammed to the floor, skidding out of control. Sparks flew as the *Predator* spun around to face back the way it had come. To his dismay, Mike found himself staring at the two VY-Crafts.

One had followed too closely, getting caught in the EMP of the Concussioner and losing power. Close enough to the entrance it managed to glide onto the runway floor and, like the *Predator*, was skidding down its length. The second had wisely held back and then took a daring dive through the invisible opening. From his position, Mike knew his options were limited. Using the top wing mounts, he fired on the approaching ship while coaxing what power he could from the port engine. The *Predator* whipped to the right, its rapidly firing gun cutting through the surprised enemy craft, which ignited in a bright flash and broke apart.

Mike cut power as the *Predator* continued to spin. A shuddering crunch announced the surviving VY-Craft's collision against the side of the CAF-47. Mike groaned at the sound. The impact pushed the two crippled ships the last few meters into the hangar where they finally ran out of momentum. With an exhausted moan, Mike lay back in his seat a moment, watching Lash run forward with an Air Force officer at his side. The Vairdec pilot quickly made it out of his ship, intent on fighting to the death. Lash's Teshian reflexes proved the better and soon the Vairdec lay dead. Mike slowly made his way down the ramp, only casually glancing at the body.

"Those emergency doors better be shut," he said.

"Already being done," Lash reassured.

Mike looked to the officer. "Are there more of you here?"

"Four of us," the officer answered.

"Good. Mechanics?"

"Yes, sir."

"Then get these ships running. We'll need them soon."

"Yes, sir."

Mike turned toward the exit with Lash walking slowly alongside.

"We made it good for a first day," Lash commented with a snarling grin.

"First day?" Mike shook his head. "War is hell."

CHAPTER FIFTEEN

"I want that medic ward functioning," Amber ordered as she strode into the SIERA controlled south bunker. "Who can get these wounded taken care of?"

Two bloodied, trembling men crouched against the wall at the colonel's feet. A young woman rushed toward them with a medical kit.

"Do you have medical training?" Amber asked as the woman knelt before the wounded.

Looking stressed and nervous, the woman glanced up to notice Amber's uniform. She gave a tentative nod.

"Nurse at Maysen Medical." Her gaze diverted to the floor as she reddened. "Just got my license, though."

"I don't care," Amber answered, stepping carefully around her so as not to slip in the blood. "Fix these two up and get them over to the ward. Report in there. You work for us now. See who else is from Maysen. We'll need everyone we can get."

Without waiting for a reply, Amber headed across the chamber. Around her the once quiet atmosphere throbbed with the bustling mass of personnel all focused on creating the bunker into a workable military center. The large central room now housed various sets of computers along with a quartered off command post. Numerous weapons lined the walls of the side chamber with armed guards at its entrance. The other small chambers acted as officers' barracks, food storage and a medic ward, the last already busy despite the fact that most equipment was still packed in crates.

"Colonel," Riechet's voice said over Amber's comlink, *"meet me in my quarters."*

"On my way."

Twisting her way through the many piles of supplies, Amber headed for a small storage room that had been converted for the general's personal use. Knocking on the entryway she stood at attention until her father turned to her with a smile. Assured that they were alone, they dropped the military persona for a moment to be a family. Riechet embraced his daughter as thankfulness and relief washed over him.

"It's good to see you safe," he said.

"It's good to see you, too."

They stepped backed from each other and once again assumed their military demeanor. Riechet shook his head.

"I'd lie if I said I didn't fear for you, but it's obvious you did very well. I'm proud of you."

"Thank you, sir. Under the circumstances I suppose all went as well as could be expected. Most were not skilled fighters."

"Well, neither are the Vairdec," Riechet replied as he walked to the far side of the room.

Amber's eyes narrowed. "Sir?"

"This is an outpost for them. Arct-Ieya's finest battalions would have landed in Celehi controlled regions. They may need Karnoss as a station, but we Humans are not the main target."

"It's logical."

"But let's not become complacent, either." Riechet turned back to look hard at his daughter. "Their weakest fighters can hold well against our best."

"As we saw."

"How many casualties?"

"Nineteen confirmed, but with no true roster the numbers are slow in coming. We have yet to hear from Gilpar's team."

"Mm. All we can do is wait right now. Keep checking northern bunkers. They may have had to enter there."

"Yes, sir."

"In the meantime," Riechet held up a sheathed sword. "I thought you'd like to have this back."

Amber's stance softened as she took the sword from her father. Carefully removing it from the sheath she examined the etching of flame running down the blade. Even in the dim light she knew every intricate detail.

"*Fire Lass*," she said softly. She allowed herself a weary smile as she looked up at her father. "You're right about me wanting this. It's funny how you never seem to miss something until it's no longer there."

The light in Riechet's eyes dimmed as he pondered the depth of her words.

David threw a pack he'd been given onto a low cot without bothering to see what was inside. Using it as a pillow, he collapsed with a groan.

"Bad day?" came a weary voice.

Looking over at the cot next to his he saw Mike stretched out with his arm across his eyes.

"You?"

Slowly Mike drew his arm back to glance over at David. "Oh, just great. Haven't been shot at like that in a while." He gave a sarcastic chuckle. "I just hope they get the *Predator* fixed. Something tells me this isn't over."

"Sadly no," Amber replied as she entered the room.

"Well, look who joins. Welcome, colonel."

Amber glanced over to where Mike watched her. "Commander."

David rolled over at the sound of her voice to watch as she seated herself on the edge of a cot near the door. Since she gave no indication of enforcing military protocol he gave her none. He was too tired. Unlike the men in the room, Amber took the time to remove her boots and gun before stretching out on her cot.

"We lost the transport with blankets and pillows," she muttered.

"Damn," Mike yawned.

David felt completely apathetic. He was drained and numb. It went beyond a physical fatigue. He was in good shape and the rigors of the activity did not exceed what he had trained for. However, the brutality of the battle was new to him. He was use to capturing his opponents and taking them in unharmed. Only once in his career had he suffered the pangs of death. Rolling onto his other side, he shut his eyes tight, hoping for a few minutes to forget it all.

A commotion in the main chamber caused David to grimace, though he refused to do more in acknowledgement. He was not in command. With both Riechets in the vicinity there was nothing for him to do. He could hear Amber moan and rise. Curiosity tugged at him to follow, but his body rejected any notion to move. Amber staggered to the door and carefully took stock of the activity beyond.

Personnel ducked as Toodat flew in, beating his leathery wings madly to stay aloft. The Manogonite was breathing irregularly, his limbs shaking, blood soaking one side of his back. With a few final desperate flaps, he lost altitude and unceremoniously collapsed upon the bed of a supply skiff. Behind, Captain Kailyn Gilpar led her battered team into the waiting arms of medics. Amber pushed her way through to come alongside her limping friend. Riechet, too, was hurrying to their sides.

"General," Kailyn panted.

Riechet gave a nod. "Captain."

"The Vairdec picked up our location when we brought up the shield."

"Casualties?"

"Thankfully only one. If we hadn't commandeered a transport, I doubt any of us would be here. De'oolay's in bad shape."

Riechet reached under Kailyn's arm to support her around the waist, assisting her to their medical ward. "You accomplished your mission. Good work. Getting as many back alive as you did is admirable."

As the general set Kailyn on a cot, she reached out to take hold of his wrist. After authorizing the removal of the intel-band she wore, she slowly removed it, wincing as the dried blood cracked and tore at her injury. With a sigh she handed it off to Riechet.

"De'oolay discovered something while at the computers. Sounds important."

Riechet gave a solemn nod. "Thank you. Now you rest." He turned to his daughter who stood faithfully at his side. "The same goes for you. You've done well. You deserve some sleep."

Amber hesitated, her eyes locked on the intel-band in her father's hand. Tired as she was, curiosity held her in her place a moment longer. However, she was a soldier whose commanding officer had given her an order. Pushing back her desire to stay, she gave a quick nod and left the room.

David could not tell what time of the day it was when he awoke. So far underground, day and night ceased to exist. Giving a grunt in response to a sore arm injured from falling debris during the battle, David wiped a finger across the timeband on his wrist. A gentle glow from the densely packed fibers indicated he had managed to sleep for close to nine hours. That was good. There was no telling when he would get such a long stretch of uninterrupted sleep again. Reluctant to rise, he rolled to his back and draped his arm across his eyes, letting his mind wander where it wished. He could not recall any dreams, yet there was a sense of having done so. He felt detached from the world around him, as if he was still fishing for reality. Reality? What was real anymore? Everything felt like a disconnected series of nightmares.

Another hour passed before he managed to convince his body to move. Jolts of pain stabbed at muscles that had grown stiff and cramped. Forcing himself to sit up, David looked about the darkened room. Mike was gone, though a newcomer lay asleep on a cot against the far wall. He was an Oxyran, a species David knew quite well. They inhabited Telamier's closest planetary neighbor of Ayzat and long ago built a region on Telamier that bordered Earthenia to the south.

Oxyrans were a short, stocky species rarely reaching heights beyond one and a half meters. As Ayzat was slightly cooler than Telamier, they possessed a short, dense hair that covered much of their bodies. Both males and females sported facial hair, though it was the females that grew theirs long as a statement of beauty. Strictly vegetarians, Oxyrans possessed only two large, flat teeth that ran the upper and lower rim of their jaws. These were often used for communication in the form of teeth clicking and gnashing – a system David never fully managed to translate.

The Oxyran in the room was a silvery-white male with darker grey striping along his head and shoulders. He was a particularly hefty looking individual whose attitude David knew most likely matched his tough appearance. Oxyrans often possessed bullish personalities that were attributed to their smaller size. His large eyes were shut tight and he clicked his teeth in response to some agitated dream. Clutched in his thick-fingered hand was a large grenade launcher with a blaster rifle resting against his back. David shook his head, imagining what this individual must be like on the battlefield.

Walking to the door, David paused briefly to look at Amber. It was difficult to imagine her as a tough, even callous, military officer while she lay asleep before him. All he saw was a woman – another Human caught in an unthinkable tragedy. Pulling himself away from his musings, David silently slipped out the door and into the large chamber beyond.

Here the activity continued regardless of the hour. Personnel came and went in orderly shifts to organize intel, manage communications, maintain weaponry and continue their vigilant care of the wounded. David walked slowly among the groups, observing their actions casually as he went. Passing the medic ward he slowed to watch as nurses busied themselves with changing bloodied bandages and doing what they could to ease the pain of their charges with hushed tones and forced smiles. Behind them, a connecting chamber glowed in the sterile brightness of operating lights. The panel that stretched across the door cast long shadows of doctors frantically patching some poor soul's body back together. David turned away. He had seen enough. Of all those that now lived in this underground sanctuary, the doctors would be the busiest. Such was the tragedy of war.

Keeping along the wall of the main chamber, David came at last upon the command center, sectioned off by shoulder-high panels and dominated by countless computers and map grids that cast their soft light upon the worn yet determined features of General Kyler Riechet. He stood tall and proud, his hands clasped behind his back, his eyes fixed on a map that blinked through a series of statistics. For a moment David stood mesmerized by the scene. He could imagine Riechet standing among the Natchuan generals of old, a sword in hand and a great Candonian warrior at his side.

"Don't hover, Malard," Riechet said without turning.

His voice made David jump. Embarrassed he backed away, intent on leaving.

"Sorry, sir."

"Get in here."

David paused as he tried to predict the general's reason for summoning him. Straightening, he stepped around the panel to stand just inside the command center. For what felt an eternity, David stood at attention, waiting for Riechet to speak. Instead, the older man continued to examine the map, fingering through bits of information without acknowledging David further. As the minutes ticked by, David began to wonder if the general had forgotten him but dared not move. At last, Riechet spoke, though he still did not turn to face him.

"Did you sleep?"

"Yes, sir."

"Good."

Again a long pause as Riechet moved to another computer. After he entered some figures, he stepped back and finally faced his young officer. David remained frozen as Riechet's scrutinizing gaze passed over him.

"The colonel spoke highly of your work at North Slope."

David stared straight ahead, avoiding locking eyes with his superior. "Thank you, sir."

"What did you do wrong?"

The question took David aback. He was unsure of what the general was driving at. What had he done wrong? Thinking back over the full battle, he analyzed each moment.

"I… I should have stayed on the road with the rest of the unit?"

"Why didn't you?"

David swallowed hard as his throat clenched. "The lower walk provided a view of the enemy the road could not. It was a way to command where the unit should focus their efforts."

"And another could not take your place?"

"Most were civilian fighters. They had no training."

"It sounds as if you did what was necessary."

"I suppose, sir."

"Then what did you do wrong?"

David felt the sweat forming on his palms and discretely tried to wipe it away. The battle had happened so fast. Everything had been chaos. His team was not well trained.

"I might have done more to protect my men."

"Like what?"

Again David struggled to find an answer. Maybe he needed to return to the road sooner. Perhaps his unit would have listened to orders. What of Hethron? Could David have stopped him from running into the path of the flamethrower? So many variables presented themselves, all of which may or may not have worked under the circumstances. Unsure of how to proceed, he glanced questioningly into Riechet's face, prepared to hear the general's criticisms.

"Terrible things happen in war," Riechet said. "Some things we can learn from and change, other things we cannot. In hindsight there are a lot of 'what ifs' that arise, but in the heat of battle there are no guarantees. Nothing works as cleanly as we'd like. The key lies in doing the best you can with the training and wisdom you have, then living with the outcome. The answer for you is, you did nothing truly wrong."

David let his gaze drop to the floor. He felt relieved at avoiding a harsh reprimand. However, he still felt confused and drained.

"Perhaps there was a way for you to do better, perhaps not. Work things through in your mind and learn what you can. But in the end, an officer must have confidence in his choices – and in himself."

David's voice barely made it above a whisper. "Yes, sir."

"I'm promoting you."

At this, David's gaze snapped back to Riechet's face as he tried to read the general's expression.

"I know this is not military procedure, but this is a time of war. Unfortunately we have neither the time nor the means for formalities. I need good officers and you are one. You are now Major David Malard."

Riechet paused to allow his words to sink in. David was use to not having promotions come quickly. The Coalition of Law Enforcement made it particularly trying to move through the ranks. Not only did one have to qualify through rigorous tests and achievements in the field, each candidate had to serve a set number of years under each rank before being allowed to move up, regardless of personal abilities. This came from having a number of Celehi involved in the workings of CLE. Though never spoken, it was well known that the slow promotions kept too many Humans, especially young ones, from outranking too many Celehi. It was a heavily debated practice, one David had learned to live with and be thankful for making it to first lieutenant. To suddenly jump from that to major was shocking. Unable to think of anything to say, David simply dipped his head in acknowledgement.

"Yes, sir."

"I trust you," Riechet continued as he retrieved David's new insignia. "You're intelligent, hard working and devoted to the people. You have the training and the heart, so trust yourself."

"Yes, sir," David repeated, though the words felt hollow in his mouth.

He took the insignia and held it numbly in the palm of his hand.

"Come."

Automatically David pivoted on his heels to fall into step at the general's left shoulder. They exited the command center and wove their way through the network of soldiers to where the Candonians quietly rested. Darkracer straightened from where he leaned against the rock wall as he watched the men approach.

"General."

"Racer. I would like for you and Phantom to accompany us to the east bunkers."

Phantom arched his back then gave a hearty shake. "Is that where they're sending civilians?"

"It is."

"At least we can stretch our legs," Darkracer said as he gave a nod to Riechet.

David watched with disappointment as Riechet grabbed hold of Darkracer's mane and swung easily onto his back. He knew he would be expected to do the same. He gave Phantom an uncertain look only to have it mirrored by the Candonian.

"Malard?" Riechet asked.

David clenched his fists. He preferred not to ride. It made him feel inferior somehow. Furthermore, he spent most of the time worrying about falling off.

"No saddle," he pointed out, trying to give some excuse for his hesitancy.

Phantom bent his knee. "I don't mind."

David gave Riechet a questioning glance to find the general watching him with a hint of amusement in his eyes.

"It's all right," he reassured. "We're only walking."

Then why must I ride? David thought. With no room for argument, he reluctantly pulled himself onto the Candonian's back.

As they walked along a narrow, dark passage, Riechet spoke.

"I know riding is still very new to you. Not many people are ever given the privilege of being carried by a Candonian."

"Then why now?"

Darkracer gave a chuckle as if he held the same question as David. Riechet looked over with a smile, his face a soft green in the glow of the portable light upon his shoulder.

"At this moment there is no reason except that I want you to have as much experience as possible. You are still in training, you know."

"All of SIERA is trained to ride Candonians?"

"All forbid," Darkracer grumbled. Phantom gave a snort of agreement.

"No," Riechet admitted, "but I want you to learn. I'm surprised by you. I thought you'd be more enthusiastic. After all, riding Candonians was a signature among Natchua."

David nodded. That much was true. However, he still felt uncomfortable.

"And you don't mind?" he asked, touching Phantom's neck.

"No," Phantom answered, "but I'd mind even less if you sat up straighter. Sit with straighter legs, point your heels toward the floor, not into my ribs."

"Sorry." Quickly David did as told.

"Good posture will help you balance," Riechet added. "Turn your feet in so your toes point toward

Phantom's head. That will give you a proper grip with your inner thighs. Hang on there, not with your feet. You'll be sore for a while, but it will go away as your body becomes use to it."

As he obeyed, David felt his center of gravity shift down to a more comfortable position. He began to understand the rhythm of the muscles beneath him and instead of fighting them to stay aboard, he moved with them. A confidence began to form. The fear of falling slowly dissipated.

"Sir," he finally said, "why am I being taught this?"

"Candonians have always been the Human's allies. Sadly many on both sides have forgotten the importance of that relationship. It is an important one that can save you both in battle. You must learn to work with them – to trust them as they learn to trust you. Together you are a stronger force than if you fought alone. As of right now, they are accompanying us not only for your sake in training, but for the purpose of making a statement."

"A statement?"

A cunning glint rested in Riechet's eyes. "A man who can sit higher than his fellow Human can stand is looked up to not only physically but psychologically. The refugees of Karnoss need leadership. To know there is a command system – some control in an otherwise chaotic situation – provides hope and comfort. Furthermore I cannot have anyone question who's in command." He paused to give a slight huff. "I understand that this may sound arrogant of me, but considering this is a state of war, government officials need to allow those of military rank to do their job. I am currently the highest ranking officer in Karnoss, and as SIERA is heading the defense operation, that ultimately places me in command of the city."

David didn't need to see Riechet's face to understand that while the general accepted the task, there was no arrogance associated with it. A great weight rested on General Riechet's shoulders and he knew it. It was a responsibility that he refused to corrupt with undue pride.

"And do not forget our position," Darkracer added. "Like you said, the Candonian alliance is easily overlooked. Our willingness to work with Humans reminds them whose side we're on. Working with the leadership only strengthens our positions in your species' eyes."

It was a point David never considered before and he silently vowed not to complain about riding anymore.

The northeast bunker system appeared much like the south system SIERA now owned. A large main chamber of carved stone acted as the central hub to numerous smaller rooms and side passages that were steadily filling with refugees. Within the main room a semblance of order had been gained and designated leaders worked diligently to set up stations for tracking arrivals, checking in supplies and handing out rations. Along the rim, the somber faces of survivors stared vacantly back, the shock of the last couple of days refusing to dissipate from their countenance.

Phantom halted suddenly, causing David to scramble to reposition himself and maintain a semblance of professionalism. Peering down, Candonian and rider saw a young boy huddled in front of them, his arms wrapped around the soft grey neck of his pet kiejaud whom he had been trying to catch. His eyes were as wide with surprise as those of the little hoofed animal. David felt pity for the boy's plight tugging painfully at his core. Phantom lowered his head to touch the boy softly with his nose.

"Go along," he said. "It's all right."

The trembling call of a young woman drew David's attention to where the boy's caregiver hurried to retrieve her charge. She appeared near tears and with shaking hands took the boy's arm to guide him and his pet away.

"What will your mother say when she gets here?" Though spoken quietly, her choked voice rang clearly through the silent chamber.

With a shake of his head, David looked away. The stress hung as a thick vapor in the still air. Through this tension a pale, trembling man cut his path toward the general, his bloodshot eyes fixed upon Riechet despite one being half-closed from an injury that had turned a deep purple across half his face. His rumpled clothing was soiled with blood though his uninhibited movement suggested the blood belonged to a different victim. Riechet waited patiently for the man to address him first.

"You're with SIERA, are you not?"

"General Kyler Riechet, commanding officer."

The man was visibly relieved by the news.

"Hansen Elliots, Karnoss councilman. We've been hoping for more leadership. I made it here last night and learned the CLE left the other day."

Riechet gave a nod. "On my orders. We need people to fight."

"True, but what can we expect for here?"

"I leave it to the city council to maintain order among the refugees. We can't afford to split our fighting forces into non-combat positions."

"Right now everyone seems to be cooperating, but..."

Elliots paused to take a careful look around. Understanding his desire to avoid eavesdroppers, Riechet dismounted to stand before him. David remained on Phantom's back to keep an eye on the chamber from above, though leaned forward to catch what was being said.

"Food will eventually run out," Elliots informed, his voice straining with the thought. "Rations are holding for now, but in a nahm or two..."

Unable to find words to convey the gravity of the situation he simply threw up his hands in defeat.

"We've been focusing our efforts on recovering food topside," Riechet reassured. "Once SIERA's stocks are stable, supplies will head your direction."

Elliots' white complexion paled even further. "Once SIERA is stable? But how long will that be? More people could come."

"Let's hope they do."

"Then what about the food?"

Riechet's expression conveyed his compassion, yet his stance and voice remained firm. "I sympathize with your situation, but if my people aren't kept in fighting condition food will be the least of your worries. My concern right now is in getting survivors to safety while weakening Vairdec forces as much as possible. I leave it to you to distribute food properly. It won't be an easy task and you'll have to make difficult decisions, but I trust you can handle the job. Encourage every able body to join the military ranks. That will decrease the number of mouths to feed here and hopefully place those with a fighting spirit where they are best utilized."

Resigning himself to Riechet's instructions, Elliots gave a terse nod. An empty glaze fell over his weary face.

"I only hope I'm not alone," he muttered to himself, his hand dragging absently over his shirt. "Nakola didn't make it."

Riechet placed a caring hand upon his shoulder for a moment of silent sympathy before returning to Darkracer's back. Without a word he motioned Phantom to follow. David kept his eyes fixed on Councilman Elliots as long as he could, sharing in the emotion of the man's loss.

After a brief assessment of the bunker's supplies, Riechet guided the way past the many smaller chambers of refugees to a sealed passage nearly invisible against the rugged rock. Unlike traditional doors, after being unlocked Darkracer had to shove it open with his shoulder, straining against the stubborn hinges as it swung aside. A blast of icy wind shot up from the yawning black depths.

Dampness filled the air, heavy with the odor of wet rock and mildew. Without a word the general signaled the Candonians to make their way into the darkness.

David gripped Phantom's mane with both hands, feeling the creature's tentative steps on the slippery path that cut along the edge of the rock. Even with the combined efforts of David's and the general's lights, barely a meter was illuminated around them. Nothing of the tunnel wall to the left could be seen and the wind howled up through the depths of the plateau.

"Stay close to the wall," Riechet instructed, his voice echoing through the void.

As much as he knew he would regret it, David wished he could see beyond he light. It was evident they were traveling through a very large chamber. There was no telling how far the drop to the left was. With his confidence and curiosity growing, David leaned to his left to see if he could see beyond Phantom's hooves. The Candonian gave a fierce grunt of disapproval in the shift of weight and David hurriedly straightened as previously taught.

As they wound their way along the narrow ledge David began to notice a change in the wind's howl. A roar now accompanied it, growing louder with each turn. After several precarious minutes along the narrowest shelf of rock, they stepped out on a wide ledge. Riechet drew a flare gun from his belt and fired off a single orb-light that grew in intensity as it suspended itself over a great chasm. Walking to the edge, Phantom allowed David to take in the sight. A massive river churned and frothed as it boiled through the veins of the plateau. It poured over the jagged rocks to cascade into the emptiness of the abyss.

David knew of the underground river system running below Karnoss. Its name was Quaradia, the Great Northern River. It flowed out of the arctic regions to cut a path toward the distant southern mountain range of the Naharan. There, as if in some great defiance of physics, it traveled not alongside the mountains, but right over the top. An ancient lava tube acted as its ladder. Water spilled in through the base, filled the tube and cascaded down the other side of the peak. From there it branched into smaller rivers. One such branch ran close to David's house and he remembered the summer days he spent on its shoreline. To see the mighty headwaters now took his breath away.

"I never knew there was so much water."

"Most of it comes from underground aquifers that push waters up through vents in the rock. The rest accumulates from whatever rain and snowfall we get. This is the city's lifeline."

A tightness formed in David's gut. "Do the Vairdec know?"

Riechet jumped to the ground with David following suit.

"I cannot be sure," he admitted as he navigated a small trail down to a flat bank level with the river. "Nothing ever came through our spy networks suggesting that they do, but there's no guarantee at this point. Let's hope they haven't. Not only does this system provide us with the necessary water, it powers the bunkers' generators. Without them, we have no ventilation. Luckily, I doubt the

Vairdec will take the time or energy to try and sabotage the waterways immediately. We're not a big enough threat for that."

"Do we want to be?"

"Yes, we do. But if we're going to expose our full force, we need to be ready to defend ourselves from the inevitable counterattack."

David watched as Riechet removed a small canister from his belt to collect some of the water. Finishing his task, he rose to stare with David out across the hypnotic waters.

"Everything in life has consequences. We as leaders must weigh all possibilities and be as prepared for the outcomes as we can. I won't lie in saying this is easy, and you will find the consequences do not always come with a happy ending."

"Then how can one make the right choice?"

"You will know."

David wished he could be as confident. Though Riechet's answer had not been entirely satisfactory, he knew there was no quick and easy answer to direct all decisions. This he voiced aloud to receive an approving smile from the general.

"You are wiser than you think. There is no one answer that takes care of all situations. Your wisdom will have to play into finding the truth behind each challenge faced. Weigh your choices with compassion, but do not forget reason and logic. Sometimes the consequences are difficult to bear regardless of the decision, but if you balance your choices between compassion and logic you can at least rest assured that you made the best choice possible. You already possess the qualities to make the right decisions. Now all you have to do is find the confidence to move ahead."

CHAPTER SIXTEEN

David, wearing his recently acquired major's uniform, slipped into his place on a bench in the newly furbished situation room, fashioned from a small side chamber next to the command center. Around him sat several other soldiers, ready to receive orders for the next mission. Above ground the sun would be dipping westward to plunge the crippled city into yet another dark and empty night. Eighteen hours had passed since he and General Riechet returned to the south bunker, giving David more than enough time to freshen up and grab a bite to eat before making his way to the command center for his assignment. Riechet spent most of those hours looking over new information from the field and preparing operatives, causing David to wonder what the limit of the man's stamina was as he had yet to see him rest.

At the moment the general was receiving the gratifying news that the water samples collected on their excursion to the river had come back negative for any contamination. Even with so far to go to achieve victory in the war, the small bit of good news brought with it audible relief from all within earshot. Riechet refrained from any emotion as he faced the assemblage.

With SIERA's new major sat seven other soldiers including Keven Arzen. The injury to his leg turned out less serious than first thought, being only a flesh wound that was easily packed and bandaged. He had rested over the past day and was eager to be moving once more. The doctors agreed that walking would help keep the leg from stiffening so Keven quickly made known his desire to join the mission. Since it did not entail combat, Riechet agreed.

David eyed his team carefully, assessing each individual who would be under his command. He was thankful Keven was among them. At least there would be one he knew he could count on in a moment's notice. The rest were SIERA trained, though many were young, newly enlisted into the Special Forces branch. Second Lieutenant Benak Macsen ranked the highest among the soldiers and David had been informed of his model performance record. It was clear General Riechet wished for David's first solo command in the war to go without incident - a point David gratefully accepted.

"Latest intel points to a pocket of civilians held up in the mid-western resort district," Riechet began. "As far as we gathered from new arrivals, they're bunkered in the Piña Dorado. With it only being a matter of time before the Vairdec claim the mid-west sector, it is our urgent duty to extract all survivors. This is not an open engagement assignment. Stay under cover and avoid enemy pockets when possible. Your only concern at this time is to bring those civilians back alive. Gather what supplies you can on the way but no deviating from the mission.

'The enemy is beginning to deploy sweepers throughout the upper tunnel systems so your breakout point will be here," he indicated a softly glowing map behind him, "at the North Winds whose lower shipping dock has not yet fallen onto the Vairdec's sensors. It's still a distance from the resort so use the night to your advantage. Take 43rd as opposed to the Avenue. The sweeps we made earlier cleared the route. Remember, the darkness is your ally, so keep moving and get back before dawn. Major Malard is in command. Good luck."

Without a word the team rose, checking over the weapons in their hands as they filed from the room. David stood by the door, giving them each a quick inspection as they passed. Before he had a chance to follow the last member out, General Riechet took hold of his shoulder.

"I'm giving you liberty to assess and choose the best course of action to accomplish this mission. Do everything you can and get the team back safely."

"Yes, sir."

"Peenah Doraydoo…"

David flinched at the ever-common mispronunciation of the resort. "Piña Dorado," he corrected. "It's... uh… Spanish."

He was surprised he had to think of it. At one time he had become rather accustom to informing people of the strange name and its history. Recently,

226

however, too many other events fought for his brain's attention. It had been a long time since the days of accompanying his parents to the various Tavishon Resort establishments. In the silence that followed he allowed himself to consider the events of his past. Behind him the rest of his team kept a steady pace through the lower transit tunnels, keeping an eye on shadows and sensors alike.

"What's Spanish?"

The question drew David out of his momentary reflections.

"A language."

"Really?"

David could sense Private Reede's desire to press him for more information. There was little to do at the moment but walk and think about the horrors of war. Discussing something other than impending doom was a welcome idea for all present.

"From Earth," he answered quickly.

As much as he wanted to relax and talk about trivial matters, as leader, David knew he must remain vigilant. However, understanding his team's need, he allowed the conversation to continue as long as it did not cause them to lose track of the seriousness of moving through a Vairdec controlled city.

"I've heard Earth had different languages," another soldier mused.

"Has," Keven returned. "I would think Earth is still around."

"What if it isn't?"

Everyone grew quiet until a disbelieving huff from Corporal Ramkah broke the silence.

"What would make you think that?" she quipped.

"Maybe the Vairdec visited."

The uncomfortable silence threatened to take over again, being thwarted by Private Reede's dislike for jumping back to thoughts of the Vairdec.

"It sounds funny to have so many languages for one people, doesn't it?"

"Why?" Keven asked. "Oxyrans have different tribal languages."

"Celehi have dialects," Second Lieutenant Macsen added.

"Only on the outer colonies."

"True," Reede cut in, "but we're Human. We stick together, right?"

"Not always," David grumbled. After all, Melina's killer was Human.

Ramkah motioned toward David with her head. "So how do you know this Spanish?"

"I don't know it," David admitted. "I just know about the name of the resort."

He would like to have known more Spanish. Unfortunately there were no tutors well versed in languages from Earth other than the one once referred to as English, now known simply as Humenan. Over the first years of living on Telamier, it became the dominant language due to its preferred use among the Founders while other languages simply faded over time. Spanish remained one of the few that was at least in part written down since, as fortune would have it, one of the Founders brought her Spanish dictionary with her from Earth. Information gleaned from the remaining pages along with folklore handed down through the Founders' books gave rise to the resort's name.

"So what is it?"

David gave Reede a quick glance. The private certainly held a great deal of curiosity.

"The Golden Pineapple."

Reede gave a nod as if it all made perfect sense. "It sounds grand."

"Depends," Keven chuckled. "What did you say a pineapple was? A food?"

"A fruit."

A soft ripple of laughter flowed through the team.

"A fruit?" Macsen scoffed. "That lavish resort is named after a fruit?"

"It must be some fruit," Ramkah said.

David shrugged, never taking his eyes off the path ahead. "I don't know. The corporate president wanted something to sound exotic and tropical. Apparently pineapples are a symbol of hospitality. It fit."

"How do you know so much about this place?"

Was there ever an end to Reede's questions?

"Because my father was the corporate vice president."

Yes, David knew the workings of the resort quite well. His father was a nephew to the wealthy Tavishon family who owned the most famous resorts in Earthenia. With a natural prowess for business he became a leading accountant for the company and continued to rise from there. It accounted for much of the wealth David had inherited, but for him, going to the resort was filled with bittersweet memories. Accompanying his parents on numerous trips, David enjoyed the luxury of the finest suites, but also endured the lonely days of long hours aimlessly wandering the corridors while his parents worked.

Half an hour later the team entered the lower shipping docks of the North Winds. Scouts had already picked the transports and supply rooms clean, leaving an empty shell of what was once a bustling work zone to one of Karnoss's most popular restaurants. The team kept their guns held at ready as they climbed a service ramp to the kitchens situated a floor below the main level. Around them the walls and counters stood blackened. A thick, charred smell filled the interior. David picked his way carefully among puddles of soupy ash. It was fortunate that the fire failed to spread to the upper floors. Most likely it started when some panicked cook knocked something onto a hot surface while making a hasty retreat.

Emerging from the service hall, David took a careful assessment of the main floor before stepping forward. All was quiet. The once lively dance stages situated among the tables were dark. Holo-boards had ceased to display their many flamboyant images. The metal bands embedded within the deep mahogany wood pillars gave only a lusterless flicker in the beams of the soldiers' lights. Tables sat in disarray. Dishes were scattered, many ending up on the floor. Glasses lay tipped, their contents creating sticky pools on the sleek table surfaces. Corporal Ramkah jumped as she stepped on a broken dish. The team paused for only a fraction of a second. They were above ground now. It would not do to stop for very long.

Stepping onto the street, David took a deep breath, thankful for the fresh air despite the danger. As instructed, he kept his team along 43rd, weaving his way skillfully among the few private vehicles privileged enough to access these roadways, skillfully keeping to the shadows. The night was his world. He had grown to love it ever since his assignment to the CLE's midnight team. The world changed when the sun disappeared. While it offered more threats, it also provided a cover of solitude David found comforting. He felt the master of his world when he could watch unseen and move unnoticed by the rest of society.

The earlier scouts clearly succeeded in their mission, and the team arrived at the Piña Dorado without crossing paths with so much as a kiejaud. Not pausing to consider the best route, David headed for a smaller door set twenty meters to the right of the elaborate main entrance.

If not for the darkness and lack of activity, the Piña Dorado could have past for its usual opulent state of business. The Vairdec had yet to defile it. From where they entered David managed to just catch a glimpse of the main entry with its massive tree-like pillars and spinning orb chandelier, now dark from the lack of power. Keeping against the wall to the right he led the way past the boutiques and various smaller shopping venues to one of the many luxury eateries within the facility. Though the route would add a few minutes to their trek, he hoped it would keep them under better cover, for the main paths through the resort were deliberately large and open. Just because no evidence of Vairdec presented itself did not mean they were not close.

The lights the team carried provided the only illumination. Caught in their beams, potted trees rose among the tables like shadowy specters, their dropped fruit creating wisps of heavy, sweet odor as it ripened around the roots. Having been genetically altered, the plants would continue to produce fruit so long as they were cared for. David felt disappointed that the trees themselves could not be moved, for they would be a valuable asset inside the bunkers. How to care for them, though, was beyond his understanding, so the most he could do was pause a moment to allow the team to grab what fruit still clung to the branches. Stuffing the precious food into pockets and each other's bags, they continued on.

They wove their way cautiously among the tables, which, unlike the North Winds, had been cleaned and diligently set for the following day. Napkins rested on the plates in neatly folded flower shapes. Utensils were polished to a high gloss. Crystal glasses sparkled in the beams of light that swept across them. Everything was set in perfect order – a wasted art.

Climbing the stairs to the upper level, David led his team silently through a pair of glass doors into a large open space decorated with vine carvings and once flowering plants. As their lights hit the open floor, the team paused, watching the beams reflect and ripple across a pool occupying much of the room. David did not wait for his team. Instead he stepped right off the edge of the tiled floor and onto the water.

Only as he continued across did the team notice the pool lay under a transparent floor that ingeniously created the illusion of open water. David glanced back with a slight glint of amusement in his eyes. Apparently these young soldiers were not accustomed to the opulent life of those who could afford to stay at the resort. Unlike his team, he knew this ballroom. It was the place where he had had his first dance with… he paused to sweep the area, reassuring himself that the team was alone. They followed quietly behind, picking their way around the few pieces of fallen apparel lost in the hasty retreat, as if to disturb them would in some way disrespect the innocent lives impacted by the takeover.

Avoiding the etched glass double doors on the other side, David headed toward another, smaller exit situated near the stage where several instruments lay abandoned. Allowing his gun to lead, David cautiously made his way into the hall. Though a smaller thoroughfare, it was not a service passage. Around them the walls glistened with etched stone painstakingly arranged to produce mosaics of exotic plants and animals. Though not as grand as the main halls, this remained a favorite path for guests heading to the resort's famous spas and health centers.

Located in the heart of the resort, the spas consisted of a series of rooms, corridors and gardens perfectly arranged for a tranquil, tropical repose. The natural mineral springs of the plateau were utilized in steaming spas surrounded by live herbs and medicinal plants that could be harvested for the freshest use. Bubbling fountains danced in an array of colors, each signifying the health properties of the water, which could be drunk upon request. A medical facility oversaw simple ailments while massage parlors promised to drive away all cares. While David figured the promise of peace would be hard kept in these times, he knew the extensive use of tropical plants and medical equipment made it necessary to run the spas on a separate generator system. It was possible the system was still operational, gathering survivors around it like an oasis.

Entering the main hub from which the various health rooms branched, he found his guess to be correct. Fourteen people huddled in small groups within the dim interior, looking undeniably frightened and forlorn. David looked between the ashen faces with disappointment. There were so few. For a resort that held thousands, it was shocking to see only a handful of people. They were a mix of Celehi and Human, three of which were staff members. A young couple clung to each other in the corner. Huddled near a dim light a trembling, wiry man tried to read. Two others sat near a stilled fountain, pausing in the mindless task of weaving together the vines from a nearby herb. A tall middle-aged woman, still dressed in her party evening wear, pushed her way past some piled supplies and a stunned employee with a clear air of authority.

"I assume you are here for us," she said.

"Yes, ma'am," David replied. "Gather what supplies you have. We're leaving shortly. Are all the survivors in this location?"

"We've walked through the rooms yesterday," one of the employees said. "Most everyone had already left. I don't know where they are."

"Fine," David said. "Let's get two teams to do one more sweep. Arzen, take Reede and Tenner and head north. Macsen, you and Ramkah go south. Go quickly. We only have a few hours."

David turned to his team to instruct them on what to do during that time but was cut off before he could speak.

"And you will give no consideration to the injured?"

David's stomach knotted. His concentration remained so intent upon getting in and out, that the thought of any injured people had embarrassingly slipped his mind. Squaring his shoulders he faced his remaining team member in an attempt to hide his inner feelings.

"McTavish, work with these people. Get them ready." With a deep breath he faced the woman. "Take me to them."

One of the staff members waved him toward a side door. "He's in here."

David followed, grateful that it sounded as if only one individual required special treatment. The medical clinic glowed softly with the assistance of the backup generator. Two doctors stood in the far corner, discussing something in hushed tones. A nurse sat staring at a readout panel while a Celehi man leaned against the wall near the door, staring blankly at the one occupied bed. David felt his energy drain from his limbs at the sight. The injured was a young Human boy, no more than seven, his head bandaged, his face pale and lifeless. At his side sat a man David guessed was the father due to the greater strain in his expression and the way he kept his hand pressed tightly against the boy's. All eyes turned to David with a mix of surprise and newfound worry as he stepped slowly toward the bed.

"How is he?"

One of the doctors stepped forward with an answer. "Difficult to tell right now. He may recover in time, but he sustained severe head trauma."

Stopping beside the bed, David gazed down into the expressionless face. "How'd it happen?"

"He was in an upper level care center. A piece of a neighboring building collapsed and sheered off that corner. Some were able to pull him from the debris."

"We continue to signal for help with nothing coming," the Celehi man said. "Where are they?"

"We are the help," David reassured.

"Soldiers?"

Those assembled glanced to the door as the older woman stepped in. With her was a hefty, gray-haired gentleman in a formal suit. David felt sure he had seen him before though at the moment could not place from where.

"There have been lots of rumors," the man grumbled. "Meteor strike, terrorism, war…"

"Invasion," David answered dryly.

The room grew deathly still. No one moved even as McTavish entered, followed by the young couple and two of the staff.

"That explains why they didn't come back," the gentleman muttered.

David tore himself away from the child's bed to approach the man. "There are more?"

"Were. I doubt they're alive now." A single sob emanated from within the small crowd. "When the power went out many of us moved to this area, but as time went on, most either returned to their rooms or, in some cases, decided to leave all together. A couple of them said they'd come back, but that's been some time now."

David gave a shake of his head. How could these people not know what had happened on the streets outside this very building? How many others were sitting confused within the upper city?

"If they didn't make it down to the bunkers, they would be easy prey on the streets."

It was a fact David hated hearing McTavish voice, no matter how true.

"Are we going to the bunkers?" the young woman asked.

David gave her as reassuring a smile as he could muster. "Yes, so gather your things. We need to leave quickly."

"But the boy," the doctor stammered. "We can't move him."

"I'm afraid we don't have any choice."

"You don't understand. The life support system won't travel with us. If he's removed from it for even a few minutes his body will shut down. There's no way we can leave now."

"I'm sorry, doctor," David said, his voice strained and low, "but there is no choice. We leave now."

"Just like that," the older man growled. "We're to just follow your orders and kill an innocent boy?"

David felt himself growing hot with anger and clenched his fist to try calming himself.

"There are no other options."

"Can you be sure?"

David refused to look at the man and instead focused on the doctors. "Are there any other options?"

They looked between each other and the nurse in helpless desperation.

"Maybe we can rig something that will hold him long enough to get him to a medical transport. With that we can get him to the hospital..."

"We're not going to the hospital."

"Why not?" the older woman asked, her voice a mix of fear and growing frustration.

"If we're to survive, we go to the bunkers."

Silence enveloped the room. The young woman began to cry softly against her lover's shoulder. One of the employees sank to the floor against the wall.

"Is it that bad?" the Celehi finally asked.

David found it difficult to look anyone in the eye. "I'm afraid it is. McTavish, see to gathering all the medical supplies you can."

With a nod, the young sergeant stepped forward to begin his work only to be blocked by a suddenly frantic looking doctor.

"Not the Provaxoline," the doctor pleaded.

David's eyes narrowed. "Why?"

Shakily the doctor motioned toward the bed. "Conner needs it."

Great, now he knew the child's name. David's mood was rapidly worsening. Grabbing the doctor by the arm, he forcibly escorted him and his colleague through the door. In the outer room, the rest of the

238

civilians busied themselves with gathering their supplies, fear and confusion clearly written on their faces. They diligently kept to their tasks, giving David nothing more than a sideward glance to be sure he was not there to instruct them. Pushing the doctors against a wall, David took a firm stance before them.

"All right, I want the truth. What are the boy's chances of survival?"

They fidgeted as they looked to each other for an answer. While they were trained medical doctors, their field involved matters of simple ailments and enhanced wellness techniques. Severe trauma was neither of their specialties.

"We just don't know," one answered slowly.

"A percentage," David ordered. "Give me one."

"Thirty, maybe, if we're lucky."

"Thirty." David turned away from the doctors to run a shaking hand through his hair. His nerves were raw and he was growing to despise the position he was in. Turning back, he looked each in the eye. "That's all the chance he's got?"

"Some have pulled through with less than that," one of them pointed out.

"Under the best circumstances, though."

David knew he was arguing with himself as much as with the doctors. A shift in the doctors' eyes alerted David to the activity behind him. Spinning about, he watched as Keven jogged up, his team halting at the entryway, guns drawn and ready. The situation was deteriorating rapidly. David motioned Keven to a side room, making it clear to the doctors to stay put with nothing but a firm gesture.

"What happened?"

"We've got a full platoon headed this way. They aren't in the resort yet, but give it ten, fifteen minutes tops. I would have called in, but they're sweeping for call signals."

"Have Reede and Tenner bring back the other team. They've got five minutes."

Keven gave a nod and turned back to the waiting soldiers, pausing for only a fraction of a second to look over the doctors. He could sense the seriousness of their predicament but, as a soldier, would not waste time asking for details outside his current duty. As Keven left, David returned to the doctors.

"The boy will probably die no matter what we do, is that correct?"

"Most likely," came the muttered reply. "Unless we get him to the hospital."

"There are no hospitals," David snapped.

He felt bad at letting his temper show in front of the doctors. They held no control over the outcome. Unfortunately, he felt he needed to vent the hurt somehow. He knew what decision lay before him and he hated to make it.

One of the doctors stared at the floor as he thought. "If someone stays here a few more days, we can see if the boy improves. We'll need to keep the Provaxoline. If in a few days he doesn't…"

"No. We're taking all meds and movable equipment. That is final."

"Oh really?" David cringed as he turned to face the older man who stepped up behind. "That's final? Just like the military, isn't it? Take care of their own – survival of the fittest?"

David hated to listen to this nonsense.

Catching Keven by the shoulder as he approached, David ushered him a short distance away.

"We've got a boy in there that can't be moved."

Keven shook his head. "We can't stay. There's no way we'll survive. We're outnumbered. Even if we managed to hold off this one platoon, it wouldn't take long for the rest of the Vairdec to show. With civilians to protect, we're not in a good position to fight."

"I know, but maybe we can beat the odds if we rush the boy to the bunkers."

"I wouldn't advise it. You know as well as I do it won't work."

David gave a short nod. Helplessness lay in his eyes. He knew what Keven was saying. He just did not like hearing the inevitable. Keven pressed his argument in hopes of aiding David's inevitable decision.

"Carrying the boy will slow us down. To keep him alive, our focus would be split between him and the safety of the team. There're too many chances of being caught. And if we have to engage the enemy we'll be at a further disadvantage. Furthermore, what happens when he dies and we're still a ways from the bunkers? What do we do with the body? Are you prepared to dump him on the streets? Taking a corpse into the bunkers is just as bad. There're too many chances of others in this group dying because of an already dying boy."

"I know."

The words barely escaped David's throat. He was in command and as hard as the decision was, he had an obligation to do what was right for the majority. It was best if he did not dwell long on the subject. Pushing past the obstinate man still hovering nearby, he headed back to the medical ward.

"I'm giving everyone five minutes," he announced as he entered. "Grab what you can and head out. We need to move now." Stepping over to the father, he looked for the first time into the empty eyes. "I'm sorry," he whispered.

The father did not respond, though David could see the resignation in his countenance.

"Typical government," the older man snarled, taking a firm stance in the middle of the room. "We're just collateral damage in your little war."

"My war?"

David spun to face him, finally placing where he had seen this obnoxious brute before. His name was Norman Gorby and he specialized in creating political mayhem with his editorials and stance as a government critic. Often radical in his ideas, he swayed whichever way suited him at the moment, sensationalizing and promoting the conspiracy that the government and military were somehow the enemy of the people. David had read a few of Gorby's doom's day reports, none of which he favored for the slander thrown toward law enforcement. Meeting him now did not improve his impression. He wanted nothing more than to storm over and punch the man senseless. Wisely he held his ground.

"Look," he growled, trying desperately to control his tone, "I would love to say we are not in danger. I would love to say we could get this boy to a hospital and save his life. In fact, there is nothing I want more at this moment. I'd carry him there myself. Unfortunately I don't have a say in any of those things. My job is to save as many lives as possible."

"Maybe the government should have thought about that before provoking a skirmish."

"We didn't provoke this war," David shouted.

Gorby would not back down. "And I'm sure the government is more ready to throw the guns in the open than try negotiating the situation down."

"You don't negotiate with..." David paused, glancing around the room. They did not know. Word never reached them as to who was behind the attacks. Now he wondered how much he wanted to share, as it would indelibly cause panic.

"With what? Faxons?"

Some of David's anger subsided as he realized he was now the barer of even more bad news. His eyes locked on Keven who entered to stand silently at the door. Somehow it felt easier to break the news with his friend nearby.

"It's not the Faxons."

"Then what?" Gorby pressed before David could finish. "Renegades? A collective? Maybe the Celehi are tired of us."

The Celehi flushed red as he spun on Gorby. "You do not..."

"It's the Vairdec," David jumped in, instantly extinguishing all fight among the party. "The Vairdec have taken the city."

The sobbing returned in the background, but luckily no other sounds of panic ensued. Norman Gorby visibly paled, his argument eluding him a moment as the words sank in. However, even with voice shaking, he refused to lose the verbal battle.

"How did our government allow that?"

David stormed up to him, getting right into his face. "I don't know and frankly, right now I don't care. Right now all I can think about is getting as many people out of here as possible. Feel free to stay and negotiate with the Vairdec when they arrive. I've just been informed that it will be very soon. I'm sure you won't have to wait more than half an hour."

Leaving Gorby speechless, David turned to the rest of those in the room. "Get everything you can. We leave immediately."

No one argued further. Numb and mechanical in their movements, they did as told, being guided through their motions by the watchful soldiers. Feeling suddenly nauseous, David approached the still silent father to place a gentle hand upon his shoulder.

"I'm truly sorry," he spoke softly, "but we have to be realistic. I have to get as many to safety as I can."

The answering voice was barely audible, sounding like the breath of the dying.

"I know."

Sweat broke out on David's palms and he felt himself shiver from the pain of what he was doing. His throat tightened as he fought to keep from looking upon the innocent little victim he was leaving behind to die. This was not his nature. This was not his way.

Everything in him screamed to grab the child into his arms and rush him to safety.

"Let's go," he whispered.

To his great disappointment, the father weakly shook his head. "I will stay with my son."

David's heart began to race faster. He could not leave two to die. One was agony enough.

"Sir, please. Your son is already dead. You will die, too, if you stay. Let's go."

"No." The word was spoken so softly, so gently, that David found it surprising how it left no room for argument. "My wife is gone. My child is dead. Let me stay with my son."

Slowly David backed away. How could he disrespect such a wish? But how could he turn his back on someone whom he could save? Or could he save him? Looking into the father's eyes, David could sense that the man was already lost. He had died with those he loved. It was all too real an understanding for David and in the end he could only give a consenting nod.

As he headed for the door, he found the room emptied of all but one of the doctors who leaned forward as David passed.

"Couldn't we leave some of the Provaxoline for the father to administer?"

David wished he could comply but knew the right choice in the matter, regardless of the pain it caused him.

"No," he whispered. "We can't afford to waste any on the dead. We need it for those we can save. I'm sorry."

Nodding his understanding, the doctor exited. David stood facing the door, finding it terribly difficult to walk through. The burden of his command and the decision he made ripped through his gut. He longed to protect the boy, but he longed in vane. Forcing back the tremble in his hand he stepped forward. As the door shut behind him, he took one look back, briefly spying the father as he stretched out on the bed to cradle his son. Then their tomb was sealed and David saw them no more.

"Move out," he ordered, forcing his words through a tightened chest and throat.

No one spoke as they packed tightly together and headed toward the exit. David hurried to place himself at the front, not as a show of leadership, but in an attempt to hide his tears.

CHAPTER SEVENTEEN

The shower room was dim and quiet as David staggered in. It consisted of a couple rows of raised basins with spigot lines running water to each one. A few proper showers existed with more hopefully on the way, but for now David figured a quick toweling down would suffice. He still felt the bitter tightness of nausea twisting in his gut and every muscle remained clenched from the stress of his mission. Stepping up to one of the basins he stripped to the waist and flipped on the spigot. For a minute he just stood there, staring into the running water as he leaned against the basin.

"Hard day at the office?"

The unexpected voice jolted David from his moment of mindless staring. A short wave of adrenaline swept through his veins at the surprise. Amber watched apathetically as David collected himself and turned to face her.

"I'm sorry," he stammered. "I didn't know anyone else was in here."

Hurriedly he gathered up his belongs, almost forgetting to turn off the water before leaving.

"No need to leave," Amber said as he reached for the spigot. "I'm not shy."

David hesitated, his hand on the control. At last he relaxed. Quietly he turned his gaze to the colonel who stood across from him, letting his gaze trail over her. There was not much reason for her to be shy. Her military jacket and blouse were the only things she removed, a utilitarian bra keeping her respectfully modest. David was surprised by the slight touch of disappointment he felt over that fact as he found himself staring at her trim form, which created a beautiful combination of strength and feminism. As she gave him an amused sideward glance he quickly turned away.

"How do you feel?"

David busied himself with the water, unsure of how to answer.

"Fine, I guess," he answered flatly, knowing to remain silent would be a slight against his superior.

"Fine? Don't lie to me, Malard."

He could only shrug. "I don't know."

Tossing her towel into the basin, Amber turned off the water and stepped around to lean against a partition to study David. Her burning stare made it difficult for David to think. He tried to busy himself with washing up only to find it increasingly uncomfortable. Though he had never been overly shy, Amber possessed an ability to strip away far more than clothing with her eyes. He felt as if his very thoughts and emotions were exposed, a feeling he greatly disliked.

"It's okay to be upset about it," she finally said. "I would be."

David carefully looked in her direction. There was no deception in her, no shallow words spoken just to make him feel better. She was much like her father that way. When he said nothing, Amber continued.

"You did the right thing. I know you've heard that already, but I wanted to add my thoughts on the matter. Frankly, I would have done the same. I would have hated it as much as you, but I would have done it." She dropped her gaze to the floor, scrapping the toe of her boot across the stone. "You know you're in hell when the best decision has to be something as sick as that."

David set his towel on the edge of the basin to look at her. The last phrase had been spoken so quietly he wondered if she meant for him to hear it. Even in the dim light he could see her face drawn tight with tension. A slight tremor rippled through her slender form and he could tell that her knuckles were white from where she gripped the edge of the basin. As a commanding officer, the decision David had faced was what Amber would experience numerous times throughout her career. He did not envy her.

"How did you…" he began.

The thought of what he was about to ask made him cut his words short. The question could be considered rude. A rather cunning smile replaced the tension on Amber's face as she glanced up at David. She knew exactly what he wanted to ask.

"How did I become a colonel at my age?"

David felt deflated. Was there anything he could keep from her? Luckily she did not seem to mind the question.

"I actually get asked that quite often. The answer comes from having very focused military parents and being an only child. I never had any real friends growing up, partly because I'm a bit of a loner and partly because we moved around so much. I knew what I wanted to be right from the beginning, so poured all my free time into study. My mother schooled me rather hard and I pushed through the standard testing by the time I was thirteen."

David gave a huff of amusement. "I always thought the family drill sergeant would be your father."

"Him?" Amber gave an amused shake of her head. "He was the spoiler. He doted on me, though never enough to soften me. I followed him everywhere, mimicking him as best I could, so when I entered the Academy I already knew more than the other cadets. It helped me move through the ranks quickly."

David nodded slightly as he took a moment to think through Amber's family life. If only she knew how lucky she was. Snapping from his trance-like state, he gave her a warm smile.

"I'm very impressed by your military achievements. You're father must be very proud."

Though she tried to hide it, David sensed Amber was actually a little embarrassed by the accolades.

"Don't praise me too highly," she said, her voice lower. "When it comes right down to it, the military promoted me to colonel for political reasons."

"Political?"

"With SIERA's ESF branch becoming joint with our allies, the government insisted on Humans staying in command. The only way was to have the two top ranking officers be Human. I was the best candidate at the time to promote and as Py'guela is a lieutenant colonel, they pushed it through to make me a colonel." Her face suddenly went ashen as she realized she was letting too much slip. "You are not to speak of this to anyone, am I clear?"

David straightened with a quick nod. "Yes, ma'am." He wondered if he should salute just to emphasize the fact that he was serious, but in the end settled for a gentler approach. "You can trust me. I swear I won't say a word."

Amber relaxed, nodding appreciatively as she rounded the basin to retrieve her belongings. A moment later Mike walked in and paused at the sight of the two.

"Is three a crowd?" he asked.

Rolling her eyes, Amber stepped around to push past. "What goes on in your mind scares me, Commander."

Undaunted, Mike gave a chuckle and moved to a place to wash up, leaving David to finish in silence. As he wiped the last of the grime from the back of his stiff neck, he paused. Tossing the towel across his shoulder, David shut off the stream of water to listen to the steady thrum of voices down the passage. He was not imagining things. The din had grown louder. Hurriedly he pulled on his shirt and gathered his scant belongings. While he felt no anxiety over the situation, he did find himself uncontrollably curious as to what may be proceeding in the main chamber.

Almost instantly upon entering the large central room, David found himself on a collision course with two adults frantically ushering four children away from a transport. Other civilians crowded around SIERA's equipment while soldiers anxiously watched the activity. Weaving his way through the crowd, David did his best to navigate toward the command center, nearly tripping on a small boy in the process. The young child gazed up at him in awe.

"Are you a real soldier?"

"Yes," David answered hurriedly, trying to step around the boy.

Unfortunately his escape route was blocked by equipment.

"Where's your uniform?"

"Uh…" How could he escape this? "I don't have it."

"Why?"

"I'm off duty."

"Have you killed any Vairdec?"

David stretched his neck to peer over the heads, hoping to find some location worth trying for, and in doing so evade the large, inquisitive eyes in front of him.

"Some," he replied.

Spying an exit in the form of a small passageway a short distance off, David stepped forward. The boy would not budge.

"When I grow up I'm going to kill Vairdec."

"That's nice, kid."

In a final act to evade the inquisitive child, David hoisted the boy up by the shoulders, turning around to place the child behind him. Before anymore could be asked, he had pushed his way through the crowd and, slightly out of breath, made it to the far wall.

"Didn't think you'd be joining a circus, did you?"

David watched Mike push his way up alongside and take a moment to scan over the crowd.

"When did this happen?"

David shrugged. "Just now, I guess."

One of the two soldiers stationed in the passageway David had originally aimed for looked up from where he stood in the dark recess of the entrance.

"Transports came in and started offloading."

David ran his fingers through his hair and shook his head. Feeling exasperated, he faced Mike for no other reason than that the pilot was close by.

"Why did they all come here?" he questioned grumblingly. "Where did they come from?"

Lifting his hands, Mike shifted away in defense. "Hey, you're asking questions I'm not in charge of answering. But a word to the wise," he shoved his hands in his jacket pockets and leaned close to speak quietly, "don't go asking these questions to those in charge. I'm sure they're getting close to murder."

David nodded his understanding. A flash of auburn hair caught his eye and he chanced a look at where Amber shoved her way past a driver to disappear once more in the milling swarm of bodies.

"I can just imagine what the general's doing right now."

"Imagine all you want," Mike replied. "As for me, I plan on executing a tactical retreat."

Tapping David's arm with the back of his hand, he motioned him past the armed guards and into the small passage. David heaved a sigh of relief upon leaving the crowd behind. He felt as if the world had opened up again regardless of the relatively narrow confines.

"Wonder how long this is going to last," he commented.

Peering over his shoulder, he hoped he would not be ordered back into the chaos any time soon.

"If the general has a say, not long." Mike gave an amused huff. "And believe me, he has a say. Best thing for us is to lie low and let this blow over. This is one battle I can do without."

Turning through a door on the right, Mike and David entered the mess hall. Large stacks of food lay against the back wall, the reason, David knew, for the armed security at the passage entrance. By now he was sure refugees were beginning to wonder what provisions were at hand and how long any would last. If they became aware of the scarcity of so many needed supplies, a likely panic-driven riot would break out, and the resources needed to ensure the strength of the Telamierian army would quickly be pillaged.

The medium-sized chamber remained dimly lit – no need to waste energy just to allow more light on the food. There was nothing gourmet here. No one complained. A small crowd of soldiers occupied the room, sitting in scattered groups around the long, narrow tables. Most, like Mike and David, had retreated in order to avoid the collision of civilian refugees. They spoke in low voices, holding conversations over the rumors of Vairdec advancements and sharing tales of harrowing survival from missions completed topside.

Collapsing into a chair against the side wall, Mike gave a groaning sigh. David slipped silently into a place across the table from the pilot. Neither said a word. For David it was a time to be quiet and observe the people around him. They all looked strained, most hiding it well under the guise of a weak smile and an occasional forced laugh. He wondered how many had actual combat experience before the war. With much of Earthenia's army set in reserve for just this type of crisis, he figured few were ever called to duty abroad. Not that many conflicts involving Humans existed abroad. David figured he was actually a minority, having dealt with brutal combat and death. A shiver rippled down his spine. It was certainly an advantage he would rather do without.

Turning his attention to Mike, David studied his mannerism intently. He was still trying to figure the pilot out. All that he heard about Mike from those in the unit was extremely positive. The man did not seem to have an enemy in the world… except Vairdec, David corrected in his mind. Even then, Mike expressed little anger or stress. It made him highly likeable, and David admitted that he enjoyed the pilot's company, counting him as a friend. If only he could figure out Mike's secret to such a laid-back persona in the middle of a war. As if to emphasize his nature, Mike was at the moment leaning with his back against the wall, balancing expertly on the back legs of his chair. One arm rested behind his head and his eyes were shut. He stayed this way until the distinct sound of hoof beats drew near.

"Hello, Racer," Mike said in a slow drawl as he opened his eyes.

Darkracer stopped beside David and gave a shake. Behind him, Phantom pushed aside a couple empty chairs in order to move in close enough to be a part of the group.

"Sometimes I wonder why we ever decided to put up with your species," Darkracer grumbled.

"Come on," Mike replied, the chair clattering as the front legs hit the floor. "It can't be all that bad."

"Oh no? Well, you don't have to worry about having your tail pulled."

A sharp, hearty laugh escaped Mike before he could cover his mouth and stifle his amusement. Clearing his throat he folded his hands on the table.

"Sorry."

David, too, admitted to the humor of the complaint, though managed to conceal any laughter behind a ducked head and tight smile. Darkracer's front hoof created an echo through the hall as he stamped, causing the other conversations in the area to momentarily pause.

"It's madness."

Mike gave a shrug. "What war isn't?"

With no good comeback, Darkracer resorted to flattening his ears and giving an angry snap of his tail.

"What do you know of the situation?" David asked.

"The refugees?" Darkracer gave a toss of his head to indicate the direction of the central chamber. "Apparently they were driven out of the southeastern bunker."

David and Mike straightened, their expressions growing more serious.

"Driven out? The Vairdec are in the bunkers?" David hated to hear the answer.

"Vairdec?" Phantom replied, sounding surprised by the notion. "I doubt there would be any refugees left if it were the Vairdec."

The men relaxed as they realized the logic of the Candonian's statement.

"From what I gathered," Darkracer continued, "the Faxons and Manogonites have united to push the Humans out of that bunker system. They'd rather not mingle with your kind."

Mike shook his head. "And yet they chose to visit a Human city in a Human region. Go figure."

"So these aren't survivors from the surface," David said, feeling disappointed at the thought.

"Some might be," Phantom answered. "It's hard to tell right now."

Darkracer blew heavily through his nostrils, causing Mike to lean back to avoid the Candonian's moist breath.

"Let's just hope the general finds new living quarters for them soon," he muttered.

"Ah," Mike taunted as he rubbed his hand across his face, "I thought you loved playing with the children."

"I leave any playing with children to you," Darkracer returned. "Frankly, I think you fit right in."

David gave a chuckle. Seeing Mike with children seemed a rather natural thing. He gave a quick motion of his head toward the pilot.

"Did you ever consider having children?"

Mike pointed to himself with a look of mild surprise. "Me?" He gave a snort and shook his head. "Can't see myself as a father, at least not right now. Though having a couple kids would be nice... down the road. You?"

David shook his head quietly.

"You and your girl never thought of family?" Seeing David wince, Mike's demeanor grew sympathetic. "Look, I'm sorry. It was a lousy thing for me to ask. Forget it."

Silence fell between the foursome. Phantom's hoof methodically scraped the floor. David shifted in his seat. He did not like the quiet, knowing he was the cause for the moment of discomfort. Clearing his throat, he eyed Mike.

"Have you ever been in love?"

Mike kept his eyes on the table. "Thought I was once. Obviously it didn't work out." He looked up with a smile. "It was a mutual breakup, though. No hard feelings."

"That's good," David muttered.

Again they fell silent. Suddenly Mike raised his hand and waved at someone he spied across the room. David tried to peer past Darkracer's large form, but the newcomer remained out of sight as he hurried over.

"Here I find you," Lash panted.

Mike pushed a chair back with his foot and Lash sank into it. "What's the trouble?"

"Beyond what is encountered out there?" An aggravated hiss slipped between Lash's sharp teeth. "When did all happen?"

David eyed the Teshian, who practically bristled with tension. His sharp nails clicked against the tabletop.

"Not long ago," Mike answered.

Phantom dipped his head toward Lash. "You were better off staying with the ships."

"I wanted," Lash admitted, "but I needed to discuss with you."

He motioned toward Mike who tilted his chair back calmly. "You didn't think to call?"

Lash gave a deep-throated growl. "Communications failed... again."

Automatically David and Mike checked their comlinks.

"If there's been a fracturing among the bunkers' signals," Mike said, "it probably affected the hangars as well."

"Do you think the Faxons have something to do with that?" Phantom asked.

Darkracer gave a shrug, a move David found surprising to be a part of a Candonian's capabilities. "Perhaps."

"Perhaps?" Lash looked between the Humans and Candonians in bewilderment. "What have Faxons to do with this?" He cursed under his breath.

"Communications fail for time and the whole war goes super nova."

"Faxons and Manogonites took over the southeastern bunker," Mike explained. "They drove the Humans out, which is why we have a population explosion. I'm sure the general will have them all routed to other bunkers shortly."

"Staying in the hangar becomes all the more welcome."

"How's the ship?"

Leaning back, Lash's red eyes narrowed. "The *Predator* progresses slowly." He paused to get Mike's reaction, though only received a quick drum of fingers as a response. "The stabilizer went out. Not difficult to fix if you have replacements, which none are here. The VY-Craft is operational."

"Oh sure," Mike scoffed, though his tone held no real anger, "the enemy ship works great. Ours..." He shook his head.

"It may come in use," Lash pointed out.

"Mhmm." Mike drummed his fingers again. "Is there a pilot for it?"

Lash spread his arms wide to make a silent presentation of Mike. The Human only shook his head with a laugh.

"I've only read about those ships."

"No one ever did more," Lash argued.

"Unless you employ the Vairdec," Darkracer replied dryly.

Mike glanced over at David who was keeping his gaze slightly averted. "Do you fly?"

"Me?"

"No," Lash quipped, "Candonians."

Phantom raised his head, his ears pricked forward. "That might be possible."

"Not on my watch," Mike muttered.

David looked between the two pilots as he rested his elbows on the table. "No. Never learned."

"Never learned?" Mike gave gentle tsk sounds as he looked David over. "You don't know what you're missing."

"I prefer to keep my feet on the ground."

"Oh," Mike said in a long, slow drawl, "you're one of those."

David could not be sure why, but he felt suddenly defensive. "So? What of it?"

Mike gave a sudden laugh at David's unease. With a wave of his hand, he blew off the connotation.

"Ease it all, co. It's your right. As for me, I was born to fly."

"Very much literally," Lash cut in.

"I come from a long line of pilots. It's kind of a family tradition. I've been flying so long I can't remember when I started."

"Birth," Lash suggested. He leaned toward David, his long, silky hair falling over his shoulder, and gave him a sharp-toothed grin. "His birth came in air."

"Really?"

"Really," Mike said. "I was born on a flight. Surprised everyone, including Mom, from what Dad always said."

David found himself smiling at the pride that weld up in Mike.

"We Teshians prefer more prepared starts to life."

Mike watched with an amused twinkle in his eye as Lash rose. "Where's the fun in that?"

Lash refused to comment further on the subject. "I will get food. That is one supply the hangar lacks a favored amount."

Mike raised his hand in gesture of farewell. "Get it while you can. Who knows how long it will last."

David kept a hard gaze on Mike as Lash took his leave. After a moment, Mike stared back, confused.

"What?"

"How do you do it?"

Mike glanced from side to side as if an answer to David's cryptic question lay nearby. "Do what?"

"Stay so calm, so jovial."

"Jovial?" Darkracer chuckled.

"So pleasant," David continued. "With everything going on, I just don't see how anyone can do that. What's your secret?"

Dropping the chair to all fours, Mike leaned in across the table, his expression growing more serious.

"It's not as easy as it looks at times. I feel all this, too. It's just," he paused to think it through, "I've seen what happens to people who let the situation get to them. Perfectly healthy soldiers have gone completely insane. Almost went that way myself, once. Then it occurred to me. There are only so many things I can do – so do what I can and don't sweat the rest. The less I dwell on the stuff that's out of my control, the easier it is to cope and to deal with the situations that are in my control. I guess that's the best way I can put it. Not very deep or philosophical,

I'm afraid, but to be honest, this is the first time anyone's made me think about it."

"Well philosophical or not, it's admirable. Maybe I can learn to do the same someday."

Mike grinned as he leaned across the table to give David's shoulder a gentle slap. "You will, just give it time. You've been through stuff I'd hate to face. I'm actually impressed by your resolve. You're probably doing better than I would."

"Doubt it," David mumbled, brushing his fingers through his hair and half hoping no one could hear him.

"Don't be so sure," Mike answered, his voice just as quiet. "After all, you're the one witnessing the fights on the streets, not me."

Phantom blew through his nostrils in a small release of his own grief and frustration. "Let's face it, we're all in hell."

"You know I'll be fine," Amber argued, looking squarely at her father. "I've got a full platoon."

She held little fear of him as her superior, especially in the quiet confines of Riechet's personal quarters.

"You know I don't like sending high-ranking officers on salvage operations. It's not protocol."

"Admit it, you're just worried about me."

"I will admit it," Riechet returned boldly, "and I still say it's not protocol."

He sank onto the edge of his bunk, suddenly looking very weary.

"You can't risk worn soldiers being turned right back out," Amber continued. "Most aren't trained for the strain and we'd just lose them. We need the supplies," she waved a despairing hand toward the door, "more now than ever, and I'm fit to lead."

"I am aware of this," Riechet said. "I just... well, I am your father."

Amber sat down next to him, staring across the small room to the roughly chiseled rock wall.

"And I wouldn't want it any other way. I'll come back. As you said, this is a salvage operation. It's not a front-on assault. I'll be careful."

"I know you will be."

"And thank you for worrying."

Riechet turned to give his daughter a weak smile. "It's part of my job."

"With worrying as a parental requirement, I'm never having kids."

At Amber's comment, Riechet burst into a short bit of laughter. "Don't rule them out so quickly - for my sake at least. You may change your mind when you meet the right man."

Amber rose to step across the room and pick up her sword that rested in the corner. "You mean *if* I meet the right man, right?"

"You will."

"Well, I'm in no hurry. There's a war to win."

"That there is," Riechet said as he rose. "Are there any questions?"

"No, sir. I know the residential district well enough."

"Are you sure you want to handle the Darson boy? I could hold him back."

Amber shook her head, strapping her sword to her waist. "He's spurred to go. I think he's getting frustrated at being down here. I can handle him. Besides, he knows the," she raised her hands to form quotations with her fingers, "'salvage' business better than most. I've also seen him in action. He's a good shot."

"Let's hope there is no action."

Amber reached over to place a hand on her father's arm. "You worry too much," she teased.

"Perhaps. I do feel better that Racer and Phantom will be watching your back."

"So do I."

Riechet watched as Amber headed for the door.

"Oh, and I'm putting Malard on the team as well."

Amber paused. Slowly she turned to face her father. "Are you sure? Begging pardon, but he just got back. I thought the idea was to have fresh soldiers."

"He's rested. His last mission didn't require a lot of energy."

"Not physically, but…"

"Emotionally he is not going to do well if he's locked up here with nothing to do but brood on the situation – especially with the number of children around. I believe he can better help himself by getting back in the field where he can focus his mind."

"And you're not going to have him lead? After all, you made him a major."

"I thought we were in agreement over that."

"I can't argue his skills," Amber said, "but he still has a lot of emotional baggage. Yes, he's leadership material, but right now?"

Riechet pressed his hands into the small of his back as he approached his daughter.

"I've been watching his behavior. I agree he is still recovering from horrible loss. I also agree that his mind is strong when it comes to making wise, and difficult decisions. He cares about the people. We need officers like that. Stoneman makes for a reliable leader to SIERA's strike force, but he lacks the finesse to work with both military and non-military personnel. I'd like to put Malard in a position to command the captain as needed."

"It's just…"

"I'm familiar with his type. He'll rise to expectations given him. But you're right, he needs a little extra work, which is why I'm not putting him in charge of this operation. He responds well to your command and can learn a lot at your side."

Amber gave a slow nod as she thought. "I trust you know best."

Mike sat on the edge of his cot, watching David gear up once more to head into the field.

"You know," he said. "I actually envy you."

"Envy me?" David slung his protective vest over his shoulders and buckled it across his chest with a shake of his head. "Don't bother."

Swinging his feet up on the cot, Mike leaned back against the wall, eyeing the LB-49 David was checking with an almost longing. "At least you get to do something. I'm stuck here."

David paused to study Mike. "Something tells me you know how to use one of these."

He held up the gun.

"Of course. My problem is, I also know how to fly a fighter jet. There aren't enough replacements for pilots if one of us gets hurt on a ground mission."

"Is it any easier? In the air, I mean – where you don't see the destruction?"

Mike winced but managed to keep his overall countenance calm. "It can be, at least from that perspective. I've known plenty of pilots who lost touch with the reality going on below. I try not to forget. To be a good pilot, you can't forget. You do, you're no better than the machine you fly."

Dropping his gun into the holster, David gave a quick nod of agreement. There were no words to follow that statement. Instead he finished strapping on his gear in silence. As David turned to leave, a figure darted past him, sliding to a halt by a far cot. Nathan hurriedly snatched up an empty satchel and, as quickly as he came, rushed out the door.

"I think he's more ready to head out than you," David observed.

"I know it," Mike admitted. "Oh, the ignorance of youth. We'll see how excited he is after a few more battles."

David gave Mike a sideward glance. It was unlike the pilot to sound pessimistic, but David knew he was right.

Mike swung his legs back over the side of the cot and sat up. "And let's just hope he lives through those few more battles."

"Yeah," David answered quietly.

Without looking over at Mike, he headed for the doorway.

"You make it back, too, you hear?"

"It's just a salvage mission."

"I know. Just make it back."

Pulling his pack higher onto his shoulder, David left without comment, mentally preparing himself to once more step out into the ravaged city.

CHAPTER EIGHTEEN

Heavily clad soldiers glared through their war masks as they marched through the corridors of the once opulent resorts, scanning for any life. Theirs was not a mission of mercy. They sought to kill. Orders strictly forbade taking prisoners unless of military rank. After all, civilians left alive would sooner or later take up arms in revolts, and this was unacceptable. Arct-Ieya herself gave the orders. If not obeyed, the penalty was death. She wanted Telamier. Her power and prowess set her in position to take it. These soldiers knew their role in her mission and dutifully swept through one resort after another, emptying each of any resistance and claiming them for the great Vairdec factions to which they belonged.

David lowered the field glasses in silence. Though some distance away, he could make out the movement and lights of Vairdec troops as they worked their way through the resort district. The flicker of a couple small fires sent dancing shadows across the high building walls. Once cleared of any possible resistance, each resort would house enemy troops and equipment, providing them with shelter, supplies and space to maximize their occupation. David slammed the glasses back into their holder on his belt with an irritated grunt. It was a fine set-up – too fine for such sobs of the galaxy.

From where he stood on the outer edge of a small shopping complex, he could only see very top of the Piña Dorado, but knew it already housed countless enemy soldiers. Too bad the buildings were reinforced. As disappointing as it may be to lose the structures, David found pleasure in the thought of bombing the entire district. Unfortunately their weapons cache did not include enough large warheads to efficiently destroy all the buildings quickly. No doubt the Vairdec understood the possibility of attacks on the resorts and were well spread among the massive buildings. Riechet's army would never be able to successfully wipe out the full Vairdec population in one decisive blow. A real pity, David thought, turning his back to the distant resorts.

"Clear northward," he stated to Amber as the colonel made her final checks of the team.

Forty-three soldiers turned toward their commander, anxiously waiting the start of their long, silent journey around the southern edge of the city to the residential district. Among the ranks stood Phantom and Darkracer along with Nathaniel Darson. Though disappointed to learn of Nathan's presence on the mission, David said nothing to indicate his disapproval of the over-energetic youth. Nine Celehi, two Teschians and the Oxyran David had first seen asleep in the officer's bunk added to the ranks.

The Oxyran he learned was Yehgrett, a highly trained weapons expert with a short temper toward any who foolishly disrespected him for his shorter stature or apparent lack of strength. Many learned the hard way that, though stout, Oxyrans were extremely strong, their dense muscle fibers providing them with the strength of four adult Humans. David chose to keep his distance when in the bunkers, partially for his knowledge of the species temper, and partially from a deep preoccupation with his own thoughts. He was curious, now, to see the Oxyran's abilities in the field, and eyed Yehgrett as the creature clicked his two flat teeth together, sniffing the wind as it ruffled through his short, dense fur.

As soon as Amber felt assured that she had accounted for everyone, she motioned with her rifle for them to follow. Their path led them east. Off to their right, the remains of the once expansive South Ridge Airfield lay as a blackened heap from the vicious attack on the night of the Vairdec's arrival. They left little standing, knowing the importance of airfields to any counterattacks. For this reason, Amber was forced to lead her team above ground. The damage was so extensive that the connecting underground lines had collapsed, leaving the only remaining southern-end path between the east and west sectors on the open streets. David glanced south to where he knew the towers of the airfield should be. An eerie sensation rippled down his spine at the sight of the gaping hole in the skyline. Nothing remained of the buildings beyond massive piles of ash and rubble.

Little was said during the trek east. Not even Nathan appeared interested in speaking. Nearly three hours passed before the residential district came into view, the team's progress on the aboveground path having been slowed considerably by streets littered with giant portions of buildings and other, now unrecognizable, debris. Despite Vairdec troops remaining on the north end of the city, aerial patrols slowed the journey even further.

The Karnoss day was just beginning to announce itself with a faint glow in the east when David set his gaze upon the southern edge of the main residential district. Like a massive fortress wall, it extended the full eleven kilometers of the plateau's eastern edge. A city within a city, it not only housed the citizens of Karnoss but maintained them as well. The harsh weather raging across the desert made prolonged exposure to the outdoors impractical, giving rise to apartment complexes conveniently situated atop shopping centers, medical facilities, educational buildings and various entertainment venues. Vast and well stocked, it was an ideal place to salvage supplies. Already SIERA and numerous other refugee groups had pillaged the district, desperate to acquire needed supplies before the Vairdec laid claim to the area. It was unclear as to how much the Vairdec knew about the supplies within the district. However, Riechet had emphasized the need to hurry, sensing a shift in the Vairdec's attentions.

The Vairdec were making their way carefully across the western and center portions of the plateau, their progress slowed by pockets of resistance. As General Riechet observed, the army Arct-Ieya sent to carry out the capture of Karnoss was comprised of lesser soldiers, weaker and less experienced than those most likely striking the powerhouses of Celehi regions. Even so, Karnoss's invaders were formidable enough and were learning quickly. The eastern edge of the city would not remain free from enemy hands for long.

Slipping through the main entrance of the Skyline Mall, David chanced a look up at the arching windows that comprised the entryway ceiling, watching the ripple of soft hues infused through the glass. The eerie glow of landing vessels heading into the northern sectors sent a wash of red across the upper regions of nearby buildings. With their lights' reflections visible to the naked eye, David knew they were flying low, and probably landing closer than first anticipated. Time was of the essence. Amber, too, observed the need for haste and began barking orders, her voice ringing hollowly through the empty space.

"Food, medicine, hygiene, blankets, clothes – in that order. No non-essential materials. Again, food is primary. Let's keep our people alive."

Amber led the way across the main plaza toward the back regions where everyday necessities were stored and sold. Once beyond the reaches of the faint hints of dawn filtering through the plaza windows, the complex fell into oppressive darkness. Small green lights blinked to life as the soldiers switched on their field lamps. A soft aura of light soon enveloped the team as they headed up the hall. David held his position at the back, keeping an eye on the rest of the team and making sure no one strayed behind. His eyes constantly tracked back and forth across the hall to ensure their safety, pausing briefly to gaze at the ghostly reflections cast upon the darkened shop windows as they passed. One Celehi slowed, finally stopping to gaze into one of the windows. David placed his hand on the soldier's back as he came alongside.

"Let's keep going," he said.

The Celehi held his ground a second longer, unable to tear his gaze from a collection of intricate Celharan works of metal and glass that glittered in the light of the field lamps.

"So sad," he commented quietly. "Save them… cannot."

"Artworks can be replaced," David reminded. "Let's save the artists."

With a gentle push, David urged the soldier on, though the Celehi's feet dragged as he kept his eyes on the beautiful figures as long as he could.

"Shame - Vairdec destroy these." He looked hard at David. "They will."

"I know." David pushed a little harder.

"I wish to destroy these myself." The soldier waved a hand in front of the glass. "Rather us over the enemy."

Still hesitant to leave the sight, the Celehi, with the continued goading of David, moved on after the rest of the platoon. David glanced back at the last of the visible works, spying a very beautiful and life-like Celehi maiden wrought of semi-precious metals, raising her delicate hands toward him from amid a sea of colored glass.

"No," he said, speaking slowly and thoughtfully, "I think not. Leave everything intact, and let our enemy see who we are."

Amber kept her team on a direct path past the outer rim boutiques, display windows and a large multi-level recreation center to head toward the inner sectors where health clinics and cafés would dominate. Making a sharp turn to the right, she halted the soldiers in the middle of a rounded cluster of businesses including a dental clinic and veterinarian office.

"See what you can find here," she said. "And make it quick."

The team spread out among the various rooms, having in many cases to break through the doors to gain entry. David followed a group of eight into the veterinarian clinic where they immediately began sweeping the area for bandages and medicines that could work effectively on sentient beings. In the back room they came upon the sad remnants of three pets, forcibly abandoned at the start of the invasion.

Though he hated to look, David felt himself compelled to glance into the different pens, spying the cold, stiff bodies of a toupsu and a kiejaud still hooked up to their now powerless lifelines. Nearby a second kiejaud struggled weakly in the corner of its enclosure, sick and starving. One of the Celehi soldiers in the room took notice as well. A second later David's stomach twisted at the distasteful sound of the little animal's neck snapping. He knew the choice was the most humane but, regardless, exited the clinic quickly in as dignified a manner as possible.

"What a waste," he murmured, thinking on the invasion as a whole.

"Malard." He glanced up to watch Amber approach. "We'll cover more ground if we split up.

Take that unit," she motioned with her ever-ready gun at a cluster of twenty soldiers, "and head around to the north end. I don't expect much left from the open market, but the surrounding food shops may have a few things that haven't spoiled. Check the storage rooms below the shops. What we need is probably a couple stories down."

"Understood."

"Stay on the short-wave and check in with your position every ten minutes. I will do the same."

"Yes, ma'am."

With a raised hand David signaled his new team to follow him back to the main hall and continue on northward. Amber kept her eyes on the departing soldiers until they disappeared around the far bend.

"Hurry it up," she called over her shoulder.

Within ten minutes she and the remaining soldiers, including the Candonians, moved back to the main hall and turned in the opposite direction, heading southeast toward a region Amber knew held another clinic along with various cafés. As ordered, David called in, confirming that his team arrived safely to the open market section of the mall. So far all was going as planned, though Amber knew not to grow careless in light of their good fortune. She continued to move cautiously, gun in hand, her eyes sweeping back and forth to examine every dark corner they came upon.

Before long the hall opened into a wide space where a colorful playground lay as the centerpiece to various small boutiques, cafés, clothing stores and a childcare service center situated on the far end. At first glance the area appeared useless to their needs.

However Amber wisely understood that boutiques carried soaps and other needed hygiene materials while clothing stores held coats, boots and other practical outfits. More so, the childcare center carried blankets and was regularly stocked with non-perishable food that could be easily handed out to fussy children. If her luck held, Amber felt confident they could load themselves with needed supplies from this one area alone.

"Remember," she told her team as she stationed herself in the center of the playground, "just the essentials. Stack everything you find here. Let's get the Candonians loaded first."

With softly spoken affirmatives, the team broke into smaller units to fan out among the various shops. Within a few minutes a couple piles of clothing, a box of soaps, two large cases of nectar juice and a loaf of dried bread lay at her feet. Breaking the loaf in half, Amber allowed Darkracer and Phantom to eat. Their conditions worried her. Since the invasion began, they had received little in the way of sustainable food. Larger in size, they would require larger amounts of food to stay fit. While they did not yet show it, having gone without a good meal for only a few days, it would not be long before their weight would begin to drop. Neither of them complained. They were a strong and proud species. Amber gave a smile as they quickly finished off the bread in her hands.

If you will not worry about yourselves, she thought, *then I shall worry for you.*

A vibration drew her attention to her comlink.

"Go ahead," she said, wiping her hands on her slacks.

"Malard reporting in. Things appear pretty well picked over. We're moving through each shop, but there's not so much as a crumb."

Amber's brow furrowed. Something about the report made her uneasy. This section of the district had not yet been thoroughly swept by SIERA.

"Any sign of refugees?" she asked.

"None."

"And the store rooms below?"

"We're heading down there now."

Amber glanced at the coordinates coming in over her intel-band. Configuring them on her map she determined David had made it to the far northern end of the marketplace. Logically he would head down a level and sweep back toward her position. So far so good, but Amber still did not like the report. Obviously scavengers not associated with the army got to the main food center first. Though the thought of losing food was disappointing, the real concern lay in not knowing who exactly had taken the food and where they were now. How many would there be? Were they injured? Would she be able to get them safely back to the bunkers? Or worse still, could the Vairdec be occupying this space already?

"Very good," she said in response to David's report. "Transmitting our co-ordinance as well. Stay alert. With that much food gone, there may be refugees in the area."

"And if there are?"

"Report to me and do what you can for them."

"Colonel."

278

Stepping around the Candonians, Amber made her way across the open play area toward the private that stood at the far end waiting for her.

"You better come and see this," he said.

The concern in his voice caused Amber to tense and she cleared the final distance at a jog. Taking her gun in both hands, she shouldered her way past the solider and into the dark recesses of the childcare center. Soft patches of green light illuminated a group of soldiers who had ceased their scavenging to form a line toward the back room. Inside, cowering beneath the steady gazes of three armed soldiers, huddled a group of nearly two dozen children and their adult caregivers. A hasty scan provided Amber with enough information to cause her to feel her confidence in a quick in-and-out mission fade. The children were quite young, all tired, hungry and weak. The adults clearly fared no better, some appearing sick.

"Who's in charge?" she asked, nodding toward the group of civilians.

They glanced among themselves, questioning each other with their eyes as to whom should volunteer to answer, thus accepting the overlooked role of leader.

"How many do we have?" Amber jumped in, turning her back to the civilians to address her soldiers.

"Nineteen total," a sergeant answered. "Six adults, three youth, ten children." He leaned closer to speak quietly. "One woman's pregnant – nearly due."

Amber gave a growling sigh but said nothing on the subject. Fixing her eyes on an elderly woman clutching a two-year old she spoke, her words intended for the full group.

"Have you been here since Rew'cha?"

"Some," came the hoarse reply. "The center was open for the festivities. Two adults and five children."

The grandmother pointed toward a middle-aged woman and a young man standing near the back of the group.

"The rest of us came from different apartments. I thought I could wait out the problem, but when my son did not come home for two days and no one came back to the district we decided to head for better areas. We were hoping power would be on somewhere. No one seems to know what's happening or where to go."

"Are we supposed to go to the bunkers?" the young man asked, his voice shaky.

"I've never been to the bunkers," a young woman whimpered.

The grandmother glanced back with a shake of her head. "No one has."

A small boy tugged on the young man's arm until he leaned over to listen to the child. Though the boy cupped his hand to his mouth as if to whisper, his voice came across clearly in the heavy stillness of the room.

"Can we go home now?"

"We're going to the bunkers," Amber announced suddenly, not allowing herself the time to contemplate the complexity of her task.

She knew she could not leave the civilians behind, but formulating a plan to move the full group quickly and safely across the city currently eluded her. If only the underground passages below the airfield escaped damage, perhaps a chance for relatively fast travel would still be possible. As it was, young, old and pregnant would all have to somehow traverse above ground without being noticed by the enemy. The original plan was to stay in the safety of the malls during the day, taking the time to gather as much as everyone could carry before using the cover of darkness to return. With weakened civilians, traveling by night would be risky, as temperatures would drop below what they could most likely handle.

These concerns she put to Darkracer who stood patiently at the entrance of the center. He nodded thoughtfully as he considered all she said, his ears twitching and his tail snapping against his flank.

"It's pointless to call for reinforcements," Amber concluded. "That just means more people to move. If only we could use a transport of some kind."

A distant rumble, barely audible through the thick walls, came as a sobering reminder of the enemy's proximity. Darkracer lifted his head high, his nostrils flared. He heard and felt the rumbling with greater clarity than his Human companion. Amber knew this well and kept quiet, waiting for Darkracer to provide her with more detailed information.

"Sounds like explosions," he said after a tense minute. "My guess is that they're two, maybe three kilometers away. The way they've been sweeping, we still have time."

"We leave now," Amber interjected.

"What of the central line?" Phantom asked as he made his way forward, his eyes trailing north in the direction of the explosions.

"That's awfully close to enemy lines," Darkracer reminded, "and it adds a good four hours to the trip."

"Above ground it would take longer," Amber said, her mind made up. "You're taking the central line. It may be closer to the Vairdec, but being underground you'll be far less detectable than on the surface. It was hard enough getting trained soldiers across in the open. I can't risk it with children."

Darkracer shifted uneasily, his hooves scraping the flooring. "I was being optimistic with four hours. I know that's the time it would take this platoon. With the refugees we need to put at least two more hours onto that."

"I don't care about the length of time," Amber admitted. "Just get them through safely."

Phantom eyed Amber nervously. "You sound like you're not coming."

"I'm not."

Darkracer stamped his foot in disapproval. "I made a promise to get you back safely."

"I'll be right behind you. As you said, children will slow you down. Most likely the rest of us will catch up within a few hours."

Amber pushed her way past the larger creatures to return to the still growing stack of salvaged supplies.

"However," she continued, "you forget that I also made a promise – to accomplish this mission. Everything salvaged so far goes with you and the refugees. I'll send a team of soldiers along for protection. The rest of us will stay behind to continue our original mission. With the Vairdec moving this way, this will probably be our last chance for supplies in this area. Malard and his team have not yet been informed. I won't leave them behind and waiting for them will delay our return to the bunkers even more. Sergeant."

Speaking rapidly, Amber did not even turn to look at the soldier she addressed, who was emerging from the childcare center. The colonel's sudden acknowledgment of her presence made her jump to attention.

"Colonel?" She hastened over to stand before her superior.

Picking up the first of the supplies, Amber began loading the Candonians.

"Get the civilians out here right away. We need to assess who can walk and who needs to be carried. Any who can carry supplies must do so. I want that group," she pointed toward the childcare center, "to be ready to move in ten minutes. Clear?"

"Yes, ma'am."

With a hurried salute, the sergeant spun on her heels to jog back into the center.

"Adosia to Malard."

The response was immediate. *"Malard here."*

"Civilians have been discovered." She paused as she lugged a case of brack seeds up and across Phantom's withers. David remained silent on the other line, awaiting further instruction. "Part of my unit is heading out in ten, central line. Report your status."

"Not much to be found on this end," David admitted. *"We're about to check the last underground storage room. Our co-ordinances are relaying."*

Amber gave her intel-band a sideward glance to see the flash of numbers appear, not taking the time to read further. She trusted David.

"The doors are locked," he continued. *"We'll be through momentarily."*

"Carry on but kick it up," Amber said, giving a grunt as she pulled hard on the cords that tied down a bundle of blankets. "We have possible enemies three clicks north."

"We'll hurry, Malard out."

Nathan dumped a load of stylish coats and hats at Amber's feet, pausing to stare rather casually at her.

"The Vairdec are coming?"

"Patrols may be close, but there's no official evidence that they are advancing. No word of this. I don't want a panic among the civilians."

Without acknowledging one way or the other, Nathan turned to head for another store. Before he could take more than a step, Amber caught him up by his pack and dragged him back in front of her. Despite his complaints she ripped the field pack from his shoulder and dumped its contents upon the floor. Nathan cursed as an assortment of jewels, currency and computer modules rolled past their feet. Amber was not impressed.

"We have absolutely no room for non-essentials. If you can't eat it, I don't want to see it in your pack. Now get into that childcare center and

284

grab every scrap of food you can find or I'll have you chowing on this the rest of the war."

She kicked a computer chip and sent it skidding into the darkness. With a muffled growl, Nathan snatched his pack and stormed off to the center. Ten minutes later, just as ordered, the civilians and nine soldiers stood ready to depart. Amber hated to sacrifice supply space on the Candonians to allow the pregnant woman, the elderly lady and the two youngest children the chance to ride but knew the importance of the decision. Luckily the rest of the civilians agreed without complaint to carry any extra items they could. Even the little five-year old boy bravely shouldered a makeshift pack filled with dried fruit and nut packets.

Amber's heart raced, though she concealed it with a firm stance. A desire to protect washed over her. She wanted to go with the first unit to ensure the safety of those in their care. Should anything go wrong along the way, she was powerless to help them. The vulnerable feeling left her uneasy. Before the war, the scenarios she faced remained comfortably within her control. Now she struggled with the thought of letting go of that control. She quietly reasoned with herself that her decision gave them the best chance to survive. It was all she could do. Stepping back, she gave one final assessment of the team.

"Head out."

Darkracer led the way with the rest of the unit clustered close behind. Amber scanned each person as they filed past her and disappeared down the shadowy hall.

"Has this area been stripped of essentials?" Amber asked without looking toward her twelve remaining soldiers.

"Yes, colonel," the sergeant answered.

Amber snatched up her field pack from where it lay at her feet and gave a terse nod. "Then let's head for..."

"Malard to Adosia," Amber's comlink squawked, cutting her off in mid sentence.

"Go ahead Malard."

"I'm relaying our position. We've discovered a large cache and need extra soldiers to load it out."

Finally, Amber thought, some good news.

"Your position's noted. We're on our way."

Amber headed off in David's direction, knowing the rest of her team would follow without question. She passed close to Nathan who was bent over picking up the dropped currency. Without breaking her stride, she gave him a swift kick in the rear. He snapped upright and hurriedly fell into line, grumbling under his breath to wisely keep from speaking aloud any of his thoughts.

Using her intel-band, Amber soon pinpointed David's exact location. Though roughly only two hundred meters up the hall, they were three stories down. It would take several more minutes to swing eastward through service corridors to come to the nearest stairwell that descended into the marked storage room. She broke into an easy jog, enjoying the physical work after the trying moments just minutes earlier. Before long her team rounded the final bend before the stairs.

Heading down, Amber recalled the arguments the city found itself in some twenty years ago over whether to put in stairwells to the growing residential district. It meant an extra expense, one deemed unnecessary at the time. After all, Karnoss held the distinction as Earthenia's power center. More power plants and generators ran on the plateau than anywhere else due to the heavy northern winds that generated them. With ample supplies of energy no one thought power outages would play into the life of Karnoss's citizens. Of course, no one at the time thought about the possibility of a violent attack from a hostile civilization. Luckily, enough members of the city government felt the lifts may occasionally break down or become overwhelmed by any sudden mass exodus, winning the buildings the much-needed stairwells.

The darkness felt oppressive in the narrow chamber and Amber slowed her pace in order to ensure no misstep in the dim glow of her field light. Half way to her goal, she froze. Instantly her gun was at eye level. Her body tensed. Behind her, the sound of weapons clicking into position briefly echoed through the darkness. Just below, another group tensed.

"Identify," Amber ordered.

"Yehgrett," came the reply.

The Oxyran chattered with the release of adrenaline as he stepped into Amber's light. Behind him, eleven soldiers lowered their weapons. All were heavily loaded with supplies. Yehgrett strode up to Amber, shouldering a pack as large as the taller Humans and Celehi carried.

"No 'shoot first' order is good," he commented.

"Indeed," Amber answered. "Malard below?"

"Yes."

"And all of you have everything you can carry?"

"Yes."

"Then I want you to head toward this location," Amber ordered, sending the co-ordinance to Yehgrett's intel-band. "We picked up civilians. Darkracer has a team headed toward the central line. I want you to join that group immediately and offer what assistance you can. Understood."

Yehgrett let his heavy-barreled grenade launcher drop back against his shoulder. "Yes."

"Then go. All of you."

Yehgrett said no more. With Darkracer's position in hand, he continued up at a greater speed than most would expect a short-legged species to achieve. Amber did not wait to watch them go. Yehgrett had served with SIERA for over a year and proved himself a very reliable soldier. The fortunate coincidence that led him to be the first packed and ready to go gave Amber a sense of relief. An Oxyran of Yehgrett's ability was a great asset to the civilian team. She gave a sigh, allowing some of the tension of the day to dissipate as she and her unit finished their descent. Yes, it felt good to see things work out favorably for once. Crossing the outer storage chamber, Amber opened the door into the room where David would be waiting.

"Colonel!"

CHAPTER NINETEEN

Amber heard the call but only comprehended the frantic nature of the tone. Her vision tunneled as a rush of adrenaline shot through her blood. The world flashed and slowed around her. A shot exploded near her head. Instinctively she twisted to the side, finding herself unable to move freely while against the doorframe. Soldiers pressed against her back, causing her to momentarily fight for her footing. She was aware of the sounds of gunfire but unable to pinpoint the shooters in the near pitch-black environment. A blur of movement caught her attention and she spun to face it, feeling the impact of something hard against her face before she managed to get off a shot. A hot, burning sensation swept up her right leg as the world tumbled away around her. Then there was nothing.

From across the room David watched helplessly as Amber succumbed to the attack, thankful for the soldiers behind her who quickly dispatched the maddened Oxyran before he managed to swing his battle-ax again and kill the colonel. There was no time to assess her situation further. Around him the very air crackled with the intensity of the sudden battle. It all happened so suddenly. One moment he and his team were filling their packs with supplies from the abundant underground cache, the next they were facing off with a vehement Faxon and his renegade group of refugees, which included a Manogonite, two Oxyrans and three Airisuns. With the amount of shooting, he was sure more were present than what he managed to account for.

It all started right after David sent Yehgrett and half the soldiers, loaded with as much as they could carry, up to meet Amber's team. With a numbing roar that reverberated through the room, the Faxon and his gang appeared through a passage across the chamber. Instantly the Faxon began accusing David and the soldiers of thievery, threatening to kill them. Try as he might, David found it impossible to defuse the Faxon's rage. A tense standoff ensued, everyone with weapons trained and ready. Luckily, no one appeared too eager to begin shooting and for a moment, David felt his confidence rising at the thought that he and his remaining team would be able diffuse the situation. And then the side door opened.

The movement and sudden appearance of more soldiers startled the Faxon into action. He fired toward Amber before she could react. A fast and furious firefight erupted in response, the built up tension on both sides snapping. As David twisted out of the line of fire and stationed himself between two stacks of food, he caught sight of the Oxyran charging the door. Though he tried to fire, his angle was wrong. A sense of helplessness washed over him as the Oxyran slammed the handle of his ax into Amber's face. David leaped from cover at the sight of her going down, only to realize he now stood in the path of the Faxon.

While those near the door took care of Amber's attacker and leaped into the fray, David found himself spun around by the force of the Faxon's arm as the creature made a swipe at him. Now it was David's turn to become enraged. Taking advantage of a stray shot that struck the Faxon in the shoulder, David lunged forward to smash his foot down on the creature's knee. Buckling slightly from the impact, the Faxon shifted his gun away from David, giving the Human the precious second to close the gap between them.

However, wounded or not, the Faxon refused to succumb easily and drove a punishing blow with his fist into David's side. David gave with the impact to minimize bodily damage but still found his vision blur and redden from the flash of pain. His right arm fell against the Faxon's chest. Unable to fire a clean shot, David used his left hand to snatch a knife from his belt and drive it into the Faxon's flesh. The howl that erupted nearly deafened David. He grimaced but continued his move. With a sudden burst of strength, he shoved himself back enough to aim his gun at the Faxon's head and fire.

Dark, greasy splatters of blood flickered momentarily in David's field light before coating the floor and surrounding crates. The Faxon thrashed, his right eye damaged, the flesh on top of his skull seared away. Understanding the difficult nature of killing a Faxon, David never dropped his guard, rightfully predicting the creature's attempt to rise and fire on him. Firing consecutive bullets into the thick skull and throat, David managing within a few pulls of the trigger to finally end the Faxon's attack. Heaving each breath, he slowly turned in a circle, aware for the first time that the fight was over.

Slowly the soldiers converged near the center of the chamber, their individual lights brightening the area as they closed ranks. David stepped among them, giving each a cursory check. He nodded at the sergeant.

"How many lost?"

The sergeant looked about her, still assessing the situation.

"Unclear. Some wounded."

"And the colonel?"

The sergeant pointed toward the closed doors of a lift with her gun. "In there."

David pushed past those standing between him and the lift to inspect the doors for himself. Sure enough, they refused to open. Banging on them with his fist, he listened, receiving no response. With a disgruntled sigh, he turned back to his team.

"How did this happen? I thought there was no power."

"There isn't," the sergeant admitted. "I don't have any more information."

To his left David caught sight of the three Airisuns huddling fearfully under the watchful eye of two soldiers. Passive by nature, the natives from the Auri system had quickly surrendered when they discovered the strength of the military. As David approached they cowered against their captors, their wrinkled faces creasing further with trepidation. They had witnessed David's attack on the Faxon, whom they assumed was the strongest creature in which to form an alliance. With him dead at the hands of a Human, they found themselves extremely vulnerable to a surprisingly stronger species.

David stood over them, watching as they shied away, looking even smaller in stature while doing so. Their long, wispy white hair did nothing to hide their dark eyes that kept darting between their captors. To a Human they appeared as old men though in fact they were quite young. The larger amount of wrinkles indicated that.

"Will you cause any more trouble?" David asked them.

They glanced between each other in confusion.

"Do you know Human speech?"

Still no response.

"Nak Celharan auh?"

Their eyes brightened and one relaxed enough to move forward. Celharan they understood.

"Deekat guinal-et coshaidar," one explained, hoping to diffuse any remaining tension with words of peace. "Deekat guinal blegerate."

"Deekat eja," David said with a nod, indicating the surrounding soldiers. "Auh carsordar-et."

An audible sigh escaped the Airisuns as they realized they would not be harmed. Clasping their pudgy hands together, they pressed their fists to their foreheads in signs of respect. It was enough for David. Reassured that the fighting would not resume, he pointed toward the lift.

"N'lad'eer. Nia zilac?"

The delegated speaker for the Airisuns stepped forward, pointing to a smoldering generator to the left of the lift doors.

"Deekat voerday meckeer. Deekat guinal-et tan'meca quoo quayd. Meckeer hendi'et."

"Mmhmm," David answered, studying the generator.

Sure enough, the generator the civilian group had used to keep the lift functional for their convenience now lay as a useless heap of smoking metal.

"Give me a hand here," David ordered a couple soldiers standing nearby.

Together they pried at the lift doors, finally working them open enough to see inside. To David's disappointment, the lift, along with Amber, was not on the other side. Shining his light up the shaft, he hoped to find it sitting just a floor or two above only to receive more disappointment. The beam of light vanished into the darkness without any trace of the lift.

"A power surge must have been jolted upward when the generator was hit," David said as he turned back to the group. "There's no telling what condition the colonel is in. I'm going up to see if I can locate the lift. Private," he nodded toward the young soldier at his side, "you're with me. The rest of you pack everything you can carry. That goes for the Airisuns, too. Head back the way we came and contact

Yehgrett. Join up with his team and get this stuff back to the bunkers."

"We're not to wait for you?" the sergeant asked.

David wiped his knife clean and sheathed it with forceful purpose. "We'll follow."

"And if she cannot be moved?"

"We'll call in for assistance. Just get this food out of here." David headed for a side staircase. "Make it quick everyone. There's no telling who else will show."

David did not wait for anything beyond 'Yes, sir' before jogging to the stairs. Even with his light, the darkness felt oppressive. The air was heavy and stale, and David found himself wheezing as he took the stairs two and three at a time. His side ached from where the Faxon punched him and he hoped that he had not cracked any ribs. Focusing on his need to retrieve Amber, David ignored his pain and slammed himself against the door, almost losing his footing as he tumbled into the main corridor of the Skyline Mall. In either direction the hall stretched as an empty expanse into the darkness. Approaching the lift, David and the private found the door shut.

"Colonel?" David called, using his comlink in favor of shouting through the door. "Malard here. What's your status?"

All he received was silence. With his fist he pounded on the lift doors.

"Colonel?"

Getting no response, he stepped back to scan the doors as he tried to formulate a plan. A sense of urgency washed through him.

"Help me out here," he said as he tapped the private, who dutifully guarded the hall, on the shoulder.

Together they tackled the doors, using their combat knives to force them open a couple inches. Grabbing either side, they pulled hard. The doors remained stubborn, only shifting a few more inches.

"Colonel Riechet?" David called

Beyond the doors all was dark. His voice echoed hollowly inside the shaft. Wedging his shoulder into the gap, David pushed hard, bracing with his feet against the frame until he managed to create a space large enough for him to lean inside. No lift. With a high-beam light he pulled from his vest, David swept the interior of the shaft, finally locating the bottom of the lift four stories above him.

"Colonel," he said, "if you can hear me, I'm on my way up."

Having never been inside the residential complex, it took several minutes for David and the private to locate the emergency stairs that wound their way from the subterranean service tunnels to the very top floor of the building. Inside the stairwell the air pressed around them. Without power to ventilate the complex, the inner regions lay stagnant and nearly unbreathable. Their wheezing breath echoed up and down the dark stairwell. A couple times David caught his foot on the edge of a step, nearly falling had he not managed to grasp the railing in time. Shaking and out of breath, the two weary soldiers stumbled gratefully into the apartment hallway. The cold, still air stung David's face, but he welcomed it after the climb. Before long he stood once again in front of the lift doors.

"Colonel," he called, rapping on the metal.

"In here."

The voice was not Amber's. Again David and the private tackled the doors. This time they found their work assisted from the other side. At last the doors yielded to reveal Nathan standing on the other side. Amber lay nearby, barely conscious. Around her a pool of blood slowly grew from a gash on the inside of her right upper leg that was wrapped with a bit of cloth. Nathan glanced back at her with an expression of uncertainty. David dropped to his knees beside Amber, sliding off his pack and rummaging for medical supplies.

"Stand watch," David ordered.

Nathan stepped into the hall to take a position near the private.

David carefully placed his jacket under Amber's head. "Colonel?"

Amber's eyes fluttered open and she gave a slight moan. Blood trickled past her left eye and down her cheek. Pulling bandages and bio-sealant from his pack, David concentrated on the leg wound. A steady stream squirted with each beat of her heart. If David failed to stop the bleeding soon, Amber would not last more than a few minutes. With a strap from his vest he made a tourniquet before carefully removing the cloth. He knew the importance of working quickly. Taking too much time would cost Amber her leg. A pre-packaged syringe of antibiotic wash cleared the wound, making it possible for David to apply the bio-sealant. He hoped it would be enough to hold the nicked femoral artery together.

"Give me a hand," he called as he pressed the first bandages into the sealant-filled wound. Nathan appeared hesitant to leave his post. Luckily the private proved more willing to take orders and knelt hurriedly at David's side. He held the bandage in place while David used strips to tie everything down.

"That should hold for a while," he said as he removed the tourniquet.

To his relief the bandages held. A rumble vibrated through the walls.

"How long a while?" Nathan asked over his shoulder, his eyes never straying from the sights on his rifle.

"Malard to Squad Four." Nothing. "Malard to Racer. Racer, come in." Silence. "Malard to Command, come in Command. Malard to Command." David glanced up at the private. "Try yours."

Doing as instructed, the private called in, only to shake his head a moment later. "Nothing."

"Darson?"

"Nothing," Nathan answered back.

After trying Amber's comlink, David sat back in defeat. *Naturally*, he thought. Another vibration rippled from further up the building.

Nathan stepped further into the hall to pivot in an agitated circle. "The Vairdec?"

"Further north," David answered wearily.

"How much further?"

"Hard to say." David groaned as he got to his feet and crouched next to Amber. "But we can't stay here."

Cramming the bloodied cloth and extra medical supplies into his pack, David picked Amber up as gently as he could. Careful not to leave bloody tracks, the team exited the lift. Amber groaned and laid her head against David's shoulder. He could tell she was regaining consciousness, though she said nothing as they made their way to the stairs. A deep, thunderous boom rolled up through the stairwell, causing the walls to creak in protest.

"That doesn't sound like they're very far to the north," Nathan observed, looking down the stairs by means of his rifle.

David looked back and forth in thought.

"We won't get far on the lower levels," he observed. "This way."

He led the way to the left, turning down side passages until he felt a safe distance from the stairs. A line of doors stood before him. Nathan moved ahead, testing each door as he went, while the private took up a rear guard. Several doors gave way, most likely the work of the Faxon-led gang. Stepping through one, David found himself standing in a modest, yet stylish, apartment with a typical Karnoss layout. Past the main entrance a raised platform held the kitchen, a counter creating a barrier between it and the rest of the house. From the kitchen a slightly lower platform housed a small dining set that looked out over a sunken living space where transparent walls gave a view of the city skyline to the west.

David led the way around the kitchen on the lower floor, past the bedrooms to the left and into the living space. Around them, the décor consisted of thick mat flooring, heavily upholstered metal furniture and numerous large, mythical statues. A smell of strong musk incense still clung to the air. Thick tapestries hung in various places from the ceiling. The whole place felt confining. Though under normal circumstances David would have found this somewhat garish environment unappealing, he now found the feeling of enclosure rather inviting. Staying against the wall near the door, David looked to his two armed companions.

"Sweep the apartment again."

He watched as Nathan and the private made their way carefully through each of the rooms. A movement from Amber drew his attention to her. She was awake, her gun in hand, ready to do her part should trouble arise. Luckily she did not demand being set down, for David knew he would have to disobey orders if she did. Putting any pressure on the leg may cause the wound to break open. It was a risk David refused to take, so he forced himself to rely on others to confirm the area secure while he held back with Amber in his arms.

"Kitchen and living space secure," the private announced.

"Back rooms secure" Nathan said a moment later.

Using the tapestries as cover, David slipped along the north end of the living space, carefully examining the wall.

"What are you looking for?" Nathan asked as he made his way from the back.

"These apartments aren't always what they seem," David explained. "This is a mid-class suite. There's usually a private lounge or access to other suites via swinging walls."

With a push of a nearly invisible panel at the far corner, the wall swung enough to admit the Humans through. Beyond lay a very small private lounge that, from the looks of things, had been converted into a religious shrine. An intricately woven blanket lay on the floor before a narrow, curtained alcove adorned with glow stones, incense and a jeweled statuette whose origins David was not familiar. Placing Amber gently on the floor against the west wall, he retrieved the blanket from its place in front of the shrine and snatched what looked like a kneeling pillow.

"Sorry," he muttered half-heartedly to the eight-limbed, multi-eyed idol.

He returned to Amber to place the pillow under her leg. She blinked and gazed at him, confused and in pain.

"Malard to Command," he called again with the same frustrating silence following.

"The explosions could be cutting out our signals," Nathan observed.

David hated to admit the teenager was most likely correct. With a disgusted groan he dropped into a sit next to Amber.

"They're not going to find us here," Nathan continued. "Not if we can't call them."

"Thank you for stating the obvious," David growled.

"Malard?"

David rose to his knees to gaze into Amber's pale face.

"Stay still. You're wounded."

"Where's the team?"

"Safe. On their way back. We have to wait for reinforcements to get you out. We're safe, though."

Refusing to say anything about the explosions and inevitable Vairdec advancement, David busied himself with checking Amber's leg. So far the bandage remained free of blood. For how long, David could not say.

"It won't be long," he reassured, checking her head wound.

Standing, he stepped into the living space again to address his two waiting soldiers. "We need to get help and I can't leave the colonel. These don't normally lock on their own, so I want you two to seal off this room from the outside," he motioned toward the small lounge, "then join up with the main group. Tell them where we are."

"Yes, sir," the private answered quickly.

Nathan only responded with a nod.

"Stay together," David continued, "and make sure there's no evidence of our presence in this apartment before you leave."

"What of the explosions?" Nathan asked. "They could level this entire complex."

"Not likely," David reassured. "Those are low levels, probably even some flash bombs. They're just making sure everything is clear. If they had wanted to

302

level the place they would have done so by now. Move quickly, though. There's more to worry about than this building dropping."

Even before the private could answer with another "Yes, sir," David was back in the lounge beside Amber. He listened to the wall panel slide shut behind him and click as they were sealed inside. The thought of being locked in did little to agitate David. He knew he could break down the wall in an emergency. What bothered him more was the sight of Amber so weak from the blood loss and the thought that her fate lay in two young soldiers making it back to the main group alive. Keeping Nathan's stealth and weaponry skills in mind, David did his best to reassure himself of his decision and focused instead on caring for Amber.

Settling next to her, he wrapped the blanket tightly around both their shoulders, pressing in close to Amber's side. Her breathing grew slow and steady. Fully awake, she listened without comment as David explained the earlier attack. Finishing his report, he helped her with some water before allowing her to lay her head against his shoulder. She was doing everything she could to keep her body under control despite the amount of blood lost and the vicious strike to her head. Knowing he could not risk her falling asleep, David searched his mind for something - anything to talk about. Unfortunately he kept coming up blank. There were always the usual topics. Family - a not-so-favorite topic for him, jobs – a topic that did not require any questions between them, relationships... David shook his head. That subject he preferred to avoid.

"What's your favorite holiday?" he asked as his mind turned to the failed Rew'cha celebration.

A feeble start to a conversation, perhaps, but he figured it was better than nothing. Amber gave a sigh. She knew what David was attempting and willing played along. Her words rolled off her tongue in a slow drawl.

"I suppose Bolarda."

David nodded his agreement. Bolarda was the largest celebration on Telamier. The entire last nahm of the year was set aside for the holiday, providing many with a twenty day vacation to celebrate the end of winter and the start of spring, which, by the Telamierian calendar, also started a new year. Every culture had its own way of celebrating. For Humans, it became a blend of old traditions from Earth and the learned traditions from the Celehi.

Recognizing it as an end-of-the-year holiday, Humans married their Earth year-end traditions with Bolarda. Decorations of natural foliage, winter flowers and numerous lights adorned homes and businesses alike, everyone preparing for the fifteenth when families gathered to play games, hold sumptuous feasts and exchange gifts. This normally continued through the twentieth, the last day of the nahm, when everything culminated in large street festivals, dancing and light shows to welcome in spring and the new year. Its length and popularity made even Rew'cha, the second largest holiday on Telamier, appear small.

David remained silent for some time as he thought about past Bolarda celebrations. He, too, looked forward to the holiday, even though the last few years of his parents' lives were often wrought with tension. Bolarda had a way of bringing with it a sense of peace and unity. Would it be the same this year? Though still three seasons away, David sensed the conflict they currently faced would ultimately interrupt any thoughts of celebrating. Even with the blessed chance the Vairdec would be routed by that time, the destruction was already so great that a holiday of laughter, peace and thanksgiving appeared impossible to achieve. The thought depressed him, and David began rethinking the wisdom of his choice in topic. However, with the invasion engulfing their lives, could any topic avoid thoughts of the present tragedies?

"I like Christmas, too," Amber continued. "In the military, combat's a way of life. I like having a night to think of peace... hope."

In the dark it was impossible to make out Amber's expression, but David could tell from the sound of her voice that she was smiling at the thought. It surprised him to hear such a sentimental side of Amber revealed. He closed his eyes as he thought about what she said.

Old records indicated how Humans split their Earth Christmas traditions between Bolarda and the Telamierian Christmas. On Telamier, the Christmas holiday focused on religious aspects kept alive largely by the Tenner family whose founders had been missionaries. Taking one of the darkest days of the year, they turned it into a night of hope, where the lights they lit shown all the brighter, signifying their hope in the love of their savior.

Though not overly religious, David never refuted the beliefs. Despite debates that continued to play out over what was true, David found it impossible to argue the compassion and gentleness associated with the missionaries' standpoint. Furthermore, true or not, the hope and peace they found through their belief was greatly welcomed. Sadly, David's family life kept him distant from any structured belief system in his youth and he had only attended one Christmas celebration. It remained an uplifting time in his life, so he allowed himself to now set his mind to that, contemplating the symbol of light in dark times as a sense of comfort for him.

He did not know how long he pondered these thoughts before he realized Amber had grown very quiet. Fearfully he gave her a shake.

"I'm still here," she answered softly.

David relaxed, hearing a bit of strength returning to Amber's voice.

"Good to know," he said. "So, you attend Christmas?"

"Every year. It's a tradition."

"And this year?"

"There's no reason not to."

David gave a huff. "You surprise me. I always took you for a strict, military officer – tough and unemotional."

"I'm still Human," Amber answered, a hint of hurt in her voice. "Yes, I am tough. I have to be unemotional. Comes with the job." She paused, the length of her silence worrying David. "Just so you know," she finally continued, "believing in peace doesn't mean one can't fight against wrongdoing."

"A real paradox, isn't it?"

"How so?"

"Sometimes if you really believe in peace, you have to fight for it."

Amber grew quiet. David allowed the silence to be shared between them until the passing minutes became too difficult to accept. He wanted to be sure Amber was not slipping away. But what could he talk about? Before he spoke, the sound of scuttling caused them both to stiffen. David reached for his weapon.

Out of a small hole in the far corner two mer'ks appeared. Their lithe bodies undulated in and out of the shadows cast by the Humans' field lights as they slunk across the floor, their claws clicking on the hard surface. While not overly afraid of the Human presence, they remained wary of strangers. Narrow muzzles twitched as they sniffed out the intruders to their little domain. One approached David cautiously, all six of its stubby legs stiff, its fluffy striped tail bristling with apprehension. David let it sniff his hand, but it came no closer as it concluded there was no food to be had. As quickly as they appeared, the two small hunters were gone.

"I wonder how long pets will last on their own," David mused.

"Don't know."

"Did you have a pet growing up?"

"No."

David surprised himself with a chuckle at a distant memory. "I had a toupsu once. Hid it in my room until my mother found it. Scared her half to death. Dad wasn't too pleased. He really didn't like animals. I never understood why he built my mom the

307

stable for some kippers. Of course that didn't last long when she realized the amount of dirty work that went into pets."

Amber pulled the blanket tighter around herself and stared at the corner the mer'ks had disappeared around. "I understand. I think my parents would've been fine with pets. We just never seemed to have time for them."

"I always wanted a dog."

"Mmm."

"One like Sarge."

"You can't get over Natchua, can you?"

David shrugged. "I latched onto the stories growing up."

He faltered before managing to go into more detail. Details would include explaining how he was left alone much of the time and how the stories were a way for him to escape the hurt of his parents' dysfunctional relationship. Amber seemed to sense this for she did not press the issue.

"A dog would be nice," she agreed. "Too bad they're so expensive."

"Wonder if there'll be any left after this."

They grew silent again. David winced at the realization that the conversations kept returning to the current state of war and scolded himself for bringing it up. He shifted where he sat, suddenly becoming aware of something sticking him in the leg. Shining his light down, he noticed Amber's sword strapped at her side. She, too, noticed and reached down to unbuckle it.

"It's funny how this has become so much a part of me. I put it on without thinking."

She placed it in her lap, allowing David to study it.

"Do you use it a lot?" he asked.

"Not really," she admitted. "It's more a dress piece than anything, but it can be used as a weapon as needed. In fact, it makes a very good weapon. However, I don't carry it onto a battlefield – too many chances of getting in the way. It usually stays on Phantom's saddle."

"How long have the Candonians been with SIERA?"

"Darkracer's been with Dad…" Amber hesitated, as she realized the military slip. "The general…"

"Dad," David interrupted. "Let's pretend there is no war for a little while, huh? We're just two Humans having a conversation."

Amber gave a huff and complied. "Dad and Darkracer were working together before I was born. Phantom is Racer's cousin. He joined as a colt when I was seven."

"Hmm, I always thought he was older than that. Guess I'm not a good judge of Candonian age."

"He's mature for his age. Darkracer's forty, I think. He never told me. He shouldn't care. He's in his prime."

"Women don't give their age either."

"Thirty-five."

"Most women."

At this Amber gave a weak laugh and laid her head against the wall. The light-hearted moment passed all too quickly and David found himself growing somber with the concern of Amber's injury.

"How are you doing?"

"Feeling it but still here."

David reached under the blanket to feel her leg.

"Excuse me," he said as an after thought.

Amber said nothing. He could feel the damp warmth of blood soaking through the bandage. Luckily it was not bleeding heavily.

"Can you feel your foot?"

"It's a bit numb." Amber caught the worried look in David's eye. "I can feel it."

Her answer was reassuring. Now all she had to do was hold on till help arrived.

"What will you do when this war is over?" Amber suddenly asked.

The question caught David off guard. He had not given the subject any thought. After all, being on the front lines, what were the odds of one in his position living long enough to see the end? He remained silent as he tried to think of what to say, apparently remaining quiet too long for he received a light jab in the ribs.

"Hey, soldier, you with me?"

"I don't know. I mean I don't know what I'd do. I never gave it any thought."

"You could stay with SIERA. You're a good edition to the team. I'd hate to lose you."

Weakly she let her head roll back to David's shoulder. David took no notice as his thoughts remained on what Amber had said. It was a good idea. However, he felt slightly unsettled at the thought of spending the rest of his life in the military. It was as if there was something else tugging at him – some other calling that he had yet to discover. He was not ready to commit to any one thing.

"Maybe. Are you planning on staying with SIERA?"

"Mhmm. What else would I do?"

"What else do you want to do?"

It was Amber's turn to be caught off guard. She sucked in air between her teeth she tried to think. In the end she just shook her head.

"Don't know. There've been times I've wondered what civilian life would be like – even envied people for it, but I think I'd go crazy if I wasn't here."

"Why?"

David waited several minutes for Amber to speak. He could tell she was thinking things through carefully, fighting back the haziness caused by her injuries to find the strength to speak.

"Because here I can make a difference," she said slowly, her words succinct and direct. "Too many believe the military's full of people who just want to kill. They think we're all unfeeling brutes with our fingers on the trigger. That's not it at all. I believe soldiers are some of the most compassionate people there are. We show it differently, but how many people are willing to walk onto a battlefield? Risk - even give up their lives? For what? For other people, many whom we'll never meet. To defend those who can't defend themselves. It's always been what I wanted to do. And if I live through this, I intend to keep fighting against any who wish to harm not only our way of life, but the people who make up that life."

There were no words to follow. David just sat and pondered Amber's testiment. They had long since been the very ideals embedded in his own heart, though lately he found it difficult to feel anything. He leaned his head back against the wall, rubbing the tattoo on his right wrist as he often did when deep in thought.

An involuntary jerk of his muscles woke David with a start. He recalled experiencing the sensation of falling only to realize he had been dreaming. The instant his eyes opened, the memory of the dream dissipated. Only the sensation remained. Sucking in the cold air, he rubbed his face and glanced at the time. He had only fallen asleep for a few minutes but still felt the twinge of anger rising over his lapse in watchfulness.

Over three hours had gone by and it was getting to be late morning. David spent much of the time staring at the far wall, not really thinking anything in particular. His mind wandered to various times in his life, surprising himself with forgotten memories such as the camping trip with his childhood friend or the time he tried to run away from home at the age of seven – getting as far as the edge of the woods behind the house. His intent at the time had been to find the lost Telamierian gateway city where Natchua was first formed. He had worn his homemade Natchuan uniform and snuck out with the replica of Alsen's sword. Luckily it was his mother who found him and not his father. Strange the things one thought about in times like these.

312

David shook his head and turned his attention to Amber. The soft breathing at his side reassured him that she was still alive. However, he could not be sure of the severity of her physical condition. Part of him wanted to wake her but he found himself unable to interrupt her rest. As long as he knew she was breathing, he'd let her be.

Laying his head back against the wall, David took stock of the past few days, mentally running through the events. He was not sure what he hoped to gain by it beyond giving his mind something new to work on while he waited for help to arrive. Hopefully it would be soon. Even though he just looked, David glanced at the time. He wondered how long it would take. Nathan and the private should have made it back to the main group by now. Had something gone wrong? Had the Vairdec found them? Perhaps he should go out to check. But what of Amber? Torn between what to do, he decided to wait a little longer. The gurgling complaint of his stomach reminded him he had not eaten in some time. As carefully as he could, David shifted away from Amber to pull his pack out from behind him. Try as he might, he failed to keep Amber from rousing from her shallow sleep.

"Sorry," he whispered.

She said nothing in return. Instead she stared at him in a daze. Placing a hand on her forehead he could tell she was slightly feverish.

"How are you holding up?"

"I'll make it," she replied, sounding as if she needed to convince herself as much as him. "People survive far worse than a cut."

"It's a bad cut, though," David argued as he got to his knees. "May I?"

With a nod, Amber allowed David to pull back the blanket and examine the bandage. Even in the dim light he could make out the dark patches of blood that had managed to seep through the layers of cloth. The bio-sealant had not been enough to close the wound entirely. The heavy pulse of blood coursing through the femoral artery proved too much for the field bandages to manage. Luckily the artery was only nicked. If the Oxyran's blade had gone a fraction deeper he would currently be rehearsing what to say to a grieving father.

Amber didn't bother to examine her injury with the same care as David. Her gaze swept the room.

"We should probably not stay in one place too long," she observed.

"Hold tight," David said, ignoring the fact that he was arguing with a superior. "It won't be long now."

"Sure," Amber huffed, "long for what? Our side or theirs?"

"You can't move," David answered honestly. "Too much and you'll tear the cut wide open. You do that and it's all over."

Amber said something under her breath David did not quite catch. He caught her meaning just the same. She was not in the habit of coddling her injuries. She was tough, and while it was admirable, David knew this time it would be her undoing.

"I'd scout the area, but I ordered us to be locked in," David admitted. "I didn't want to risk unnecessary exposure."

"Two of SIERA's officer's locked in a civilian lounge," Amber grumbled. "I wonder if this will go in permanent records."

"Sorry, ma'am, but I wasn't going to leave your care in the hands of those I had with me." He rose to examine the wall panel. "I could break through the wall if I have to," he reassured. "It's your call."

"As much as I want to get back to base, we could wait a little longer," Amber grumbled.

David returned to kneel beside Amber. Before he could settle back against the wall, her hand shot forward to grip his wrist. He froze, having immediately picked up on the unwelcome sound of footsteps. A second later, voices became audible. David eased himself up to one knee, pushing back the rush of adrenaline as he reached for his gun. The language was distinctly Vairdec.

CHAPTER TWENTY

Though unable to translate the conversation, David began creating a mental picture of what lay beyond the wall in the main apartment. There had to be at least four Vairdec. They would be weaving among the furniture and tapestries like predators on the prowl, their low voices discussing what possible targets lay in wait for them. David fingered his gun in preparation.

A squealing cry grated on the nerves down David's spine. It belonged to the Vairdec's special pets. No doubt the larkrae's sensitive sense of smell had picked up a scent – a Human scent, Human blood. Mentally David began to run through the scenarios that would likely surround the battle to come. Where would he need to aim first? What direction would he take for cover? How would he protect Amber in the process? The low thrum of the Vairdec's voices grew in pitch and speed. Furniture scraped across the floor. Something tipped over to add a bone-jarring crash to the growing shouts and screams. David half-rose, but Amber caught him by the arm, motioning him to stay down. The screams were not only that of the bloodthirsty animals. They were Human.

As relieved as David was to know the Vairdec were not about to crash through the wall, he felt a wash of illness at the thought of the Human victims just beyond his reach. He could hear their pleas and knew they fell on deaf ears. How could he sit quietly and listen to that? Again he began to rise, and again Amber forced him down. She was right, no matter how painful it was to admit. It would take too long for David to break through and go on the offensive. Even if by some miracle he managed to enter the room alive, with no knowledge of the Vairdec's placement or exact numbers, it was a suicide mission. He would be outnumbered and gunned down before getting off more than a couple shots. It was futile to attempt anything, but forcing himself to stand down came as even more torturous.

The pleas grew intense until they turned to horrified screams. With the sickening whack of heavy metal against flesh and bone, the screams diminished by one. The cries bore through David's being. Even in the dark his mind's eye allowed him to visualize the whole brutal slaughter. How could he stay where he was? He felt cowardly kneeling there behind the wall. Another attempt to help ended with Amber's hand tightening around his wrist. In her eyes lay her own anguish. She hated the decision as much as he. What could they do, though? Their deaths would be guaranteed if they moved and the Humans beyond the wall would still meet the same terrible fate.

Sweat slicked David's palms and burned his eyes. Nervously he fingered his gun, while his heart beat hard enough to break his ribs. *Breath steady*, he told himself, *you know how. Steady.* The Human sounds of terror and agony mingled with the squeals of larkrae and the Vairdec's amusement. Footsteps suddenly added to the noise, coming straight for the wall. A few shots and the wall reverberated with the impact of a falling body. Instinctively David raised his gun in preparation to fire, but the wall remained unmoved.

All the Human noises ceased. David kept his gun trained at the wall, his muscles as tense as springs ready to let loose. If this was it, he planned to go down fighting. His hatred for the Vairdec had increased dramatically in those few minutes. As the time ticked by, he began to realize the Vairdec were moving on. Their voices trailed off to another part of the apartment. Something crashed in another room; then the voices grew even dimmer. Slowly David lowered his weapon. Every part of him was shaking. Lowering himself to a knee, David leaned against the wall. He let his breath out in a slow, steady hiss.

A crash threw him back, the wall trembling from the impact. Raising his gun once more, David prepared to fire from where he lay. Amber, too, held her gun at the ready while her free hand pressed against the wall as if to hold back the assailant. The crash came again, followed by the noise of rapidly digging claws. They could hear the larkrae's snarls as it raked the wall. David wanted to tear the creature apart with his bare hands, and if it got inside, he intended to. Any second now.

Amber's sword flashed from its sheath. Despite her injured leg she pushed herself up and jammed the blade into the small space between the sliding wall and its frame, adding a layer of security to the already sealed panel. Heavy boots beat the floor as the Vairdec approached. It shouted angrily as the animal continued to attack the wall. Dropping to the floor, it sniffed and squealed, creating a terrible ruckus with its high activity. The Vairdec halted at the wall, just feet from where Amber and David crouched. This was it. A hand ran across the paneling above David's head. Then, to his surprise, he heard the disapproving squeal of the animal and the footsteps began to recede. From further in the room came a questioning few words that the handler answered to in a gruff tone. The larkrae continued to protest as the Vairdec left the apartment.

Ten minutes of dead silence passed before David found it possible to convince his muscles to relax. Careful to conceal any trembling, he sat once more beside Amber. Neither said a word. Instead they stared into the dark corners of the room, allowing their thoughts to wander where they wished. Many musings passed through David's mind, but after nearly an hour he found himself surprised at his inability to recall any coherent thoughts during that time. Growing aware of his stiff muscles he shifted and turned his attention to Amber.

"Are you still with me?"

Amber gave him a weary look. "Hmm."

Placing his pack beside him, David pulled the canteen loose and handed it to Amber. Gently she pushed it aside.

"That's yours."

"So? Don't like sharing or something?"

"We all have equal rations. I have my own."

David stubbornly kept the canteen in front of her. "You need it more than I."

Frankly David figured any water he tried to drink at the moment would come right back up. The thought of what lay beyond the wall made him nauseous. Amber, on the other hand, needed to stay well hydrated so he insisted until she relinquished with a sigh and drank. Handing it back to David she gave him a slight motion with her head.

"You do that a lot."

"Do what?"

Amber reached over to take David's wrist. As she did, he became aware that he had begun subconsciously rubbing his hand over the tattoo.

"Nervous habit, I guess," he said, feeling to his surprise a hot wash of embarrassment.

"So the Hawk is a nervous animal, huh?"

"I think I have reason to be."

Amber pressed her hand into his. There was nothing suggestive about the act, only comforting, encouraging, for both their sakes. David found himself staring blankly at her hand, the extent of the recent devastation washing over him.

"What good are we?" he whispered.

"What do you mean?" Amber asked, drawing her hand away.

"Putting our lives on the line? Defending those who can't defend themselves? I'm hiding here listening to people die."

320

Amber slumped back against the wall, her breath hissing between her teeth.

"So you think I'm a hypocrite?"

David lowered his head, shaking it slowly. "No. Not really."

With a huff, Amber rubbed her eyes wearily. "I suppose I might sound like one. But what choice did we have? There was no possible way to help them. You would never have made it out in time. We would have only added to the body count."

David stared hard at the wall.

"I know," he admitted, "but it doesn't make it any easier to accept."

"No, it doesn't."

"Let's just hope we can stay alive long enough to defend those who can be saved."

A heavy thud beyond the wall brought David immediately to his feet, gun in hand. Standing over Amber he listened intently to the sound within the apartment. Amber, too, drew her weapon, though she made no effort to move. The scrape of furniture grated on David's nerves. He hated all the hiding, all the waiting. Fingering his gun, he allowed the solid weight of the weapon to focus his mind and calm him in preparation for battle. A familiar curse bounced off the wall.

David relaxed. The phrase was distinctly Human, spoken as the newcomer stumbled upon the carnage left behind by the earlier Vairdec. As much as he wished to step from hiding, David remained fixed. There was no telling what the Human on the other side would do if surprised. The unpleasant encounter with the Faxon and his gang was still raw,

321

making it difficult to consider trusting anyone. Carefully he leaned forward to listen. More movement. The Human was not alone.

"You were right about smelling blood," the voice said. "Fia!"

With a sigh of relief, David holstered his gun. Amber did the same. They recognized the voice.

"Luckily I don't see the colonel among them."

David pulled Amber's sword loose so those on the other side could draw back the panel. Nathan appeared momentarily in the open space before being shoved aside by Darkracer who squeezed his head and shoulders through. Spying David, he blew through his nostrils with relief.

"Good to see you," David said, equally relieved.

"Right where I left them," Nathan replied as he wrenched his gun out from between the wall and Darkracer's heavy body.

"The colonel's hurt," David continued. "The leg's badly cut. I'm pretty sure it's the artery."

"So I heard," Darkracer said. He squeezed his way further in to look over Amber carefully. "Colonel?

"Hey, Racer," Amber greeted quietly upon seeing the worried Candonian's face.

"Thank goodness you're alive," he replied in earnest.

"The civilians?"

"We left them in the care of a refugee group headed for the deeper bunkers. When Darson and Boenhiem arrived with news of what happened I headed straight back here to look for you. Phantom and Yehgrett also came."

David shouldered his pack and did a last assessment of Amber's leg. He found the bloodstains worrisome.

"Took you long enough," he grumbled as he slung Amber's pack across his arm.

He did not intend to be so abrupt with the rescue team, and blamed the fear for Amber's safety for the rude approach, though neither did he apologize. Darkracer blew angrily, creating a burst of hot wind across the back of David's neck.

"Blame the Vairdec, not us. They're moving down from the north and we had to work our way around the back side of the district. We even had to engage a patrol."

"You make it sound like a bad thing," Nathan answered haughtily.

Yehgrett chuckled his shared sentiment. "Looks you saw action also," he replied as he scanned the room.

"Heard," David corrected. "To be honest, I'm glad I didn't see anything."

"It must've been real pissin' not to help these people?"

David was thankful that he could neither see nor get to Nathan at that moment since the wall separated them. He sucked air through his teeth, attempting to calm himself. He didn't need to hear those words despite agreeing with them. Amber, too, appeared slightly annoyed by the comment but was too weak to respond. Instead she just shook her head as she pulled her sword from David's tight grip and sheathed it. David lifted her into his arms. Darkracer came to their defense against Nathan, backing from the wall to glare over his shoulder.

"With the colonel injured, I'm grateful Malard had enough sense to stay where he was. If they were the same Vairdec we came across they would have been far too many for one person to effectively attack, especially from this position." Darkracer motioned toward the small opening in the wall with his head. "He would have given up not only his life but Colonel Riechet's while providing no change to these victims' outcome."

"Thank you," David answered as he stepped into the room, giving Nathan a glare of his own.

The youth pulled back. "Stop the snap. I was the one that locked you in, remember? I know you couldn't do anything." He turned away, scanning the room. "Fia," he said under his breath. "Where'd they come from?"

"Other apartments, probably," David answered. "The Vairdec were searching this room when they were dragged in."

Though grateful for the thought of departing, David felt sickened by having to view the carnage. The remains of three women and an elderly man were strewn through the confines of the apartment, blood coating furniture, walls, even the ceiling. Gingerly he stepped around the woman lying against the movable wall, feeling a bit uncomfortable at having to walk through her blood. Chancing a quick glance down, David's stomach churned. Her features were nearly nonexistent from the larkrae attack.

Pulling his gaze away from her one remaining eye, David focused his attention to the daylight streaming in through the large transparent wall. Though pale – dimmed by the hazy remains of drifting smoke – it instilled a sense of renewal in him. As much as he thrived in the deep shadows of night, the long days of viewing nothing but darkness left him thankful for the simple appreciation of the view of sunlight. As quickly as the observation was made, David found himself drawn back into the moment.

"The team," Amber stated quickly to avoid focusing on the bloodied corpses. "Are all accounted for?"

"They are," Darkracer said. "But let's not worry about them. All I want to do is get you to safety."

"What about other people?" Nathan asked. "Could there be other survivors?"

Darkracer shook his head. "Not likely."

"Do a bio-sweep anyway," Amber ordered. "Scan the residence as we go."

"I prefer to just get you back safely," Darkracer replied as he knelt, allowing David to place Amber across his back.

David jumped into the saddle behind her to ensure she stayed aboard.

"It wouldn't hurt to check, though," he insisted, the thought of listening to the people dying still grating on every nerve.

Yehgrett and Nathan hurried from the apartment to start their sweep of the surrounding apartments while Darkracer made his way carefully to the door. From atop the Candonian, David found himself forced to duck to keep his head from bumping the ceiling. The door proved a particular challenge, but luckily construction took the tall Celehi into consideration, and doorframes were cut to a standard of nearly three meters. It allowed for just enough clearance for the riders who lay across Darkracer's neck.

In the hall they found Phantom standing guard, his body quivering as he listened to distant Vairdec activity. Upon seeing Amber's state, he gave a soft squeal of alarm and pressed his velvety muzzle against her cheek. He nickered softly, communicating in a way only he and the colonel fully understood. Reaching out with a weak hand, Amber gave him a gentle pat.

"I'll be fine," she reassured.

"We better hurry," Phantom said. "There's no telling how many more are on the way."

She and David rode through the hall, heading south along the upper level for as long as the team could safely manage before coming at last to the nearest staircase. With the stairwells built for only Humans and similar bipeds in mind, the path proved too small to ride the Candonians down. Though Amber was a relatively easy burden, the earlier excursions, the stress and the heavy air all worked together to leave David shaking and panting. Once free of the stairs, Darkracer stepped close and lay down. Again David carefully set Amber across the saddle before swinging up behind her. Unashamedly she leaned against him, allowing him to support her as Darkracer climbed to his feet.

No civilians were found on the way, coming as a mixed blessing in David's mind. He wanted to save as many people as possible, but knew they would slow the return trip. He could not be sure how much longer Amber would hold on. Nathan and Yehgrett climbed more hesitantly onto Phantom's back. Neither of them knew how to ride. Only the urgency for speed convinced them to climb aboard. With daylight revealing the streets they needed to traverse, there was no time to lose.

David closed his eyes and allowed Darkracer to find his own way through the dark lower recesses of the complex. With nothing urgent for him to do, he began wondering how he managed to get himself into the predicaments he did. Misfortune liked to haunt him. This was supposed to be a simple salvage operation. Simple. Was there ever anything simple in a time of war? So much had happened to him in so little time. So much - and so little of it was good. Could this really be his lot in life? Was he destined to witness first hand all the horrors a lifetime could possess? Why him? What could he do about it? So far it felt as if he had accomplished very little.

He could not tell how long his mind drifted through these depressing questions before a blast of arctic air slapped him back to the present. The chill of the outdoors constricted his breathing and he found himself tightening his grip around Amber. Even mid-spring in Karnoss felt like winter back home in San Terres.

"Hold on," Darkracer said over his shoulder.

Beginning at a trot, Darkracer steadily increased his speed until he and Phantom were racing

through the rubble-strewn streets back toward the safe
confines of the bunkers.

CHAPTER TWENTY-ONE

The warmth and strength of Darkracer's shoulder felt comforting to David as he pressed his back against the Candonian, watching the medic ward spring to life upon their arrival. Thankfully the trip back had gone without incident. Amber wavered in and out of consciousness along the way, relying on David to protect her as they traversed the city. David still felt the twinge of chivalry that rose in him during the ride. As the gallant knight he valiantly carried the fair maiden to safety. A chuckle escaped him as he shook his head. What a dreamer. What a fool.

The sound of David's chuckle drew Darkracer's head around. The Candonian found nothing humorous in the present situation and boldly spoke his mind.

"It's not about her injury," David reassured.

He pushed off from Darkracer's shoulder and walked away. Why did the moment have to be ruined like that? There were so few thoughts left to lighten David's spirits, could he not have at least one brief moment? Not in war. Shaking his head despairingly,

David made his way toward the command center to give General Riechet his report of the recent events. Arriving at the entrance, he held back, waiting and watching for the proper moment to interrupt the general's work.

Riechet stood over the central graphics table, its three dimensional imaging depicting the city of Karnoss in surprising detail. With him stood Yehgrett and three individuals David did not recognize, all clearly civilians by their clothing and mannerisms. The two men were around Riechet's age, though one had disregarded his physical health, having grown rather portly from opulent living, David was sure, as he observed the rich fabric of the man's suit. The other was trim and modestly dressed. At his side fidgeted a young woman with short brown hair and large eyes. Their conversation seemed centered around the resort district and they motioned often to the towers of the Piña Dorado. With a nearly unnoticeable motion of his hand, Riechet zoomed in on the towers.

"You may come in, Malard," he said without looking away from the map.

David hesitated a brief second as he tried to understand how Riechet knew of his presence without looking up. Stepping across the small room, David stood at attention by the general's side. He saw from the corner of his eye the civilians stop their conversation to look him over, the young woman taking more time than the men. A moment later Riechet straightened to turn his attention to David.

"The report, sir," David said, handing off the data.

Riechet took and pocketed it with an approving nod. "Thank you, Malard."

"I knew a Malard once," the portly man said. "Quite some time ago, when I was just starting to work for the Tavishon Corporation."

"My father, Benjamin Malard, worked for the company."

"Ah yes," the man said with a nod. "Vice president if I remember correctly."

"For a time, yes."

"Didn't he die?"

"Yes, sir, he did."

"I'm sorry."

"Enzio Shikoa," Riechet introduced, motioning with his hand toward the gentleman. "Tavishon's corporate manager."

"Shikoa," David acknowledged, giving the man a brief handshake.

Riechet nodded toward the other two. "Calvin Jomiyo and his daughter Sherlain." David shook their hands as well, oblivious to the slight blush that came to Sherlain's cheeks. "They're architects we found that may be able to help in our next operative."

David turned his attention to the map though kept his questions respectfully to himself. He already knew that Riechet was planning strategic offensives for various places around the city. What remained unknown to him were the specifics of the attacks and their exact locations. It surprised him to see the resorts being a part of the plan.

"We're fortunate so many professionals survived," Riechet went on to say. "I considered bringing down the resorts from the beginning and now have the intellectual support needed to pull it off."

At this revelation, David ventured to question. "Bring them down, sir?"

"At least what we can of them."

David's brow furrowed as he studied the image rising before him on the table. Though not terribly sentimental, he found the thought of the Piña Dorado's destruction rather disappointing. With a cock of his head, he examined the building from another angle.

"How, may I ask, is this to be done?"

"There's a cistern beneath the south tower," Mr. Jomiyo stated as he focused the map on the resort and its underground system. "With this larger space underneath, we may be able to successfully compromise the foundation."

Reaching out to the image now dominating the table, David spun it slowly to take in all angles. During this he kept a wary eye upon Riechet less he overstep his privileges with the general. For the time being Riechet appeared content to allow David to consider the strategy and add input.

"Wouldn't they have considered a compromised foundation before the building of the tower?"

"The cistern was made after the tower was in place," Manager Shikoa explained. "The resort was originally tapped into the main mineral springs below the plateau, but since that is government property, they were competing with other companies. Building this," he motioned to the boxy outline of the cistern, "put the waters directly in Tavishon control."

"At least the portion that was pumped into it,"
Mr. Jomiyo added.

Shikoa gave a quick nod. "Yes. They
reinforced the tower with several support beams
through the cistern. It's quite strong." He paused to
check David's reaction. When he got no clear
indication of David's thoughts, he continued with his
explanation, a crafty smile appearing on his round
face. "But, there is a weakness. To make the waters
even richer, extra minerals are added into the cistern
and kept heated. The healing properties are
wonderful, but they have begun to wear away the
infrastructure. A few strong explosives on the support
beams should weaken the entire underground
system."

David waited to be sure Shikoa had finished,
letting silence dominate the room as he thought, his
chin cupped in his hand. Turning his gaze to General
Riechet, he observed a pleased look gleaming in the
officer's eyes. Yes, Riechet already knew all this and
more. He probably had the entire operation ready to
implement. What he wanted now was David's
thoughts on the operation. This was a test. Feeling
himself suddenly under pressure, David sucked in a
deep breath and straightened.

"Weakening the cistern's supports and
bringing down the resort are two different things," he
said thoughtfully. "There's more to this, is there not?"

Though he spoke toward the three civilians,
David's gaze trailed toward Riechet to see if he might
give some clue as to what he already knew. He gave
no indication of helping. Clearly the general wanted
to see how David thought through a problem. David

turned his attention to Yehgrett to find the Oxyran quietly working on one of his guns. Apparently he had already provided the needed information about explosives to the conversation and held no interest in going further.

"Is water still being pumped into the system?" David ventured.

Mr. Jomiyo shook his head. "With no power the backup generators are dead now."

David's eyes narrowed as he bent over the table. "Then how are the Vairdec getting power?"

"They brought their own power systems."

The sound of Riechet's voice caused David to straighten. Stepping away from the image, he prepared to concede to the general. Riechet held his hand toward the table to silently usher David back to it. He felt completely at a loss but conceded to his commander's wishes. After several minutes of pondering each possible scenario, David shook his head in defeat.

"With the underground systems and transits, the cistern looks too deep to do much damage. Wouldn't this entire area," he pointed to the layers of storage, transit tunnels and maintenance blocks between the tower and the cistern, "have to be detonated as well? Do we have that amount of explosive power?"

"No," Yehgrett admitted.

David looked at Riechet questioningly. The general stood with his arms crossed over his chest, watching with such a calm expression that David could come to no other conclusion than the fact that Riechet was just waiting for him to come up with the same plan as he already made. David's mouth ran dry and he struggled to swallow. There was just no way to do this. Knowing he had no choice but to come up with something, he spent the next several minutes in silence, trying to work through every possible method while doing his best to ignore the impatient stares of the three civilians beside him.

"Is there enough water in there to create steam?" he finally asked as he gave Riechet a sideward glance.

Was that a proud smile he saw tugging at the corner of the general's mouth? Riechet stepped forward to finally speak more on the subject.

"Better than that," he said. "Apparently the minerals they added to the water are rather volatile when combined with the right temperatures and chemicals. They rapidly expand into a gaseous form."

A bit of light sparkled in David's eyes. He was beginning to understand. With the support beams blown and the gas rapidly building up, the cistern would burst under pressure. It was brilliant, but almost immediately his stomach sank.

"What about the pipes? Won't the gas escape through the pipe system?"

"Not if we can block them off," Sherlain spoke up, pushing past her father to stand by David. "There are only two pumps, one on either side. We know the east one – that's the larger of the two."

Her voice trailed off as she stared at the model.

"Unfortunately we don't have the actual print of the building," Mr. Jomiyo said. "The second pump was placed after the original design. We know it's on the west side but no more than that."

"You said the waters are heated?" David asked after a moment of thought.

"Correct."

"Preeko Corner."

The group looked curiously at David.

"What?" Manager Shikoa said, his eyes widening in surprise.

"Preeko Corner." David leaned past the slightly blushing Sherlain to turn the model and point toward a corner of the west side shippers tunnel system. "When I was young, I and a couple other boys from the resort use to go down there. It was called that because the giant pipe that ran along the wall was heated and drew preekos out. We liked to catch them."

Sherlain gave a shudder, not liking the thought of a wall crawling with six-inch long fuzzy rock worms.

"I never knew what the pipe was for," David continued, "but Preeko Corner is right…" he traced his finger through the maze of shipping tunnels to the point, "there."

With some quick work, Mr. Jomiyo used the point to create a pipeline down toward the cistern. A broad smile quickly spread across his face.

"It fits. I think we found our missing pipeline."

"Good work, Malard," Riechet said, placing a hand on David's shoulder. Keeping his hand in place, he ushered David toward the entrance of the room. "I had a feeling you were worth adding to our discussion. And now I'm adding you to more." He handed David a datapad. "With the colonel injured, you're taking her place during the upcoming offensive. Your team's mission is outlined in the pad. Study it and be back here at oh-four hundred." Riechet stopped at the situation room's entrance and gently pushed David out. "Eat and get some rest. I'll need you alert when we're ready to roll."

Before David could speak, Riechet disappeared. For a moment David just stood rooted to the floor, unable to decide what he should do first. Looking down at the datapad, he drew in a deep breath.

"Here we go again," he muttered.

CHAPTER TWENTY-TWO

David yawned deeply and gave a shake of his head. The last fifteen hours had come and gone all too quickly. Besides the hours of studying his role in the offensive, David spent what time he could at Keven's side as his friend prepared to accompany Bravo's team back to the Piña Dorado. Keven reminded David that his mission was the safest of the four due to its stealthy underground nature, though David still understood the danger involved. After wishing his friend luck and a safe return, he had tried in vain to get some rest. However sleep maliciously continued to elude him, so at last he decided to make his way to the situation room early.

With nearly forty minutes before four o'clock, most of the other officers had not yet arrived. Only Mike sat in his designated place facing the center table, which glowed in a three-dimensional model of the northwestern half of the city. His eyes remained on a computer board set before him. David slipped silently into his seat across from Mike and took the time to scan over his own board. The list of his assigned Delta Company scrolled along the left side. Not much else was visible at this time.

"Welcome aboard."

David looked up to acknowledge Mike whose eyes remained on his computer.

"Thank you," David answered quickly.

He knew it was unwise to try engaging further in conversation. Mike obviously had far more important things to deal with. He continued to listen to whatever activity was on the other end of his headset, occasionally moving some information around as new stats came through. David watched him quietly, observing Mike's demeanor as the pilot worked.

"Copy that," he said after a while and leaned back in his seat.

His eyes met David's and David quickly looked away, not wanting to appear as an intruder to Mike's duties.

"Bravo Company is already in place," Mike explained without being asked. "They're having to drill through the rock above the cistern to drop charges."

Mike said the last part in a yawn, rubbing his eyes wearily before giving his stiff muscles a much-needed stretch. Finally he set his gaze firmly on David.

"Are you ready?"

"I suppose. I've never really done this before."

"Just remember, it's easy to forget you're safe when you hear firefights break out. Don't let it get to you. If you do, you end up forgetting to focus on what you're supposed to. Let the boys being shot at worry about getting hit."

"Understood."

David turned his attention to his computer board again, scrolling once more through the names of his team. He wanted to be sure he could account for every member. Delta's mission was simple – create a wall along the southeastern edge of the Quarshia Water Plant so Charlie Company could take out the main pumps and pipe lines, thus disrupting the surface water supplies the Vairdec were using. Riechet saw fit to engage in this second offensive against the water plant during the resort attack in hopes of confusing and splitting the Vairdec forces.

Most of Delta Company consisted of those considered good marksmen and were being designated as snipers. Nathan was among them. *What were the odds?* David wondered. Others were heavy ground-pounders including a couple Oxyrans and the Faxon Amber released from prison for the North Slope battle. Couple them with the son of the Pho'Max mob family and David knew the job before him could easily become a taxing one.

All too soon, the other officers entered. Captain Kailyn Gilpar seated herself on David's left, dutifully watching over Charlie Company while Captain Stoneman sat at David's right to watch Echo Company. Two medics stood to one side. David knew they were there to assist in giving medical advice as needed, but it gave him a foreboding feeling over the high likelihood of casualties. Turning his attention to his board, David cleared his mind of such thoughts and prepared for the task ahead. All he needed to do was watch over the team providing cover for those blowing the water plant. Captain Stoneman would see to those using the chaos as an opportunity to fire rockets down on the Vairdec transports stationed on the desert floor near North Slope. Mike saw to the team now almost ready to bring down the Piña Dorado's south tower. Everything was ready. Last to enter the room was General Riechet. He wore a clean uniform jacket and walked with an air of cool confidence. Standing near the center table he placed his hands behind his back and looked to each officer in a moment of silence.

"Ladies and gentleman," he said, his voice relaxed yet authoritative. "Let's go to work."

"They're coming in fast."
"Hold your ground."
"You'd think the resort would've taken them out."

"Cut the noise," David snapped as he switched his viewing to the eastern side of his company's line.

They had split into four smaller units spanning along the bottom and middle sections of a line of buildings facing the water plant from the east. At the moment Delta was nervously watching the lines of Vairdec heading up from the south away from the resorts. Bravo Company's mission succeeded as planned, and the Piña Dorado's south tower imploded due to its compromised foundation. At the moment there was little word on the number of enemy casualties, though it was already reported that the top of the tower struck a nearby complex, causing a short, but devastating domino effect. Everyone back at command hoped it would be enough to reduce the seemingly unending stream of Vairdec that swarmed Karnoss's streets. Now, despite being confused and dazed, the Vairdec's fighting rage exploded. Knowing Karnoss's army had set an offensive line at the water plant, they rushed northward in a frenzied desire to fight. It was exactly what General Riechet expected and wanted, hoping to catch the advancing enemy in the crosshairs of his waiting snipers.

"Tengali," David said, "stay focused south. Cover Arthurson."

The snipers holding position on the southern edge of the line of buildings held their attention on the Vairdec rushing 2nd Lieutenant Arthurson's position on the street just below them.

"Vairdec north. Vairdec north," came the computerized call of Quesree, a civilian Manogonite assigned to fly between the northern and central snipers of David's Delta Company.

"Heads up, Miloe," David relayed. "Keep those Vairdec off Charlie's back."

Charlie Company, under the eye of Kailyn Gilpar fanned out around the water plant to engage as many of the enemy as possible while they rigged the central plant to blow. If all went well, they would not only disrupt all water supplies to the surface, but cause significant casualties to the currently attacking Vairdec. Out of the corner of his eye, David saw General Riechet making his way around the table toward Kailyn. He remained calm and focused, filtering through all the voices of the companies coming through his headset via a small control tucked in the palm of his hand.

"Gilpar," he said, "send Frolnarak north to assist Delta."

"Affirmative," she replied before relaying her order.

"I can't get a clean shot," David heard Nathan complain. *"Do I go north or south?"*

"Hold your position," David snapped. "Let them come to you."

"But I could..."

David withheld any further comments he thought about the youth. He could hear Delta's leader Captain McTavish chewing Nathan out and ordering him to remain where he was. Let the captain deal with the situation. David flipped his focus to the southern units. His stomach knotted as the life status on one of his street fighters suddenly flat lined. He chanced a quick glance up at Riechet to see him looking across the table to where the medics stood. Though expressionless, the general knew of the death.

"Gilpar," Riechet said, his eyes still locked on the medical readout, "ETA to detonation."

She pushed information around her screen as she continued to listen to Charlie Company.

"Three minutes."

"Don't break. Hold the line."

David's attention jumped to his street fighters who he could see were drawing further from the buildings as the Vairdec swung westward.

"Arthurson," David said, "pull back. Draw fire northeast to McTavish."

He could hear Lieutenant Arthurson shouting orders to those around him to head back for the buildings. A signal at David's left hand announced another fatality. He found himself instinctively glancing toward the medics, spying two from Charlie Company also going down. A quick look in Kailyn's direction told him of her agitation. Riechet stepped up behind her and placed a hand on her shoulder. She calmed slightly at his encouraging touch.

"Malard, bring Delta's north unit around to flank Charlie. Send Toodat to assist the south streets."

After relaying Riechet's order to the northern unit, David flipped open communications with Toodat.

"Toodat, get to the south streets. Cover from the air." He looked at the readout of Delta's individual positions. "Arthurson, get your unit eastside."

"Tell that to the mob."

David growled, vaguely aware that Riechet's eyes had turned his direction.

"Pho'Max," David snapped, "do as ordered. Draw the Vairdec east."

Before he could hear any argument, Toodat's voice screeched over his headset in a stream of Manogonite curses.

"Toodat, what's your status?"

"They not supposed to."

"Toodat!"

"VY-Crafts. VY-Crafts."

David's throat tightened as his heart raced ever faster. "Positions. Where…"

The sound of roaring engines cut him off. His attention shot to the general for support. Aircrafts in the area came as a variable they had hoped to avoid. The operation's timing coincided in large part with a sizable storm blowing in from the north. While the buildings provided enough cover for those on the streets, flying in the high winds would be terribly risky. Apparently the Vairdec either did not know this or, more likely, did not care. Riechet's eyes narrowed, but he still showed no signs of panic.

"Soerin," he said in an even tone, "link to all company leaders. Follow those birds."

"Yes, sir."

Mike's hands flew over his board as he reconfigured his tasks, tapping into spy rigs set prior to the attack.

"Malard, pull the snipers down. Everyone stay out of the open. Gilpar, ETA."

"Sir, estimated 60 seconds to blow."

"Malard, swing full Delta north. Force the Vairdec's flank around to Quar 3."

David immediately obeyed, relaying the information to the unit leaders and hoping their teams still had enough sense to listen. He could hear the heat of battle out on the street as he spoke with Arthurson. The unmistakable roar of a Faxon drowned out the lieutenant's last response.

"Say again," David said.

"We need cover."

With the snipers evacuating their positions from higher up in the buildings, providing cover would be near impossible for a while.

"Toodat, Quesree," David called. "See what you can do to help Arthurson."

"Bring them to me," Nathan's voice cut in. *"Come on. Bring them here."*

David made a fist as he noticed Nathan's position had not moved.

"Darson," he snapped, "get out of the building."

"Bring them here," came the stubborn response.

A scream of engines whirred through the headset. A second later came the rumbling sounds of an explosion. For a second David worried that Nathan's building had been attacked, but after a quick check of life statuses, confirmed that the maverick sniper was still in one piece.

"Detonation successful," Kailyn reported.

Regardless of the feelings within the room, no one took the time to celebrate. Riechet's demeanor never changed. He continued to watch in silence – listening, watching, waiting.

"One bird down," Mike announced. "Explosion knocked him. Three birds still up. Pulling west and low. Wind factor increasing. They won't be able to fly down Quar 2 or Maji."

Mike traced the board in front of him with his finger, his movements appearing on the center map as green lights running down the indicated streets.

"Gilpar," Riechet said. "Begin moving your team along Quar 2 to Strausse."

"Rocket launched," Captain Stoneman said, still following Echo Company's attack on the transports below North Slope. "Air's grown hot."

Riechet lifted his eyes to the captain without shifting from his position. "Is there time for another launch?"

"Negative. Rock shelf compromised."

"Pull out. Head south to join Charlie."

David kept his head down as he focused on his company's various positions. Delta's leader, Captain McTavish, had managed to make his way up to Nathan and was keeping an eye on the rest of the team from his vantage point. David still advised against it but reminded himself he was not in the field. Hopefully the VY-Crafts would remain at bay. Those on the ground had, as Riechet ordered, pushed the Vairdec down Quar 3 in time for the large explosion on the east side of the water plant. With many underground lines traveling nearby, the street burst from the impact, killing many of the enemy soldiers trapped on its surface. Now they fought against the rushing water from broken water mains, slowing their progress and giving SIERA's forces the opportunity they needed to do as much damage in the short time they still had before Riechet ordered them out. Delta's snipers from the south side of the line were about to join the street fighters pressing down the middle when David caught the general's order directed his way.

"Malard, send Delta's south unit around the Hub to flank the Vairdec pinning Charlie. Break Charlie out and head to Lynbrooke."

"Sir." David scanned his board as the little points indicated each soldier's movement.

"Tengali," he called, "take…"

The soldier's life status suddenly flat lined. David felt the heat rising through his body and fought through it as he pulled stats up on the next in command.

347

"Tenner, take Gevlick, Reequay and Gregor and haul it west. Break through to Charlie at Hub Q-7. Toodat, can you cover them?"

"Not in the air. VY-Craft!"

"Stay off River Drive," Mike warned. His voice suddenly broke through David's line to speak with Tenner who was rallying those around him to do as David said. "Keep in the smoke and have one eye on the sky."

"Toodat," David continued, "head north. Back up those on the ground. McTavish, get out of the building."

"On our way."

Riechet's calm voice cut in through the chatter. "Gilpar, send your northwest units east on Strausse. Start evac."

"Yes, sir."

"Malard, have Delta hold till Charlie passes."

"Yes, sir."

David could hear Delta scrambling to hold the line of Vairdec as they waited for Charlie Company to clear the area. Knowing there was little he could do to help, David kept silent, allowing those in the midst of battle to deal with the situation as they saw fit. As long as they did not break the line and retreat before ordered, he would let them be. It was a helpless feeling and David tried to busy himself with checking the remaining soldiers' stats and periodically glancing at Riechet to try and read any change in the general's demeanor. Riechet gave him none. He was focused, neither completely at ease nor overly tense. He shouldered his immense responsibility with poise and dignity, never forgetting the value of every life in his

348

hands. His eyes jumped between the medical readouts and the central map as he took in the status and needs of every company with an intellect far beyond what David could comprehend.

A voice directed to him pulled David's attention toward the soldiers sent to assist part of Charlie Company.

"We've broken through, but Vairdec are turning back. We need more cover."

"Toodat," David said.

"Coming in."

"Malard." David's eyes turned up to Riechet. "Have Delta's northern units flank Charlie and begin planned evac."

"Yes, sir."

"We've got you in sight," McTavish's voice jumped in, directed toward the returning members of his Delta Company who had just rescued the remaining members of Charlie. *"Take Quar-5 off Lynbrooke."*

After relaying Riechet's order, David kept silent to allow Delta's leader to give orders to those he could see from his vantage point. He and Nathan had been making it down from the building as ordered, but apparently were forced back up and over to the southern complex in the process. The unexpected event swung in favor of the returning Delta and Charlie soldiers who now benefited from the cover needed to escape the pursuing Vairdec line.

"Continue on evac," David said as he watched the soldiers' movement.

They swung south and east, heading toward the various tunnel systems. Nathan, McTavish and the Manogonites brought up the rear.

"Vairdec are in the tunnels," Captain Stoneman announced as he kept his eyes on Echo Company.

"Continue as planned," Riechet said. "Malard, have Delta's flanking members hold in Tunnel 55."

David instantly relayed the order to McTavish who pulled up short with Nathan and three other members. Though unable to see the other companies' soldiers from his screen, David knew Echo was fast approaching Delta's position.

"Cover for Echo," he told McTavish.

The time that followed seemed intolerably long, though only a couple minutes passed before McTavish's voice came through David's headset again.

"Echo is through. Repeat, Echo is through."

At the same time, Captain Stoneman was announcing the same to Riechet.

"Companies report in," Riechet ordered.

Those around the table checked in with their field officers to account for all the surviving soldiers. One by one they confirmed that everyone made it into the tunnels.

Riechet straightened a little more and gave a quick nod. "Lock the back door."

"Lock back door," David relayed.

"Lock back door," Kailyn echoed along with Stoneman.

Another painfully long interlude ensued as everyone in the situation room waited for the tunnel entrances to be detonated, thus blocking the Vairdec long enough for SIERA to escape to the lower levels. At last David heard what he wanted to hear.

"Door is locked," he announced.

The rest were announcing the same.

General Riechet gave a slow, approving dip of his head. "Bring them home."

With that he stepped through the situation room's door and disappeared into the main chamber. The medics began their calls to the medical ward to prepare them for the specific needs of the returning soldiers. David, Kailyn and Captain Stoneman continued to watch as the three companies made their way through the tunnels. Mike, too, stayed in his seat, looking for the first time very tired. He watched with the rest, though his Bravo Company already made it back. Finally all the survivors were safely inside the bunker systems. With exhausted groans, those in the room tossed their headsets on the boards in front of them and stiffly rose. Kailyn gave Mike a cursory glance as she headed for the door.

"Where did those VY-Crafts go?"

"Winds must've gotten too strong," Mike said. "It sounds like one almost struck a building and they all headed back over Tralex."

"Too bad it was just *almost* struck a building," David replied.

Captain Stoneman gave a huff. "And heading over Tralex disrupted Echo's mission."

"Did they get anything?" Mike asked.

"One transport and a couple skiffs."

"I guess that's better than none."

David gave a slight smile at the glimmer of Mike's unending optimism. Glancing at the time he found it surprising that just over three hours had gone by. It felt far longer. Walking into the main chamber, he paused, his eyes fixed on a point a short distance across the room. There stood General Kyler Riechet, tall and proud as he faced the doors the returning soldiers were entering. Though exhausted, the general would not leave until every surviving soldier stepped through those doors.

CHAPTER TWENTY-THREE

Amber sensed her father stood beside her before she opened her eyes. With new arrivals in the medical ward, the choice had been made to move Amber to the officer's quarters again where a partition separated her from the rest of the group. General Riechet remained quiet about his feelings over the partition though as a father he appreciated the decision. He never liked mixing the sexes in one living space, but with limited rooms there was little choice. Thankfully his officers held high standards. Of course it did not hurt that they all knew and feared the consequences should any misconduct become known.

"How did it go?" she asked as she slowly opened her eyes.

Riechet seated himself on the edge of the bed and looked at his daughter with a tired smile. "All considering, as well as could be hoped. The Vairdec will find it difficult to access any water in the upper city."

"Good. What of casualties?"

"Ours or theirs?"

"Both."

"Well," Riechet leaned back as he thought, "we have little way of knowing the losses on the Vairdec's side, but the resort tower came down as planned. With few patrols out at that time we're hoping a good number were buried in the rubble."

"And ours?"

Riechet heaved a weary sigh. "Fewer than expected, more than I would like."

"As always."

"Ordering people to their deaths is a part of my job I will never get use to."

Amber slipped her hand into his. "That's why they love you. You care for the troops. They'll do anything for you. I think they all knew the risks, but for you they'd go anyway."

"Is this supposed to make me feel better?"

Amber gave a slight laugh as she propped herself up on her elbows. "Guess not."

"How are you feeling?" Riechet asked in an attempt to change the subject.

"Better. A little sore perhaps but not too bad. In fact, I'm not sure why I'm still in bed."

Riechet placed a hand on her leg. "You've been running a fever. That deserves bed rest."

"The fever came down this morning."

"That's good, but I'm not going to let any complications arise."

Amber lowered her voice. "You know you shouldn't give me special treatment."

"As a general, yes," Riechet said, leaning in to speak just as quietly. "As a father, no. However," he leaned back again, "if it makes you feel better, there's no activity at this moment. A portion of our army is recovering from the last offensive. Unfortunately we don't have the numbers to keep up a steady barrage. We'll keep to smaller engagements. I'm sure the Vairdec will be on high alert for a while. At this time you have no excuse to be up."

"I'm restless."

"We all are. Just let the leg heal. I'll keep you informed as needed."

Amber lay back on the cot. She still felt weak and tired but was not about to admit it, even to her father. With no room for argument, she complied with his request and soon fell asleep.

By the next day Amber's high fever returned. David found his moment of quite reading on his cot interrupted by a sudden burst of activity as two of the doctors hurried into the room to disappear behind the partition. Setting the reader down, David stared at the partition, listening to the hushed tones on the other side. He dared not interrupt though found his concern steadily growing. After all, it was he who stayed by Amber's side through her ordeal. He still felt a touch of responsibility to her. Riechet entered moments later, heading directly to his daughter. David remained frozen in his seat, following the general with his eyes. When Riechet reappeared, he sprang to a stand, refraining from calling out or approaching him in anyway. His movement was enough to catch Riechet's eye.

Riechet studied David, knowing the sudden stand went beyond military courtesy. David wanted to know what was happening and was too smart to demand any explanations. Weaving among the few cots between them, Riechet approached.

"The fever went up," he explained. "It appears there's a bit of an infection."

David's shoulders slumped as he took in the news.

"I should have done more to clean..."

Riechet cut him off with a raised hand. "You did everything you could. As I've said before, thank you for bringing my daughter back alive. Personally, I'm indebted to you, though that shall remain between us."

"Of course, sir," David said.

His gaze trailed toward the partition and Riechet followed the look. Forcing a smile, Riechet stepped away.

"She'll make it," he reassured, his voice strained from the stress. "She's strong and stubborn, just like her mother."

David watched silently as the general left. Sinking to the edge of his cot he tried to imagine what Amber's mother must have been like. He wished he knew more about her, but it would be unwise to ask Riechet to explain the details. Swinging his legs onto the cot, David lounged back against the wall. He picked up the reader again only to find himself unable to focus on the words. Though he kept it in front of him, he continued to watch the partition, hoping Riechet's last statement was not just a father's optimism.

For the next twenty-six hours, doctors and nurses regularly came and went from the officer's quarters. David found it difficult to concentrate on anything else as his thoughts continued to draw him back to the trying time when Amber's life rested in his hands. Though he believed Riechet's words over the fact that nothing else could have done, it did little to keep him from replaying every moment in the field as he tried to think of what more he might have achieved. David could not decide if guilt or simply concern for a friend aggravated him. Whatever the emotions, he felt deeply connected to what was happening.

At Riechet's approval, he kept watch at Amber's side from time to time to allow the medical staff some much needed rest. During those hours David let his mind wander to when he first met the bold, feisty redhead. Despite the anger he expressed that night, he had immediately held a deep sense of respect for her. She was proud, confident and smart – like her father. Much of his desire to stay at Amber's side stemmed from the admiration David held for the general. Kyler Riechet was a unique man; dignified and compassionate. He was all-military, yet retained an approachable demeanor. David found solace in his presence. The Riechets were honorable people, and for that, David remained loyal to them.

Upon the third day Amber still showed little sign of improvement. Few officers managed any amount of sleep even though the doctors remained quiet out of courtesy to them. David was not the only one who felt a sense of loyalty to the Riechets. Mike regularly woke at every little sound and Kailyn often hovered near Amber's bed. Even Toodat occasionally perched on top of the partition to check on Amber's progress. As much as Riechet admired his officers for their concern over his daughter, he finally decided to move her to his own quarters to ensure that his army's leadership got the rest they needed. The war would not go on hold just because the colonel was ill.

After the attack on the Piña Dorado and the Quarshia Plant, the Vairdec's patrols grew more vigilant. No longer were the citizens of Karnoss considered frightened, oppressed refugees attacking in small, unorganized militias. So far there was no news of extra Vairdec troops coming to Karnoss from other points on the planet. Doing the calculations, Riechet figured other, stronger resistances around the globe kept Arct-Ieya from sending reinforcements to their little city. Karnoss was a strategic place for a northern base with its inability to be easily ambushed by anyone other than those within the city but not strategic enough to risk pulling too many soldiers from the hot spots around major Celehi centers. That suited Riechet just fine. Even the increased patrols by the Vairdec already stationed above did little to faze him. Indeed, he foresaw such a reaction to his offensive maneuver.

With units searching for resistance along the streets and upper tunnel systems, Riechet focused his tactics on guerilla warfare. Small, elite teams slipped in and out of the city, killing any Vairdec foolish enough to blunder into their crosshairs. They held the advantage of the familiar territory, but the Vairdec still posed a formidable threat. They were cunning and eager to fight, showing no hesitancy to tear into anything that moved. As dangerous as the missions were, Riechet was pleased with the slow yet steady progress his devoted army maintained.

Days slipped by. While civilian refugees remained sectioned off from SIERA, the growing discomfort reached the ears of the military on a daily basis. David found his duties jumping between attacks on the Vairdec and checking the levels of tension among civilians. Luckily the CLE and remaining political body of the city retained much of the control despite the slowly growing fear. Rumors of impending food shortages were beginning, and the cramped living quarters often caused already frayed nerves to snap. Quarrels were becoming all too common. David concluded that going after Vairdec was the more favorable of his duties.

He had just returned one evening from a tunnel mission feeling rather good despite all the tension within the bunkers. Nine Vairdec soldiers lay dead from the attack David and his team achieved, making for the highest enemy casualty list in the last five days. Furthermore, Amber had pulled through. Thanks to the ingenuity and persistence of the doctors, she not only recovered from her high fever but would also keep her leg. She spent much of her time sitting in the main chamber, watching the activity and participating as she could in decision-making. Entering the main chamber, David greeted her with a salute before heading toward the officer's quarters. Amber returned the gesture with a salute of her own. Kailyn sat beside her, following David with her eyes until he disappeared through the side chamber. A smile appeared as she shook her head.

"What?" she asked, spying Amber's judgmental gaze.

Amber only rolled her eyes.

"Good news ladies and gentlemen," Mike suddenly called out as he sauntered across the room. "All the showers are finally fully working."

A cheer rose among the assemblage.

"And," Mike continued, "thanks to yours truly, the water is warm."

Another cheer. Mike raised a hand to quiet the group.

"However, with energy shortages as they are, all showers are to be no longer than five minutes each." A ripple of groans and mumbling ensued. "Anyone caught going over will be forcibly removed in their sweet nothings."

Amber shook her head at the amused chuckle that came from the pilot. A signal from his comlink drew his attention from his announcement. Without a word he left the room. Amber watched him exit, curious as to the nature of the call. A bit of frustration began to build in her. She was used to knowing everything that happened around the bunkers. The nature of his response to the call indicated that it was an official order. She hated being kept in the dark.

"Well," Kailyn mused, breaking into Amber's brooding, "there's a few soldiers here I hope lose track of time."

"Kailyn Gilpar!"

She just smiled at Amber. "Think Mike would pull you out?"

"He wouldn't dare." She paused to consider it. "Though I think I'll take four minute showers."

Another signal came through, this time from Kailyn's comlink. Glancing at Amber, she rose slowly, the playful banter lost.

"What is it?" Amber asked quickly.

"The general's calling a meeting."

"Without me?"

Kailyn shrank back from the severity of Amber's tone. "I don't give the orders. All I do is follow them."

Amber said nothing in response. Instead she struggled to rise. Her leg was still numb and soon she collapsed back into her seat.

"Fia," she said under her breath.

"I'm sure the general will fill you in," Kailyn reassured.

"If not, you will."

Kailyn held her hands up as she backed away. "Only if the general allows me to. He outranks you."

Amber gave a frustrated grunt and waved her friend off. As Kailyn departed, David appeared and headed in the same direction. Amber first thought to call out to him. In the end she only forced herself to rise and, with the help of crutches, limped back to her father's quarters to wait.

David sat between Kailyn and Mike with Lash and the Candonians stationed across from them within the tight confines of the situation room. Riechet stood at the door, waiting patiently as De'oolay joined. Her movements were slow and strained from the pain. The injuries incurred during the North Slope attack sadly never fully healed. The shimmer indicative to Celehi skin had not yet replaced the pale, chalky look that expressed her body's continued stress. However, her eyes gleamed, her mind as strong as ever. She held her head high, still proud and elegant despite her confinement to a chair. Quietly she maneuvered herself close to the table to take control of the computer that sat upon it.

"When within the military wing during the time of the North Slope attack," she began, "I found success in retrieving additional data from computer units still in operation. According to the best intelligence available, one outer perimeter Spynix satellite was not discovered by the Vairdec. It orbits a further distance from Telamier with part of the year behind Ayzat, but we hold the ability to send a signal to it using the right frequencies. Possessing information on Vairdec tracking systems, I believe I can bypass their decoding abilities to send a message through."

The room remained silent as everyone considered the news. Spynix was a military system that, as the name suggested, managed secret intelligence gathering of deep space activity for the Telamierian armies. Though invented in part by Humans, it was Celehi owned. Only specialized, high-ranking officers within the Earthenian army maintained access to the satellites and their findings. Not used as a primary source of communication, the Spynix network faired poorly at sending long-range messages. While David wondered at this, he figured the incredible prowess of De'oolay allowed her to think of something. Anxiously he waited to hear what that might be. The others appeared just as eager for they leaned forward against the table. Undaunted by the intense and undivided attention of her audience, De'oolay allowed the information to scroll before them.

"No communication systems set in Karnoss can connect with the satellite. The systems at SIERA Headquarters hold the needed power to do the task - theoretically."

Mike shifted back and crossed his arms. "Theoretically?"

"Contact with headquarters became lost two days ago. No reconnection at this time."

"How long will it take to reconnect?" Darkracer asked.

De'oolay glanced at him with a faded shimmer of faint yellow. "Too long. The satellite will be too far within a few days."

"So who's going?"

General Riechet looked hard at the inquisitive Candonian.

"I'm afraid you are," he said, receiving a surprised snort from Darkracer as a response, "at least as transportation. A Human on foot will not be efficient enough."

"Granted." Darkracer gave a dip of his head before looking among the occupants of the room. "So who is the rider?"

David felt the following silence as a heaviness pressing against his mind. Something in his gut warned him as to the answer before any words were spoken.

"I am."

All eyes turned intently upon General Riechet. No one spoke. What could they say or do when the general had clearly made up his mind? However, the announcement came as a heavy blow. Darkracer finally broke the silence, his hooves scraping the rock floor as he shifted uneasily.

"Is that wise?" he bravely ventured. "I cannot see the reasoning behind the commanding officer leaving his army."

Riechet slowly seated himself beside De'oolay, appearing suddenly very weary, even sad.

"It would not be the first choice, but unfortunately in this situation, I am the only person who can contact Spynix. The system must recognize me. This is a mission I cannot instruct another person to perform. If we are to get a message to Celhara, I must see it through."

The uncomfortable, silent heaviness returned. David felt his body begin to ache though he dared not move and break the stillness. Moving only his eyes, he studied each face, determining everyone was trying to process the information, thinking through possible scenarios and formulating questions.

"May I?" Kailyn finally managed. Riechet gave her a nod. "What do we know of other people's attempts to contact Celhara? We certainly can't be the only ones who would try, can we?"

"Likely not," Riechet admitted, "but we have no confirmation either way. Because of that, we must assume we are completely alone. If others are trying, then we will lend our voices to theirs and hope that at least one makes it through. If we are alone, then we still must try by any means possible to call for help."

Lash slowly lifted his hand from where it rested atop his crossed arms. "Where be Celhara forces? Do they know our trouble?"

"Again, we have no confirmation, so must assume they do not know what has happened. At this time the possibilities are countless as to why we have not seen any response from them. They may simply be unaware, or they, too, may be under attack."

"Making a message to them pointless," Darkracer grumbled.

"Maybe," Riechet said, "but they being at war is pure speculation. We still have a duty to try everything within our power and not assume the worst. Furthermore, there is a chance that in calling the Celehi for help our message will reach other allies, such as Hardiban."

"Can it reach the Vairdec?" Phantom wondered.

De'oolay gave a slight shake of her head, too sore to manage more. "Not in reason. They hold no access to Spynix. Our allies will understand a coded message before our enemies."

Through the exchange, Mike remained uncharacteristically quiet, his eyes unwavering in their focus on the bit of table in front of him. David watched the pilot with equal intensity, noting the strain in Mike's usually calm features. It made David's heart beat a little faster as he began to fathom the seriousness of the mission. At last Mike spoke, his voice slow and steady, his gaze remaining on the table.

"To contact a satellite like Spynix will take a great deal of energy. The Vairdec have energy detection, do they not?"

Everyone looked to Riechet. David easily observed the tension building in his features despite the general's quiet mannerism.

"They do."

The news caused David's heart to drop. Now he understood Mike's unease. He turned his gaze away from the general, unable to look him in the eye. Dropping his hands into his lap he clenched his fists, listening with growing stress to the conversation. Darkracer, too, caught on to Mike's concerns.

"If the Vairdec can detect energy outputs, it will lead them straight to headquarters."

"Yes." Riechet's voice remained deceptively calm.

Kailyn looked between Riechet and Mike with worry growing in her eyes. "But that would mean they would attack, correct?"

Riechet responded in his calm, even tone. "Most likely."

"Energy waves of headquarters will bring many," Lash said. "Their army will attack in full."

Riechet leaned forward to place his hands, palms down, upon the table. "It is a likely scenario."

"Can Valor Peak withstand a full attack?" Kailyn asked.

No one seemed ready to answer such a question. David's stomach knotted as he waited for Riechet's inevitable response.

"Not likely."

Darkracer gave a violent toss of his head, his hooves clattering loudly in the confines of the room as he stepped back in a sudden fury.

"This is a suicide mission, isn't it?"

"Racer," Riechet said, his voice gaining a touch of authority, "control yourself."

"We have to think of another way," the Candonian continued. "You cannot go, not with that risk."

"Everything has already been considered. We need to take advantage of this opportunity. I am the only one who can, so it is my duty to take on this mission, regardless of the risks."

"Your duty is to this army."

"Racer, stand down."

"You are the leader of this army. You cannot leave."

General Riechet stood with such speed and force that his chair toppled over. The rest in the room shifted back in shock as the usual passive nature of the general was suddenly replaced by a fierce, authoritative power. He glared at Darkracer with fire in his eyes, his hands now fists upon the table.

"Darkracer, I order you to stand down now!"

Darkracer took a step back, his head held high on a stiff neck, his body rigid. He gave a stomp with his hind foot, but said nothing more. General Riechet continued to hold his position over the group, his posture clearly stating his resolve in the matter.

"We all have our duties to this city and our planet. I cannot, nor will not, be exempt. If I am the means to a possible end to this conflict, then I will do my part regardless of the sacrifice, just as each of you have pledged to do. I admit it is not an ideal situation, but it is one that cannot be avoided. This is not a guaranteed suicide mission and I intend to use all the caution I can and use whatever means within my power to return safely. Now I have brought you here to tell you what will happen, not ask your permission." Riechet relaxed and placed his hands behind his back. "I will prepare each as needed in order to see that this army continues functioning properly in my absence. Under proper military standards, leadership will fall to the next highest rank."

David noted a cloud of grief fall across Riechet's features. He knew that it would not be long before Riechet faced the most challenging moment of his departure.

CHAPTER TWENTY-FOUR

"How do you feel?"

Amber had grown familiar with the question, as it seemed to always be the first words anyone asked her. She had begun to take little notice of it, until now. This time she gave it full attention as she detected the strain in her father's voice. The question went beyond the immediate concern for her wellbeing. Sitting up, she attempted to prove her answer with action.

"I should be back to normal in a few days."

Kyler Riechet sat beside his daughter and placed a hand on her knee. "You let the doctors decide that one. And no ordering them around. You may know your job, but they know theirs. You won't need to be in the field for a while."

"Perhaps, but..."

Riechet raised a finger to stop Amber's argument.

"Listen to them," he said.

A minute passed in silence. Amber studied her father's behavior with a well-trained eye. He had something more to say and was having trouble saying it. When he spoke, it was obvious he fought to keep his voice steady.

"I am placing you in charge of SIERA."

Amber felt her body flush with sudden emotion. Her mind throbbed for a couple seconds before she brought herself back under control. However, her heart continued to pound madly while her limbs grew numb and shaky. Few reasons existed for an officer to hand over command. Her father would not say this unless a good chance existed in him not living much longer. She wanted to speak only to find the words catch in her throat. She sat in numb silence as her father continued.

"In order to send a distress signal to Spynix I'll have to return to Valor Peak. While I'm away, you have full control. We'll need to do an official sign over of power so if I do not return there will be no question. You are to share leadership responsibilities with Lt. Colonel Py'guela, but if he does not make it, Commander Soerin will be your second. I want you to treat him as an equal. Even if you are the official commanding officer, never think you're above council."

"Dad." The word was forced out through a tight throat.

"I'm confident you'll know what to do," Riechet forged on despite his growing emotion. "I've taught you all I can and you have the skills needed."

"I…"

"And don't try to be stronger than you are. Know your weaknesses as well as your strengths.

Rely on others to fill the gaps, but do not forget who and what you are. I know you'll get through this."

"No. Dad, general, I…"

Amber struggled between the pain of her personal feelings and the duty she held as a military officer. She knew she should not argue, but this was not just her commanding officer, he was her father – her only family.

"If all goes well, you'll not have to worry about this."

"No."

"I do intend to come back."

Riechet spoke truthfully, though both he and Amber knew the odds were stacked heavily against him.

"I should be the one going," Amber choked.

Riechet placed a tight grip on her hand. "You don't have the clearance for Spynix. Even if you did, you haven't the strength yet."

"In a few days I'll be…"

"We don't have the time."

"The general shouldn't be…"

"Amber." Riechet's voice was firm, causing Amber to grow silent and look for the first time into her father's eyes. She saw the struggle embedded in them. Grief formed in the words he spoke.

"I'm afraid I have to do this. You have a long life ahead of you and this unit needs you as much as they need me. It's my turn to go. If I'm meant to return, I will, but for now…" He faltered. Even in the dim light Amber could see his eyes glisten with growing tears. Blinking them back he drew his daughter into an embrace. "I love you so much. I'm so proud of you. Never forget that."

Amber felt her countenance collapsing. In her father's arms she was once again a helpless little girl. She clutched him tightly, letting a single tear fall.

"I love you too." A heat rose in her. "You'll come back. You're going to come back. Everything's going to be okay."

Riechet drew her back to arms' length to look upon his daughter with love and pride. "I sure hope so."

A soft rustle turned their attention to watch David step up to the doorway. He kept his head low, his body slightly turned away, feeling awkward at the interruption.

"Forgive me, general, I…"

"Come in, Malard."

Breathing deeply, David stepped into the room. "Sir, I request permission to join you."

Riechet refused to answer right away, causing David to second-guess his decision to come forward at all. He glanced over at Amber for some hint of a reaction, though she just stared back with the same grief she expressed toward her father. After some time in thought, Riechet drew in a long, slow breath.

"This is a very high risk operation," he said. "I'll be walking right into heavily patrolled territory. The signal will alert the enemy. I will not order anyone to go that is not vital to the mission."

David stood tall, determined to follow through with his decision. "I understand the risks, sir, and with all due respect, I believe that I am vital. No soldier should go on a mission alone – even with

Candonians. It would be good for someone who can carry a gun to watch your back. Phantom already agreed to join the mission. Sir, I'm alone. I have no connections to anyone. If I don't make…" He faltered, looking between the Riechets as he considered how best to proceed. "In any case, my ability to fight if the need arises can increase the chances of a successful mission."

Amber glanced hopefully at her father. David presented a very convincing argument. As grieved as she was at the thought of her father taking on such a dangerous mission, hope rose with the idea of him having backup. Riechet, too, understood the value. With a thoughtful nod, he stood to step up to David.

"You're point is noted and your service is accepted. However, I emphasize this is a mission I do not order you on. You go of your own free will."

"I understand, sir."

A smile replaced the hurt on Amber's face. David tried to return it only to find himself too tense. Despite his conviction his heart still raced.

"Very well," Riechet said. "Considering you will be accompanying me, it would only be fitting to provide you with the proper attire. Come."

Riechet waved David over to a corner of the room where a large case sat beside Darkracer's saddle. Amber watched from the bed as her father drew back the lid and removed a brimmed hat. Handing it to David, he proceeded to remove other clothing items including jackets, slacks, boots and gloves. David turned the hat over and over in his hands. Though light, it was a hard material, making it more helmet than hat. Nonetheless it retained a stylish appearance; a sleek design of such a dark purple it appeared almost black. Curiously he glanced at the other items.

"Exactly tailored after the official Natchuan uniforms," Riechet explained.

David recognized the look immediately but still found himself in awe over Riechet's words. While the first uniforms worn by Natchua were nothing more than an eclectic mix of clothing brought with the Founders from Earth, it took little time for them to adopt the usage of Celehi materials in order to create a distinct outfit based on the look they most commonly wore in the early battles.

Lightweight black shirts were worn under sturdy doublets of the same dark purple as the hats. The slacks, too, sported the color, and had a weave so dense and strong that blades had trouble tearing it. Knee-high black boots protected the lower legs, having just enough of a heel to fit comfortably against the stirrups of a Candonian's saddle. David admired the simple yet incredibly elegant look of the ensemble, running his thumb over the non-reflective gold of the doublet's buttons, intricately molded with the crossed sword symbol of Natchua. It was by far the most incredible uniform he ever saw.

And he knew the value of the uniform went beyond its physical appearance. Technological advancements transformed the uniforms into ideal stealth armor. The purplish material could deflect most laser strikes while the doublet provided protection from numerous projectiles. It also protected against the elements, keeping a person cool, warm or dry as needed. Turning the material back and forth, he watched the sheen of the threads bend and refract in the light. The color and nature of the material made it more difficult to spot in the shadows. He even heard tell that its refractive abilities caused it to thwart certain frequencies, making a wearer nearly invisible to sensors while heat trapping fibers confused heat seeking devises. Other field uniforms possessed similar qualities, but the Natchuan uniform continued to stand out as a highly specialized, if not expensive, outfit.

While one full set impressed David, Riechet produced two. He found words hard to come by as Riechet piled the pieces into David's arms.

"How did you manage to get two of these?"

"Two? There's more than this in my arsenal." He gave David a wink.

"How…" David began.

"Natchuan members tended to be succeeding generations of the original Founder's family lines. However, over time many have done away with passing the Natchuan legacy to the next generation. The line of Daniel Riek is an exception."

David already figured Kyler and his daughter could trace their lines back to Riek as their last name suggested. The man was a founding member of Natchua as well as Jonathan Alsen's closest friend. The lineage was a prestigious one even though, nearly two hundred years later, most people thought little of their ancestry. With less than seventy pairs of Humans making up the foundation for the entire Earthenian population, most people traced their lines to numerous family names. In fact, many of the original family names became so common and overused, that Humans began to change them either in part or in full. Even David's name changed over the years from the much longer Malaradienan. To keep alive a legacy of one founder's line was, as Riechet mentioned, an exception.

David was thankful they chose to be the exception. While Humans still looked upon Natchua with respect, being such a vital part of their history, little was done to keep more than the memory alive. After only three generations, Natchua officially disbanded in the wake of new military establishments. The roles the first members performed were delegated among various new units and government positions and the region of Earthenia became officially recognized as an independent nation. As Candonians slipped back into their native forests, Natchua, like the cavalry of old Earth, became nothing more than legends and history lessons. Until now. Kyler and Amber Riechet could easily be considered the closest living examples of Natchua. It was humbling for David to realize.

"It may be a little big," Riechet said as he placed the hat on top of the pile of clothes in David's arms, "but I think it will do just fine."

True to form, Riechet was correct. The sleeves and pant legs proved slightly too long, but with the boots and arm guards, David found them easy to adjust. With an extra pair of socks, the boots fit comfortably. The doublet was adjustable in size, so in the end, David looked himself over with pride, feeling as if the uniform had been made just for him. He chose to wear his own combat gloves, pulling them on as Amber watched. Her eyes narrowed as the bit of hawk tattoo visible from behind the sleeve disappeared under the black leather of the gloves.

"I've been told you were called the Hawk in the CLE."

She appeared not to notice as David winced at the memory.

"Hmm," she mused. "A hawk of the night. It kind of suits you."

Looking over at her, David could not tell if she was joking with him or speaking seriously. However, pressing matters forced him to push it from his mind. Riechet, dressed in an identical uniform, handed over David's weapons. Strapping them on, he stood at attention before his commanders.

"Do I look like Natchua?"

"Like Alsen himself," Amber toyed gently. "Almost."

Standing with care, she limped over to another case to pull out two black, cloak-styled coats. Handing one to her father, she placed the other over David's shoulders.

"Now you're Natchua," she said.

"You'll need these, too," Riechet added, his tone far less sentimental.

David took a pair of tinted field glasses from him. He recognized them, though they were not part of standard equipment. Like the vision-aid headbands, these provided him with night vision, but included an array of special sensors to read infrared, temperature variations, distance calculating and numerous other helpful qualities, all triggered through a connection with his intel-band. Knowing he would need to be constantly aware of possible threats among the canyon rocks, David was thankful the specialized glasses were in SIERA's arsenal. As he pocketed them, the moment of awe over wearing a Natchuan uniform faded. The reality of the mission hit home. Riechet collected Darkracer's tack and David followed suit with Phantom's. Without a word, the general motioned David to accompany him into the main chamber.

The Candonians waited patiently beside the command center. With them stood Mike, Lash and Kailyn. De'oolay wheeled herself away from the computers to watch as well. Amber limped over to stand at Phantom's head, instructing David on how to properly saddle him. Though her instructions were well stated, he was thankful when Mike stepped forward to assist. The mood remained somber as the last preparations were made.

Before long the Candonians stood in full uniform, their powerful black forms draped with blankets that matched the Humans' clothing. The saddles were attached not only by a cinch, but by a wide breast collar adorned with inlays of leaf patterns culminating into the Natchuan symbol at the center, all made with the same dull gold metal as the doublets' buttons. The masks gave the creatures a fierce look, and David could not remember a time when he had seen Candonians look so regal. He situated himself in the line of officers, standing closest to the Candonians. Before Amber joined the line, David watched as she slipped a sheathed sword into its place on Darkracer's saddle. The Candonian turned his head to watch, neither he nor Amber saying a word. David followed with his eyes as Amber joined her fellow officers. Moments later Riechet stood before them.

"Colonel Amber Adosia Riechet, I, General Kyler Thomas Riechet, commanding officer of Earthenia's Strategic Intelligence and Enforcement Regional Agency, hereby hand over active command to you until my personal authoritative order releases you or you are decommissioned by the Earthenian Military Board. Executive control lies with your command within this above stated division. If objection stands, senior officers of the effected military division may now speak."

No one moved.

"Commander Mikander Armon Soerin." Mike stepped forward. "You are witness to the transfer of duty."

"I am," Mike said.

"Then signify."

Mike pressed his thumb against the pad Riechet held.

"Captain Kailyn Shaleeah Gilpar." As Mike stepped back, Kailyn took his place. "You are witness to the transfer of duty."

"I am."

"Then signify."

Kailyn did as Mike had done and stepped back.

"David Jonathan Malard."

David heard only his name. The rest passed without comprehension as he thought of the event's significance. Luckily he didn't need to hear the general's words to know what to do. As he pressed his thumb against the pad, he watched Riechet closely, observing the strain that came over him. There was one more officer to address.

"Colonel Amber Adosia Riechet, do you accept your duties?"

"I do."

David's gaze darted to her, hearing the equal strain in her voice.

"Then signify."

Upon doing so, Riechet took a step back and saluted his daughter. She returned the salute, standing tall and brave before him. He turned to the other members, saluting them in turn, then, without a word, mounted Darkracer. David gave the assemblage a salute as well before pulling himself into Phantom's saddle and riding out of the chamber and into the dark corridors with General Riechet.

CHAPTER TWENTY-FIVE

Several winding miles passed without a word. All four remained lost in their own thoughts. While none of them particularly expected to die, they each knew the chances remained high. David felt more grief for Riechet than himself. The general had someone to go back to. He had a daughter that loved him and countless people who looked to him for guidance. Perhaps for that reason David felt so compelled to join the mission. Perhaps he was meant to see Riechet safely back to those people, even at the cost of his own life. He did not mind - not entirely - for he had no one to return to. If he was to sacrifice himself in the war, doing so in this manner meant more to him than a random fatal strike upon the streets of Karnoss.

With nothing but tunnel walls to view and the steady beat of the Candonians' hooves, David tried to picture himself alongside Jonathan Alsen on his way into battle. The task needed little imagination - dressed as he was, riding a Candonian and heading off to face the Vairdec. How strange that, after two hundred years, history was repeating itself.

The deep grinding of stone on stone drew David's attention to the black wall before him. He shifted in the saddle, feeling sore after the hours of riding. A blast of icy wind swept past, howling as it wound its way through the tunnel system. A moment later they stood outside, beneath of blanket of stars. David breathed deeply. The air moving along the Tralex Desert floor smelled refreshingly sweet after the confinement of the bunkers and battle scarred city. Stretching his stiff shoulders he gazed up at the heavens, awestruck by the effect. It looked so close, so peaceful. With Karnoss shrouded in darkness, the natural light from the millions of visible stars spread like a blanket of jewels over his head. Galaxies became visible to the naked eye and David wondered what troubles plagued the distant worlds. Were there others in his position, looking up and wondering if there remained any hope in the universe?

Pulling himself away from the hypnotic glimmers of distance space, he turned his attention to Riechet. The general, too, sat looking at the stars. His gaze remained fixed on the sky until the low, resonating thud of the door behind them broke the nighttime silence. They were now cut off from the world they once knew. An almost imperceptible shudder ran through Riechet and he closed his eyes, allowing his head to drop. Darkracer continued to face the trail though his ears swiveled back to catch the mood of his rider. Riechet reached forward to bury his fingers into the thick mane of his companion.

A second later he straightened and drew in a deep breath.

"Let us be off."

The long dark ride progressed in silence. Though David highly doubted the Vairdec would ever hear them, the mood remained so somber that it lent itself only to quiet contemplation. The Candonians picked their way carefully across the rocky terrain, often navigating large areas where not even a semblance of a trail existed. With the Vairdec aware of the canyon road, there was little choice in usable routes. Safety lay south of the canyon wall. Hidden by the mountainous rocks to David's right, slow moving air ships thrummed ominously along, carefully hunting the canyon on their nightly patrols. Their massive engines vibrated through the rocks and the occasional deathly pale light of their search beams washed close overhead. Never had David been so thankful for his attire. The uniforms served their wearers well, keeping them hidden among the shadows even when an unexpected ship swept over their location on its way further south.

Five hours remained before dawn when Darkracer and Phantom finally came to a halt in front of a solid wall of rock. There was no indication that a doorway of any kind existed and David gave the entire area an inquisitive investigation as he tried to see where their path would lead. It appeared they had reached a dead end. Riechet never looked about him, knowing exactly where he was. With his comlink he mentally sent a signal out ahead of them. A click then hiss announced the acceptance of the general's electronic command. Faint lines snaked their way around the hidden door as the camouflaged sealant broke apart. Moments later they were walking up a confining tunnel of stone while the secretive door sealed tightly behind them.

David pressed himself against Phantom's neck. The solid rock of the mountain closed in around him, giving him little clearance on all sides. From time to time he felt the brush of the walls against his legs and the ceiling remained just inches from his head. He would have preferred to walk, but the Candonians continued at a fast clip, covering the distance at as great a speed as they could manage within the tight confines. David shut his eyes. There was nothing for him to do at the moment and seeing how close the rock was around him provided no comfort. He focused on the surging power of the muscles beneath him while planning as best he could for the tasks ahead.

In an unexpected instance, the world opened up around David who took an audible intake of breath as he felt the mountain lift away from him. They had made it into SIERA's headquarters. David straightened with a satisfied sigh, opening his eyes to see where they had entered. The glasses adjusted quickly to the light, providing him with a clear view of the barracks' main corridor, its long line of doorways stretching into the darkness on either side. Only the soft emergency lights glowed along the upper edge of the walls, creating deep shadows around door crevices and side corridors. Nothing stirred. Even the air moved at a sluggish pace. Oppressive silence clung to every corner.

Darkracer wasted no time in setting off at a brisk trot toward the far end. Everything remained void of life as they made their way through the lower levels of headquarters, passing training centers, medical wards and mess halls and finally up into the heart of the facility. Only when the control center came into view did Riechet dismount. David followed suit, forcing his stiff leg muscles to move after the long hours of riding. They hurried past a few on-duty soldiers who only received a quick salute from the general.

"Sir."

Jylin Py'guela's response was instantaneous upon Riechet's entry to the control center. The Celehi stood at attention as Riechet crossed the room and took his place in front of the main computer. David held back with a couple of soldiers who followed them in. Though the bulk of SIERA had journeyed to the Karnoss plateau, eleven were left behind under the command of Lt. Colonel Py'guela. Over the course of the last nahm, they diligently watched the war's proceedings and gathered every scrap of information possible both on enemy movements and overall planetary controls.

"Py'guela," Riechet said, his eyes never wavering from the screen, "how's our security?"

"Holding, sir. Full lockdown still engaged and outer shields are operational."

"Very good. Take a team to manually check the blast doors of this level. Lock all down."

"Yes, sir."

Without questioning the reasons behind the orders, Jylin signaled his soldiers to their duties. David shifted back as they passed.

"Malard," Riechet continued, "hold a rear guard at the door. Phantom, stay with him. Racer, keep your eyes on breach status."

They took their positions without a word. David pressed his back against the doorframe. His fingers tightened around the grip of his drawn weapon. His eyes fixed on the bend at the end of the passage. Would the Vairdec come? What would it be like if they did? Would they storm the place or send in a missile? What would it be like to be blown up? David gave a stern shake of his head.

Stop this. Just do your job. Everything's fine.

Still, David found himself tensing for some unexpected attack to come from the very air. As the minutes ticked by, he chanced a quick glance at Riechet. The general remained focused on his task, his hands dancing across the computer's controls as various readouts and images flashed before him. David spent no time in trying to decipher what he saw. His task was to watch the corridor. Letting his gaze sweep back to the hall, David immediately took a defensive stance at the sight of movement. SIERA's soldiers jogged toward him. Observing the unit's movement, David relaxed slightly, noting that their jog, while hurried, was not driven by the urgency of an attack. Jylin pushed to the front and made his way into the control room.

"Confirmation of lockdown security complete."

Riechet paused to look back at the soldiers holding the corridor beyond the control room's door.

"Good. It will buy us some time. Hold the hall for as long as possible."

Jylin glanced questioningly between Riechet and the computers.

"What are we to expect, sir?"

"Anything."

Jylin took his place next to David, giving him a look of concern as he drew his weapon. David glanced back without saying a word. What could he say?

"Incoming."

Darkracer's sudden warning turned their attention for a brief moment. David fingered his gun in anxious anticipation and pressed his back firmly against the doorframe. Seconds later the walls shuddered. A low rumble followed. Before any of the soldiers had time to wonder as to this, a second, more powerful explosion jolted the corridor. They braced themselves as best they could as the floor lurched under their feet. Two more explosions followed in rapid succession.

"Malard, Py'guela."

David and Jylin hurried to Riechet's side.

"The Vairdec are breaking through outer defenses. Once those fail, they'll storm the place." He pointed to the screens Darkracer continued to watch. "They want survivors if they can get them. I can't leave until the message passes on from Kelapore. Py'guela, take half the unit and hold the Eastern-Three Corridor. The hangars are their likely breach point. Hold as long as possible then retreat to the plateau. Do not use the canyon. Do not allow yourself to be captured."

"Yes, sir."

Jylin turned sharply and headed for the door. David refused to make eye contact. He knew what not being captured meant. Suicide was mandatory over being taken prisoner – especially for officers.

"Malard."

"Sir."

"You are the last line of defense. Hold this corridor for as long as possible."

"Yes, sir."

David returned to stand with the five remaining soldiers. With a few short orders he organized them into two formations, one facing each direction of the corridor. They dropped to their knees or braced themselves against the walls as explosions continued to shake around them, growing ever nearer. David stood in the middle, continually sweeping both sides of the corridor. All he could do now was wait.

CHAPTER TWENTY-SIX

"Fire!"

"Get back!"

David heaved back on a nearby soldier's arm, nearly launching him backwards into the control room. The rest dove for cover as David slammed his fist against the door panel. He could already feel the heat as a wall of fire swept through the corridor. The oxygen felt as if it was being ripped from his lungs as the door slammed shut, reverberating angrily under the onslaught of sudden flames. David stepped back as heat began to seep through the metal causing it to glow slightly in the view of the glasses he still wore. When the last explosion hit, he half expected a missile to drop right through the ceiling on top of him. His ears still rang from the noise it had created. To his surprise, everything held fast, but only seconds later Darkracer frantically shouted his warning of the oncoming fire. Now they were trapped.

David looked to the general who shot him a quick glance before returning to the screens. With the rumbling in the corridor growing softer, David slowly backed toward Riechet, his eyes trained on the locked door, his finger on the trigger.

"Come on, Larrett," Riechet muttered.

The sound of his voice broke David's concentration of the door. He stopped behind Riechet's left shoulder and turned to watch the information scrolling on the screen. He could see their computer system was speaking with the computers on Telamier's moon of Kelapore. Though he possessed the knowledge to decipher further into what the computer was saying, the increasingly intense explosions kept his mind on the attack. The words and graphs flowed meaninglessly past him. He didn't care. It was not his place to follow the screens anyway.

"Sir," he began.

He longed for more instructions.

"Racer," Riechet cut in.

"Corridor's clear," he reported. "Systems are coming online."

"Malard."

"Sir."

"Keep them back."

"Yes, sir. Open it," David called to the soldiers as he pointed to the door.

They obeyed without question and followed their leader bravely into the scorched corridor. The fire passed through so quickly that very little smoke lingered. Everything lay in darkness. The intensity of the heat had knocked out the upper lighting. As David stepped down the passageway, the eerie blue glow of emergency strips struggled to life along the edge of the floor. He stopped at the bend in the hall, motioning his team to halt. Ensuring that an equal number of soldiers took position facing the opposite direction, David dropped to one knee and trained his weapon along the far side of the corridor.

Come on. Come on. David did not particularly want to face the Vairdec, but the waiting for something to happen proved intolerable. Hadn't Riechet managed to get a message off by now? What was taking so long? Logically he understood the difficulty in getting a message past enemy frequencies, crippled satellites and to a spy system not originally configured to take messages, but with the enemy pounding their location it was difficult to be patient. He chanced a fraction of a second to check the time. Gritting his teeth he focused once more across the hall. He did not like the time he saw.

All the explosions had ceased after the fire swept through. The Vairdec would not give up so easily. It must mean they were in the facility – hunting. But where? Since no warnings came from Darkracer, David assumed the watchful sensors of their security system had been destroyed in the bombardment of missiles. They were sitting blind in their own headquarters. With the wait David began to take deep, controlled breaths. It was time to focus – time to be calm. The fight would come to him.

"East side!" Phantom shouted, his hoof beats reverberating off the walls as he leaped into the hallway.

Those facing the opposite direction joined David to reinforce the eastern stretch of the corridor.

"How many?" David called back, never taking his eyes from his target on the wall.

"Unclear."

A couple of the soldiers shifted anxiously. Phantom stationed himself behind them, to keep watch over their heads. Holding his gun steady, David slipped his hand down along his thigh to retrieve a grenade. As he drew it up, he rose to a crouch and activated the device in one smooth motion. Shadows played against the wall and heavy boots echoed toward them.

"Brace yourselves," David ordered.

Leaping for the wall across from him, David threw the grenade down the hall. He chanced a quick glance at the menacing war masks of his enemy before dropping on his side and rolling to place his back toward the sudden explosion. Little heat emanated from the grenade as it centered its blast among the bodies of the Vairdec, though David still felt the shock wave as it shoved him against the wall. Bits of armor and Vairdec anatomy pelted his protective clothing. Using his feet to push off the wall, David slid around to face the onslaught and fired from his low position.

The blast succeeded in slowing their approach, but they were already reorganizing and firing back. David picked off the leaders to force those behind to struggle over the bodies of their comrades. A laser shot struck David's arm at a shallow angle, its energy easily displaced by his uniform's fabric. Another struck the hat whose helmet-like properties held back the searing energy of the shot. David ignored the near hits as he ceaselessly fired into his enemy's midst. Despite the barrage of firepower he and his team laid down, the Vairdec continued to slowly press closer.

Getting to his feet, David backed around the corner toward the control center door. He felt the other soldiers pressing at his back. Their stress was palpable, but they held the line, firing relentlessly. David stumbled slightly as the soldier against his right shoulder staggered from a hit. With a push from David, he righted himself and fought on. Another jerked backwards to slam against the wall and slide down, leaving a red smear behind.

"Down!" Phantom shouted.

Holding his position in the back, he dutifully watched every move the Vairdec made. One weapon in particular was on his mind. The moment he saw the flamethrower appear, he gave the order before wheeling around to take cover inside the open door of the control room. The rest of the soldiers flattened themselves against the floor just as the weapon's mass of energy swept toward them. For a second time David found himself enduring the wash of the flamethrower's power as it passed overhead. He was no more use to it than the first time. A boiling rage stirred in him. From his position he saw the boots of the Vairdec approaching. Having to evade the blast of the flamethrower, SIERA's soldiers had no way of holding the Vairdec back. The two armies were about to collide.

Leaping to his feet, David slammed himself against the chest of the lead Vairdec, knocking the alien's weapon aside. The alien's bone-breaking grip held David's own gun from finding its target. For a brief second David found himself staring into the mask of some grotesque creature. Hatred seethed through him. With his free hand he snatched the combat knife from his belt and drove it down past the body armor and into the creature's neck. Another Vairdec grabbed David's wrist, attempting to rip the knife from his grasp. David kept a firm hold on it while firing on another pushing his way forward even as the one holding his wrist forced David back. The soldiers fired into the swarm of Vairdec. The crushing grip on David's wrist slackened and he pulled free in time to fire into the mask of one bringing his weapon to bear on a soldier at David's side. It took several shots to fell the brute, costing David valuable seconds needed to evade an incoming shot from the opposite side.

A searing heat ripped through David as the projectile cut across his neck. The sudden intense pain blinded him for a second. Luckily, the close quarter fighting saved him from a hit in the face as the Vairdec intended. A solid object impacted with the side of David's head, sending his field glasses tumbling into the fray. He staggered, caught sight of the shooter taking aim again, and threw himself against the chest of the closest Vairdec while firing first. Staying pressed against his enemy kept the one behind from readily using his gun. David's shot proved better and the Vairdec shooter stumbled from the impact. Unfortunately the enemy's gun fired as he fell, missing its chance at a kill shot, but sending a four-inch metal bolt through David's right leg.

David felt his leg give way beneath him. He took a desperate step back to remain on his feet, receiving a second heavy blow to his left shoulder and chest. The impact sent him backwards, right into the arms of General Riechet. Supported by the general's strength, David fired three quick shots into the press of Vairdec. A gruff order from somewhere within the group caused the soldiers in front to lower their weapons and charge the two Human officers. A glint of steel swung past David's head to decapitate one of the lead Vairdec. David ducked aside as a spray of yellowish blood splashed across his face. Despite the unbearable pain racing up his leg, David knew he had to stay on his feet. As he reached for the wall to brace himself, a body pressed against his back to hold him up.

"Time to go," Darkracer said into David's ear.

David took hold of the Candonian's saddle and continued to fire on the Vairdec to provide Riechet with cover. The Vairdec struggled to contain the general, having been ordered to take him alive. However, none were able to get close to the Natchuan blade he wielded as it cut through the air and through them. Darkracer knelt down.

"Come on!"

Giving a cry of pain, David swung his injured leg over the Candonian's back. Together they turned into the fray to aid Riechet. Darkracer struck with his hooves and teeth while David fired upon any who raised a gun. Riechet sliced through the chest of a soldier who futilely tried to get around behind. A moment later, Riechet swung nimbly up behind David. Wheeling about, Darkracer sent a bone-crushing blow into a soldier's skull before galloping off down the hallway. Gunfire erupted behind them. Darkracer gave a cry. David felt the creature give way beneath him. With great determination the Candonian stayed on his feet and continued on. Riechet agilely twisted to seat himself backwards behind the saddle and threw a grenade into the Vairdec's midst.

The impact caused Darkracer to stumble just as an incoming shot struck Riechet in the shoulder. Out the corner of his eye David caught sight of the general slip. Gripping the front of the saddle to steady himself, he grabbed Riechet's arm. Hitting the floor with his feet, Riechet used his and David's combined strength to leap back onto the galloping Candonian, facing forward once again. David could hear a groan escape from between Riechet's clenched teeth but could not get a clear view of him.

"You okay?"

"Keep going."

Riechet's cryptic answer worried David. Sadly he was in no position to check on him further. The other SIERA soldiers had already retreated with Phantom to a side passage and now lay down cover fire as Darkracer neared. Without warning a shower of rubble rained down around the riders. Darkracer's foot caught on a giant slab of the ceiling that crashed in front of him, sending him somersaulting. David and Riechet were thrown sideways into the wall. Hitting the floor on his side, David felt the bolt in his leg twist from the impact, tearing through his flesh and sending a stream of hot blood into his boot.

Dazed from the fall, he felt little of the pain as he struggled to his feet, his leg growing numb in the process. Riechet accepted a hand up and they leaned against the wall to assess the situation. The corridor had completely collapsed inward, cutting them off from the side passage and the rest of the team. Luckily it also cut them off from the Vairdec.

Riechet winced as he raised his sore arm to look at his intel-band and assess his team's positions. The readout on his wrist flickered erratically.

"Racer. Are you still there?"

"I am," came the strained reply.

"Are you hurt?"

A pause. *"I'll live."*

"Get the survivors out of here. We'll go by way of the bunkers and meet you at ground level."

"Will you be all right?"

"You can't do anything for me here, Racer. Just go."

"Be careful."

"And you."

A soft blue glow was all that lit the area around David and Riechet. Though they could not see each other clearly, they both knew the other was injured. Riechet caught David up under the arm to help support his weight.

"Can you walk?"

"Yes, sir," David answered, though he feared he was not being completely honest.

Without his night vision glasses, David relied on Riechet's guidance as they made their slow, painful journey down a couple levels toward the bunkers. Often they found themselves in near blackout conditions. David kept his mind trained on each step he took. It was becoming increasingly hard to get his leg to move as he wanted. Every time he put pressure on it a burning pain shot through his body. Breathing grew more difficult. It was possible he had cracked a few ribs.

Riechet, too, struggled with the pain of his injuries. David could hear the labored breaths next to him. There was a limp in the general's walk and the bolt remained lodged in his shoulder. Neither let the other fall. The strain of their injuries would not outweigh the dedication they held to see each other to safety. They struggled on together, spitting out blood from time to time and leaving red smears against the walls they used to support themselves. At last they came to the long hallway of barracks. From there they could use the side tunnel down to the lower reaches of the mountain and finally out onto the desert floor. Once there, Darkracer and Phantom would carry them back to the safety of Karnoss's bunkers.

The door was a blessed sight for David. For a brief moment the pain subsided in the wake of the relief he felt at being so close to escaping Valor Peak. Riechet stepped forward to override the door's security. As he waited, David turned to rest his back against the wall with a groan. A bolt slammed through his chest, smashing the breath from his lungs and sending a new white-hot pain coursing through him. The bolt scraped against his ribs, stopping short of a kill as the protective vest kept it from cutting through David's heart. Across the hall he could just make out a couple dark figures. He tried to raise his gun only to find his body terrifyingly slow to respond.

Then Riechet was there, standing between him and the attackers' shots. David saw the shots but strangely the sound ceased around him. Getting his gun up, he prepared to join the fight only to watch Riechet slump. Desperately David reached out despite his own physical state, intent on holding the general up and getting him to safety. The door stood open at their backs. Riechet turned in David's arms to face the young man. His breathing was shallow, his body rapidly weakening in David's grasp. Behind them, the Vairdec begin moving in for the capture.

Pulling the glasses from his face, General Kyler Riechet looked directly into David's eyes. Life was ebbing from him but David refused to believe this was the end. Though he longed to speak to Riechet, his voice was cut short by the agony in his chest. With all his strength he tugged at his mentor, his leader, his friend, desperately trying to pull him through the door. The Vairdec were almost on top of them. With great courage and determination, Riechet reached down to remove something from his belt. Still looking into David's eyes, he gritted his bloodstained teeth.

"Live," he said.

Then he shoved David backward through the door. David raised his gun as he watched the Vairdec grab hold of the general, but the force of the shove sent him off his feet. His back slammed against the hard floor, knocking out what little air was still in his lungs. The world reeled around him. Helplessly he tumbled down a shallow slope. An explosion ripped through the walls. David felt himself being pushed up against the wall; then everything went black.

CHAPTER TWENTY-SEVEN

Black. No light. Blindness? Darkness.

"Kyler!"

Words lost. Emptiness. Groping, struggling, searching. Where am I? Alone? Dead? Buried? Warmth – a presence.

"Who's there?"

A strength. A warm breath. Words – but what?

"What are you saying?"

Just climb. Get aboard. Be carried. Be saved. But pain – pain! Searing, burning, agonizing pain. From the leg. From the chest. The body ripping apart with pain.

"Get aboard. Just ride."

Am I on? Am I moving? Are you there? Where are we? Where will we go? What will we do?

"Kyler!"

"Hush now."

Hush.

Awake! From what? Dreaming?
Unconscious? Dead – dead and now alive. Or still
dead? Where is this place? Movement. Sound.

"Who's there?"

"Shh!"

Stillness. Fear – of what? What's there?
Where are we? Open your eyes. Look. See. Can't!
Still blind? Still dreaming? No, night. Wind, shadow,
rock, stars. Where's the stars? Get up. Pain! Oh, the
pain!

"Shh!"

Light! Pale, blue, unearthly. Moonlight? No –
sweeping, steady… angry. Where's my weapon?
Where's my defense? No feeling! Can't feel anything!
It's getting closer. What is it? What will happen?

"Just hold on."

Hold to the shadows. Quiet… quiet… quiet.

So cold. Where am I now? Muscles rock with
motion… floating, floating through space. We're
moving. Where? Oh the pain! Every breath fire. Can't
breathe! And cold, cold, ever so cold…

A rattling wheeze; labored, strained. Hold
your breath… It continues. Not mine. Scraping stone,
drumming head… and wheezing, never-ending rattle
– in, out, in, out. Where's the light? All is dim.
Heaving, gasping! The ground lurches below. Again!
Again! Each lurch a cry; each pause the rattle, the
wheeze.

"What's happening?"

"Must climb. Stay with me."

I'm with you. Where are we? What's happening?...

"Get down!"
Hard surfaces - rough, icy, unfeeling. A solid ground. Electric agony through the leg. No voice. No cry. No breath! Warmth – heavy, pressing black warmth.
"Don't move."
Don't move.
What's out there?
"Lie still."
What will happen?
Brightness! Blinding white – burning eyes, chilling blood. Oh the roar! The roar drives knives into the brain. The screaming! The wailing! Make it stop! Just go away. Please! Go away!
Sudden silence. Darkness – oh glorious, most welcome darkness. No scream, no roar, only the wheeze, only the rattle.
"Come."
Yes, come. Work body, work. Rise. Move. You must rise!
Again upon the warm, steady movement. Again safe – for now. Climb, just climb.

Day? Night? Awake? Dreaming? Alive? Dead?
"Where?"
"Shh."
The rattle. The wheeze. The endless rhythm. Gasp. Wheeze. Join the steady rattle below.

A veil lifts. Sight? Yes! Streets? Walls? Why do they move? Why do they sway? What's the throbbing? No more. No more!

"Stay with me!"
Electricity! Fire! Agony! Red flashes and screaming sirens in the brain. Rolling, thundering, all around endless drumming. Wind stings – burns! What's happening?

New electricity. New fire. Where? From behind! The world compresses – slowing in the face of the fierce speed. React. React! No thought. What to do? What to do? Turn and face it. Return the fire.

Thunder rolls beneath. It twists. It turns. Harder. Stronger. Faster! Lurching. Buckling. Falling away.
"No!"
Not now. Rise!

Silence.

The wheeze. Oh the faithful rattle of breath below me.

Is it day? Is it night? Silence.

So this is what it means to die…

403

... "David? David, look at me. David, come back."

CHAPTER TWENTY-EIGHT

"Where's the scan?"

"I need this guy's readout."

"Get me some more whole blood."

The tinny voices echoed from some far off realm beyond the swirling void - hazy, distorted, incoherent.

"Do we have more Provaxoline?"

"Hold on, soldier."

"The Lord is my light and my salvation: whom shall I fear?"

"Nicky! Nicky!"

"Wye-auh, moot."

"Eja."

So many whispers floating through the emptiness. Who were they? What were they about? What is happening?

"Is he awake yet?"

"No ma'am, not yet."

Pain – horrible, agonizing, unending pain. It burned through every fiber, every part screamed under the fire. Every breath had to be fought for. Muscles tensed from the stress of each gasp, sending flares of hot red light through the brain.
"Doctor."

"David?"
He knew the voice, but from where? Why did it focus his mind from the usual chaotic swirl of sound and sensations around him? It was directed to him. It spoke to him. But who was she?
"Colonel."
"Coming."

Demons appeared first through the fog of his mind – demons with grinning faces and fiery eyes. They surrounded him, mocked him, beat him. They drove spikes through his flesh and sent fire through his blood. Their roar relentlessly pounded against his temples. Screams of pain ripped through the shadows around them. He wanted to fight them off but his arms and legs refused to move. He was helpless against them.
"Don't!"
"Hey, it's okay."
What was that voice? It was not the demons. Where was he coming from? Was there something touching his hand? Was somebody there? Who are you?

"David?... David... Hey there."

David blinked again. It was hard to focus. Where was this image coming from? Was this real, or in his mind? For a long time he stared at the face of the woman looking down at him, trying to understand what he saw. He thought he recognized her; only he was too confused yet to place from where he had seen her before. She just stared back, a smile – sad and weary – on her worn face. It broke David's heart to observe such deep sadness in her. Why it hurt him so, he couldn't quite figure out.

Other hurts began to grow more apparent. As the fog continued to lift from his mind, the world and all its sensations grew sharper. The noises around him no longer echoed in some distant corner of existence. Soft voices tucked in the shadows, the scrape of furniture across the floor, footsteps – all became recognizable. The world opened further around him. Even in the dim light he could make out dark images of people moving around, weaving about in a slow, methodical fashion. Chemical smells stung his nose.

But above all the other senses, David found his sense of touch return in the most agonizing manner. His whole body ached. Painful jolts ran up and down his right leg and his chest burned with an indescribable fire. It choked him. It raked his lungs. Heat and nausea swept across him in merciless waves. His sweating temples beat out a torturous rhythm. Why did he feel this way? What had happened? A warm hand pressed into his and for a moment he managed to draw his focus away from the excruciating pain of his body. The woman leaned slightly over him.

"How are you doing?"

How was he doing? What kind of question was that? His body was ripping itself apart. He opened his mouth to speak but his throat felt hot and tight. His tongue felt swollen, sticking to the roof of his mouth. All he managed was a choked groan. The woman looked away, keeping her hand pressed against his.

"Doctor."

The click of shoes on stone preceded the doctor who stepped into David's view as he came alongside the woman.

"Colonel?"

"Is it possible to get this man some water?"

"Yes, ma'am."

Colonel? Somehow it fit. David allowed her to adjust the pillows so that he lay slightly more upright. Though every movement raked him with pain, he held his tongue, unwilling to complain in front of the woman who obviously held great concern for his wellbeing. When the doctor arrived with a cup, she took it and helped David drink. The water tasted good despite how much it hurt to swallow. After a couple sips he turned away, unable to endure the pain any longer. Setting the cup aside, the woman held his hand, studying his face for a long, silent moment.

"Can you remember anything?"

"Of what?" David managed to ask aloud.

A strained look came over the woman's features. Tightening her lips in a forced smile, she glanced away and gave a tense, short nod. David wished to help ease the obvious hurt. She meant something to him. What exactly that was and why, he could not say. With great effort he gave her hand a squeeze. She looked back at him with tears rimming her eyes. Hurriedly she swept them away and straightened.

"You get well," she said, her voice taking on a no-nonsense tone. "You hear?"

Not allowing David to answer, she quickly stood and disappeared from his sight. David kept his eyes on the place she had sat until unconsciousness overtook him.

"Of course he was going about 6 Gs, inverted no less. The C-Class can smooth it out while pulling 12 Gs in a low atmospheric rocket-climb, but that's not recommended with the B4-Slipwings, especially without the FBG-suits."

David opened his eyes to look at the man beside him, watching in silence as he continued to talk, more to himself than anything, as his gaze wandered the room.

"I prefer the sharper maneuvers of the B4s, but you can't deny the Razorback's style...and you are listening," he ended, looking down at David.

Reaching over, he placed a friendly hand on David's shoulder.

"You gave us quite a scare for a while, but, sorry to tell you, the doctors say you're going to live."

David returned the smile, though not with the same enthusiasm. He still felt disoriented. He longed to speak, to ask questions, but nothing came to mind. The man at his side didn't appear slighted by David's silence and gave his shoulder a gentle squeeze.

"I'm glad you're all right." He paused, letting his gaze trail up and down David's bandaged body. "More or less. How do you feel?"

"What happened?"

The look on the man's face grew somber. "You don't remember?"

"No."

Leaning back in his chair, the man gave a heavy sigh. "Right now that may be a good thing. Don't worry about it. We're all glad you're back. Just get better."

The man prepared to stand, leaving David suddenly frantic. He didn't want to be left alone yet.

"Wait," he managed, weakly reaching out to touch the hand of his companion.

Pausing, the man settled back into his seat.

"What is it?"

"Well... uh..."

David wasn't sure what he wanted to say or even hear. His mind kept jumping about, unable to hold any one thought for long. Visions, ideas, feelings all bounced chaotically around inside him. What did he want to say?

"Who are you?"

The somber expression deepened. Leaning forward the man looked straight into David's eyes.

"You really don't remember anything, do you?"

Fear rose through David. Was this more serious than he thought? What was happening to him? What was he suppose to remember?

"Wha..."

"What do you remember?"

"I don't..."

David fished through his troubled mind for some concrete memory. There was the pain - he definitely remembered that. He remembered unrecognizable voices and the movement in the dark around where he lay. He remembered...

"Where is the woman?"

"Riechet?"

How should he answer? David sensed that the name held some meaning. Was that the woman he saw earlier or was there another? He couldn't be sure. The man at his side kindly assisted him.

"Colonel Amber Riechet. Tall, red hair, tough."

"Colonel. Yes, they said colonel."

"But you don't know her?"

A shudder ran down David's spine. There was a sense of familiarity about everything and everyone around him. Unfortunately, no matter how hard he tried, he could not place how it all fit together.

"Why am I like this? What happened to me?"

Pity showed on the man's face. "Do you remember anything about the war?"

David felt his stomach knot. War? Could that really be the answer? Somehow it made sense. Sadly he still could not think of any specifics revolving around this revelation. Defeated he shook his head.

"Don't worry about it. I've no doubt you'll remember everything soon enough. At that point you may want to forget it again."

David's heart beat a little faster. No doubt lay in his mind over the truth of the man's words. Between the thought of war and the pain he was

411

experiencing, what happened must have been horrifying. However, David still longed to know the details. Whatever horror awaited him in the return of his memories, it could not be so agonizing as having lost a part of himself.

"I'm Mike, by the way," the man continued. "We're friends. In fact you could say we're blood brothers now. You lost a lot of blood."

"You gave me blood?"

Mike shrugged it off. "It's what soldiers do for each other."

Giving David another squeeze of the shoulder, Mike rose quietly and walked away. David let him go without complaint. Too many things rested heavily on his mind. Soldiers? A slight sense of comfort rose in that knowledge. He was not some passive victim to someone else's conflict. He was an active part of whatever war they were facing. It gave him a sense of purpose and courage, and despite his continued pain, he found himself able to slip into a more peaceful sleep.

When David awoke, he had no sense of time or place – only a sense of panic over the realization that he could not breathe. He choked and gasped, his body beginning to convulse as it fought for oxygen. Fluid bubbled in his throat. Heat flashed through his body. What could he do? He tried to move but nothing happened. Voices sounded around him and hands grabbed at his arms. The disembodied figures hurriedly turned him on his side and he could feel thick, sticky fluid drip from his mouth.

"What's happening?" Amber demanded as she shoved her way to David's side.

"Could be a slow bleeder. Most likely ARDS" the doctor replied hurriedly. "Possibly a bit of pneumonia as well."

"Could be? Possibly? Don't you know?"

Strong hands grabbed Amber's shoulders from behind and pulled her back.

"What can be done?" Mike asked from behind her.

The doctor knelt by the bed to tear away the bandage around David's chest. "We need to drain the lung first."

Two other medics were already in place, handing over supplies as they prepped David.

"A chest tube will help," the doctor said.

A nurse looked up from her place on the other side of David's cot. "Are we anesthetizing first?"

"No time." The doctor glanced over his shoulder at Mike. "Hold him down."

Mike stepped forward to place one knee on the cot and press his weight against David's shoulders.

Amber paced nearby. "Get him more oxygen."

"We need to clear the lung first," the doctor replied.

"Where's the oxygen machine?"

"Surgery."

"Colonel," Mike said, his tone grave, "he'll be fine."

"Is it pneumonia?"

"I don't know," the doctor admitted, not looking at the colonel. He counted down David's ribs to find the place for the catheter.

"I'm not losing him."

Mike gritted his teeth. "Colonel."

Amber ignored him. "What medicine do we have on hand?"

"Amber! Go!"

Mike's voice was so fierce that even Amber was stopped in her tracks. Her eyes narrowed and her fists clenched. Keven stepped around her, having heard the commotion. Catching sight of him, Mike nodded toward the cot.

"Could you hold his legs?"

Without a word, Keven complied. Amber turned away to storm toward the medical ward's door. Behind her she could hear David's cry of pain as the thick needle was jammed through his side and into his lung. She cringed and hurried from the room.

"Don't you ever speak to me like that again!"

Mike stood quietly a half hour later in what use to be General Riechet's quarters. The fluid had been successfully drained from David's chest and the doctors were doing what they could to keep his lungs clear. The task proved difficult with shortages of supplies, but they were trained for fieldwork and continued to fight for their patient despite the setbacks. All remained confident that the crisis had been averted, though Mike still found himself shaken by the event. Apparently Amber, too, felt the effects of nearly losing yet another close colleague. Her stress boiled over into rage now directed at Mike. He supposed he had it coming, and, knowing Amber as long as he had, took it in stride. She paced what were now her quarters without looking Mike in the eye. Her frustration clearly showed in her features.

"Do not forget I am your superior. I will not have you disrespecting my authority. I don't care who you are. Do I make myself clear, commander?"

"Yes, ma'am."

"This is my command now whether I like it or not. I know that, you know that. But if the rest are to follow I must have the respect of my officers. Is that clear?"

"Yes, colonel, it is clear."

Amber stopped her pacing to look hard at Mike for the first time. She stepped up boldly to him and narrowed her eyes.

"But what?"

Yes, she knew him as well as he knew her. She understood his subtle tones, the unspoken words, the thoughts beyond what he was willing to say out loud. Knowing they were beyond the earshot and prying eyes of the rest of the division, Mike dropped his guard to look Amber square in the eyes.

"Are you ready to lead?"

"How dare you! This not my first command. I've been training since I was five. I'm as qualified as any military officer..."

"I'm not questioning your qualifications," Mike cut in boldly. "Amber, you just lost your father."

"I'm fine."

"You lost your only family."

"I'm fine!"

"No you're not."

Amber's argument caught in her throat, giving Mike the opportunity to forge ahead.

"I've been watching you. Don't think I don't know what it's like. Your stress is through the roof. You're attacking everyone. You've given yourself no time to grieve."

"There is no time."

"Make time – even a couple hours; a day. No one will think less of you. We're all grieving. Kyler was as much a father to me as he was a friend. He meant a lot to many here. You're right, we can't give up fighting because of this, but if you don't come to terms with what happened, you'll never be the leader I know you can be."

Amber turned away.

"You're not alone, Amber."

She did not respond and Mike stepped cautiously forward.

"Amber?"

He could hear a soft sob escape her. Here in this small closed space there was no rank, no authority or protocol to follow. There were only two people suffering a terrible loss. Quietly he reached out to take her shoulder and gently turn her. She did not pull away. Lying her head against him she let the tears silently fall.

CHAPTER TWENTY-NINE

When David finally recovered enough to observe his surroundings he discovered he was not alone. At first he could not be sure who or even what lay next to him, but it was apparent that something large rested beside his cot. His neck and shoulders complained with electrifying stabs of pain as he forced them to work. Carefully he turned his head toward the object, noticing the soft rise and fall of a large black mound. Wanting to see more, he twisted further, his body protesting in a sharp cough as his airways constricted. The mound stirred and a head rose from behind, twisting on a long neck to peer over its shoulder.

Darkracer's nostrils twitched with the satisfaction of seeing David awake. Shifting his body with a groan, he situated himself more comfortably to look down at his injured friend. His eyes smiled at David and for a while they just stared at each other. David felt a sense of comfort wash over him at the sight of the Candonian. He knew this creature. Though at the moment he was unable to place the name, the familiarity surrounding his presence caused David not to care about the lapse of memory.

Straining against the aches, David lifted his arm to brush the back of his hand against the Candonian's soft jowl.

"Hi," he whispered.

The eyes smiled even more at him. "Hello there."

"I know you."

"Yes."

Darkracer already knew of David's amnesia. He often asked about David's progress while he, himself, recovered from his injuries. The two of them had been through so much together. It took three terribly trying days to navigate the desert floor, climb the plateau, slip through the city and finally back into the safety of the bunkers. It began when Riechet and David failed to show at the designated meeting place. Sending the rest of the team on with Phantom and Jylin, Darkracer retraced his steps, hunting all the while for any sign of either of the missing members of the team.

Nearly a day was spent in his searching. Often he tried calling only to receive dead air over his comlink. Something had gone terribly wrong. With each passing hour, Darkracer had grown more frantic. He traversed the tunnel systems tirelessly, ignoring the injuries to his legs and head. The fall when the ceiling collapsed resulted in much of the skin and flesh being torn from his knees. A long gash ran from between his ears to the back of his left jowl. His continued movement repeatedly broke open the wounds and his front legs cracked and oozed from layers of dried blood. Nonetheless he pressed onward. He refused to retreat until Riechet and David were safe. He would find them or die trying.

Despite the danger, Darkracer often called out to them, his voice echoing among the dark tunnel passageways. The mask he wore kept him oriented in the dark, but the labyrinth beneath Valor Peak continually mocked him with one empty passage after another. At long last, Darkracer's sensitive ears and nose led him to where David struggled weakly in the blackness. The sight of the man's injuries shook the Candonian to his core. A steel bolt glimmered from where it lay embedded in David's vest, and by the overwhelming smell of blood, it had obviously pierced his chest as well. His right leg barely supported him. Blood held his shirt collar firmly to his sliced neck. Still more horrifying, there was no sign of Kyler Riechet.

David remained disoriented, blind by lack of his night vision glasses and by the obvious state of shock he was experiencing. He slumped against the wall, reaching out to grope the darkness. His voice was harsh and cracked but he continued to call out for Riechet.

"Kyler!"

Darkracer approached to gently touch David on the arm. The man recoiled for a second then reached out toward him.

"Who's there?"

Darkracer closed the distance between them, gently nuzzling David.

"It's me, Racer. It's all right; I'll get you out of here. Where's Riechet?"

419

David appeared confused, unable to comprehend the words.

"Kyler! Oh god. Oh god he's... he's... Kyler!"

"He's what?" Darkracer asked, trembling as he prepared himself for the answer. David only collapsed to the floor in grief-stricken shock.

"Why him? Oh god, why him?"

Darkracer had heard enough. Deep down he knew his search ended here. There was no reason to continue the hunt. Kyler Riechet was gone. The realization left him feeling weak. He wanted to collapse next to David and give up, only that was not his way. Steeling himself, he pressed his nose against David.

"We have to get out of here. I have to get you back to the bunkers."

"What are you saying?"

Darkracer eased himself down next to David, ignoring the scabs on his knees that cracked open to release a new stream of blood.

"Get aboard. Just ride."

It took a moment for David to struggle into the saddle, but he still held a strong sense of survival that kept him from giving in to his agony. Darkracer took heart in David's conviction. Together they would make it. Yes, together. Clenching his teeth, he rose. As he did, David reached out once more.

"Kyler!"

"Hush now."

It was night when Darkracer emerged once more onto the desert floor. A full day had passed without his knowing, buried as he was in the depth of the mountain. Facing the east, Darkracer stared a moment at the plateau rising before him. It looked so close. One jump and he would be there. If only it were true. As quickly and quietly as he could, Darkracer began his stealthy journey.

Much of the way David lay draped across the saddle, barely conscious. Darkracer rarely spoke to him. He focused all his strength and energy on each step, fighting stubbornly through the pain and grief.

It was still dark when the whir of engines began to buzz in the Candonian's ears. Desperately he scrambled off the small path he was following to press in among the rocks. David stirred.

"Who's there?"

"Shh!"

The engines remained soft, announcing a small spy ship, probably unmanned. They were dangerous. They maneuvered into places other ships could not and they saw and heard everything. David struggled to push himself up in the saddle.

"Shh!"

Darkracer shifted further in among the rocks and bent low as a pale blue light washed overhead. The unearthly hum throbbed in the Candonian's sensitive ears. Instinctively he froze, allowing his dark coat to hide him among the shadows. After a few more passes, the ship went on its way, leaving the Candonian and rider once again alone.

"Just hold on."

For the rest of the night and into the morning, Darkracer labored on. He refused to stop for anything. Every minute on the desert floor was another minute closer to death. He had to reach the plateau. The loss of blood began to blur his vision and weaken his step. Thirst overwhelmed him. Before long his parched tongue and throat began to crack and bleed. The desert air sucked the last of the moisture from his breath and he wheezed under the strain of his journey. The cold threatened to break his lungs.

By midday they stood at the base of the plateau. Remarkably they succeeded in eluding the patrols. Darkracer knew it came from a combination of his species' instinctive stealth, the dark color of both his body and David's clothing, and just sheer luck. If only luck would remain on their side. They needed it now more than ever. Without Riechet, there was only one way into the city. He would have to climb a narrow trail that cut its way up the side of the southern cliff of the plateau. Never did that mass of rock appear so immense. Throughout the torturous day he struggled up the trail, lunging forward in order to keep climbing steadily upward and not lose his footing.

"What's happening?" David groaned.

"Must climb. Stay with me."

They had almost made it to the top when a ship's engines announced the enemy's approach. Darkracer faltered a moment as he realized they were trapped on the side of bare rock. Only the long shadows of evening and a small jutting of stone offered any protection. There was no time to waste.

"Get down!"

As he cried his warning, Darkracer dropped to the ground. David tumbled from the saddle to lie between him and the cliff wall. He gasped in pain. Pressing himself against the man, Darkracer froze.

"Don't move," he whispered. "Lie still."

The rock around them began to shake as the massive ship swung around the far eastern edge of the plateau. Its blinding lights washed over them and the roar of the engines threatened to burst Darkracer's eardrums. He could see the bulk of metal block the view of the desert beyond, filling all his vision. He was not well versed in the different ships so knew nothing of what kind was passing by. All he knew was the danger it posed. Luckily it continued its sweep around the edge of the plateau before gaining altitude and turning south. At last it was gone.

"Come."

Once David was securely in the saddle, Darkracer rose wearily to finish his climb into the city of Karnoss.

Entering the city came both as a relief and a frustration. Darkracer was thankful to have finished his climb, but Vairdec patrols had shifted further east and south, which in turn forced Darkracer off a direct course to the tunnel system that would lead him to the bunkers. Throughout the night and into the third day he traveled slowly along the abandoned streets, trying to break through patrol lines. Fear rose steadily in Darkracer, not for his own safety, but for the one on his back. Often David grew so still that Darkracer would pause to look over his shoulder, dreading the thought of finding his rider dead. To his relief, David continued to prove himself a true fighter.

By late evening, their luck finally ran out. Weak and tired, Darkracer failed to hear the subtle movements of a hunting pair of larkrae until he and the vermin blundered into each other. The animals instantly raised the alarm, screeching with frenzied delight over the smell of blood. They leaped from the low ledge they had been traversing and spread the leathery skin between their legs to sail straight at Darkracer's head. Instead of turning to run away, Darkracer lunged straight into them, knocking them from the sky before galloping down the street. Already the animals' cries had brought their handlers and shots began to fly past. Darkracer weaved along the streets, using rubble to shield him from the shots coming from behind.

"Stay with me!" Darkracer shouted, hoping David still possessed enough strength to stay aboard.

More patrols joined the chase, trying to block the racing Candonian in. Darkracer's speed kept him ahead of the enemy. Sadly he knew he could not outrun gunfire for long. To his amazement, David suddenly pushed himself up in the saddle and returned fire. Though his shots were less than accurate, they succeeded in slowing the Vairdec's progress. Just ahead lay the entryway to a transit tunnel. Darkracer immediately recognized it. They were close. Summoning he last bit of strength, he leaped for the ramp. His front feet struck the sloping ground and gave way.

"No!"

Darkracer felt a hard pull on his mane as his rider cried out. David was forcing him up. He would not let him fall. Rolling back onto his haunches, Darkracer managed to right his front end in time to land upright on the floor of the transit station. By the time the Vairdec entered, their quarry had disappeared. The hidden maintenance tunnel guided the two weary soldiers away from harm, drawing them deeper into the core of the plateau, and to safety.

Darkracer blew softly through his nostrils as he replayed the terrible journey taken with David. They had been through so much together. Darkracer had never been very close to anyone other than Kyler Riechet and his daughter. Now he felt a certain kinship with this young man. David was special, just as he had expressed to Riechet in what seemed another lifetime. A great burden lifted from the Candonian's mind as he gazed down at David, knowing he would live.

He thought back on when he had finally arrived at the bunkers. The relief was overwhelming. Not until he dragged himself the final length of tunnel into SIERA's chamber did he realize just how frightened he had been for David's life. At that time David had collapsed once more and lay draped across Darkracer's back. Darkracer could barely stand. His feet dragged heavily on the floor, which lay only inches from his bowed head. Blood dripped from his legs and nostrils. He hardly noticed the number of people around him.

Mike and Keven wasted no time in pulling David down and carrying him to the medical ward. Only upon seeing David being taken care of did Darkracer feel his task finally complete. Amber knelt by his head as the Candonian succumbed to his own weakened state and collapsed. Other members hurried to assist, but Darkracer noticed none of them. All he saw at the time was Amber as she held his head in her lap. Her eyes spoke of the grief welling up inside.

"Racer," she had whispered. "Where's Dad?"

Darkracer closed his eyes at the memory of her words. The look on her face still haunted him.

"You carried me."

The soft voice caused Darkracer to open his eyes again. David stared up at him, trying hard to grasp lost memories.

"You carried me," he repeated.

"That's right," Darkracer answered. "I carried you."

David struggled to remember when and why. Nothing came to mind. He only knew he had been on that great creature's back. He remembered the sensation of the muscles churning beneath him and of the wind against his face. Where had that all happened?

"Were you with me when this happened?"

"I found you and brought you back."

A look of disappointment fell across David's face. No one seemed to be able to tell him what had happened. In fact, they were all hoping he would tell them. Why? What significance did his situation hold?

"Thank you," David said quietly.

Darkracer could sense the troubled spirit within the man. He stretched his head forward to touch his velvety nose to David's cheek.

"Do not fret. You will remember soon enough. What needs to be known will be known. In the meantime, be as thankful as we are that you are alive."

David liked this Candonian. They lay next to each other without speaking, allowing each other's presence to comfort them. Soon they were both asleep.

"Get the survivors out of here. We'll go by way of the bunkers and meet you at ground level."

Riechet's voice rang clearly through David's dream. He could feel the strong arm of the general wrap around him to keep him upright. They struggled slowly through the dark passageway. An icy, still air hung around them. Their footsteps sounded unnaturally loud within the enclosed space. David fought to breath. He could hear Riechet struggling to do the same. It was a terrible place to be, but David didn't want to let his mind take him anywhere else. He didn't want those arms to leave him. He didn't want to stop hearing the sound of the man at his side. The passage opened up around them, revealing a dark, desolate chamber. Doors lined the room.

No, David wanted to say. *Don't go through there. Go back.*

But he was powerless to stop the events. Though his mind screamed at him to change the scenario, he continued on with Riechet at his side – continued on toward that black, sinister door.

Not there. No. Let's go away. Not to there.

To that door they went anyway, and Riechet stepped away from David's touch.

Run, David's mind screamed. *Run!*

Instead, David just stood there against the wall. He knew what was to come but could only brace himself for the impact. The figures rose up right out of shadows on the floor. A burning pain ripped through David's chest. He couldn't move. No matter how hard he tried to get his body to respond, he continued to stand there, staring at the slowly approaching shadows.

Riechet's hands grabbed him by the arms. He was being propelled backwards. Those eyes, those pleading, dying eyes! David didn't want to see anymore. He tried to grab hold of Riechet.

Don't go. Don't do it.

"Live."

That one word drove through David's mind so sharply, so clearly, that he found himself paralyzed. This was it. He couldn't watch. He couldn't turn away.

"No. No, Kyler. No!"

He was falling, falling backwards. There was no impact; only a sense of suspension as a wall of fire engulfed Riechet. Then the world dropped out from under David.

"Wait!"

David's body screamed in protest over the involuntary jerk as he woke. For a second longer he still felt the sensation of falling and held his breath to see what would happen. When nothing did he exhaled painfully and lay still. He didn't want to move. He didn't want to think. Something stirred at his side. A warm breath caressed his cheek. A soft touch nudged him.

"Are you all right?"

Shakily David reached into the darkness to tightly grip the Candonian's mane.

"I remember," he choked.

CHAPTER THIRTY

David lay propped against the wall on what was now Amber's bed in General Riechet's old quarters. The decision was made to move him so that he could speak confidentially with the officers who at the moment surrounded his bedside, taking in the report he had just finished. All remained very still. David fidgeted with the edge of his blanket. The chest tube in his side hurt and his leg and lungs burned. He barely noticed any of it. All he could do was think about that terrible night and what Riechet had done. He carefully chose the information he gave, sharing what needed to be known while sparing, especially Amber, from some of the more graphic details. Riechet's last word David kept to himself.

Quietly Jylin turned away and left the room with Kailyn. Mike followed after giving David a comforting touch on the shoulder. Darkracer stayed where he was a couple minutes longer before exiting as well. Amber sat on the edge of the bed, alone with David. Neither spoke. What was there to say? The discomfort of the silence outweighed any of the other discomforts David felt. He wished he could quietly leave as well.

"I'm sorry," he ventured.

Amber looked up from where she had been vacantly staring into the corner. With obvious effort, she gave him a weak smile.

"You're not to blame."

David looked down at his blanket. "Still."

Amber's hand slid over the top of his. She waited until he lifted his gaze to hers.

"There was nothing you could have done. He made the choice. He... he did what had to be done."

She gripped his hand tightly and turned away.

"Now what?"

"Now," Amber drew her hand away and stood, "we fight on – keep going."

Walking to the case that once held Riechet's Natchuan-styled uniform, Amber reached inside and drew out an object wrapped in cloth. Quietly, almost reverently, she carried it to David and placed it on his lap.

"Mike, Darkracer and I talked about who should inherit this. It just felt right to be you."

David looked curiously between Amber and the object. It was long and a bit heavy. Carefully he removed the cloth. His breath caught in his throat. Lying across his lap was *Excalibur's Legacy*. The sword hilt glimmered in the dim light. Its sheath looked newly oiled, the embossed leather sporting a beautiful pattern of leaves and stars. With a trembling hand he ran his fingers across it. How could this be his? It was too much. He gave a firm shake of his head.

"I can't accept this."

Seating herself once more at his side, Amber looked hard at him. "It is not respectful to decline the inheritance of a Natchuan blade without justifiable cause."

Justifiable cause? Where should David begin? "If this is an inheritance, it should go to you."

Amber shook her head. "I carry *Fire Lass*. No one can own two Blades of Norian."

David stared at her. Where did these rules come from? He didn't recall reading about them in Alsen's journals. Was Amber making them up? Her expression said otherwise.

"I'm not Natchuan."

"Technically no one is," Amber explained. "Some may be direct descendents, but since the group is no longer recognized it is more of a personal choice to follow what was learned by them. The blades, however, have always had a tradition of ownership. They stay in the possession of a person until death, then pass on to the next most worthy holder. At least one other sword holder must approve the choice."

"What makes me worthy?"

"You hold a respect for Natchua most have lost. You also trained directly with my father and hold to the same devotion as the Natchuan officers. You are also probably the best expert on Jonathan Alsen. Who better to carry his sword?"

David stared at the blade for several minutes. He found himself running out of excuses for being chosen to carry the sword. However, he still felt unworthy of it. The image of Riechet wielding it returned to his mind. He had moved with incredible power and grace. The sword danced with him a deadly dance, both beautiful and fierce. How could he, David, ever accomplish such perfection? His brow furrowed. Funny, he couldn't remember Riechet returning the blade to its place on Darkracer's saddle. He must have done it so quickly when mounting that David never noticed. Of course he had been focused on the attacking Vairdec and figured such details would naturally go unnoticed during that time. Still, it surprised him that the sword was here at all.

"What am I to do with this?"

"Each of the twelve keepers do a variety of things with the blades. These were never meant to be locked away and forgotten. That was something specifically explained early on. However, they were always to be respected and used appropriately. That is why a sword holder must be among the ones to choose a successor to a blade. We want to know whoever holds one shows it the proper respect."

"Indeed." David tried to lift it, finding himself still too weak to do much more than raise it slightly from his lap. "But shouldn't these be in the museum? After all, I would think they would be considered national treasures."

"They are," Amber confirmed, "but there was a collective will put down by the founding Natchuan officers that stated the blades would never be put on public display and every keeper must do whatever it takes to keep the blades from falling into the wrong hands. More so, they are never to be together except in battle."

"Why is that?"

"It's not explained but we hold to the will. That is why the blade is now yours. It's obvious you will care for it properly and I know you won't let it fall into the wrong hands. As far as what you are to do with it, that you will have to decide."

David studied his new treasure with a mixture of awe and apprehension. This was a responsibility not to be taken lightly. After all, this was the actual sword wielded by Jonathan Alsen, the sword that led soldiers into battle, not the replica hanging on the wall back home. His first thought was to wrap it up and seal it in a special case where no harm could come to it. But was that right? This was a symbol of the Humans' courage and strength. Furthermore it was a tool, and tools were meant to be used. After all, Riechet used it to save David's life. The sword was two hundred years old and still looked as it did when first forged. It was just as strong and sharp as ever, so treating it like delicate glass would actually be disrespectful. No, David would follow Kyler Riechet's example. He would learn to wield it and keep it in use… somehow.

"I…" He searched for the right words. "I am honored to be this sword's keeper and I will try to do what is right not for the sake of the sword but for the sake of your father's memory."

Amber's smile broadened. "Then our choice of successor was correct."

"May I ask a favor of you?"

"You may."

"You once said you would show me how to use a sword. Can I hold you to that?"

Taking hold of David's hand, Amber placed it and hers across *Legacy's* hilt. "You can. But first, you must heal. Get some rest, and be at peace. Don't blame yourself for my father's death. As hard as it is to accept that he's gone, it would also have been hard to lose you. I'm glad you made it."

Before David could respond, Amber stood and left the room, leaving him to settle back with *Excalibur's Legacy* at his side.

The next day David insisted on returning to the main medical ward. He did not want to appear to be receiving special treatment. He also knew as commanding officer, Amber needed her space. *Excalibur's Legacy* went with him, kept safe in a case sitting under his cot. He was still too weak to do anything with it, so he instead allowed the knowledge of what lay in his possession guide his thoughts to the stories he had read from Alsen's journals. The thought of learning to use the sword motivated David to work on healing, though it was six days before the doctor felt confident enough to remove the chest tube and another five before David felt strong enough to do anything more than lie around all day.

During his recovery, David spent much of his time observing the other patients within his line of sight. Some slept fitfully, refusing to respond to those tending their needs. Others struggled to get their broken bodies to once again respond to their unspoken commands. Still others ceased responding all together. These last were silently mourned as their tattered remains were reverently wrapped and hurried from the ward. Where did they go? David wondered.

How could one bury the dead when the living shared their quarters in this deep underground tomb of rock? How many now lay in death shrouds? How many more would join in the days to come?

A wailing cry jarred David from his rest. The screams of incredible pain emanated from the partitioned operating room. Like several others on cots around him, he struggled to lift himself enough to look in the direction of the sound, wondering what calamity had befallen yet another person. The screams reached a higher pitch. They were clearly that of a woman's. What was happening? What terrible injuries had this woman received? Why hadn't they put her under yet? David groaned, lying back on his side and turning his head from the OR. He felt very sick. The screams and cries continued for countless minutes.

Make them stop! David tucked his head into his arm. He couldn't take any more of this. There was just too much suffering; too much death. *Just make the cries stop!* All grew suddenly silent. The screams ceased. Had death claimed another? Then a new sound rose, softer and gentler than before – the wail of a newborn baby.

CHAPTER THIRTY-ONE

As the days came and went, David continued to heal, strengthened by the encouragement of those around him and by the courage shown in his friends. First he forced himself to stand for short periods of time. Mastering that, he took slow walks around the ward, his steps always watched by at least one of the ever-present young nurses. David found himself overwhelmed by the dedication they held for their work. With nothing to do in the bunkers, a couple young women from the civilian quarters chose to volunteer their time caring for the injured soldiers coming in from the field. They were never far from David's side, making sure he had everything he needed and remained as comfortable as possible, even going as far as to sit for hours working the kinks from David's sore neck and back. It was encouraging to know that the city's civilians really cared about the work he and the other soldiers were sacrificing their lives for.

David lost track of time during his slow healing. It seemed an oppressively long time. Finally he chose to ask a close-by nurse if she knew how long the war had been going. To his disappointment, she, too, did not know. For everyone the days blended together in a ceaseless cycle of hopelessness and death. With no indication of night and day, only the time ticking away on people's timebands reminded anyone of the truth. With no timeband of her own, the nurse hurried away to find the answer to David's question before he could stop her from going through the trouble.

Standing by his cot, David slowly rotated his shoulders, forcing stiff muscles to work and noting the depressingly limited range of motion of his complaining body. It felt good to stand, despite the unending pain. He had become use to the pain. Shoving the thought of any discomfort to the back of his mind, David took a few strained steps forward. The young nurse walked quickly toward him, appearing intent on helping David who motioned her to hold back. She did as requested, a look of disappointment on her face.

"I found out what day it is," she announced, placing her hands behind her back to show she would respect David's wishes. "It's Triedi twelve." She hesitated, looking embarrassed. "I'm afraid I don't know how many days that makes it. It's midmorning, though."

She glanced up at David with a hopeful smile, pleased that her effort received her a smile back.

"Thank you."

"Is there anything I can get you?"

"No, I'll be fine. Thanks."

The nurse held her ground. She seemed incapable of deciding what to do. Presently she flashed David a second smile and ducked away to tend to some business a few cots down the row. David watched her go, deciding after a brief moment not to puzzle over young women's behavior. He wanted to heal as quickly as possible. Even stuck in the medical ward he was aware of the comings and goings of colleagues still facing the front lines. He hated not being able to help.

Turning to face the far wall, David made the short, two-meter journey toward it. His leg burned, sending stabs of pain up and down its length with every footfall. To keep his mind off the physical trauma, David worked out the math involving the date. Rew'cha fell on Regetch three. Working through the pain, it took David a little longer to run the numbers, but by the time he headed back to his cot, he figured that forty-eight days had passed since the Vairdec invaded.

Forty-eight days. David sank to the edge of his cot in thought. Just over two nahms? Thinking of it that way, it sounded as if hardly any time had passed at all. Try as he might, though, he could not think of life without the war. How fascinating and terrible it was that a single event could supersede all past events in one's life until nothing but the present moment existed. True, David could pick memories out from the years of his childhood, of his training days in the CLE Academy, even memories he hated to remember, but they all seemed distant, like dreams. None of them felt real anymore. Only the war was real, only the pain.

An exuberant cheer roused David from his thoughts. The nine other patients in the ward were enthusiastically greeting a voluptuous, slender woman with long, black hair and a swagger achieved only by someone who knew of her importance. She was of medium height with delicate features, rich dark eyes and full lips that drew back in a genuine smile as she greeted her bed-ridden fans.

"Can you believe it?"

David jumped as Nathan enthusiastically threw himself down next to him. The jolt of pain instantly made David regret his sudden movement and he glared at his intruder. Nathan had shown a level of friendliness over the past days, visiting David and checking on his progress. While he did not particularly dislike the youth, David continued to feel uncomfortably suspicious around him. He heard tell that Nathan now knew of the Malard's wealth and wondered how long it would be before the over-active teenager asked for a favor. Right now Nathan's eyes were locked on the woman.

"Lameena Narheen," he said rather dreamily, "she is so t-bow, isn't she?"

David studied the woman carefully. Tempting beyond words? That may be taking it a little far, but he agreed she was a beautiful woman. However, he refrained from speaking his thoughts aloud to Nathan.

"She seems like a nice woman."

"Nice?" Nathan shot David an offended look. "She's got to be one of the sexiest..."

"Keep your voice down."

"...desirable..."

"Nathan."

"…temptingly amazing women around."

"She's also married."

"Yeah, well he's not here."

If David had the strength, he would have left. Even without the strength he considered giving it a try but Lameena was already approaching. She extended her arms as if greeting an old friend. Nathan nearly jumped to his feet, only restrained by a sudden grab from David.

"You must be Major Malard," Lameena said, her voice sweet and melodic. Yes, it was easy to see how she managed to create such a following.

"Yes, ma'am."

She gave a pleasant chuckle as she sat on the empty cot across from him. "I'm not military, so just call me Lameena."

"Sure thing," Nathan answered before David could speak.

The singer gave him a confused, slightly suspicious look. David figured he could relate.

"And this is?" she inquired.

Nathan was not about to let David lead the introductions. Reaching out to take her hand, he slipped across the empty space to sit next to her.

"Nathaniel Darson, sniper. I'm the best shot here."

"I'm sure you are," Lameena answered, her eyes remaining on David. "I've heard a lot about you."

"Thank you," Nathan said, not realizing he was not the subject of the conversation.

"There isn't much to hear that isn't true for others," David answered as he carefully lay back on his pillows. "I'm just a soldier, same as them."

He gave a slight motion toward the rest of the ward. Lameena kept her eyes on him with a smile.

"I was told you're also modest. They say you gave us a chance at calling for help."

David winced. "That wasn't me."

"Oh? They also say you're a living miracle – that you shouldn't be alive."

"That is you," a new voice answered.

The three looked up to watch Keven approach. "Not many have the will to keep going for three days with a bolt in his chest."

David felt himself flush. He didn't like the attention. Riechet was dead; he had been unable to protect him. After making the decision to sacrifice his life if needed to ensure Riechet returned safely, it was he, David Malard, that sat alive and recovering while those who knew the general mourned. He did not want any congratulations to accompany his grief.

"Everybody makes sacrifices," he muttered. "Many don't have the privilege of coming back to be congratulated."

After a brief silence, Lameena gave a firm nod. "You are right. However I would still like to honor you, and all those here, if I may." She stood to look around at the expectant faces. "You have all sacrificed so much. I want you to know that we are grateful to you."

She turned back to David with a smile. Removing a small audio box from her jacket pocket, she tapped in an arrangement that flowed with a soft, melodic tone, beautiful yet sorrowful at the same time. Cupping the box in her hands, Lameena turned so all in the room could see her as she began to sing.

"As stars and moons glow on darkened veil
I close my eyes and let dreams prevail
Of morning dew and soft love's kiss
Let now my heart alight with this
Let now my heart remind me still of this

When moons grow dim, when stars bleed red
When stirring fires grow cold and dead
Beside me be, remind me this
Of hearts alight and soft love's kiss
Let now my heart remind me this

When sorrows fill my troubled heart
When hope lies smothered 'neath the stone
Oh lift my eyes and let me see
The moons, the stars... eternity.

Sing now my sorrowed heart to tell
That soon the world will all be well
That peace will flow throughout this night
That in the end the dawn glows bright
Let now my heart alight with this
Let now my heart remind me still of this

Of hearts alight and soft love's kiss
Let now my heart remind me this"

CHAPTER THIRTY-TWO

David woke the next morning with Lameena Narheen's song still running through his head. He was familiar with the tune, as most people knew at least one or two of her many numbers. In fact, he knew enough to realize some of the words of the original song had been changed. It seemed as if the present situation affected everything. With his eyes still shut, he let his thoughts wander back to when he first heard the song. It was at a concert, not that he was much of a fan. That was left to Melina. She was the one who followed the artist's career, often playing her songs around David and even encouraging him to dance from time to time. He resisted at first. In fact, he resisted many of Melina's advances in the beginning.

Growing up alone and slightly distrustful of people, romance came with some difficulty to David. It was Keven who insisted that David not spend his entire life alone. Noting the casual attraction between his best friend and his sister, he threw himself diligently into the role of matchmaker. After some failed attempts to get them to formally meet, Keven succeeded and David found himself warming up to the idea of having someone to care for. Melina shared many of his interests. Both of them being CLE provided them with a means to gain common ground and they grew steadily closer.

Melina fascinated David. She was playful without being foolish. Her laugh was contagious, making David forget the woes of his past. Though gentle and feminine in many ways, Melina was also tough. Whenever David tried to resist, she was the driving force that got him out to parties, dances and numerous other events David would have otherwise avoided. She brought fresh air into David's life. But that was only a short-lived breath, so quickly vanishing with a single inconceivable act.

David had pulled back in light of her absence. He withdrew inwardly, falling deeper into a despairing loneliness than he had ever experienced at any other point in his life. Only the war kept the full impact of his grief at bay. He let the event consume him, secretly hoping it would eventually take his life even though he still fought to survive. But what if he did survive? What if the war ended in victory for Telamier? What life awaited him? Could he find a means to really live again? Riechet's last word echoed through David's mind. Live. What did it truly mean anyway?

Sitting up, David reached under his cot and withdrew *Excalibur's Legacy*. The weight felt good as he rested the blade in his lap. Strength lay there - a steady, unyielding strength. Carefully, almost reverently, he unwrapped it from its cloth to examine the intricate scrollwork on the hilt. Tracing it with his fingertips, he set his thoughts on the hands that once wielded such a mighty weapon. A soft nicker alerted David to Darkracer's presence. The Candonian lay in a small, secluded alcove across the room, almost invisible within the shadows. Rising slowly, David approached him with sword in hand.

"You are recovering well," Darkracer said as David stepped up in front of him.

"As are you," David answered.

He seated himself on the blankets the Candonian rested on and leaned back against the great creature's side. For a while they remained silent, both staring thoughtfully at the blade David balanced, point down, on the floor in front of them. Finally David spoke.

"I found some form of writing in the etch work."

"Mhmm," came the thoughtful reply.

"You know about it?"

"I do."

"What language is it?"

"Telamierian."

"Do you know what it means?"

"Leader. Guide. Protector."

Unsheathing the sword, David raised it toward the light to inspect the words once again. They contained a strange mixture of flowing script and hieroglyphs David had never encountered before. A lost language by a lost people – lost in war with the Vairdec. How painfully ironic. With a heavy sigh, David lowered the sword to his lap.

"I don't deserve this."

"There are those who feel differently."

"I know." David laid his head back against Darkracer's side to stare at the ceiling. "A leader? Guide? Protector? Am I really all that?"

"Are you?"

David gave a huff. The Candonian's ability to twist a conversation around exasperated him at times. However, David could not deny Darkracer's wisdom. Not up to the challenge of squaring off with the creature in a battle of the mind, David searched for a different topic of conversation. Looking back down at the naked blade, he ran his fingers thoughtfully down its length.

"The Blades of Norian," he spoke, his voice barely above a whisper. "The twelve swords gifted to the Humans by a species they never met."

He shook his head at the tragic twist of fate.

"And yet you owe your existence here to the Telamierians."

"Yes," David answered dejectedly as he sheathed the blade, "a lot of good that's doing us now."

"Would you be free of trouble if you lived on Earth?"

David only shrugged. He didn't wish to answer, as he knew Darkracer was right.

"What of the Candonians?" he asked. "What gift did they ever get?"

"My kind coexisted with the Telamierians. There was no need for any welcome gift."

"You know a lot about the Telamierians, don't you?"

"More than most, which I'm afraid is very little nowadays."

"Do you know why these are called the Blades of Norian?"

"There are theories. Most likely it was the name of the Telamierian who had them forged. They knew of the sword's symbolic significance among Humans. It must have appeared a fitting gift."

"More than fitting – necessary."

David grew quiet as he thought of how the swords had saved the lives of the Founders when they were thrust into battle. Over all these years the swords continued to save lives. The thought of Riechet wielding *Legacy* to rescue David from certain death struck a raw nerve. It was time to think of something else to talk about.

"The Telamierians seemed to know a lot about Humans. Did they visit Earth?"

"Well," Darkracer began, shifting in what felt to David as discomfort over the subject, "I have no knowledge of the Telamierians' travels. Perhaps they did. I do know the Candonians moved through the gateways."

"Is that why there are Candonian creatures on Earth?"

At this Darkracer gave an angry snort. "Those are not Candonians."

"I know that, but they do look a great deal like you. In fact, looking at the pictures I can't tell the difference."

"Looks can be deceiving."

"Why do they look like Candonians then?"

"The horse?"

"Yes."

Darkracer did not answer right away. With the minutes ticking by, David began to wonder if his companion would speak at all. He had not expected the subject to be so uncomfortable for him. Just as he began to wonder if he should try a different subject, Darkracer spoke.

"We are connected," he answered softly. "Candonians use to enjoy the freedom of traveling between worlds. They possessed a special sense that guided them to the energy sources of the gates. It is possible that it was they who taught the Telamierians the gates' secrets. Whatever the case, small bands of Candonians could always be seen crossing between the worlds in the early days. Some of the younger members enjoyed the freedom from the Telamierian herds so much that they began forming their own rogue herds on Earth.

'However, in doing so they began to lose their sense of identity. The longer they stayed on Earth, the lazier and more complacent they grew. They lost their ability to sense the gates and became trapped. Interbreeding, the offspring grew ever more wild until they were even mating with the local species of similar appearance whom the Humans were discovering made useful beasts of burden. What little Candonian sense was left melted away with the promise of another species providing for all their needs. The horse you see upon the pages of Earth books was born."

David understood now why his question brought discomfort. To be a species connected to the existence of a non-sentient being must feel like a great dishonor. Could Humans end up the same way?

Had they in some other world? David's eyes narrowed as he pondered the many questions flooding his mind.

"How do you know all this?" he asked.

"This is a piece of our history carefully passed from one generation to the next so we do not forget what happened long ago. None of us wish for it to happen again."

"And yet legend has it Candonians continued to travel through the gates."

"Yes, we went through the gates all the way up to the Telamierians' annihilation. We never forgot what could happen if we stayed, though."

"Why did the travel stop?"

"The gates are very difficult to find under the best circumstances. They break down around artificial energy sources. With the first Vairdec war, so many machines and weapons came to Telamier that the gates all but disappeared. After years of their absence, we Candonians lost our ability to clearly sense them. I'm afraid there is no going back to Earth."

"Too bad. This would be a good time for it."

"Now David," Darkracer gently scolded, giving him a push with his nose, "you don't really mean to say that you would abandon your home or your people?"

"It would be good for the people to leave this place."

"You don't know that. Besides, if Humans ran back to Earth, you would be no better than the Oxyran nation returning to Ayzat. I hear a lot of angry talk over the feeling of abandonment. Was it, though? Is it any different than what you say you want for your own people? Be careful not to say one thing and do another."

David sat in defeat. He could not argue against the wisdom of the Candonian. A sense of shame gnawed at his gut. He had not really meant to abandon what was his home, or those who would be left behind to face the Vairdec. It was only frustration talking. Nonetheless, Darkracer was right. David knew he needed to use better judgment in what he said. *But still*... a small part of him argued. It felt so tragic to be unable to escape the Vairdec's vicious campaign? Would any Humans be left in the end?

"Don't give up," Darkracer said, his velvet muzzle warming David's cheek. "There is still a lot to live for."

"Live?" The word sent a shiver down David's spine. "If the Vairdec have their way, we'll never get the chance."

"Oh David, there will always be challenges. We can't wait for the perfect time to live our lives. Otherwise, we'd lose a great deal of what it means to live."

CHAPTER THIRTY-THREE

Moera Sveeleet

It spilled from the lips of every Celehi who nervously glanced skyward to their one small moon circling Celhara. Settled into orbit around that moon was a delegate's ship from beyond the super system – a Vairdec ship. Like the rest, Colony Relations Supervisor Rykorik El'loray found himself gazing up at the hazy sky more often than normal, wondering what the next days would bring. Shouldering his way past a small group on one of the many east quadrants' bridges spanning the canals branching their way through the decadent city of Luequara, he broke into a jog to catch one of the speedways heading for the center capital.

Settling back against the cushioned wall of the transport, he closed his eyes with a slight ripple of yellow. He had been so happy to return to the main world after four years abroad. Not to say he disliked his work, but during the last year he longed to see the great cities of Celhara once again. The rich, unspoiled Celehi culture beckoned to him. Unlike the off-world colonies, the civilization of Celhara remained deeply rooted to the traditions and standards built over the centuries. No foreign species settled on its borders, no intermingling and subsequent ways of life tainted the centuries of culture. While alien species visited Celhara from time to time, the world remained, for the most part, alone due to its place on the edge of the Chorbix Super System. Even Celehi who lived in off-world colonies rarely felt the desire to settle back on the distant main world.

El'loray was an exception. He was naturally drawn to the deep-seeded traditions of the home world. The many cultures and styles of living seen within the outer colonies never swayed him. His job merely sent him from colony to colony to make reports on their progress, needs and any specific requests their leaders wished to pose to Celhara. His duties took him all the way to the furthest colonies on the small planet of Krul and back again, with extended stays on Haevor, Telamier and Hardiban. Now home, he hoped to relax and enjoy the chance to reengage with Celhara, discussing philosophy at the oiling spas, participating in garden awakenings, maybe even watch a lighted dance performance. His hope in all that failed upon his arrival.

He rolled his head dejectedly to the side, watching the glittering city streak by beyond the tinted window. Vairdec. Of all the species to suddenly show, it had to be them. It came as little surprise, though. Ever since the Celehi embarrassed the Vairdec on Telamier, the latter species hovered at the edge of Chorbix from which they were banned, subsequently staring down their old enemy whose planet happened to orbit just beyond the border. Sooner or later El'loray knew a declaration of war would come. But why now? Why did it have to happen during a time when he found his presence indispensable at the capital? What were these negotiations about anyway?

"Oask troduc," the automated voice announced as the speedway slid to a halt outside the capital building.

El'loray stepped through the door with a small crowd of various capital workers, subconsciously glancing skyward once again. The moon lay out of sight of Luequara, but he still felt the eyes of the Vairdec glowering down upon his shoulders. Ducking his head, he slipped beneath the first tier of the building and headed for the lift. No one sitting along the rounded sides of the glass lift's interior spoke. Fidgeting hands, furtive glances and ripples of color vividly expressed the undercurrent of tension. El'loray refused to look at anyone. Enough lay on his mind, especially the one nagging question that bothered him since he received his meeting notice last night. Why him?

After climbing walls and sweeping along the roofs of the various tiered levels of the building, the lift finally came to rest at the central meeting chamber where representatives from across the globe now congregated. Luequara was an ideal place for the talks to commence. It floated on an inland sea, secluded from the other vast cities of Celhara by towering cliffs and mountains that protected it from storms and, at this moment, any possible attack from Vairdec. Though a relatively trusting species, the Celehi learned over time the value of adding extra defenses to their cities. The surrounding cliffs housed numerous cannons and an impressive pulse-shield able to knock attacking ships from the sky with electro-magnetic waves.

El'loray crossed the hard, shimmering floor without a word, even his footsteps silenced by the sound absorbing qualities of the tiles. Above him the porous ceiling glowed with the morning light captured by the buildings internal reflectors and amplified throughout. Around him the walls gleamed with life-like murals of historical events. El'loray rippled a subtle yellow as he flinched, catching sight of a Vairdec image out the corner of his eye. A battle scene from Telamier, he noted. A similar mural decorated the central capital of that colony world. Hurriedly turning away from the sight, El'loray made his way to what appeared to be a solid wall. In reality it was an imaging system that instantly read the metallic band on his upper arm and let his pass through to the large chamber beyond.

Many of the Celehi delegates already there looked his way, only to return to their quiet conversations without further acknowledgement. One stately, older man approached with a nod.

"Bota auh'nia."

El'loray returned the nod. "Bota."

He chose not to answer how he was. No one needed to hear it said to understand how each felt. The Vairdec faction leader would right now be stepping into the ambassador quarters of the moon's negotiation hall to speak with them. Following the older delegate to a seat along the outer rim of the circle, El'loray took note that all ten of the Celehi leaders were present. Celhara was a one-government world with ten equal rulers chosen every seven years by popular vote. With all ten present, along with numerous subsidiary leaders and city chiefs, El'loray felt suddenly out of place. Just as the last few Celehi entered the building, the image of the Vairdec leader appeared in the center of the room.

El'loray gave an involuntary shuddered as the figure materialized. He had only seen image representations of Vairdec, never one so real, so close, before. Even though he was still looking at an image, this time it represented someone very close, able to respond to anything said or done within that room. The Vairdec stood as tall as a Celehi, but his build suggested greater physical strength and stamina. He carried no weapons, presenting himself as one who held no reason to rely on them even if the need arose. Instead of the armor and war mask prevalent in Celehi art, he wore a distinguished grey and black military suit offset by an orange half-cape draped across one shoulder. His eyes were dominated by giant black pupils encircled by brilliant swirls of green and gold. Countless tiny hairs covered his skin in a dense, velvety layer of pale gray-green. An impressive black mane covered his head, neck and shoulders, falling around his face in gentle, silken waves.

But it was the face that captured El'loray's full attention. Without the gruesome masks the Celehi so readily associated with Vairdec, he found himself looking at one not too different from so many sentient beings he encountered in his travels. The face was slightly angular with strong, rugged cheekbones and brow line, both, El'loray observed, being softer and rounder than that of the Celehi. He had a visible nose and a mouth that, contrary to Celehi lore, did not brim with froth and fangs. There was a calm, almost pleasant, expression upon the Vairdec's lips.

"Greetings," he spoke, his Celeharan nearly perfect, "my name is Nor-Yahvan of the Eevgiah Faction. I come not in a state of war, but of negotiation between our civilizations."

He gave a respectable pause, allowing the leaders to authorize his continuation. The Celehi did not respond immediately. Instead they looked between each other, receiving nods from each member to be sure they were all in agreement. El'loray watched the proceedings intently, but his mind was not on the current actions. Nor-Yahvan. Where had he heard that name before? And what of the Eevgiah Faction?

Receiving the approval to proceed, Nor-Yahvan gave a slight bow and continued.

"It has come to the attention of the Eevgiah that a rogue faction has tried in folly to declare war upon your great nation. Not all Vairdec agree to this warring behavior, and the unprovoked nature of the rogues' actions have led Eevgiah to turn upon them in favor of peace with the Celehi. We are a strong and well stationed faction, and our coming to your borders has quelled the aggression."

A couple of the leaders leaned toward one another to speak in hushed tones. After a few brief words, one rose to face Nor-Yahvan.

"It was not one rouge faction that declared war upon us, it was three large, seemingly well-established factions intent upon our destruction. We know several ships slipped over our borders, for many of our scouts and long-range communications have been destroyed."

"A regrettable incident, I assure you," Nor-Yahvan replied. "However, if I may humbly correct you, it was one faction so disconnected and scattered along the border, the scanners could easily mistake it for two. As for the third, that would have been the presence of the congregating Eevgiah. We are large and powerful, no doubt causing undue concern to Celhara - to that I apologize. The rogues have made it difficult for us to contact you until now, despite our strength. However, the immediate danger is over. As for those who slipped into the super system, I offer my aid if allowed to enter with a few tactical ships to hunt down these renegades."

Again a polite pause. The Celehi turned to one another to discuss the matter. El'loray kept his eyes on Nor-Yahvan. Where had he heard that name?

"Sir," one of the leaders spoke, rising slowly as he did, "if I may ask, what is the name of this rogue faction and why did they choose to attack us so brazenly? While we understand our two species hold no open compassion for one another, I did not believe Vairdec to attack without specific cause."

"A Vairdec of justice will not attack without specific cause," Nor-Yahvan corrected. "However, it appears this faction has little justice. They are deeply rooted to the humiliation of banishment, no doubt connected to the war of so many years ago. Most

Vairdec care little for that moment in history, but it is not my faction's specific history so we will not heed it. A few feel otherwise. As for the name, they are not a recognized faction within Vairdec society, having formed through a variety of discontented individuals."

It made sense, El'loray admitted. Nor-Yahvan was conducting himself with great poise and courtesy. He spoke the truth and showed little fear of deceit. So why did this feel so wrong? His thoughts were broken by the question posed by a nearby delegate.

"What of Arct-Ieya? It has come to our attention that she is the leader to this act of aggression. I can imagine she would feel justified in attacking us."

El'loray focused hard on the Vairdec, trying to catch the subtle changes in Nor-Yahvan's mood. He remained hard to read but El'loray took note of the longer pause taken before a response came.

"Arct-Ieya does have justified reasons to attack," he admitted, "and I will not speak either way for her. The humiliation was great and her standing became fractured within Vairdec society. The strain, I fear, has broken her. She resides far beyond this system, perhaps beyond the galaxy itself, as we have not heard from her for well over a century. Most likely you picked up communications from these rogues who use her name as a means to rally others to their cause. I have heard such myself. Regrettable but understandable."

More hushed discussion flowed through the ranks of Celehi. El'loray's gaze wandered the room. The leaders hid their thoughts well, and he found it difficult to tell whether they believed Nor-Yahvan's words or not.

From across the room, one rose respectfully. "You say that the vast majority of this rogue threat has been neutralized by your faction. If this is so, why should we consider assistance from you?"

El'loray's attention shot back to Nor-Yahvan. It was a very good question. How would the Vairdec respond? A slight smile graced the alien's soft features.

"As Vairdec, we are far better equipped to hunt our own. This is a vast system and Vairdec technology includes sensor blocks and visual cloaking shields. Without the proper knowledge of our ships energy outputs you may never find the rogue ships."

This acknowledgment of Vairdec power rippled uncomfortably through the Celehi ranks. The consideration of cloaking technology among the Vairdec came as nothing new, but to hear it confessed by one of its leaders unsettled the Celehi nonetheless. Nor-Yahvan waited patiently for the delegates to finish their hushed conversations. At last one of the planet leaders rose.

"Would you provide us with the information on these rogue ships' signatures so we may conduct a proper hunt?"

"That, I'm afraid, is a privilege beyond our relationship status."

More hushed discussions. The speaker remained standing, looking hard into Nor-Yahvan's image, though it was clear he was listening to those around him.

"We will consider your offer of assistance within the super system and give you our answer in the morning," he announced.

Nor-Yahvan gave a bow. "As you wish."

The image faded and the Celehi were left alone in the room.

"We cannot allow Vairdec ships into this system," one delegate spoke out.

Another just shook her head. "What choice do we have? We know the Vairdec are in the system already."

"Have communications been reestablished with the outlying colonies?"

"Not all. Those on the far reaches are not yet responding."

"Which are those?"

"Vezbree, Krul, Gil'landra and Telamier," El'loray answered before realizing he had just joined in the conversation.

Several pairs of eyes looked his direction. A leader of the western sector motioned to him.

"Colony Supervisory El'loray?"

"I am he."

"Can you add any insights from your work among the colonies?"

El'loray rose respectfully. "Not on the Vairdec invasion. I never crossed paths with any rogue ships and only the last colonies I visited spoke of possible aggressions. I returned with the Mor'vayat convoy deployed to assist when war was declared. Apparently they were the only close colony that brought aid."

"That is correct," another leader said. "Only our colonies farthest from this border that possessed the means to send military aid were requested to do so. Those furthest out never arrived."

El'loray cocked his head in thought. "Telamier would have sent a convoy. They should have arrived by now, should they not?"

"We sent word for them to turn back when the Vairdec withdrew. With the information we have on a thwarted battle plan, we felt it unnecessary to have them come all this way. Furthermore, if rogue Vairdec are still in the super system, we wanted them to be on alert for them deeper in the system."

"And to return to protect their planet," another leader added.

"I assume they received this message?" El'loray asked.

"Yes, we received confirmation of the order, but that was when communications ceased. We have not been able to reach them since."

"How long ago was that?"

"Over two nahms." A pause followed as the exact time was checked. "Forty-nine days ago."

One of the leaders rippled with exasperation. "That long ago?"

"When will communication be reestablished?" a delegate asked.

"That is still unknown," a representative of the satellite controllers answered. "Hopefully soon, but if satellites were destroyed deeper in the system, it will take far longer."

"And what of repair vessels being deployed? I have heard some disturbing news."

"At least one has fallen to these rogues. It is difficult to mobilize the proper units with Vairdec so close in our orbit. We will need military protection when venturing further into space."

"Supervisor El'loray."

El'loray turned his attention to a leader across the room.

"What strength did you see in communication technologies beyond our own colonies? The Vairdec may have targeted Celehi satellites, but they would likely avoid other species."

"Well," El'loray began, "Hardiban is, of course, our most likely point of contact despite its distance from us. The Teshians are strong allies. They also have a growing colony on Telamier, as do the Manogonites."

"I would not wish to rely solely on Manogonites," a voice in the crowd grumbled.

"The Humans are also strong allies with us," El'loray continued. "However, they share much of the same satellite networks. They have no contact with their home world, so long distance communications are shared with our technologies."

"Humans," one of the leaders mused, "they are a small colony, are they not?"

El'loray gave a quick nod. "Yes, their population is quite small, but they control a vast region in conjunction with the Candonian species on Telamier. Their military prowess has served them well. In fact, Humans, not Celehi, lead the joint military division that involves studying Vairdec and their tactics."

"I know of this," another leader spoke. "Their joint spy network has given us several useful insights into Vairdec mannerisms."

462

"Can it help us now?" someone asked.

"We do have officers here who trained with their units for a time. They are already deployed to watch Eevgiah's leader."

A delegate in military dress spoke up for the first time. "Their training occurred over two years ago. It is known that Humans have continued to run covert operations which may have given them further insights into Vairdec tactics."

One of the leaders gave a firm nod. "Then we must contact them as soon as communications are reestablished."

"Again," came the argument, "that may take time as we cannot get repair teams to venture far enough from our immediate system."

"Perhaps we should let the Eevgiah Faction assist."

The comment caused a heavy silence to fall over the crowd. The eldest of the leaders slowly rose and lifted his hand.

"If I may make a proposal. We all have much to consider and it may be best if we are given personal time to contemplate the nature of this decision. Let us give ourselves the next hours in solitary contemplation then return to express our considerations in full."

A general agreement rippled through the room. Moments later El'loray found himself back on the main street, gazing up at the sky, still trying to understand the reasons for his overwhelming anxiety.

That evening El'loray restlessly paced his apartment as he thought. He first considered heading for the public oil den to indulge in the luxury of some much deserved pampering. Unfortunately he knew the rich oils massaged into his iridescent skin would have little effect at calming his turbulent mind. So instead he paced. It angered him that Nor-Yahvan's identity kept eluding him. He heard it once before – but where? The hours slipped by at an alarming rate. Before long the decision on whether or not to accept the Vairdec's help would come. Personally he was against the idea despite no solid evidence available to support his feelings. Or was there?

Collapsing onto a bench, El'loray let his feelings ripple freely over his skin. A display of yellow, red and orange played in the greenish hue of the glow orbs beside him. Nor-Yahvan. He must have heard the name on Telamier. It was one of the few places where study of the Vairdec remained truly active; the Human's Strategic Intelligence and Enforcement Regional Agency saw to that. El'loray rose to continue his pacing. While on Telamier he spent a nahm studying with the group near the Human city of Karnoss. Humans certainly proved themselves an industrious species, he mused. No, no! Focus. What had he learned? Those who summoned him to the meeting that day had felt what he learned in his travels was of some importance or he would not have been called. He just needed to remember. But that was nearly a year ago. Much had happened since then.

Hurriedly he looked to his journals, sweeping through list after list as they flashed in front of him. Several screens were dedicated to SIERA, though none of them mentioned Nor-Yahvan. He knew all this even before checking. The journals were the first things he checked upon returning to his apartment after the meeting adjourned. Everything in his notes also lay in the hands of the Celharan military. So why search them now? He felt himself growing frantic. With a final exasperated sweep of his hands he shut down the journals and collapsed onto the bench once again.

Calm yourself, he ordered inwardly. *Relax first.*

Taking a deep breath, El'loray closed his eyes and began to meditate on his travels, reaching further and further into his mind as he rewound the events of the past year. Karnoss – it was a glamorous city, fascinating but certainly too gaudy to suit his tastes. Tralex Desert – what a strange place to build a tourist city of entertainment. Everything was so bleak, so desolate and rugged. Valor Peak – central headquarters of SIERA. It was an ingeniously placed facility – Celehi design, of course. But now the Humans claimed it. Humans... General Kyler Riechet, yes, that was it. A respectable Human. El'loray liked him. Had he said anything about Nor-Yahvan? Nothing came to mind. There were many Humans around. Since El'loray spent most of his time among Celehi colonies, the time with SIERA proved a most interesting cultural experience. Human personalities varied so greatly. Some, like the general, presented themselves with proper dignity. Some preferred to joke and play. Joke and play... joke and play... El'loray had overheard many a conversation during meals. He understood little of what was spoken, preferring to stay close to the Celehi officers assigned to the division. The conversations now played without reason through his mind. Voices grew clearer.

I'm glad I'm not Vairdec. I'm not sharing one woman with a bunch of other guys.

You'd prefer it the other way around, wouldn't you?

Share the love.

Laughter. More joking. Humans seemed so preoccupied with sexuality.

You just don't want to consider yourself dominated by a woman.

Hey, you can dominate me any time.

Sounds like our girl is up to four now.

Four? Arct-Ieya?

That's the word. Weren't you at the last set of classes?

Had other duties.

Had other duties, yes, El'loray had just returned to the division himself. He missed hearing whatever was in those classes.

Well, sounds like the sick little bardroe's moving up in the universe.

Numbers count for something, I guess.

Yeah, but according to the classes it sounds like she actually likes this Nor-Yahvan guy.

Ah, is she going soft?

The conversation slipped from El'loray's memory as quickly as it came. His eyes snapped open and the multi-colored ripples washed away with a stream of white. Nor-Yahvan. Nor-Yahvan was Arct-Ieya's mate – a favorite mate at that. And if there was ever a Vairdec who posed a threat to the Celehi, it

466

was she. As much as the bench weighed, it still managed to scrape the floor under the violent leap El'loray took from it. He must let the leaders know of this. Reaching the communication board, he was surprised to find it already activated. Someone was trying to contact him. Opening the line, El'loray faced a government official and close friend who never failed to pass news of decisions from the government head to El'loray.

"You look concerned," he observed.

"I am," El'loray admitted hurriedly. "I must speak with the leaders right away. It's about the Vairdec."

"No need," the official answered with a shake of his head. "Apparently communications have opened with some of the outer colonies."

"Telamier?"

"Not yet, but it sounds as if rogue Vairdec ships have been spotted along trade routes. They're extremely elusive. Authorized forces are having trouble catching them."

"What about Telamier?"

"I just told you, communication has not been reestablished with them. Our satellites are not working that far out. The leaders are impatient and determined to fix this problem as quickly as possible so they're taking any help offered."

El'loray knew what this meant, and though he hated to ask, found himself doing so regardless. "Have they granted the Eevgiah Faction access to the super system?"

"They have. They didn't even need a tiebreaker council for the vote. Nor-Yahvan is moving a seeker team in as we speak."

CHAPTER THIRTY-FOUR

"Keep it out a little more or it can bounce back into your face."

David adjusted his sword's position and blocked Amber's strike once more.

"Better," she said, allowing her blade to slide off his block. "Stay aware of your blade's angle. Norian Blades can handle an edge block but many others can't. Get in the habit of protecting your sword's edge regardless."

David enjoyed sparring with Amber. It gave him something to do. Without the uses of the highest level of medical technology, his recovery ground to a torturously slow pace. At least he fell among the lucky few who were recovering. Already his workouts stretched to a full twenty-minutes. Regrettably his movement remained stiff and sloppy compared to Amber's graceful steps. David found the need to constantly remind himself that her studies dated back to her youth while his skills still lay at a beginner's level. At least swordsmanship held a 'last option' status on the battlefield. While David lacked any true skill with a blade, his accuracy with a gun remained one of the highest within SIERA.

With a flick of her wrist, Amber brought her sword around to land it on the back of David's leg.

"Keep your focus on me, not the blade," she instructed. "And don't rely on the sword to block every blow. Sometimes the best defense is to just move."

Easier said than done, David thought as he felt the stiffness in his leg beginning to grow. However, he gave a firm nod. Amber sensed his fatigue and rested her sword against her shoulder.

"Call it a day."

"Yes, ma'am."

As David retrieved *Legacy's* scabbard from the corner of the small workout chamber, he found himself grow suddenly weary with a wave of grief. Holding the sword in both hands, he let himself slump against the wall, sliding down to a sit with a heavy sigh.

"Are you all right?" Amber questioned as she hurried to his side.

"I'm fine," David reassured, "I was just thinking."

Amber seated herself next to him, resting her sword across her knees. "About what?"

"What if the message doesn't go through?"

"That was always a possibility."

David hesitated to say more. A strain was evident in Amber's voice. However, David longed to put into words the disturbing thoughts that plagued him day and night.

"It wasn't fair to lose him," he said, tracing the etching on *Legacy* with his finger. "I just can't stand thinking it may be for nothing."

Amber refused to speak for a long time. David held his tongue, unwilling to push further into the subject. Instead he rested his head against the stone behind him and closed his eyes. When Amber finally spoke, her voice barely made it above a whisper.

"He believed. I guess we should, too. No effort to end this war is in vain. Whatever happens in regards to that message is out of our hands. Who knows, maybe all of this," she made a broad motion with her hands, "all this fighting is for nothing. We still fight, though. It's all we can do."

Before David found any words to answer her, Amber rose and exited the chamber.

Across the super system, another also wondered if his efforts were for naught. Though El'loray immediately relayed the information he remembered about Nor-Yahvan to the leaders, to his dismay he faced nothing but skepticism. They questioned his failure to include the information in his official journals and wondered about the accuracy of a casual conversation overheard a year before. These questions proved difficult to answer, and in the end, he, like the rest of Celhara, grudgingly contended with the Vairdec entering the system close to their home world.

Surprisingly Nor-Yahvan stayed true to his promise. He worked quickly alongside the Celehi and successfully brought to justice four rogue Vairdec ships. El'loray refused to watch the public executions of the ships' captains. Though the actions convinced the leaders Nor-Yahvan truly sought peace, El'loray felt uneasy about the Vairdec's presence. Many times he questioned himself over whether he actually remembered that infamous conversation correctly. If his memory was correct, that meant Nor-Yahvan lied to the Celehi. Arct-Ieya had not disappeared a century ago. In which case, why was her mate assisting the Celehi now? What motivation drove him? Once communication with Telamier came back online, El'loray planned to insist on making the first call. There was someone he urgently needed to speak with.

Nor-Yahan's seeker ships swept past his view port as they prepared for yet another run through part of the system. This time he planned to go farther in than from the past runs. Already many of his ships were on route. How simple the Celehi remained, how trusting and naïve despite the centuries to learn otherwise. Their desire to placate in order to avoid conflict would cost them a prize colony. The agreement he established with them felt almost too simple. Enter the system with only a small number of predetermined ships and be escorted by Celehi watchers. The watchers proved easy to elude for short periods, allowing what appeared as less destructive seekers to deploy an array of war vessels from their camouflaged holds. Already a growing barricade lay between Telamier and its strongest allies of Hardiban and Celhara. They would wait in secret until Nor-Yahvan ordered them to Telamier.

Acquiring Arct-Ieya as a mate proved a more strategic decision than first thought. The Eevgiah

Faction held a respectable reputation among many of the larger Vairdec factions spread across numerous super systems. To openly engage in an attack on a planet he held no acceptable claim to would be deemed shameful. Arct-Ieya's claim, however, remained quite acceptable by Vairdec standards. If she managed to neutralize the planet and set a permanent claim to it, Nor-Yahvan, as her favored mate, could settle his faction on Telamier with no question from other Vairdec factions. Once he established Eevgiah on the planet, the combined forces of Arct-Ieya and Nor-Yahvan would be unrivaled by any who may consider reclaiming Telamier for themselves. Not even the Celehi with the full force of their allies held the power to stop them. All that remained was to wait for Arct-Ieya's signal to join.

David found it difficult to sleep. That's all he seemed to be doing. His restlessness steadily increased by the day. Having been moved to the officers' quarters, he found himself immersed back into the news of daily missions. Amber held to the tactics of her father, sending out smaller teams for quick engagements meant to slow the progress of the Vairdec while reducing their ranks any way possible. Without efficient numbers of soldiers to stage a large offensive, it was the best they could do.

So far the Vairdec kept their hunt for the resistance in the crumbling residential district and upper tunnels. With enough hiding places still in the city for soldiers to conceal themselves, the Vairdec thankfully remained ignorant of the thought of digging further down. It made the missions no less dangerous. Every time a friend headed to the surface, David feared it would be the last time he would see that individual. It always came as a great relief when they returned, wearily collapsing onto empty cots.

Such was the case with Keven, now a captain and resident to the officer's quarters, who at the moment was shedding his soiled field gear with little care over where it dropped. After peeling off a filth-ridden shirt, he eased himself onto the edge of his cot and looked across at David.

"Good to see you back," David admitted.

"Thanks," Keven answered with a groan. "Sorry I haven't been around to see you much. I've been taking a lot of duty top side."

David shrugged it off. He understood. As Keven leaned back against the wall to stare at the ceiling in obvious physical and emotional fatigue, a feeling of helplessness washed over David. He wanted so desperately to take the stresses of war from his battle-worn companion.

"I meant to visit more," Keven continued. "After all, you're the closest friend I've got around here." He paused and David watched a new wave of grief form in Keven's features. "In fact you may be all that's left of who I knew before the war." He pushed off the wall, allowing his body to slump forward with his elbows on his knees. "I shouldn't be here."

"You're a valuable member of this division."

"What of San Terres?"

David grew silent. What of San Terres? The question vexed him more often than he liked, especially since lying around recovering gave him little else to think on. He hated to imagine what the city might look like now. After all, it was his home, as it was Keven's. David found himself unable to look at Keven, knowing his friend left far more behind than he. Another agonized groan escaped from behind Keven's hands. David slowly rose, crossing to sit beside him and place an understanding hand on his back.

"I'm sure they're still alive. Your parents are smart and resourceful."

"I was selfish," Keven confessed, his voice filled with grief. "I couldn't handle things, so I left. I never thought about what they were going through. Now I'm not there for them when they need me."

"It's not your fault. Besides, there're a lot of people here that need you."

Keven looked up to try giving David a reassuring look.

"I know," he admitted, "but I can't stop wondering about it at times."

David gave a nod. He understood his friend's struggle but had no words to help him. Fortunately Mike provided a distraction as he entered to drag himself into bed with a groan. David could smell the combination of dirt, sweat and blood that so commonly clung to everyone's clothing, hoping the later did not belong to his friend. Carefully he looked the pilot over for injuries. Not even the valued fighter pilots were exempt from ground missions now.

"You know you're lucky," Mike said without looking David's direction. "The only way to get any rest nowadays is to get shot."

"Are you hurt?"

"No. Not lucky enough for that."

At this, Mike opened his eyes to look at David, trying to give him a weak, reassuring smile.

"When was the last time you got any rest?" David asked.

"Three, four days ago. Can't be sure anymore."

Though he knew he was not at fault, David felt a twinge of guilt tug at his gut. He felt so weak, so inadequate, lying around the bunkers all day while his friends suffered – even died. David held his gaze on Mike as the pilot fell into a heavy, dreamless sleep. Ready or not, he knew it was time.

"Commander," the communications specialist nearly hissed.

The older Teshian responded quickly yet calmly to her petty officer's call. Her duty aboard the solar system scout module added to a long list of commands, providing her the experience to handle any situation with poise. Initially her orders consisted of patrolling for smugglers closing in on the vicinity of Hardiban. With a surprising call from her commanders, she learned of the authorized entry of Vairdec into the super system. How arrogant of the Celehi to allow such a move without consulting their allies. It caused her now to be on high alert for not just smugglers but suspicious Vairdec activity. Any call from her officers made her bristle.

"Proceed," she ordered.

Only with her response did the specialist respectfully turn his gaze from her and back to his readouts.

"We seem to be picking up a distorted signal."

"From where?"

"I am unclear to that. I will try locating its source."

As the specialist worked, the commander crossed to her post and climbed the two steps to a platform where she stood gripping the rail. The move signaled the rest of the bridge to raise their alert level. All of this happened without word or alarm. Every Teshian grew more focused on their tasks of sweeping the surrounding space for answers to the signal. Finally the specialist set his gaze back on his leader.

"Commander, it appears the signal is passing through a deep space satellite."

"Owned by?"

"Celehi presumably."

"And the message?"

"Nothing is deciphered yet. It is a message of some kind, though."

"Ensign," the commander called, "assist."

The ensign joined the specialist and together they began the work of piecing the weak signal together. No one spoke. Despite the growing curiosity among those on the bridge, each worked at his and her tasks without so much as a glance in the direction of the two busily working on the message. Only the commanding officer kept her gaze trained upon the specialist and ensign, her red eyes narrowing to slits as she thought over the possible results of their work.

For an hour they toiled, struggling to patch together the weak fragments garbled over a distant satellite transmission. At the commander's instructions, the ship headed toward the signal, closing the distance and creating a stronger return. With the message finally coming together, the announcement that it was coded and generating from links with a Spynix satellite created all the more tension. Regardless, the crew remained trained upon their own tasks, knowing to turn from their duties to watch would be a breach in protocol. A slight glimmer of pride appeared in the commander's eyes. Her crew conducted themselves with great professionalism. If trouble lay ahead they would be ready.

"Commander." The specialist's voice sounded irritatingly loud within the confines of the bridge. "This is a military base alert from Telamier."

"To whom was the message intended?"

"There is no indication. The coding is basic military script for all allied systems."

The commander gave a slight nod of understanding. She may be a lower rank among the professional Teshian military personnel but held enough training to know that such a code meant the message had gone out as an all hail, intended for anyone who would listen. Well, she was listening.

"What do the Celehi say?"

"It is not the Celehi, commander. This came from the Earthenian military."

"And they are?" she asked.

She waited patiently as her crewmembers continued working through the code to decipher the full message. A junior officer quickly went to work on answering her question, scouring his computer for the needed information.

"Commander," he said, waiting silently for her to make eye contact. "Earthenians are of the Human species."

She gave a nod and he turned away. Humans. She had heard of them. They were close allies to the Celehi and had shown their worth among Teshians. This message now felt even more urgent to her. While she knew her crew worked as quickly as they could to reveal the full message, her patience was growing thin and she dug her long nails into the railing. The ensign suddenly leapt from his chair. Realizing his error he hurriedly seated himself again with head lowered.

"Commander."

"Proceed," she stated before he had time to finish his address of her.

"Telamier is under attack. The Vairdec are taking the planet."

The tension electrified throughout the bridge. While Telamier was nothing more than a colony planet, they all knew the implications. The Vairdec not only entered a super system from which they were banned, they had come in a state of war. What other worlds would meet the same fate? Furthermore, many Teshians worked and even lived on Telamier. As an ally, those on Hardiban must heed the call.

"Open a communicate with the High Military and relay this finding to the nearest Celehi network."

The specialist shook his head. "I'm afraid I cannot. We are getting interference."

"From what?"

"Commander," the helmsman called, "I am picking up faint readings of Vairdec ships. They appear to be headed our direction."

CHAPTER THIRTY-FIVE

David held himself as straight as possible. It no longer hurt so much to do so. Yes, he was ready.

"Colonel."

Amber's response was subtle as she sat behind her quarters' desk. Only her eyes turned to him.

"Major."

Her guarded demeanor caused David to hesitate. Collecting himself quickly he forged ahead.

"I would like to report for active duty."

A visible slump came to Amber's shoulders. She appeared almost saddened by his worlds.

"I would like the doctor's report first. Get yourself in for an exam."

David set the datapad in front of her. "Already done."

Amber only pushed it aside. "Are you sure about this?"

"Yes, ma'am."

"You almost died, you know."

David hated to be reminded. "Yes, ma'am."

"In fact you were technically dead for three minutes."

At this David remained silent. He had not been given that information before. It gave him a strange sensation in the pit of his stomach but did little to alter his resolve.

"Any one of us could die at any time. I am no exception, nor should I be."

Amber's hands clenched into fists as she stared almost hatefully at the report on her desk. Despite the intolerable silence, David held his tongue, waiting patiently for the verdict. At long last a fatigue appeared in Amber's expression. She had surrendered.

"You shall replace Stoneman as commanding officer on tomorrow's harvest mission. Our two sub-T fields are still intact and I'd like to keep them that way. You shall accompany the fresh guard unit and oversee the gathering of harvestable crop. This is not an engagement mission, so avoid the Vairdec at all cost."

David surprised himself by the disappointment he felt.

"Those fields are valuable," Amber continued. "Do not tip off the enemy."

"Yes, ma'am."

Another salvage operation, David thought as he left Amber's quarters. At least no possibility lay in a repeat of his last salvage mission – Amber would not be accompanying them. Scanning through the names, he found only three he recognized. Phantom and Toodat raised his confidence level in his team and seeing Darkracer's name set his mind further at ease.

While he had insisted in his readiness, his heart still raced at the thought of joining the fight again. Was he ready?

Entering the mess hall, David quickly spotted Mike seated by the back wall. It saddened David to see the state of his friend. Mike slumped against the table, his head resting in his bandaged hand. His hair, grown out since no one cared to take the time in detailed grooming nowadays, fell partially across his dulling eyes. The activity around him went unnoticed. His flight jacket lay limply across his thinning frame. David wondered if his own appearance was similar to the pilot's.

"How have you been?" he asked as he seated himself across from Mike.

Raising his head slowly, Mike gave a warm smile. At least that hadn't changed.

"Well enough. What of you?"

"I'm back on active duty."

Mike straightened, his eyes fixed firmly on his friend. "Really? The colonel let you back?"

David gave an affirming nod. "She didn't seem to want to, though."

Mike turned his focus to the table. "Well, I guess it's not easy for her – ordering people away, not knowing if they'll come back."

"It's a position I certainly don't envy."

"Agreed. We only have to worry about coming back."

A long silence followed.

"So," Mike finally said. "What's your mission?"

"Escorting the new guard to the sub-T fields and watching over harvesters. Not exactly high risk."

"High enough, not to mention important. Food is scarce nowadays."

David nodded slowly. It was disappointing that the government had missed such an important detail as providing enough food for the bunkers. Since an attack on the scale they now faced never came to mind during preparation, only food enough for two nahms was ever stored. Furthermore, the amount was calculated for the average population of Karnoss nearly three years prior. The added civilians involved with the festival and SIERA's numbers were sadly overlooked. The only thing keeping everyone from starving came from the fact that a large number had already died.

"Who's on your team?"

It took David a moment to register the question and form a response. That response time would have to change in the next few hours.

"Not many I know. Toodat's in, as are the Candonians. None of the other names look familiar."

"You've been out of the game for a nahm. It doesn't take long for personnel to change during war."

"I can see that."

Mike reached across the table to slide David's datapad toward himself and glanced over the names.

"Not many regulars here. I'm not surprised. The colonel has to hold back trained fighters for combat missions. In fact, I'm surprised to see Toodat. I guess a couple good guns are wise, though. We've had an increase in young volunteers, so those strong enough and savvy enough to make the trip are harvesters." Mike paused as he read the list through. "Yeah, like you, I don't know many of these names. It's hard to keep track of everyone with all the comings and goings."

Mike grew more somber with the last words and silence dominated the table.

"Pecquin I know," he ventured in an attempt to draw both his and David's thoughts away from the growing casualty list. "He's one of the Airisuns."

David knew whom he was talking about. Though he had not known the individual's name, he had been present when the Airisuns were discovered in the company of the Faxon-led renegade that nearly took Amber's life. While he knew the Airisuns played no role in the attack or the colonel's injury, David felt himself growing agitated by the prospect of having any of them on his team. Quickly he shoved the thought aside.

"I've had little experience with Airisuns."

"Don't worry," Mike reassured, "they're actually a very friendly species – especially these. They've remained overly grateful for being allowed to join the bunkers."

"So why aren't they with the refugees?"

"They volunteered for duty. They don't have any combat skills, but the mind of an Airisun is quite amazing. They learn fast and don't readily forget information. They're already speaking our language as well as keeping track of inventory and troop movements. Some have likened the species to walking data files."

"You seem to know a lot about them."

Mike shrugged. "I'm a pilot. I get around."

David wanted to hear more, curious now as to the nature of Mike's past. Though he considered Mike a close friend, David realized he still knew very little about the man. However, he kept the burning questions to himself. At the moment, Mike clearly appeared to be fading fast.

"Why don't you get some rest?"

Mike sat up with a smile, trying to feign a sense of energy. "Love to. And I will once the report on the *Predator* comes through."

"She's still not operational?"

"She flew earlier this nahm. We tried to see if we could make a run south to the Naharan Range. It would be huge if we can connect with any remaining military down that way."

"And?"

Disappointment clouded Mike's eyes. "Never made it. The Vairdec are holding more heavily in the mountains than we thought. We might not even have a military anymore."

"I thought Earthenia was a lesser target for them, that most of their forces were around Celehi centers."

"That's what we all thought." Mike ran a hand over his stubble-covered face. "Maybe they were. Maybe there aren't enough Celehi left to worry about."

So this was it, David thought. If what Mike said was true, there was little time left for any of them.

The Teshian commander nearly growled at the news coming over her private line. As critical as the discovered message was, there would be no way to send it to Celhara without risking its interception by the ever-watchful Vairdec. Her ship barely escaped the last ship, which forced them off course and further from Hardiban then she liked. Nor-Yahvan admirably succeeded in subtly confining each of the super system's most powerful planet nations.

Teshian leadership cautioned against any plan to send their armies from Hardiban to Telamier without Celhara's direct involvement. Regardless of the weak nature of the excuse, such a move on the Teshian's part could be viewed as an unwonted attack against Arct-Ieya and enough reason for Nor-Yahvan to declare war without bringing shame to his faction. With his ships closing on the borders of Hardiban's system, the move would be exceptionally risky for the Teshians. Since the Vairdec saw this as a Celehi matter, only if the Teshians responded to a specific request from Celhara could they avoid a strike from the Eevgiah Faction.

Under such close watch, the message would have to be delivered to Celhara in person. The commander's new orders were to do just that. Luckily her former orders acted as a perfect cover. With the volunteering of some visiting Celehi, she would have her smugglers who, by law, must be returned to their home world to stand trial. It made for the perfect excuse to head for Celhara, but first her ship needed to return to Hardiban for fresh supplies and the "smugglers". Then came the long trip to Celhara. The commander feared their efforts might be too late.

David looked over his team while trying to hide any signs of disappointment. They were young, malnourished and worn. Many showed signs of the inevitable fear associated with missions above ground despite their efforts to hold back the emotion. The harvesters consisted entirely of young adult volunteers too valuable to remain cloistered in the bunkers yet too inexperienced to head into battle. The guards assigned to take the place of those already at the fields were more mature and held the training necessary to face the enemy if the need arose. Pecquin and another Airisun David figured was Narquin kept to one side, their expressive eyes and wrinkled brows giving them a perpetual appearance of worry.

The worst state of the group, though, was that of the Candonians. Over the past nahm David gave little notice to their appearance and now found it shocking to see the amount of body mass lost. Their hipbones and withers pushed against their tightened hides and David could easily count many of their ribs. Despite it, they held their heads high and bravely refrained from any complaints.

Toodat joined last, choosing to walk instead of fly. David observed the Manogonite now moved with a slight limp. A partially healed gash ran from his neck to his chest. Only eyeing David briefly, he took a short, hopping flight up to Phantom's back and settled there, gun grasped in both hands. Before David stood the most somber team he ever knew.

"Well," he said after clearing his throat. "Let's move out."

The team chose to remain silent along the way. Though no Vairdec movement appeared on their scans, no one felt like talking much. The hard times weighed too heavily upon them. Whether through combat or starvation, carrying the dead to the lowest bowels of the plateau now stood as an almost daily ritual. No one knew who the next to take that final journey down would be. Vairdec continued to populate the upper reaches of Karnoss, their numbers appearing as strong as on the first day. The efforts of SIERA felt increasingly more pointless.

And then there was Riechet's death. Even those who never met the general sensed the loss. No matter how capable Amber proved herself, she could not stave the hopelessness brooding in the slowly dying mass of victims buried beneath a ruined city. As he walked, David began to understand the importance of his mission. Bringing back food meant more than another day to live. It meant hope in that day.

Since the underground tunnels along the south end remained permanently blocked, the team's route took them through the South Ridge Airfield, which provided a measure of protection among the massive piles of rubble created when the Vairdec invasion began. Barely anything recognizable remained. Keeping his gun at the ready, David cautiously led the way into the labyrinth of stone and metal. He wore the only night vision visor in the group which caused them to crowd close behind him, trusting his every step to be the best one to take.

An acrid odor surprisingly still wafted through the slight breezes whistling down the corridors of colorless debris, bringing with it wisps of dust and ash from a tragedy that felt an eternity ago. David hugged the shadows, leading the way along what little path he managed to find through broken aircrafts, buildings and countless pieces he no longer recognized. Shards of partially melted glass crunched underfoot. In the distance came the heavy moan of metal as a sudden gust of eastern wind shoved against a dilapidated vessel that had toppled long ago onto the lower runway. Overhead came a groaning reply. David and his team flinched, throwing wary glances upward at the charred remains of a massive craft lying on its side, a wing bending over them and encasing them in shadow.

Stepping from its cover and onto the broken runway, David took in a sweeping view of the once extravagant airfield. Blown out buildings created canyons that glowed eerily in the last remains of a crimson sunset, spilling blood red reflections across the ashen ground. Twisted cables entangled wings, engines, pieces of tower – all lifeless bits of metal and wire. One half of the nearest tower still rose above the wreckage, casting a black mark across the team as it blotted the light from its only living spectators. They kept to its darkness, hurrying in breathless silence to reach the relative safety of the far side where the mountains of debris would once again close around them, concealing their presence and burying the evidence of their passing.

Making it to safety, David paused to glance skyward, awestruck by the sheer size of the walls engulfing him. The sky appeared sickly gray overhead. Stars hid from sight despite the fast-approaching night. Here the air grew stale, choked by the dust and ash that swept down its hollow corridor. Taking a tentative step forward, David felt the heavy crunch before hearing the dull announcement of the breaking bits under his foot. Glancing down, his light shone ominously upon an upturned hand, twisted, blistering and black with most of the flesh burned away to leave evidence of blackened bone curling up at him. A glint of gold around the wrist flashed in David's light. The rest of the arm, part of which lay crushed under David's foot, remained hidden in a thick layer of dust. Refusing to turn in the other direction less he come face to face with some grimacing corpse, David steeled himself and hurried onward along the narrowing corridor created by the canyon of rubble. It grew darker the further in, every few steps creating stomach-churning crunches underfoot.

A soft murmur drew David's attention back among his team members. Amidst the pale, frightened teenagers walked Pecquin and Narquin, huddled shoulder to shoulder, muttering back and forth in what David could only guess were words of encouragement. Every few steps they extended their hands to gently touch one of the young Human's shoulders or arms, patting them softly and giving little nods and whispers. The two Airisuns seemed to draw courage from each other, letting it spill outward to those around them. David let a twitch of a smile play at the corner of his mouth then returned his focus on the path ahead. For their sake he had to remain wary.

A subtle movement caught David's eye. Before he had time to register the impact of the observation, he found himself inexplicably back on the San Terres rooftop with Melina at his side, the same movement catching his eye, signifying the presence of David's most hated enemy. His heart raced. The air cut short as his throat tightened. Warnings screamed in his head. Instinctively he swung his gun toward the movement and fired. He wanted the Assassin dead.

At the sound of Toodat's high-pitch scream, David jerked back to the bleak airfield. The Manogonite streaked by his head so fast that the momentum spun David around and into a crumbled wall. A sharp pain swept up his knee as he fell against the jagged stone, but it never fully registered. His mind snapped into the moment – into battle. The Candonians swung around to become shields to the harvesters, shoving them back into protective crags while the soldiers leaped into action with David.

Wails rose up from behind and David dared to make a quick assessment of those in his charge. Darkracer was trying to push Pecquin back but the Airisun resisted. His hand gripped Narquin's who lay on his back, half his face obliterated. Nothing but a charred and bloodied mess remained. The extent of the damage clearly indicated the instantaneous nature of Narquin's death.

"Get him back," David snapped at Darkracer with a backward sweep of his hand in Pecquin's direction.

The last thing he needed was another casualty. David was fuming. Yet another death, and under his watch. How could he have let this happen? For a moment all went deathly still. No movement betrayed enemy positions. Toodat had gone eerily silent. Leading with his gun, David headed cautiously down the path, scanning every possible hiding place for danger.

A shudder ran through him as another ear-splitting screech emanated from Toodat seconds before the creature dove from a high point on David's right to collide with a body concealed up ahead. The blaze of a shot lit the area, providing David with a clear target. He didn't hesitate to pull the trigger, causing the Vairdec to stumble from the shot. David clenched his teeth in growing rage. He had hoped for a kill. Ducking a shot, he took a position along the far side of the rubble with the soldiers at his back. There was no telling how many Vairdec were stationed ahead of them.

From somewhere among the debris came the screams and snarls of the attacking Manogonite. David knew there would be no way to help Toodat, but having experienced the ferocity of the species first hand, figured there was little need to worry. Gunfire erupted once more, remaining sporadic, even hesitant, as if the Vairdec were trying to figure out a battle plan. David and his team slowly began pushing them further down the path. Time was running out. The Vairdec had to be killed before more of the enemy converged on their location. With a lull in the shooting, David suddenly lunged forward. The heat of his anger nearly blinded him. Unprovoked the Vairdec came and took so much from him. He watched people die by their actions. He was still watching.

No more, his brain screamed. *Enough of this!*

Four of them huddled in a small space among some twisted metal. All appeared slightly smaller in stature than what David remembered, or had he just been out of the game long enough to misjudge their size? Either way, they were hated enemies. The wails from Pecquin still echoed in his mind. The image of Riechet dying before him remained vivid. There were the screams from the Avenue, the burning flesh from the transit station, the dying boy in his father's arms. So much blood, so many tears, so few left alive - someone was going to pay.

Before any of the four Vairdec managed to turn their defense, David leaped in among them. Rapidly firing bullets into their bodies, he quickly dispatched two. Another tried to rise only to be shot from behind by the soldiers still stationed on the path. He stumbled forward, getting a round of bullets through his throat before he could regain his footing. The barrel of the remaining Vairdec's rifle came to bare on David. The Human held no fear, no preservation for his own life. Throwing himself forward, David grabbed the barrel and ripped the weapon from the surprised Vairdec's hands. The butt of it slammed back into the masked face, once, twice, three times. Falling to his hands and knees, the Vairdec clawed his way up among the debris and made a desperate attempt to escape.

David refused to let him. Lunging at his prey he caught the Vairdec around the waist before he managed to clear a few feet. They rolled across the ground, their bodies bashed by shards of rock and metal. David was impervious to the pain. Leaping to his feet, he flung a violent kick into the Vairdec's head, sending him sprawling. David followed, yanking the knife from his belt. As the Vairdec turned and pushed himself to his knees, the world suddenly took on a surreal horror, everything detaching itself from solidity, from any reality.

Before him lay the bloodied, terrified face of some strange yet beautiful creature. The eyes glowed with unnatural elegance. The face was soft though twisted with pain and fear. But David could no longer control his movement. His body acted upon the impulse brought on by so much pain of his own. Something remained clear enough in his mind to ensure him that before him knelt his enemy. Empty hands raised before him – hands covered in blood – his blood, the blood of his people, the blood of his nation, Riechet's blood. Crying out in fierce rage, David threw himself upon his enemy, his blade cutting deep into the pale green body. Golden-yellow blood enveloped his vision. The knife plunged again and again, tearing through flesh and sinew, digging into bone, spraying blood. The cry of his dying enemy was lost among the bitter cries breaking past his own lips. Only when a powerful shove from the side sent David staggering back did his world stop reeling.

Darkracer pressed his body against David's to push him back from the mangled corpse. His words were not condemning, only reassuring that it was over. David stood shaking and panting. What had happened? Where was he? A couple seconds were needed to register the last minute of battle. He staggered away from the nearly unrecognizable body at his feet, feeling sick and weak. The soldiers hurried over. One handed back the blood-encased knife David had not even noticed had been dropped. Taking it in a trembling hand, he looked over the men under his command.

"Sir," one of them said, "the enemy's neutralized. There is no indication of survivors."

"We should leave quickly," Darkracer said. "We don't know what message they might have sent."

Though the soldiers glanced nervously skyward lest an attack come from above, David remained impervious to any thought of danger. Quietly he walked back to where the rest of the group waited. He checked them over without a word, ignoring the expressions of fear he received over his blood-covered appearance. Slipping the knife into his belt, he gave a quick motion with his head.

"Let's go."

All but Pecquin started forward. David could see the conflict in the Airisun's eyes as he stood over his friend's body.

"We can't take him," David said, his voice growing softer.

The rest of the group paused to look back, pity showing in their eyes.

"He cannot find rest without burial," Pecquin choked, tears in his eyes. "His spirit will break loose and not be found by Vetond."

One of the girls among the harvesters stepped away from the group to pick up the biggest stone among the debris she could manage. Without a word she carried it to where Narquin's body lay and set it at his side. She then repeated the process. Darkracer scanned the area with nostrils flared.

"Sir," he said quietly to David, "we must move on as quickly as possible."

David remained transfixed by the scene before him. By now the other harvesters had joined to pile rocks around the body. Darkracer shifted nearby.

"Malard."

Slowly David stepped toward the burial team, pausing long enough to pick up a stone of his own to add to the site.

CHAPTER THIRTY-SIX

Subterranean fields, commonly known as sub-T fields, existed all over Telamier. To economize on agricultural space, massive underground chambers grew an array of crops while either more crops flourished or feed animals grazed just above. Proper lighting and humidity kept crops growing despite the trials faced on the surface. Times of drought, plagues of crop-eating wildlife and disease rarely destroyed the extensive subterranean networks of fields.

Karnoss, too, boasted these fields, but they were only two relatively small ones compared to the agricultural centers of Earthenia's southland. With just too much rock to dig through and too much expense involved, adding more fields proved uneconomical. Furthermore, with only so much space in which to build a city, not much was left for use of fields that took away from the underground needs of buildings and transit lines. These two fields sat on the southwestern-most point of the plateau, directly beneath the few greenhouses and processing plants used to provide the posh clientele with at least some freshly grown produce. Now they were all that stood between life and death for Karnoss's population.

David held back as the harvesters hurried into the midst of the fields. Despite the sparse crops, they expressed genuine excitement at the sight of the growing produce. As a reward for their services, each was given a large tak root to eat as they worked. The Candonians grazed on bits of leaf and stalk matter, carefully picking their food to ensure the health and stability of each plant. Each was so precious now. Above, the greenhouses lay in ruin. The Vairdec saw to that nearly a nahm ago. Luckily Amber and her father both had the foresight to gather all that could be saved before the strike. Some of the plants were even moved below where, thankfully, the Vairdec remained absent. Would it be enough, though? David could not be sure as he scanned the fields. The rows looked so sparse.

As the harvesters worked, being guided carefully by Pecquin who had memorized the harvest dates for each crop, one of the soldiers coming off guard duty explained how the system ran. Most of the crops consisted of grains and vegetables. Since the dense rock lay only a few meters below the imported soil, any plant with large root systems failed to flourish in this underground environment. The light and water were provided by the same system keeping the bunkers functioning. Sadly, the pollination system had not faired so well. The controls to the automated pollinator lay in ruins along with the greenhouses meaning only careful pollination by hand ensured the continuation of any crop. A biologist was found among the survivors and after some exploration into botany he successfully mapped out a plan for both when to harvest and when to pollinate. It turned out to be more difficult than first thought and some of the plants faired poorly despite everyone's best efforts. Others continued to thrive, creating the horrible temptation among the hungry masses to strip them of everything before any could reseed. Though the Vairdec were indeed a threat, the guards were actually there to fight against unauthorized refugees. If any refused to turn away, the guards held the authorization to shoot to kill. It sounded cruel, but David understood the necessity in keeping the greater population alive.

After several hours of steady work, the harvesters sat back to rest among well-stocked packs of food. With nightfall still several hours away there was no need to hurry. Four of the teenagers sat in a circle, stripping open the long, thin stocks of the pilmar grain to pour out the mineral rich seeds into containers brought just for that purpose. The Candonians stood nearby to graciously accept each empty stalk. Though of little nutritional value, they at least filled the stomach.

David seated himself where he could watch the entryway. He felt obligated to keep a vigilant watch over his team despite the reassurance from the soldiers that this place proved to be the most uneventful location on the entire plateau. Those guarding the fields viewed the job as five days of leave from anything other than placing bets on the speed a plant could grow. David held no doubt at what they said being true, but after the earlier encounter with the Vairdec, he found it impossible to let down his guard.

At last the time came to return with their bounty. Darkracer and Phantom carried the bulk though everyone shouldered a pack save Toodat who took his place once more on Phantom's withers. With the memory of last night's attack still vivid in David's mind, he made the choice to turn northward into the lower end of the city rather than chance the airfield that by now may be alive with investigating Vairdec. Hopefully, if that were the case, they would remain occupied there and leave the northern route alone. If not, David knew they still retained a high chance of escaping notice since Amber chose to direct the fighting on the other end of the city to keep the enemy from spending too much time investigating the area holding their valued food supply.

Her wisdom proved valid for after the long trek through the darkened city, David and his team arrived at the bunkers without incident. Like her father before her, Amber was the first to greet the team. A smile forced its way onto her lips as her gaze fell upon David only to quickly fade at the sight of the blood staining his front. With a quick scan of the group she gave a sharp nod. David figured she deduced the full story just from the team's appearance and the absence of one member. David still stepped aside to provide her with the full story. However, he carefully skirted the details of his attack on the last of the Vairdec. Amber listened without emotion. When he finished she appeared suddenly very tired.

"Let's be thankful it was only one," she said. "Good work, Malard. You did well under the circumstances. Can I trust you to escort this food to the distribution center?"

"Yes, ma'am," he replied, struggling to hide his own weariness.

The distribution center lay between SIERA's bunker and those holding non-fighting personnel. Ignoring the grumbles and complaints from numerous refugees, those entrusted with the rations carefully counted through the food stocks and portioned it out according to each group's needs. Fighting personnel always received larger portions, which caused a growing animosity among the refugees. New stocks of food had to be delivered under tight security and, though they kept a low profile, armed guards remained on alert beside the distributors at all times.

Upon entering the chamber a sudden din rose that caused David to cringe. Inadvertently he placed his hand on his gun, keeping it there as he passed the eager crowd that materialized upon the very mention of the food's arrival. The packs hurriedly passed from David's team to the distributors and instantly the work began. People crowded forward to watch. They all knew the futility in trying to grab any but the mere sight of the food being lifted from the bags filled them with renewed vigor. David scanned the crowd of gaunt, colorless faces. How much longer could any of them endure?

Stepping back, he felt something bump against his leg, which followed by a squeal of alarm. He jumped aside, twisting on his bad leg. Painful heat rose up into his hip and, had he not caught Darkracer's mane, he would have ended up on the floor. Catching his breath and dignity David glanced down to where a small girl huddled in the arms of what David figured was her older sister of about seven years of age. The younger was no more than three and stared up at him with large, green eyes watery with tears. Ignoring the throbbing, David carefully knelt in front of the girl.

"I'm sorry," he said, "did I hurt you?"

"She's all right," the older girl answered. "She's just scared of guns."

She pointed at the weapon strapped to David's hip.

"I see."

Slowly he drew the gun from its holster, keeping a hand out in front of him to reassure the child. Having removed the weapon, he held it behind him, giving Darkracer a few whacks on the leg with the barrel before the Candonian reluctantly bent down and took the gun in his teeth. David held his empty hands before the girl.

"No more guns."

As he spoke, he subtly pulled the edge of his jacket over the hilt of his knife. No point in showing the girl that, especially since he still needed to clean the blood from it. In front of him the little girl buried her face into her sister's side.

"Atien never liked guns. Daddy always had to hide his."

"Where is your father?"

The older girl pointed directly at David's chest. Looking down he followed her indication to the insignia on his uniform.

"He worked for the army. He was SIERA."

David's mouth ran dry. He didn't like the sound of 'was'.

"Have you found him?"

The girl only shook her head. "He's dead," she answered matter-of-factly. "So is Mum. She was on the Ave. Atien is scared of soldiers. She thinks they'll take her away like Daddy."

What could David say to that? Was there any comfort to give?

"Atien," he began, encouraged by the sight of the watery, green eyes. "Your father was a brave man. There are bad creatures in the world that want to hurt us, but people like your father won't let them. We're here to keep you safe."

The words felt so inadequate, so trite. David figured it best to leave quickly but before he could stand, Atien broke away from her sister and flung her arms around his neck. David froze, unsure of how to proceed. Slowly he let his arms envelope the child. She buried her face against his neck, never making a sound, just holding him. He in turn held her, his heart racing but his mind, for a brief moment, at peace. Kneeling there, David found Amber's words break through the swirl of his thoughts.

I believe soldiers are some of the most compassionate people there are. We show it differently, but how many people are willing to walk onto a battlefield? Risk and even give up their lives? For what? To defend those that can't defend themselves.

Still holding little Atien, David lifted his head to her sister. "Do you have anyone?"

"We're staying with the Vonan family," the girl answered. She reached out to grip David's wrist. "They're this way."

Not knowing what compelled him, David lifted Atien, allowing her to continue clinging to him as he followed the excited older sister. They twisted their way among crowds of refugees who politely stepped aside, many pausing to stare a moment at the sight of a soldier carrying a little girl.

"What's your name?" David asked, finding himself having to pick up the pace as the girl hurried along.

"Leelanie."

"Well, Leelanie, I really should..."

Should what? Return to the distributors? His part in that was over. Return to his own quarters? Probably. So why did he still follow behind Leelanie with Atien gripping his neck tightly enough to choke him. As quickly as she began, Leelanie came to a halt, nearly causing David to fall over her.

"This is our place," she announced proudly, pointing an eager finger into a small alcove where a lamp revealed in its soft glow a few mats covering the stone floor. In the corner slumped a tattered stuffed toy. Folded neatly beside it were a few sparse pieces of clothing. So little.

"It's very nice," David said in an effort to sound encouraging.

"Delilah and Kamien live here with their mum. We pretend we're sisters." Leelanie seated herself on one of the mats and took the toy up in her arms. "They don't have a daddy, either. He's with CLE."

David tried to swallow and failed. "I see."

"Oh," came a startled reply.

David turned to see a frail young woman standing with her two girls behind him.

"I'm sorry," he began, "I…"

"I hope they haven't been bothering you," the woman cut in. "Leelanie tends to do that."

She shot the girl a disapproving glance, which caused her to hang her head.

"It's all right. She's a delightful little girl." A smile appeared behind the toy. David smiled back. "Thank you for showing me your place, but I should be going."

Carefully he set Atien next to her sister as their caregiver entered with a small bundle of food.

"Thank you," the woman whispered as her eyes briefly met David's, "you all mean so much to us. I know it's hard. If it helps in any way, this is the reward for your sacrifice."

She motioned to the four girls as they eagerly took up the food, smiles forming on their small faces. They lived with so little, but at least they lived. They had a future because men and women like David chose to throw themselves between death and these innocent children.

"Yes," David managed. "Thank you."

As he slowly rose, Atien suddenly jumped to her feet, giving a little cry as she caught David by the wrist.

"I have to go," David insisted.

"He has to go help the others stop the bad creatures so we can go home," the mother explained. "You want that, don't you?"

Atien didn't answer. She just looked sorrowfully up at David, tears forming once more in her eyes. David knelt before her.

"They need you here, Atien. You can help them be brave. I have friends, too, who need me. You wouldn't want me to leave them, would you?"

In reply she huddled up against his chest. David gave the woman an imploring look.

"She's probably remembering her father," she said.

"Your father and I have the same friends," David ventured. "Don't you want me to go help your father's friends?"

"They all die," she cried.

David found himself unable to move. He could not leave this poor child with thoughts like this. But what could he say? She spoke the truth. Seating himself beside her, David placed an arm around her small shoulders.

"Some die, yes, but not you, not your sister. Just wait. One day all of this will be over and you will step into the sun and see the blue sky again. There will be birds and trees, and who knows, maybe you'll find other family and friends. And when you dream, you know what?"

"What?"

"Those you can't see when you're awake will be there. Your father, your mother. They're still watching."

"I'm afraid to sleep," Atien whimpered as she crawled into his lap. "Mum and Daddy aren't there. Only monsters are there. They're going to hurt us."

David shot an imploring look at the child's caregiver who only gave him a sorrowful shake of the head in return. There was little anyone could do to calm the nightmares of the children these days. However, David couldn't bear the thought of leaving the poor child in such a state. But what could he do?

What force compelled David next remained a mystery. The words sprang to his mind and the tune formed almost before David was aware of it. In that dark little alcove, David began to sing a lullaby he had once heard many years before.

"Rest your head my dear, sweet child
Let your dreams start to glow
For I am here, there's nothing to fear
Sleep peaceful, my love, till tomorrow
I am here to vanquish your fears
So play in your dreams till tomorrow."

"Yes," he said upon finishing the simple song, "your parents are still protecting you. And so am I."

CHAPTER THIRTY-SEVEN

So many eyes, so many pleading looks. They all reappeared in David's mind as he tried desperately to fall asleep. Atien's beautiful green eyes captured his heart once again only to materialize into the fearful plea seen glinting back at him from the Vairdec. David threw himself onto his other side, his agitation keeping him from relaxing. How could he compare an innocent Human child to an enemy soldier? A slight rustle nearby drew David's attention around to see Mike prop himself up on his elbows.

"You all right?"

"I'll be fine," David grumbled, trying to keep his voice soft enough not to wake Kailyn.

"Upset about the Airisun?"

David said nothing.

"Don't be," Mike continued. "Bad as it sounds, few missions end with everyone returning. There was nothing you could do."

David admitted his reaction thwarted the Vairdec's ambush. The only thing was, he knew he had not responded to the presence of Vairdec, but to a memory. If he had not been firing at the Assassin of his mind's eye, could he have stopped the shot that killed Narquin? According to witnesses, the angle was wrong for David to do anything more than he did. In fact, his hypersensitivity alerted everyone to the movement kept any other kill shots from finding their marks among the team. All this did little to keep David from feeling the stress over what may happen should his vivid memories return. Luckily, such concerns were not the only things on his mind, allowing him to honestly skirt the subject.

"I killed the Vairdec," he said before he could stop himself.

Mike's brow furrowed in confusion. "Yeah, so? I'm glad you did."

David shook his head. "It's not that, it's…" With a growl he rolled to his back and stared at the ceiling. Mike's stare burned into him. He was not getting out of an explanation.

"I saw the Vairdec's face – his real face. It wasn't horrifying or grotesque. In fact it was almost beautiful."

"I've seen them," Mike admitted. "It's true they have a rather universal elegance about them. That's why they wear those masks. Perhaps they didn't think they could be taken seriously otherwise. I guess the masks are better at expressing the inner being."

"That's just it." David shifted to his side again so he could look Mike in the eye. "There was nothing hateful or vicious in those eyes. The Vairdec was afraid. He was actually afraid. He looked like he was pleading for mercy."

"Maybe he was, maybe he wasn't."

The casual tone of Mike's response surprised David. Mike picked up on David's look.

"They're an intelligent being, remember. It's only right to consider they have emotions. I heard Riechet say those assigned to this city are the ones with less experience – young ones most likely."

"Great," David groaned. "Now I'm killing children."

"You took out an enemy soldier. It's your job."

"And it's their job to take us out. Which is right? Are we no better than they are?"

David surprised himself with his question. Deep down he knew the answer. Nonetheless, satisfaction lay in verbalizing his thoughts. He heard Mike take a deep breath.

"If we attacked them unprovoked, I guess so," Mike answered. "I've heard it said that the just side of a war is determined only by the side you are on. In a way I suppose that's true, but I don't think it's completely accurate. As far as I'm concerned, a moral absolute plays a role in any conflict. For us, we were attacked without provocation. Our enemy wants only to kill us and take what's ours. Anyone bent on destroying the innocent for their own gain has lost their right to say their fight is honorable. We are defending ourselves. The Vairdec didn't have to come."

"And is it honorable to cause suffering in the killing?"

"I don't follow."

As much as he regretted reliving the attack, David filled Mike in on the details of the Vairdec's last moments. When he finished, a long silence followed.

"You have a lot to be angry about," Mike finally said. "It would be hard for any of us to react differently in a situation like that, especially if we had been there to witness Riechet's... I suppose from a moral standpoint you could have handled it better, but sadly war brings not just the best but the worst out of people."

"So how do we walk away with any dignity?"

Mike gave the question a great deal of thought, leaving enough silence between them that David rolled to his other side again in an attempt to get back to sleep.

"By recognizing the worst and not repeating it," came the whispered answer.

How could this be? El'loray continually asked himself that as he sat once again in the council chamber in Celhara's city of Luequara. A Teshian patrol ship carrying Celehi fugitives sat in its assigned dock nearly halfway around the planet, as was protocol. It's commanding officer sat among the Celehi leaders here, which was far from normal procedure. Everyone was pouring over the information brought. None seemed to know what to do with the message being given. Questions of its validity bounced back and forth, causing the Teshian commander to bristle. She remained poised, though, and listened with a scowl. El'loray, too, grew increasingly frustrated. He knew the Celehi would not proceed until they were certain the message was authentic. It would then take time to decide how best to proceed with Nor'Yahvan in the area. With this news the Vairdec had suddenly become a very real threat.

Thoughts of those he met on Telamier played through El'loray's mind. He had made many friends on that distant planet. Many of the Celehi colonists he could identify by name. There were also Teshians in their tropical paradise region of Antidine and the Humans of Earthenia. El'loray feared all he knew of them would remain as memories. If the message was true, what hope did any of them have?

Two days passed since David returned from his harvesting mission. Now he was back in the situation room with the rest of SIERA's leadership to hear about the next plan of attack. Amber stood with Jylin at the front of the room. De'oolay sat nearby. Seated with David were Mike, Lash, Yehgrett, Kailyn and Toodat with the Candonians standing on either side. Keven, sat on David's right. Captain Stoneman, newly returned from a mission, was the last to enter. With such a group present, the importance of the operative was painfully clear.

Amber began the minute Stoneman was seated. "De'oolay has been able to identify a weak signal coming from the Naharan Mountain Range."

Darkracer's ears pricked at the mention of the mountains. "Ours?"

"Yes, meaning we are not alone." Amber ignored the relief sounding around the room. "Our communication has never been the best down here in the bunkers and the Vairdec have unfortunately made it worse in recent days. We need to get a network set up with the Naharan, but that will mean returning to the field station. The system's integrated into the building which should strengthen the signals."

Memories of Valor Peak tightened David's muscles. "Won't this alert the Vairdec?"

Amber, too, shifted slightly with her unease over the memory. She struggled to keep her eyes focused on David as she spoke.

"There is a possibility in that, but unlike before, we're not sending a message off-world. This may remain too weak for any detection."

"For stronger certainty, I will send shadow signals from numbers of communication points," De'oolay added. "By chance the Vairdec detect a message from this city, they must choose from the numbers of false locations. The field station scrambles signals sent away to bases in Earthenia. A trace will prove most difficult."

"This isn't to say there will be no risk involved," Amber said. "The Vairdec have remained on high alert."

Kailyn glanced between her colleagues. "Can we wait for things to settle down before trying to respond to the signal?"

De'oolay shook her head. "The risk proves high for losing connection."

"We also need to know what's happening outside this city," Amber said. "It's to our advantage to respond quickly."

Kailyn held up her hand. "I'll go. The field station was my assignment."

514

"It was mine also," Toodat clicked. "I want to go."

"Granted," Amber said with a sharp nod. "I need both of you on this. This is a high priority operative so I want high-level fighters backing them up. Malard, you're senior officer to the mission. Yehgrett, Arzen, Gry'toena, Darson and Motgomery are on the list. I cannot stress the importance of this enough, nor the danger. Stay alert. That whole sector is heavily patrolled. I want quick, clean, and quiet action from you. This is not an open engagement. Your mission is to make contact with our forces in the south and gather all the intel you can. Get it back here with their power coding and stay alive."

The icy morning air felt crisp and refreshing. David's head cleared with each deep breath. Underground living never suited him. So many of David's past missions took place in the dead of night. While David always enjoyed the night, he honestly missed the sun. He took pleasure in seeing the day, watching for a few brief seconds as a touch of pink fingered its way across the pale expanse of desert sky.

Moving in daylight held its risks, especially since their path led them north into the more heavily patrolled section of the city. However, moving during the day now held less danger than at night. The Vairdec had grown increasingly watchful every time the sun set since that typically brought out attacks from Karnoss's resistance. Amber hoped morning would bring a changing of the guard and enough time for her soldiers to slip through. So far it proved a wise choice, as the streets remained quiet.

The team had already traveled several long kilometers through the tunnel systems to emerge just west of the business sector's hub known as Dukara Square. It was a wide expanse of giant inlaid stones, fountains, waterways and sculptures surrounded by a diverse array of high-end exhibition halls, offices, conference centers and guest residence with Government Hall's main tower to the south in direct line of sight with the square's centerpiece – a glistening red and white statue of a woman. Her name was Jezine Dukara, the fourth president of Earthenia and a pioneer in Human-Celehi relations, since she married a high-standing Celehi ambassador. One of her major contributions consisted of overseeing the construction of modern day Karnoss, her influence in the Celharan government allowing for the assistance needed to take the city from the small mining community to the elegant metropolis it was now. At least what it once was, David considered as he slipped under the figure's shadow. What would Dukara think with her city in ruin, its citizens dying? The cold stone face appeared to have lost its noble serenity, replaced with a silent sadness brought on by the shadows of the broken buildings surrounding her.

Kailyn, with her extensive knowledge of the city's layout, led the way along the eastern edge, hugging the buildings for as much cover as possible. Darkened windows stared down at them. Anyone could be watching. David kept watch between the team, which he followed from his position as rearguard, and the many points where enemy snipers could be lying in wait. Everything remained silent. Hastening across a narrow open street, the team took refuge under a high street that wrapped itself along the upper portion of the guest residence tower meant for visiting dignitaries and ambassadors. David hated to think of the unwelcome visitors possibly living there now. With the street overhead and the many artistic obstructions throughout the square, Kailyn skillfully guided the soldiers from one concealed location to the next, slipping ever closer to where the field station sat just one street over from the square.

David skidded to a halt next to Keven who covered for him as he joined the team at the edge of the square. Though David made it safely across, Keven kept his eyes trained on a window above and to the left. Reading his friend's behavior David prepared to fire if necessary and followed his gaze. Nothing. A scuttle at his right shoulder told David of Toodat's approach.

"What's seen?" his electronic collar spoke in conjunction with his clicks and hisses.

Keven and David kept scanning the windows.

"I don't know," Keven admitted. "I thought I saw some movement up there. It's gone, though."

"If they're really up there, I doubt he's gone for good," David said.

Kailyn's voice spoke over David's comlink. *"Sir, what's the hold up?"*

"Possible enemy movement upper southeast," David explained. "No further indication. Let's haul it. Hopefully they'll lose us near the field station."

"Doubt it," Keven whispered.

David shared his sentiment. Unfortunately there was no choice but to continue on at this point. No place would be safe. They tightened ranks at the edge of the street to look across at the low military-run building housing SIERA's field station. Keven held tight to David's shoulder, sweeping up and down the street with the scope of his gun.

"Why couldn't they have built a tunnel system straight into the station?"

"Security reasons," David answered flatly.

Keven rolled his eyes. "Sure. I feel much safer."

Toodat made his way across the street first, fluttering briefly as he fought a gust of wind channeled between the buildings. He quickly secured a lookout point on a ledge above the door and, after a careful look around, motioned for the rest to follow. Kailyn and Motgomery raced across followed by Yehgrett and Gry'toena. A single shot flashed from the eastern corner of the street. Yehgrett shrieked with anger, twisting to the side as Gry'toena's body smacked the street. Nathan joined with the Oxyran's fire as David and Keven repositioned themselves to strike from another angle.

David could see two Vairdec at the corner. Another lay in a growing pool of thick, glistening blood, having been surprised by the speed and ferocity of Yehgrett and Nathan's initial attack. From the corner of his eye, David saw Toodat scrambling across the walls of the building toward the Vairdec's location. He needed to keep the enemy distracted.

"Cover me," he shouted before Keven could object.

Taking a reckless leap into the street, David dropped, keeping his feet in front of him as he slid on his hip to where Gry'toena lay. As he expected, the

Vairdec tracked his reckless movement. Shots pelted the dead Celehi, spraying David with sticky blood. Yehgrett remained crouched nearby. Hurriedly wiping the blood from his stinging eyes, David caught the Oxyran around the shoulder and propelled him across the open space to the field station's wall. Kailyn caught David's wrist and yanked him out of range.

In those few seconds Toodat cleared the wall and swept down on the Vairdec. The enemy soldier closest to the building spun outward from the ambush, nearly knocking his comrade to the ground. Nathan's bullets slammed through the back of the Vairdec's head. The second found himself pelted by Keven's shots. His armor held for only a moment under the barrage David and Nathan helped lay down. A second later the team was all huddled in the field station's doorway.

"There were only three?" Kailyn asked.

"Looks that way," David answered with a nod.

"Vairdec scouts move in groups of five."

David glanced hurriedly over his shoulder. "Look alert, then. If they're watching us we need to clear out."

"What of the mission?" Keven asked, sweeping his gun up and down the street.

"Come on," Kailyn offered.

Signaling with her hand, she sent Toodat over the rooftop and out of sight. The rest followed into the building. Unlike his first visit, David found the lobby depressing. The windows drew in less light since a fine layer of dust now coated their surfaces, brought there by winds carrying smoke and debris from battles fought in the days and nahms before. Only a crumpled heap of leaves remained of the plant and the waterfall had long since ceased to flow.

Instead of heading for the secret entrance Amber used before, Kailyn led the way to the far end of the lobby and down a side hallway. Though all stayed eerily quiet, David made a point to keep a close eye on every door they passed, peering into darkened lecture halls and laboratories while pressing the team from behind to keep them moving quickly. Keven glanced back as they passed the last of the rooms.

"Reminds me of our training days," he muttered.

David only nodded. It reminded him, too, of his days of training at the CLE Academy. It was in a military lecture hall much like these that he first met Keven. The meeting would lead to the introduction of Melina.

A flash of pale morning light brought a grateful David from his painful memories. Kailyn pushed her back against the doorframe of an exit that remained hidden from view until the moment she activated it. No one questioned her as she ushered them out of the field station and into a back alley. Toodat swept down from a perch above to land on the opposite building's ledge. He gave a short nod in the direction of the western span of street.

"This way," Kailyn called back.

David cringed at the volume of her call. It echoed down the narrow street. There was little doubt the Vairdec would hear. To add to it, Toodat gave a snarl and fired a shot down the street before dropping from his perch to follow the team into the next building. They raced through halls and open rooms, less cautious now as urgency to escape took hold. Breaking through the other side, Kailyn turned to the right, heading east along the building only to slip back into it by a small door that all but Yehgrett and Toodat had to duck to enter.

Now David understood the reason for the noise. They were leading the Vairdec away from the field station. With luck, the enemy would continue to search for them on the streets, considering them on the run. Doubling back, they could slip underground and leave the Vairdec hunting in vain.

Instead of returning to the field station, Kailyn entered a small room in the second building and dropped to her knees. Pulling up a corner of flooring she revealed a lock pad. A second later the floor slid aside to expose a passageway leading down into pitch-blackness. Not until everyone had entered and the entrance was once again sealed did Kailyn explain.

"It's an emergency exit to the station's bunker. Luckily they had the foresight to give access from the outside. I never thought I'd be using the exit for an entrance."

At last they broke into the field station's secret, lower rooms. Kailyn wasted no time in racing straight for the control room.

"Yehgrett," David called out, "put a watch on the back door. Arzen, Motgomery, go with him. Darson, back up Toodat."

After seeing everyone to their stations, David joined the Manogonite who crouched on the floor near the control room, his yellow eyes scanning the dim corridor, his fingers twitching across his rifle. A soft stream of muttering growls rippled up from his chest but the collar didn't activate for translation. None was needed. David knew how he felt. Nathan knelt at Toodat's side with his gun in position to fire. There was nothing to target down here and with any luck it would stay that way. However, David, too, kept his gun up and ready. It just felt better. At his back he could hear Kailyn working the computers. His stomach tightened at the eerie déjà vu sensation sweeping over him. Glancing over his shoulder he half expected to see Riechet there.

"Anything?" he ventured.

"Not yet, sir."

Her hands flew over the controls almost as proficiently as De'oolay's. Not wanting to disturb her further, David resumed his watch.

"We got them," she suddenly said.

David fought the urge to leave his post and join her at the computer. The news came as the best he had heard in a long time. They were not alone. The Earthenian army was still out there and fighting.

"How much time do you need?" Toodat asked without looking back.

"I'm sending the colonel's message out now."

Nathan relaxed his stance slightly to look back at Kailyn. "Are they coming to help us?"

"I don't know yet."

David understood the dangers of becoming too optimistic. The Vairdec knew what they were doing when they chose Karnoss as a northern base. No army could ambush them with the open desert surrounding the city. The Vairdec controlled the skies. Standing there with nothing to do but consider these things, David began to wonder if it was for this reason Riechet chose to station SIERA here in the first place. Considering the Vairdec's tactics in advance, he would have wisely seen the need to keep a strong fighting force in the area. It was moments like this David realized how much he missed the general.

"Gilpar to Command. We've got contact. Relaying message. Stand by for response."

The minutes ticked by.

"Affirmative," Kailyn said in response to some order heard only over her comlink.

David's comlink suddenly came to life with Amber's voice.

Malard.

David kept his eyes on the passage. "Malard here." He listened quietly for a brief moment before lowering his gun with a sigh. "Copy that. Malard out." Holstering his gun, he looked over at Toodat and Nathan. "Stand down. Looks like we'll be here a while."

"How long's a while?" Nathan wondered, reluctantly lowering his rifle.

"A few days at least. The colonel wants to set up a relay system here and keep up communications with the southern army for as long as possible."

"Do we have what we need to stay?" Nathan wondered.

"Yes," Toodat said. "The door across the hall leads to bunks and a cantina. There's enough food to last us half a nahm if we ration. We'll be fine."

A shockwave from an explosion threw them against the wall. David felt a surge of adrenaline. This couldn't be happening again. It just couldn't be happening!

"Fia!" Nathan gasped. "What was that?"

Yehgrett, Keven and Motgomery appeared suddenly around the corner.

"Enemy's at the back door," Yehgrett snarled. "We're in secondary lock down."

Kailyn glanced over the computers in frustration. "There's no indication of disturbance. The sensors aren't reading any of it."

"Well it's happening," Keven said.

Yes, David thought, it was happening, and he knew the ending. It was Valor Peak all over again. How could he be so unlucky?

"Command. Command," he called. "This is Malard. We are under attack."

Amber slammed her palm against the consol table. How did this happen? The Vairdec seemed to have appeared out of nowhere.

"De'oolay," she snapped.

The Celehi shook her head in exasperation. "I hold connection with the field station security. No attack reads on my system."

"They overrode it," Amber answered in growing rage. "They must have known about the field station all along and were just waiting for us to show."

"Enemy platoons coming on the site."

Jylin hurried in with Mike. They looked over the readouts in growing concern.

"Can we get them out?" Mike asked.

"I don't know," Amber said.

"They are sending a lot of firepower," Jylin observed. "They must think that is our center."

"At least it's not," Amber replied, "but I'm not losing our people without a fight."

"Colonel," Mike said. "Permission to engage."

"Is the ship ready?"

"Yes, ma'am."

"Are you ready?"

"Affirmative."

"Permission granted. Blow those krashka sobs from the streets."

CHAPTER THIRTY-EIGHT

"Command's got all the messages we can get from the south army," Kailyn informed as she grabbed up her weapons and raced from the control room.

"Fine," David answered. "Get to the exit."

"Thought it was taken," Nathan said.

"Back door's taken," Toodat corrected with a snarl. "Head the way we came."

"How many doors does this place have?"

"Go!"

Another explosion rocked the center and the team pitched forward. An acrid odor rushed down the tunnel to meet them, followed by a blast of heat.

"Back! Back!" Yehgrett hollered.

They pushed back against one another. Toodat cut through the air above them, scraping their helmets with his talons in the tight space. Clinging to the wall, he worked a panel and sent a concealed door slamming into place, blocking the tunnel. The angry roar of another blast rumbled just beyond.

"I trust you know enough to live out there," Lash's voice crackled over Mike's comlink.

Mike would be unable to use the ship's communication board, as he was seated not in the *Predator* but the confiscated VY-Craft.

"I've tested her out," he reassured. "Just watch yourself."

"Same as you."

Mike waited with growing anticipation as Lash guided his own ship toward the hangar doors. The Max-180 would be the first to leave. If any were watching outside, their attention would be drawn to Lash's ship, providing Mike with his chance to slip out and join any VY-Craft squadrons in the area. It was a beautiful plan in theory, but, despite his confident words to Lash, Mike knew the incredible risk of the mission. His friends needed him, though, and he refused to leave them to die. With a signal from the ground, he headed out.

As expected, the Vairdec converged immediately on Lash's ship as he headed into the city. Mike fell into line with the other VY-Crafts, fighting desperately against the urge to attack right then and there. Luckily, at the speed they took, they were sailing over the field station in a matter of seconds. Below, the Vairdec held position outside the building with two large assault vehicles and a platoon of eager soldiers. Lash circled in as low as possible to send a barrage of super-heated lasers into their midst, scattering them in all directions. It was all he had time for as the VY-Crafts opened fire.

Kailyn slid to a halt in the main corridor, causing the rest to pile in behind her. Sparks and smoke poured down the stairs from the lobby entrance. The Vairdec were blasting the building apart looking for a way down to their quarry. Toodat let out an ear-splitting scream and swept past the team. Motgomery stumbled from being struck in the face by one of the Manogonite's wings, momentarily pinning Keven to the wall before David pulled them both back. A larkrae streaked past. The rest spilled through a hole in the ceiling to swarm Toodat. Razor sharp claws and teeth from both sides ripped at each other, spraying the surrounding walls, floor and ceiling with larkrae and Manogonite blood. Kailyn fired into the fray, killing two of the larkrae before David pulled her back. The hole above continued to widen. The Vairdec were about to enter.

"Toodat!" Kailyn screamed.

"We've got to go," David shouted back over the deafening screams of the bloodbath before him.

Keven pulled at Motgomery's arm to draw him back down the corridor before grabbing Yehgrett.

"I know another way," he said.

"Get moving," David ordered.

Kailyn held back, reluctant to leave Toodat behind. He had been brought to the floor and was twisting and rolling among countless snapping jaws. With Nathan and David's help, Kailyn began to thin out the larkrae swarm. Several creatures littered the floor, torn into pieces by the powerful fury of the Manogonite. Despite it, Toodat was weakening. David knew he had one chance and took it. He raced into the fray to grab Toodat by a wing. He could feel the burning sensation of larkrae claws tearing through his arm as he attempted to drag Toodat back. The Manogonite sputtered weakly, his neck flayed open, his mouth and nose filling with blood.

A larkrae suddenly leaped for David's face, forcing him to let go to defend himself. In that moment a series of laser blasts pelted the wall where David stood. One shot struck Toodat as he rose. He let out a hiss, falling back as the remaining larkrae swarmed him once again. David glanced up to see a Vairdec soldier taking aim at his face. A shot from Nathan caused the enemy soldier to retreat long enough for David to stagger back to Kailyn and Nathan's sides. Kailyn continued to scream at Toodat to get up but it was clear that was not going to happen. The larkrae looked up from their mangled prize to leap for fresh prey. With a final cry of defeat, Kailyn pushed the code to seal off the corridor in front of them. David gripped her shoulder.

"Let's go."

A larkrae dropped from above onto Nathan's shoulders. Infuriated by the animal's bloodlust, David grabbed it by a back leg and yanked it to the ground. Before it could jump back he slammed the heel of his boot into its head, repeatedly stomping on it until there was nothing left but a disfigured mess of broken bone and blood-drenched flesh.

"Where do we go, Gilpar?" he demanded.

Kailyn took the lead to a small door at the end of a narrow passage. Squeezing through it, they entered a maintenance room for the computers. The low thrum of the machines filled the small space and the air grew stifling. Kailyn paused.

"We can't let them get the computers."

Not waiting for David or Nathan to answer, she pulled an explosive from her belt. Setting the timer she reached into the mess of machines to place the charge.

"Exit's that way," she said, pointing with her gun toward a ladder.

David hastened up to press against the trap door overhead. Kailyn shouted the code up to him and a moment later he hoisted himself into another maintenance room above. Nathan and Kailyn quickly joined. The hall beyond was clear. As they ran down it the floor rocked from the explosion below. Another followed from the side, blasting smoke from one of the lecture halls. Blinded, David never saw the Vairdec until the gloved hands wrapped tightly around his neck.

"Still with me?" Lash growled as he evaded shots.

Mike followed close behind, allowing his wingman to lead the pack further into the city.

"Don't worry," he called. "I'm with you. Just don't shoot me down."

"I hold your signature."

"Let's just hope they don't," he said, indicating the surrounding VY-Crafts. "I'm on your three."

Rising above the skyline, Lash pulled the Max-180 into a sharp bank to the right, sailing over the top of Mike as he turned into him. Firing rapidly, Mike caught an incoming VY-Craft by surprise.

"Oops," he muttered sadistically, "my mistake."

Falling back into line with the rest of the VY-Crafts, he followed Lash as the Teshian drove his ship down into the city again, avoiding shots as he dipped around buildings and under roadways. Mike muscled his way toward the front of the pack, keeping in line with Lash as his partner headed back toward the field station. A shot from the armored vehicles below glanced off the Max-180's right wing.

"Watch yourself," Mike called. "Firing left and low."

Lash heeded the warning and easily avoided the missile Mike launched, allowing it to slip past and down to its intended target. One of the vehicles burst into flames. A series of harsh, Vairdec calls began filtering over Mike's ship's communication board.

"Yeah, same to you," Mike muttered.

David struggled a moment in the Vairdec's grasp before Nathan's shot slackened the enemy's hold. Behind them, Kailyn gave a cry. David spun about, trying to see through the smoke as it dissipated. Two Vairdec kept a firm hold on her. The third, protected from Nathan's earlier shot by armor, lunged back to grab David once again. David felt his arm wrench backwards and he was forced to drop his weapon. Nathan slipped along the wall, firing at the Vairdec until David found the grip slacken once again. He threw himself back to slam the Vairdec into the wall. The arms tightened around his chest. Another Vairdec rushed in, receiving a blow to the stomach from David's foot. It was a futile move. The

Vairdec grabbed David by the ankle, further disabling his fight.

Nathan found himself trapped between his two struggling teammates. The Vairdec could not reach him in the confines of the hall so focused their attention on dragging down their captured victims first. Torn between targets, Nathan turned to the nearest enemy and fired on the Vairdec grasping David's foot. Unlike Kailyn's captors, who were currently using her as a shield, those holding David found themselves exposed by the twisting struggle of their prize. The shot slid cleanly through the Vairdec's neck and blood poured over the front of his vest. David swung his free foot up and around, connecting with the Vairdec's head and sending him to the floor. Nathan turned his attention to David's other captor, who, under the blows of David's attack and another shot from Nathan, attempted to retreat to where Kailyn was held.

David yanked out his back-up weapon and fired before the Vairdec reached his goal. Unfortunately Kailyn was being dragged back under heavy guard. Neither he nor Nathan could get a clean shot. The sound of running footsteps warned of more Vairdec coming up behind. To David's right the wall ended to reveal the lobby beyond. It was clear – for now. But how could he leave Kailyn?

"Get out of here!" she screamed.

A shot burned past David's ear, averted slightly by Nathan's return fire. Not even Nathan would be able to hold back what was coming. If any were to escape, they had to leave now. David sent Kailyn an anxious look.

"Go! Now!" she continued to scream.

David refused to listen. He couldn't just run away. Directing Nathan to hold any soldiers coming from behind, he lunged forward, staying in line with Kailyn to avoid becoming a clear target to those staying at her back. Throwing his full weight against Kailyn the two of them managed to throw the Vairdec off balance. David wasted no time yanking Kailyn forward, out of the grips of her captors and straight for Nathan and the lobby. Placing himself between the Vairdec and his retreating team, David fired a continuous stream of ammo as he hurriedly backed away.

Thankfully the lobby was still empty. They would have to move fast, though, for David knew in less than a minute their only remaining escape route would be blocked as Vairdec repositioned themselves for the capture. Coming up behind Kailyn and Nathan, his world spun momentarily as the floor rushed up to meet him. Skillfully he tucked and rolled to the side, ending on his back to train his gun behind him. Kailyn struggled weakly to rise. Her sudden fall had caused David to trip over her. Blood poured from her lower back. As Nathan provided cover, David grabbed Kailyn by the arm in an attempt to pull her to her feet.

With a cry of pain she shook her head. "I can't."

"Yes you can," David argued. "Get up."

He pulled harder, realizing he was doing all the work. Kailyn's legs refused to support her.

"I can't," she repeated.

Wrapping his arm under hers, David lifted her enough to begin dragging her forward. Shots flew past as Nathan laid down a steady stream of cover fire. Their escape ground to a dangerously slow crawl. Despite all his efforts, David knew their time was up. Kailyn also understood and tried to push David back.

"Run."

"Keep going," David insisted.

Kailyn pulled her trembling left hand up to grip her intel-band. Before David could stop her, she activated a lethal injection into her wrist. Her body lurched forward, nearly taking David to the floor with her.

"What the…" Nathan began.

David didn't give him time to finish. With nothing more to do for Kailyn, he turned his attention to Nathan. Grabbing the kid by the arm, David threw him toward the exit. Behind them the Vairdec quickened their pace. An all too familiar sight reflected in the windows ahead. He pounced on Nathan, dropping to the floor with him as the inferno swept overhead. The windows burst violently into the street. With his eyes fixed on the open air beyond the lobby, David scrambled to his feet, gripping Nathan's vest to send them both out of the field station and into the light of day.

Lash navigated his ship down a narrow canyon of buildings with the VY-Crafts in hot pursuit. Mike held his position at the front of the pack, successfully blocking the Max-180 from any who wished to shoot from behind. Angry words spilled over the ship's board from pilots who found their target unattainable. Mike knew little of what was being said, but he could imagine he was losing any camaraderie with the Vairdec. Fine by him. A shot across his flank alerted him to the end of his ploy.

"Fine," he snapped.

Dropping his ship, he spun around, flying backwards while firing up at the ships sweeping in from behind. His sudden attack threw the pack off course. One swerved into a building. Another spiraled down from a hit to the wing. Reducing his speed, Mike let the rest sail over him. Making a smooth rotation, he came up behind the pack and fired off a steady stream of lasers, catching the back craft's thrusters and sending it down as a spectacular fireball.

"Not bad," he mused, looking approvingly over his ship's consol.

"I've got Malard caught on Dukara Square," Amber's voice cut in. *"Can you clear the way?"*

"I'm on it," Mike answered.

David and Nathan ducked a steady stream of shots that smashed against the decorative metalwork stretching as a wall from a walkway they managed to reach to the overhang of an adjoining exhibition hall. It created a long, straight tunnel that now provided the only means of protection for the two soldiers. Though laced with countless openings, the weaving pattern of metal thwarted many of the Vairdec's shots. David stared down the length of the building as he considered their options.

"We can't stay here," he said.

There was only one thing to do. Steeling himself for the run, David broke from his crouch to race for the other side of the tunnel. Lasers and bullets seared the air around him, most smashing into the metal to David's right. He ducked to the side, shielding his face as shards of metal and ammo pelted him relentlessly. He could feel the sting of several pieces of shrapnel but kept going. At least his body armor took most of the hits. Diving forward, he slid the last few feet to the other side where a more solid barrier provided some protection.

The scream of engines announced a single VY-Craft entering the square. There would be no way to ward off an aerial attack. While David frantically looked for a safe route, the ship veered to the side, cutting through the Vairdec ranks. David wasted no time considering his fortune. With Nathan making it to his side, he hurried for another protected location.

Mike banked around the exhibition hall for another shot. As he rounded the building, another VY-Craft came into view. It never fired. Instead it increased its speed and raced straight at him. There was no room to maneuver. All Mike could do was watch.

David heard the VY-Craft go over him. A second later the sound of smashing metal and explosions overtook the area. At this David chanced a look back to see a ship screaming down toward the square. One wing was sheered away and flames lapped at its side. Worse, it was headed straight for him.

"Move!"

He and Nathan broke from cover to cut across the square. The VY-Craft smashed into the ground at the base of Jezine Dukara's statue. The remaining wing ripped across the supports, the impact causing the structure to tilt. As the ship spun, the back end slammed into the weakened base, sending up a column of fire. Jezine Dukara succumbed. David watched as the statue tilted forward slowly at first, then faster as it surrendered to gravity. He slammed Nathan in the back to send him toppling forward out of the way. Sliding on his hip, David cleared the space. The ground shook beneath him as tons of stone crashed into the square.

Shakily David rose. Choking on the course dust billowing around him, he pulled Nathan up and toward the far end where a transit tunnel waited. David never felt so relieved to leave the light of day for the dark confines of the tunnel system.

"Malard to Command," he called, his voice shaky and weak.

"Command here."

Amber's voice sounded so good.

"Received heavy casualties. Gry'toena, Gilpar and Toodat confirmed lost. I and Darson are cut off."

"Where are you?"

David relayed their position as he and Nathan stumbled for the lower walkways of the transit center. Luckily the Vairdec remained too preoccupied with events above ground to follow.

"You're clear through the main line. Cut down at 273 but watch for sweepers. They're all through the mid-ways."

537

"Wonderful," David grumbled to himself.

"Affirmative," he said a little louder.

Neither he nor Nathan spoke as they headed for 273. They kept to their own thoughts, letting the rhythmic sound of their footfalls drive them onward. David understood this was not the time to ponder what had happened. Instead he focused on the present moment. He listened to his breathing. He counted footsteps. He watched dark corners.

Entering 273, Amber's warning came into stark reality. The low throb of the sweeper warbled through the shadows just ahead. Finding a side tunnel, the two soldiers ducked out of sight and pressed themselves against the wall. The mechanical orb's pulsating sound grew closer. Placed in the tunnels by Vairdec, the machines swept every centimeter of the tunnel system for life forms. Any indication of such would elicit a violent shooting response. If fired upon, they would explode, vaporizing everything within a twenty-meter radius. David hoped this one would stay on a programmed track that would bypass the side tunnel. The throbbing grew louder.

Out of the darkness crawled the rounded devise, moving across the roof on six thin, metal legs. Its scanner swept one wall then the next. As it passed the side tunnel, it let its beams stretch down the length. David pressed his back into the wall. Beads of sweat trickled down his neck. Luckily he and Nathan stood just out of the sweeper's reach. Its legs clicking across the ceiling, it continued down the line. Nearly a minute passed before either soldier dared release his breath. Happy to still be alive, they hurried on their way.

"Did Kailyn kill herself?" Nathan asked after a long silence.

They had made it to the lower end of the midway. Not long now and they could drop down into the deepest sectors of tunnels that would lead them safely back to base.

"Captain Gilpar had no choice," David answered sharply. "The Vairdec would have killed all of us. She knew that. We couldn't save her and she wasn't going to be taken alive. None of us can risk becoming a prisoner."

"I guess." Nathan did not sound so convinced. "Would you have done it?"

"If I had to, yes. Could you?"

Nathan took his time to respond. "I don't know. I think I'd try to fight to the death."

"And if you couldn't?"

"You can go ahead and shoot me."

David paused, watching silently as Nathan took the lead. An almost teasing glint appeared in those young eyes. Nathan was keenly aware of David's discomfort with him. While neither ever tried to make friends with the other, a mutual understanding had slowly begun to form between them. David sensed a maturity beginning in the youth. Perhaps there was hope for him yet.

"Wait!"

David threw his arm across Nathan's chest, throwing him back a few feet in the process.

"Are you…"

"Shh."

Nathan held his breath and they focused their senses on the chamber ahead. There, the barely audible ripple of clicks. Nathan shouldered his rifle.

"What is it?"

"Mines."

"You sure?"

"Detecting them is one of the many lessons of the CLE."

"Congratulations," Nathan replied with a hint of sarcasm. "So how do we get through?"

David did not answer.

"Colonel," he called, "we've got mines."

"Fia," Amber growled. She leaned over De'oolay's shoulder for a closer look at the readouts. "They must have just laid them."

"Shall we go back?"

"Negative," Amber answered. "We're detecting patrols approaching from the east. You need to keep moving forward."

David gave an exasperated scoff he hoped remained too quiet for Amber to hear.

"I don't see how," he said. "What are your suggestions?"

"I say we fight the Vairdec," Nathan said, already turning to head back the way they came.

David reached out to catch hold of his vest collar while keeping his eyes fixed on the minefield. There had to be a way. Triggering all the mines was out of the question. They had been perfected to react to the pressure of forward movement with only the one touched going off. None of the others would respond to the explosion and it would take too long to clear each one, especially with enemy soldiers closing in. No doubt the first explosion would bring them rushing to investigate the location. Traversing above the mines might work if they were carrying the proper equipment, which they were not.

"Do you carry field glasses?"

De'oolay's question drew David from his contemplation of the problem.

"Affirmative."

He pulled them from his vest pocket. As was standard, he relied on the vision-aid headband more than the glasses since the latter could be knocked off more easily in a battle. Having made the choice to carry them for backup came as a wiser decision than he had first thought.

"Find a swipe switch on the rim right side."

David ran his finger along the rim until he felt the slight indentation. A faint chirp of the mechanism followed his touch.

"All right."

"Put them on. Open your patch-link system."

David followed De'oolay's instructions while his curiosity grew. He was anxious to fully understand her plan. A second later his intel-band glowed a small code panel.

"Enter the following; gamma two eight niner kilo."

A second later David gave a nod. "Done."

As he spoke, a ripple of iridescent green and blue passed over his vision. Then the glasses returned to their normal night vision properties.

"Now what?" David asked.

De'oolay's fingers danced across the controls of her computer. Amber watched in tense silence at her back. The main screen jumped a couple times before revealing a steady image of the chamber David faced.

"My computer and your glasses are linked," De'oolay explained. "I see what you see. Keep straight ahead. I will try reprogramming the visual system of my computer to show heat signatures."

David couldn't hold back the crafty grin. Now he understood De'oolay's plan. The mines pulsed a very slight heat wave too faint for standard equipment to detect. However, with the work of the sophisticated computers back at base, the telltale waves would give the deadly weapons away.

Nathan held his position as rear guard while David remained motionless, staring straight ahead. He felt rather useless, doing nothing and relying on a trigger-happy teenager for protection. Genuine relief washed over him when the word finally came through.

"I see the mines and will guide your walk. You trust me?"

"Do I have a choice?"

De'oolay rippled green with her amusement. "No."

Stepping forward, Amber placed an encouraging hand on De'oolay's shoulder. Her eyes trailed to the points in the tunnel system alerting her to Vairdec activity. The enemy was drawing nearer.

"Hurry," she whispered.

"The field is four meters long. Please understand clearly. Go only the direction I say. Understand?"

Nathan pressed close to David's back.

"Perfectly," he answered for them both.

David felt his adrenaline start to rise as the instructions began.

"One step forward. Another. Another. Stop."

David and Nathan froze instantly, every muscle locked into place.

"Look down more," De'oolay instructed. *"Look side to side."*

The task surprised David with its difficulty. Though he knew only his feet needed to remain perfectly still, it took a second to convince his head to move.

"Step right."

David hesitated.

"You stand clear for fifty-centimeters round."

That's it? David wondered. Slowly he eased himself to the right.

"Half step more. Stop. One step forward. Left. Slight more... more. Stop."

David teetered slightly as he froze, his heart racing a little faster with every "Stop". He could sense Nathan's tension behind him and was thankful the kid was able to keep his head about him. Biting his lip, he continued to follow De'oolay's instructions.

"One step forward. Right – slightly! Stop."

Thirty seconds ticked by, then a minute. All remained silent.

"Command," David said, his voice coming out in a whisper. "Command, come in. Malard to Command."

Amber's voice broke the silence. *We're here. Hold your position.*

"What choice do we have?" Nathan grumbled.

De'oolay glistened a near perfect yellow. Before her the screens blinked erratically.

"The Vairdec are close to their location," she said to Amber after blocking the communication line with David. "Their sweeps disturb our signals."

"Can you hold it?"

"Not long."

"Get them through."

De'oolay scrambled to hold her computer signal together. "If the Vairdec find their location, they can detonate the mines remotely."

"De'oolay," Amber growled through clenched teeth.

"I can block the Vairdec's tracking system with our system. It will hold for a short time only."

"Just do it."

David heard the click of Nathan's rifle as he swiveled carefully to aim back down the passageway.

"How long do you think we'll have if the Vairdec show?"

David refused to look back, not wanting to disrupt any view De'oolay had.

"Not long," he answered.

His hand slowly wrapped around his gun.

"Two steps forward then one right."

The sudden instruction grated David's nerves. Carefully he complied.

"Never thought I'd be dancing with you," Nathan muttered.

"Let's hope you're a good dancer."

"Same."

"Step forward and left. Same time - diagonally!"

David wavered unsteadily on one foot as he tried pivoting to compensate for the direction. Nathan's hand grabbed his arm and a second later David's foot came down without incident.

"Might want to specify that one first," David said once he caught his breath.

"Apologies. One step right. Two forward then one diagonal right."

"Hold up."

David could hear the urgency in De'oolay's voice. It did little to help his situation.

"Diagonally forward and left."

"Do you realize her thought of a step and ours could be different?" Nathan said over David's shoulder.

"Shut up."

De'oolay's yellow was paling to white as she fought to hold back the Vairdec's searching signals. Amber remained as a silent, steady presence at her back.

"Diagonally forward and right. Moot, moot. Short step right. Forward. Forward again. One step right."

A small mark on the wall ahead indicated where a camo-net concealed a slight bend in the tunnel. Beyond that stood the hidden door to the lower levels. Every fiber in David wanted to break into a run. They were so close.
"Forward. Left. Left."
Come on, how many mines could still be ahead?
"Diagonal right. Yes. More. Forward. Forward. Right."

De'oolay flashed white. Her screens flickered and a series of signals streamed across the right-hand monitor.
"Jump," she shouted. "Now!"

David wished he had received some confirmation that he was not going to be jumping right onto the last mine of the field but knew there was no time to waste. De'oolay's frantic cry said it all. From where he stood he was in direct line with the bend. As instructed, he leaped for it. The buzz of the camo-net wrapped around him as he passed through. Black walls closed around him. At the same instant the tunnel behind ripped apart with a deafening explosion. The ground lurched beneath him and he slammed against the wall. Nathan's body smashed into his back.

In an instantaneous moment, David found himself lying on the ground, his back pressed against the wall. Beneath his hands the floor felt hot and rocked gently from side to side. A shake of the head warded off the swaying, which he found was his own jostled equilibrium. His ears rang with a high-pitched squeal. Dust and ash rolled lazily around him. How had he ended up like this? Had he blacked out? A couple shallow gulping breaths helped bring back the last minute.

"Malard, come in. Darson. Malard."

The voice slowly grew audible as it repeated its call again and again.

"Malard here," he choked. "What happened?"

Amber slumped, using the back of De'oolay's chair for support. Her heart continued to beat madly against her chest.

"The Vairdec discovered your location," De'oolay explained while Amber recovered. "They remotely detonated the mines."

"It won't be long before they discover the doorway," Amber said. "Get through and lock it down."

David struggled to his feet before helping Nathan rise. Still unsteady, he pulled a couple charges from his pack and placed them on either side of the door.

"Just what we need," Nathan grumbled, bumping up against the wall like a drunk as he tried to walk, "more bombs."

"We can't let the Vairdec gain access the lower tunnels."

"No, really?"

David ignored Nathan's sour attitude; feeling a bit unsettled himself. Grabbing the front of the teenager's vest, David shoved him through the low door before joining and sealing the entrance. A few seconds later the walls shuddered with the muffled explosion that buried any evidence of the door.

CHAPTER THIRTY-NINE

Inside the bunker's main chamber people moved about with frantic agitation. The place throbbed with tension. It grated on David as he stumbled along trying to orient himself toward the situation room. After the events of the day, the activity made David's nerves feel as if they were being scraped raw.

"David!" Keven's elated call caused David to jump. His friend took no heed and threw his arms around him in a heartfelt embrace. "I was beginning to worry."

"It's good to see you, Keven," David answered, wearily pushing him back with a hand on his shoulder.

"I thought you were right behind us. When I looked back…" Keven groaned and shook his head. "The Vairdec closed in behind. There was no way back. I can't believe Yehgrett got us through. You would never think he was carrying that many weapons. This has been one hell of a mission."

David heard little of this. He staggered weakly from a bump to his back as a soldier hastened past and turned his attention once more to the situation room.

"I've got to report in."

"Not with the colonel. I'm afraid she's inconsolable at the moment."

David felt a flood of concern wash through him. As quickly as the concern came, it dissipated into understanding. She and Kailyn had been close friends. This day could not be easy for her.

"Can't blame her, though," Keven continued, looking suddenly very weary himself. "Last thing she needed was to lose another officer."

Kailyn's last moments flashed to the front of David's memories. He had sensed her fear and acceptance, and it pained him to remember.

"There was nothing we could do for Gilpar," he said quietly in hopes of comforting himself.

"She got it, too?"

The question startled David. "What do you…"

"I didn't see anyone else come in," Keven said, his voice growing with concern, "but I figured more than you and the kid made it back."

David's eyes narrowed. "You didn't know about Gilpar?"

"No. We're still trying to put everything together."

David's heart beat faster and his head began to hurt. Something deep within him caused him to tremble. He hated to forge ahead with any questions but needed to know. "What officer were you talking about?"

Keven resisted looking into David's eyes. "It's nothing. Forget it."

"Keven."

"David, I don't have all the information," Keven snapped back. He, too, was growing more agitated. "I just... I thought you knew."

"Knew what?"

When Keven took too long to respond, David began scanning the chamber. He felt nauseous even before catching sight of Lash standing near the command center. The Teshian appeared ready to attack, shaking with anguish. Only one thing could make him that upset. Several times the question stuck in David's throat before he managed to crack the words.

"Where's Mike?"

David never felt the hand on his shoulder. In fact, he barely heard the words.

"I'm sorry."

The ground heaved beneath him. The world spun. He staggered, staying on his feet only by the strength of Keven's hands on his arm. Still moving forward he strained against his friend's hold.

"David," Keven said.

Getting a slight handle on the world, David twisted in Keven's hold to face him. He wanted to speak. He wanted to voice some sort of thought or emotion. All he managed was a shaky hand raised to hold Keven in his place as he pulled away to stumble hurriedly for the officer's quarters. There was no thought on what he would do there. Honestly he did not completely comprehend where he was going. David only knew he had to get away from that chamber. Barely staying on his feet he crashed through the cots to fall forward. Bracing his hands on the wall, he glanced over to the empty cot still holding Mike's pack. Again the world rolled unsteadily. He couldn't stay there. He couldn't breathe.

David spun about and retreated from the room. The passage appeared dark and narrow around him. He could feel himself bounce off something large, unable to register as to who or what it was. He wanted out. He needed air. He needed space. His body shook with nausea.

"David!"

The call went unheeded. David allowed his feet to propel him along. Slamming through the door, David stumbled to the nearest shower before growing violently sick. As wretched as it felt, once his stomach slowed its heaving, David's vision returned. The world no longer swirled around him. Now he could think. The thoughts that shot to the forefront made him wretch again. Melina lay dying just out of reach. A father lay down next to his son to die with him. Riechet's life left his eyes even as he spoke his last word. Pecquin cried out. Kailyn collapsed. Now Mike. That unending optimism, those laughing eyes - gone. Just like Riechet. Just like Melina. Gone.

David's stomach heaved but there was nothing left in him. Spitting bile-filled saliva into the drain, he laid his forehead against the shower wall and clumsily turned on the water, allowing the icy stabs of droplets to bore through his burning skin. Why? Why did everyone he ever cared about leave him? Why was he surrounded by such senseless death? Why? Why?!

David slammed his fist into the wall. The pain never registered. Blood from his knuckles swirled unnoticed down the drain with the water.

"David?"

The voice was soft, pleading. It broke through David's agony. Slowly he rolled his head sideways to glimpse the speaker. Darkracer stood behind him, pain clearly showing in his eyes. Stepping forward, the great creature lowered his head against David's chest. David allowed himself to be gently pushed out of the shower's stream. Weakness overtook him and he rested limply against the Candonian's head for a moment. Neither spoke. There were no words adequate enough. Too much grief pressed David. All the deaths, all the loss weighed him down. For so long he had tried to hold it in. With Melina he lost himself in drunkenness. When Riechet died he was too preoccupied in just staying alive. Now all the grief came to a head. Feeling drained from his limbs, and David sank to the floor. He leaned against Darkracer's leg, allowing the creature's large form to shelter him as he broke down and wept.

CHAPTER FORTY

The following day Darkracer was summoned to Amber's quarters. He stepped silently through the door to join Phantom in the small space. Amber sat on top of her desk to accommodate the size of her two guests. Her features were worn, aging her appearance by several years. No longer did her uniform fit a shapely body. It instead hung loosely from a frame that had lost much of its weight from stress, fatigue and lack of nutrition. Dark lines shadowed her eyes. She remained hollow in her expression. The fire in her had dimmed.

The last twenty-six hours had drained her completely. While Kailyn's fate had to be accepted, she had insisted on holding out hope for Mike. The crash site was too extensive, though, and a rescue team was out of the question. The Vairdec converged on the site almost immediately. Even if he survived the crash, no hope remained in him surviving an enemy attack. She ran a bony hand over her pale, expressionless face much the way her father would when grief and stress overtook him. Her breath hissed between her teeth as she looked over the patiently waiting Candonians.

"We're leaving."

Darkracer lifted his head slightly at the news, refraining from speaking in order to allow Amber to explain further. Those two words seemed to have drained her, though, and she remained silent.

"The three of us?" Phantom ventured.

"Four," Amber corrected. "I'm taking Malard. He's the only one left who can ride efficiently."

"I assume we're headed for the Naharan Range," Darkracer said.

The Naharan was his homeland. He was mountain bred and born. The prospect of leaving his tomb of rock for forests and green grasses caused a slight tremble to ripple through his muscles. However, he also knew his duty as well as Amber's. As excited as he felt, he found himself questioning the idea.

"Can SIERA afford to lose its colonel?"

"Yes," Amber answered quickly. The firmness in her voice warned against further argument. "Lieutenant Colonel Py'guela will be taking command. The soldiers all respect Jylin and he's as capable of leading this unit as I am – maybe even more so." She paused, gritting her teeth angrily.

"The army in the south is fractured," she forged on. "They call for field officers, especially officers with a greater understanding of the Vairdec. We can't ignore the call to help. If there's a chance we can assist, we need to take it. Besides, you two will die if you stay here much longer. You're of better use in the south and so am I."

"If we can reach the south," Phantom replied.

"I thought a run that direction already failed."

"There's been a shift in the Vairdec's aerial forces. We have a window and I'm going to take it."

"Is the decision based on war tactics or is it personal?"

Amber's fire momentarily flared in her eyes as she glared at Darkracer. "What difference does it make? Regardless of personal feelings you must see this is the most logical decision at this point in time. They've lost too many officers and need the leadership. I can't ask anyone else to go – they don't have the riding skills needed to get through the mountains. Now this is my final decision."

Lowering his head, Darkracer surrendered his argument. Amber spoke the truth. She was the most capable to handle the task. Giving a sigh, she softened and reached out to touch Darkracer's face.

"SIERA will be fine without me. They'll understand. Py'guela agrees this is the best way. The necessary promotions have been set in place. There's more than enough to lead here. After all, SIERA was never meant to fight in one clumped unit. We were always meant to spread out to other units as needed. It's time to do so."

Darkracer wondered if Amber said all this to verify it in her own mind but stayed silent.

"Does David know?" Phantom asked.

"He will shortly," Amber said. "Lash is finishing the preparations for the *Predator*. We'll be leaving at sundown."

Without waiting for a response, Amber dropped from her perch on the desk to push past

Phantom and Darkracer. They watched her exit, staying a moment longer as they both silently contemplated the turn of events.

David sat alone on his cot, looking over the empty officer's quarters. Not many occupied the cots anymore. Riechet's death brought about Amber's departure. Now Kailyn and Mike were gone. Even Toodat's empty perch was difficult to look at. David felt so numb. There were no more tears, no more raw emotions - nothing. In a way he wished he felt something but there was nothing left to feel. All his senses were dulled. Amber's approach didn't even register.

"Malard?"

The sharpness in her voice snapped him from his hollow thoughts. He turned his attention to her but lacked resolve to stand in her presence. She didn't push the point. Instead she crossed the room to stand over him, angling herself to keep her back to Mike's cot.

"The Earthenian Military calls for officers in the south. You and I are heading for the Naharan. We and the Candonians fly out tomorrow evening. Prepare to leave."

David stared past her to the dark wall opposite them.

"Malard?"

His lifeless eyes rolled up to meet hers. Another mission? Another team of those he cared about? Who would he watch die this time? Amber? Darkracer? The words escaped him before he registered the meaning.

"Find someone else."

David never meant to show disrespect to Amber. He cared deeply for her position and had not forgotten the respect the Riechets deserved. He just couldn't bare the thought of any more death. Amber stared back in disbelief.

"Excuse me?"

David averted his gaze. "I can't."

"Can't? Can't what? Can't go? Can't fight? What?!"

Her voice bounced angrily around the room. Yehgrett slid to a halt in the doorway. With a click of his teeth he hurried away. David continued to sit emotionless on his cot.

"Get up," Amber snapped. "That's an order."

A heat rose through David's core.

"Or what?" he snapped back. "You'll arrest me? Shoot me? Go ahead, you'd be doing me a favor."

"What is wrong with you? You're better than this."

"Am I?"

"Yes."

David grew silent. Amber's abrupt answer took him aback. She hadn't paused to think nor did her reply sound trite. She really believed what she said. So why didn't he believe it? Suddenly very tired, Amber's shoulders sagged.

"David, we all want an end to this. Unfortunately the other side has a say in when that happens. You think you're the only one suffering from the losses?"

Amber paused to collect herself. David heard her stifle a sob that escaped before she managed to bring her grief under control.

"Don't do this," she continued softly. "We need you."

"No you don't."

"Don't argue with me." Amber's voice rose once again. "You are still a part of this army."

"Maybe I don't want to be."

Now Amber's pause signaled her fight to control her anger, not her grief. David knew he was way out of line. He just didn't care anymore.

"What did you expect? People die. It's upsetting, I know, but why don't you do something about it instead of running and hiding? If you have the power to stop it, then do it!"

"I don't have the power to stop it," David shouted back, rising to face Amber. She was no longer his colonel. She was just another person and his frustration boiled over. "All any of us do is watch more and more die. For what? The enemy keeps coming. They'll always keep coming. And no matter what I do, I keep watching people die. I'm through. I can't do it anymore. I won't be apart of all this bloodshed."

Amber stood unmoved before him. "You really think we can't make a difference?"

"You believe otherwise?"

"Yes, I do, just like my father did."

"And look where it got him."

Amber's fist connected with David's jaw so quickly he never saw her move. He crashed back onto the cot, his ears ringing from the blow. He knew he deserved it. He would have done the same if anyone had spoken with such disrespect. The words came from his pent-up anger, not his true convictions. Unfortunately there was no room for apologies in this argument.

"Get out."

David looked up at Amber, surprised by the strain in her voice. Hurriedly she wiped the rogue tear from her cheek.

"Get out," she repeated with more conviction. "If you won't serve, SIERA will not serve you. Go hide with the other children. You're through." She swallowed hard, clenching her fists to control her shaking. "Goodbye, Malard."

David let his eyes close as Amber turned her back on him and disappeared from the room. His head slowly sank to rest on his upturned knees. What had he done?

David couldn't be sure how he ended up in the lower lounge of the Morning Star Resort. After Amber's order to leave, he had grabbed up his sparse belongings and did just that. Only instead of joining the refugees, he hit the streets. Perhaps subconsciously he hoped to cross with the Vairdec long enough to get himself shot and killed. He still retained too much dignity to kill himself, but letting the enemy do it sounded morbidly inviting. He might even take a few of them with him since he still held enough sense to carry his weapons. As luck would have it, the streets remained quiet, allowing him safe passage all the way to the resort district of the city. Was there some higher power cruelly bent on keeping him alive? For what purpose? He certainly couldn't think of any.

Carefully he looked around the plush room, surprised by the lack of looting that had taken place. The Morning Star sat southeast of the Piña Dorado. Perhaps when the larger resort collapsed during Riechet's ingenious attack, the Vairdec never saw fit to continue their habitation of the district any further south of the debris field. Still, it felt strange to stand in a room frozen in time, appearing much the same as it had the night of Rew'cha.

Though trapped in the darkness of a powerless city, the windowless room fought the shadows with a series of glow stones embedded in the wall along a solar-charged panel. With the daily charge from the desert sun, the stones continued to illuminate the room without the care of Human intervention. Perhaps it was this feature that drew David into the sheltered space, enclosed from any prying eyes passing by outside. Only he had no memory of consciously thinking his way to any location. Finding the room empty, he decided to settle in for a while.

Around him several tables still held an assortment of glasses, some tipped over, all now empty of their contents. Upon closer examination he observed the dried droppings of some creature. Apparently wayward pets or street savvy feral animals had picked clean any food and drink not claimed by scavenging sentient beings. Since the fare in this part of the resort consisted mainly of alcohol, he mused at what the scene must have been like when they passed through.

Crossing to the far end, David stopped at the stage. It was a small platform designed for lesser entertainers of dance and theater to wow audiences more with their sultry looks than their artistic achievements. A couple iridescent sashes lay discarded on the edge of the stage to suggest that. With a groan, David collapsed back into one of the long, plush benches at the stage's base, staring into the blackness of the ceiling while subconsciously rubbing at his wrist. What had gotten him to this point? Everything felt so surreal. As he let the events of his life play randomly through his mind, he began questioning the validity of most of it.

His hand was on the trigger of his gun the same instant he sensed the presence of another in the room. Years of training kicked in. It overrode any earlier disregard for his survival and set him poised to defend himself. He twisted nimbly in place, using the back of the bench as a shield. His senses immediately went to work at locating the figure and bringing his weapon to bear on him. A gun aimed back at his head, glinted in the soft glow of the stones only a meter away. Before either gun went off, each shooter caught the eye of the other. Both weapons sagged in response. David found himself barely able to hang on to his gun as he fumbled to holster it. If his life was not crazy enough, now he was hallucinating. It just couldn't be! The apparition looked so real he swore he could touch it.

"David?"

The voice, it sounded perfectly natural, perfectly real. Pushing back from the bench, David staggered to his feet, backing away from the image until he bumped into the stage. The vision broke into a relieved smile and approached with a heavy limp. Blood coated his front. A gash lay partially concealed by his hair. Was this the way David really remembered him? David glanced from side to side, looking for some escape. He had never been a strong believer in ghosts till now.

"David! I never thought I'd find you here."

David said nothing. As the figure grew closer he tried to scramble up onto the stage. The vision turned out to be faster and swept David into a hug before he managed to retreat. The embrace was real. The apparition was now a solid, breathing Human. Shakily David reached out to grasp the man in shock. Alive? Was he really alive? Seconds later he was holding a lost friend at arms length and staring disbelievingly into his face.

"Mike! You're alive?"

"I think so."

Mike gave a painful laugh, suddenly appearing very weak. With David's assistance, he collapsed onto the bench with a sigh. There was so much David wanted to ask but all he could do was stare. Mike lay his head back and shut his eyes.

"I never thought I'd live to walk away from a crash," he muttered. "Those ships are stronger than they look."

"Are you hurt?" David asked in his excitement. Instantly he recognized the stupidity of his question. "How badly are you hurt?" he restated.

A slow shake of the head answered him. "Can't tell. Not enough to keep from walking. Probably some broken ribs. The leg hurts but I don't think it's broken. But hey," he opened his eyes slightly to give David a weak smile, "if you can make it back with a bolt sticking out of you, I think I can get back a little dented."

David pulled out his canister of water and handed it over. He wished he had taken some medical supplies. When he left, he had removed the supplies from his field pack. At the time it seemed unthinkable to take from soldiers in need, especially since he didn't care about his own outcome. Now his noble decision felt utterly wasted. As much as he hated returning to the bunkers, he concluded he would see Mike safely back. After a long drink, Mike revived enough to sit up and take a careful look at David.

"Are you still trying to make it back too, or are you on another mission?"

Shame burned in David's chest.

"Neither," he answered quietly, shifting in his seat so he could lean back against the bench and not look Mike in the eye. "I'm no longer with the army."

"Why? What happened?"

David stared down at his empty hands. "I couldn't handle it anymore. It's just too much."

A hand squeezed his shoulder. "Something tells me you're going to make it through this."

"That's my problem." David turned back to Mike's bewildered face. "I'm cursed or something. Perhaps it's some cosmic twist of fate, but it seems like no matter what I do, I end up watching everyone I know die while I somehow cheat death. It's not as pleasant as it sounds."

"No, I understand."

David studied Mike carefully. A sense of foolishness began to take hold. Mike had cheated death as often as he. Mike cared about the same people. He, too, suffered from the loss of Riechet. There were also numerous soldiers from SIERA David held no great connection to but certainly were friends of Mike. And were there others unknown to David that Mike grieved for? The look in his eyes suggested such.

"How do you keep going?" David asked.

Mike gave a stiff shrug. "I don't know. To be honest, sometimes I don't. You've been hit with a lot of heavy losses over a short time. That's hell."

David could only nod slowly.

"Perhaps it will help to remember there are still some of us alive."

For the first time in a long while, David smiled. "Up to a few minutes ago, I didn't think you were."

"To be honest, I didn't know if you were alive, either. I don't know what I would do if you hadn't made it. It tore me apart the first time we thought we lost you."

"Don't kid yourself," David said gently. "I'm not that important."

"Oh?" Mike trained a steady gaze on David. "There're a lot of people who care about you. Don't go around thinking you're the only one losing people." Mike's expression sobered. "The sad reality is that war and loss go hand in hand."

"Which is why I can't stay. Maybe I'm selfish. Maybe I'm weak. I just don't want to suffer these deaths anymore. Especially not after I found out what my next mission was."

"Which was?"

"Amber and the Candonians are headed for the Naharan. They need officers there. Jylin is now running SIERA. I was to go with Amber."

Mike lowered his gaze. "I see."

"I watched Riechet die, Mike. I was there. Toodat was shredded in front of me. Kailyn died in my arms. I've seen so many die and there's just no way to stop it. And when I thought you were gone… Oh, Mike, the last thing I needed was to add Amber to the list. Just the thought tears me up. Amber, Darkracer – who's next?"

"Well I certainly don't expect it to be me."

The voice made David and Mike jump. Neither had heard anything until then. They turned in their seats to face Darkracer standing a short distance behind them. Mike shook his head with an impressed smile.

"Racer, your stealth is astounding. How long have you been there?"

"Long enough to let my excitement over seeing you alive wear off so I don't act like some giddy colt." Darkracer stepped forward to rest his head gently against Mike. "It's wonderful to find you alive, my friend."

"It's good to see you, too," Mike answered. "What is it about this place? Everyone I know seems to be showing up. Anyone else coming we should know about?"

"No," Darkracer said. "I'm here because I followed David."

David drew back, unsure if he liked the sound of that.

"You followed me?"

"Yes." The Candonian's eyes bore into him. "Do you really think I'd let you walk away without any explanation?"

"I was hoping you would," David grumbled.

"I'm not that kind of creature."

David turned his head away from his friends, unable to bare the sight of them.

"Oh, David," Darkracer said, his voice soft as he touched his nose to David's shoulder. "I know everyone says you're too good to leave, but I think it's because you are good that you did. You can't stand death and suffering and there is nothing wrong with that. Just remember that whether you hide here or stand with us, our fates are not going to change. The only thing that changes is who you are in the end."

David said nothing. What could he say? He felt so conflicted. Who was he? What was he to do? How could he keep going? Too many were dying. Then again, many still lived. Mike was sitting next to him. Darkracer was at his side. Amber was waiting, as was Keven. Even Nathan had come through. Was he really just running away from them? What about those in the bunkers in need of help? They were still alive. He promised Atien he would protect her. How foolishly easy it had been to break that promise.

"Come," Darkracer said to Mike, "I need to get you back."

Mike hesitated. David didn't move though he knew Mike was waiting for him to follow. Part of him wanted to, but he remained frozen on the bench. He listened silently as Mike rose and followed Darkracer toward the exit. Something clanked as it was lifted from the floor. A moment later David felt the Candonian's hot breath against his cheek and something heavy dropped down next to him.

"I thought you should have this," Darkracer replied before returning to where Mike waited.

David's throat tightened as his fingers wrapped around the object. He didn't need to see it to know what it was. However, he dared himself to look down at the sword in his hand. *Excalibur's Legacy* – a Natchuan blade, the sword of Jonathan Alsen. General Riechet's sword. Rolling it back and forth, David let the dim light bounce off the hilt. A passage from Alsen's journal echoed through his mind.

It's a strange thing, how fate lands ordinary people into extraordinary circumstances. I may be just a man, but through perseverance the measure of one man's life can become far greater than he originally perceived.

"Wait," David called.

CHAPTER FORTY-ONE

"I don't need to hear this," Amber snapped.

Nathan held firmly to his place next to the *Predator's* ramp. Despite all he had been through, he still displayed little regard for military respect.

"I rode before." He motioned to Phantom who stood nearby. "I can do it again. They could use a sniper out there."

"And they can use a sniper here. Darson, you're good, I'll give you that. You're needed here. You know these streets. Our best tactic is to ambush."

"Is it any different in the mountains?"

Amber's patience was growing thin. However she found herself hesitant to force Nathan to leave. Her team had tragically been reduced by half. If she showed up in the Naharan with only Phantom, the morale of those waiting for assistance would be crushed. Even if David and Darkracer were with her it would be a hard sell to those who called for help.

Jylin stepped around the *Predator* to study Nathan.

"Colonel," he said, motioning Amber aside. Once out of earshot of Nathan, he continued.

"Perhaps you should consider taking Darson. We have many good shooters left. You could use at least one other gun with you."

Amber gave Nathan a wary glance. "I don't know."

"He respects you more than me. I do not think he will readily take to my command. It may be for the best."

"Perhaps you're right," Amber admitted, a hint of anger still in her voice. "If only..."

Her voice trailed off as she shook her head.

"Malard made his choice. He can not be relied on."

"And Darkracer?"

"I know little of Candonians. It disappoints me, though."

"I'm losing it." Amber stepped further away, keeping her back to the *Predator* as if the mere sight of her face would tip off the others to her thoughts. "What's happening? I can't keep anyone together. How am I going to be any good in the south? I'm not my father."

"No," Jylin admitted, "but you learned well. You will not fail."

"I wish I had your confidence."

Jylin's skin rippled a light red followed by hues of purple. "I wish you had more going with you."

"Karnoss can't afford to lose any more."

"But if it will help win the war."

"At the expense of the refugees? We can't compromise their safety." She gave a relinquishing sigh. "I'll take Darson along only because I can't think of a good argument against it. The rest are in your command. They appear understanding of that."

"They are." Jylin stepped back to salute Amber. "It has been an honor serving with you."

Amber returned the salute. "And with you."

She stayed where she was until Jylin disappeared from the hangar. This was it.

"All right," she called as she headed toward the *Predator*, "Darson you're with us."

Phantom raised his head and gave a shrill whinny that echoed around the wide chamber. It was not the thought of Darson joining that elicited such a response. Following his gaze, Amber's heart skipped a beat. Darkracer cantered toward them. On his back sat two riders. A cry nearly escaped her and she covered her mouth quickly at the sight. Mike was alive! And David rode with him. Lash shoved past Nathan as he hurried toward them. Darkracer slowed, coming to a stop before Amber.

"I see we're just in time," he said.

"What right did you have to leave like that?" Amber replied, her voice failing to sound as angry as she wanted it to be. "And you," she addressed Mike, "what are you doing here? You should be in the medward."

"And live with the thought of him flying my ship?" Mike answered as he pointed to Lash.

The Teshian gave a growling laugh as he assisted David in easing Mike to the ground.

"Don't worry," Mike said once he had his feet under him. "I saw a doctor before heading over here. I'm patched up and ready to fly. The ribs hurt, but the hands and head are working fine."

Amber's eyes narrowed as she studied him, still not convinced by his reassurance.

"But you just survived a crash."

"I'm not saying I'm not good." Mike gave her a confident wink and headed up the ramp. "Lash, I need you as a wingman." He paused to look back at Amber. "If the colonel approves."

"Granted," Amber said. She was still in shock at seeing Mike alive.

David jumped to the ground. He was happy to see Amber, though found it difficult to look her in the eye.

"Colonel," he said softly, saluting as he spoke, "permission to join."

Amber returned with a hasty salute to hide the tremble in her hands. "Permission granted."

With a weak nod, he headed for the ramp.

"Welcome back, Night Hawk," she whispered as he passed.

David glanced at her questioningly, trying to decide what she meant by the name. He followed her gaze as it trailed down to the sword at his hip. Both his hands rested on its hilt with a bit of the hawk tattoo showing below his sleeve. Amber gave a nod as if coming to some conclusion only she fully understood. The briefest of smiles traced her lips. David returned it as best he could, still unsure of her words but thankful for the acceptance.

"Come everyone," Amber suddenly called out, turning on her heels to head into the *Predator*. "We have a war to win."

GLOSSARY OF TERMS

Super System
> A designated group of solar systems within a galaxy

Telamier (tel-uh-meer)
> Planet of the Ilus System known for its rich natural resources and diverse cultures

Earthenia
> The region of the Human race on Telamier

Regions
> Recognized land owned and governed by a specific species group

CLE
> Coalition of Law Enforcement – a universal agency that oversees public law in all regions of Telamier

SIERA
> Special Intelligence and Enforcement Regional Agency – a special forces and intelligence gathering unit of the Earthenian military

Nahm
> A designated twenty-day period of time, eighteen nahms make up the Telamierian calendar year

GLOSSARY OF SENTIENT BEINGS

Airisun (air-ih-suhn)
> Native to Arisus; short, timid species who live in peaceful colonies, known for their ability to rapidly assimilate and process massive amounts of information

Candonian (kan-doe-nee-uhn)
> Native to Telamier; identical in physicality with the horse but of great intelligence and the capability of interspecies communication

Celehi (kel-le-hee)
> Native to Celhara; commonly tall and slender with prominent brow and cheek bones, displays their emotions through ripples of color across their skin
>> Pale Blue: neutral
>> Dark Blue: happy, joyful
>> Green: amusement or flattery
>> Purple: embarrassment
>> Orange to Red: degrees of anger
>> Yellow: anxiety
>> White: extreme fear, terror
>> Gray to Black: degrees of grief

Faxon (fax-uhn)
> Native to Borfax; large, muscular creature with tough, leathery hides and pronounced muzzles, fierce in reputation

Manogonite (muh-nog-uh-nite)
  Native to Manog; a medium-sized winged
  creature with muscular back haunches, slender
  arms, large ears and fangs

Oxyran (ox-ih-ran)
  Native to Ayzat; short, stocky creature with
  dense fur, large eyes and broad teeth, known
  for their short tempers and exceptional
  strength

Teshian (tesh-ee-uhn)
  Native to Hardiban; a graceful species
  with quick reflexes, respected for their
  diplomacy and strong sense of personal
  identity

Vairdec (vair-dek)
  Unknown native homeland; long-lived
  humanoid creature with black, silky mane
  and short, velvety body hair, nomadic by
  nature and highly skilled in the art of war

PRONUNCIATIONS

Arct-Ieya (är-kt eye-uh)

De'oolay (dee-oo-lay)

El'loray (ehl-lore-ay)

Jylin Py'guela (j-eye-lin p-eye´gue-luh)

Karnoss (kär-noe-ss)

Kiejaud (kee-jauh-d)

Larkrae (lär-kray)

Malard (muh-lärd)

Mer'k (mare-ck)

Nor-Yahvan (nore-yä-van)

Yehgrett (yay-gret)

JOIN THE ADVENTURE

Learn more about the world of Night Hawk at
www.nighthawkseries.com

About the Author

Born with a passion for storytelling and influenced by film, author Jolene Loraine has begun her publication career with stories of fantasy and adventure, rich in action and imagination. Along with writing, Jolene is active in film making, participating in the independent film community of the Pacific Northwest. She has also studied swordsmanship, puppetry, horsemanship and theater.

Author's Note

For the past twenty years *Night Hawk* has grown and developed into what you read now. I have many to thank for it. To my mom, Jeanine, and good friend, Carrie, I say thank you for all those writer's meetings dedicated to honing the many characters and ideas into a workable story. To Jenelle and Nick for being faithful fans throughout the years. To my dad, whose creativity and faith have been strong examples for me to follow. And to all the countless people who have encouraged, supported and assisted me in my ventures. This has been an amazing journey and I am pleased to say this is only the beginning.

Made in the USA
Middletown, DE
15 July 2019